HIGHEST PRAISE FOR DIAMOND HOMESPUN ROMANCES:

"In all of the Homespuns I've read and reviewed I've been very taken with the loving rendering of colorful small-town people doing small-town things and bringing 5 STAR and GOLD 5 STAR rankings to the readers. This series should be selling off the bookshelves within hours! Never have I given a series an overall review, but I feel this one, thus far, deserves it! Continue the excellent choices in authors and editors! It's working for this reviewer!"

—**Heartland Critiques**

We at Diamond Books are thrilled by the enthusiastic critical acclaim that the Homespun Romances are receiving. We would like to thank you, the readers and fans of this wonderful series, for making it the success that it is. It is our pleasure to bring you the highest quality of romance writing in these breathtaking tales of love and family in the Heartland of America.

And now, sit back and enjoy this delightful new Homespun Romance . . .

COUNTRY SUNSHINE
by Teresa Warfield

Praise for Teresa Warfield's national bestseller *Prairie Dreams,* a Diamond Homespun Romance:

"Passionate love scenes [and] warm, loving characters who depict the strength of the heartlands make this a touching and memorable read."

—**Rendezvous**

Diamond Books by Teresa Warfield

PRAIRIE DREAMS
COUNTRY SUNSHINE

COUNTRY SUNSHINE

TERESA WARFIELD

JOVE BOOKS, NEW YORK

This book is a Diamond original edition,
and has never been previously published.

COUNTRY SUNSHINE

A Diamond Book / published by arrangement with
the author

PRINTING HISTORY
Diamond edition / September 1994

All rights reserved.
Copyright © 1994 by Teresa Warfield.
Cover appliqué illustration by Kathy Lengyel.
This book may not be reproduced in whole or in part,
by mimeograph or any other means, without permission.
For information address: The Berkley Publishing Group,
200 Madison Avenue, New York, NY 10016.

ISBN: 0-7865-0042-5

Diamond Books are published by The Berkley Publishing Group,
200 Madison Avenue, New York, NY 10016.
DIAMOND and the "D" design
are trademarks belonging to Charter Communications, Inc.

PRINTED IN THE UNITED STATES OF AMERICA

10 9 8 7 6 5 4 3 2 1

This one's for you, Mama.
It's homey, set in Iowa . . .
Yep, this one's for you.
Let me take you back.
Back . . . to the old days.
I'm thrilled that you're proud.

ACKNOWLEDGMENTS

As always, big thanks must be extended to my family. Putting up with a writer's lifestyle and erratic schedule is no easy task. In my experience, I've never seen a more supportive family. Sometimes "thank you" seems inadequate.

Tom Marlin . . . I know you're still on a wanted poster somewhere in the West (grin). But, shucks, that doesn't bother me, Mr. Renegade! Thanks for your support and, of course, your ear when times are rough. What an incredible friend you've become. Now, let's stop being sappy and get to work, shall we?

Hugs to my sisters, Donna and Barbie, and to Beth Sprosty, for being so supportive by running out and buying my books right away. What fans!

Thanks to fans in general. Without you, I'd still be playing at a hobby. I hope you enjoy this one.

PROLOGUE

The *Gazette* article arrested Robert Kingston's attention:

A visit of a few days to Dubuque will be worth the while of every traveller; and for the speculator and man of enterprise, it affords the finest field now open in our country. It is a small town ... one of the most delightful sites on the river, and in the heart of the richest and most productive parts of the mining region; having this advantage over most other mining countries, that immediately over the richest (and in fact all) of the lead mines, the land on the surface produces the finest corn, and all other vegetables that may be put into it. This is certainly the richest section of the country on the Continent, and those who live a few

1

years to witness the result will be ready to sanction my assertion that it is to be the mint of our country.

George Catlin's praise, his description of the town, and his opinion that it was perfect for "the speculator and man of enterprise" was all Robert needed to read.

Interest piqued, he folded the newspaper, tucked it under his arm, and walked off whistling down Eighth Avenue.

CHAPTER

ONE

1845

From his position near the boardinghouse room's one window, Robert glanced in frustration at the street below. A number of people, wagons, and horses traversed Dubuque's main passage, leaving prints in the mud. The women lifted their skirts to avoid dirtying them, but not nearly so delicately or with the grace of New York's genteel upper crust.

Their clothing was different, too. Plainer, Robert thought. Without pretense. And despite the heat of the summer sun, he counted only five parasols. Most of the men were lumbermen and lead miners who wore shabby garb, carried odd-looking tools, and welcomed the activities within the numerous saloons at night.

How well Robert knew that; he had arrived in the thriving town yesterday afternoon, thinking to sleep after ridding himself of the dirt that had collected on his clothing and skin during the journey. The trip had taken him west across Pennsylvania to the Ohio River, and there he had boarded a steamer bound southwest to the Mississippi—with stops along the way to pick up and deposit passengers. Once on the Mississippi, the riverboat had turned north, passed St. Louis, then entered Iowa Territory. The trip had not been pleasant; the steamer had been crowded with people. Robert liked fresh air and sunshine, but the masses had proven to be too much.

He had hoped to spend a few days resting before throwing himself into the business that had brought him to Dubuque. Instead, the noise from the saloon rowdies had kept him awake most of last night.

And now there was the current problem.

He was tired and irritable despite the four cups of coffee he had drunk in the dining room only an hour ago while waiting for Jacob Fletcher—his friend and business associate. Last evening Jacob had said they would meet at ten o'clock this morning. Robert had contemplated a fifth cup of coffee, then decided to wake Jacob, having little patience for tardiness.

Besides, he hadn't exactly liked Jacob's parting words to him upstairs last evening: that they might not be able to get the prime land they wanted in Dubuque because a rather uncooperative individual held title to the land.

Jacob had looked sheepish and embarrassed when he said that, running a hand through his reddish-brown hair, then down over his green eyes. But the parting words had come just as Robert stepped out into the hall and Jacob was closing his door, and Robert had decided to take up the matter in the morning.

But this morning the "matter" seemed worse. It seemed ludicrous.

Robert put an open hand high on the window frame and

leaned into it. If what he had just heard from Jacob hadn't been so troublesome, he might have laughed heartily.

Shifting, he pulled a small gold box from a frock coat pocket. "Cheroot?" he asked Jacob, turning slightly. Jacob shook his head, declining the offer.

Robert lifted a cigar from the box and soon had it lit. Smoke swirled near the window. The sweet, pungent aroma of tobacco began wafting about the room.

"If the land is so *right*," he began, "if the site is in the heart of Dubuque and can be seen well from the river . . . if a hotel built there would prosper . . ." He shifted again, this time to face Jacob, who sat in a chair before a small secretary—if the rickety piece of furniture could be called such. It was actually no more than a slab of wood situated on four poles. Two drawers were built into it. "Then there is no problem, title or no title. We simply buy the lots from the lady and we build."

Jacob ran a hand across his mouth. He was unshaven, his normally bright eyes were dull, and the temper and determination that usually drove the man were nowhere in sight. When someone or something disturbed Jacob Fletcher, he usually reacted with resolve. Not so right now.

Actually Robert had noticed the change yesterday, when he stepped from the boat and spotted his associate standing on the riverbank. Something had been different about the man then . . . But Robert had been tired, and so he hadn't dwelt on wondering what the difference was.

He was still tired, but now he knew: He saw defeat in Jacob's slumped shoulders, in the way the man ran his hand down one side of his face, then over his mouth again, then propped an elbow on the secretary and his jaw in a cupped palm.

Drawing heavily from the cheroot, Robert worriedly studied his associate.

"I don't think you heard me," Jacob said slowly, wearily. "The lady won't give up the title. She's determined to hold onto the land because her family came here in the thirties and settled on those two lots. As soon as the land office opened seven years ago, her father and grandfather claimed them under preemption—the right to buy the land on which you settle. By then her family had been there for five years."

"You offered her a tract outside the city?" Robert asked.

"I offered her a dozen tracts. Two dozen."

"And the last time she aimed a rifle at you and told you to leave."

"Yes."

"And you left. You just . . . left. Without talking more. Without trying to convince her."

Jacob scowled, then grunted. "What the hell would you do if you were staring down the barrel of a loaded rifle? You wouldn't stay and talk!"

Robert tossed his head. "She's a woman, Jacob. She wouldn't have shot you. She was trying to frighten you. Apparently she succeeded."

"I'm telling you, Robert, you don't know this woman. She knows how to handle a rifle, and she *would* have shot me! We've done fine business together for ten years. Hotels in Pittsburgh and Cleveland—cities that are growing fast and where there's money to be made. But I'm not willing to die just so I can be rich. Just so we can build another hotel."

"She wouldn't have shot you," Robert insisted.

"You didn't see her face. You didn't see her eyes."

"Absolutely fierce, was she?" Robert couldn't help teasing, though this was certainly no teasing matter. He flicked ashes at a nearby spittoon. "I cannot believe she would have shot you."

"She would have!" Jacob said indignantly, showing a bit of temper finally. That relieved Robert; at least Jacob hadn't changed as much as he had feared. "And don't think for a minute that the cut of your clothes will keep her from shooting *you*, my fine friend! You know absolutely nothing about the woman."

Robert gave Jacob a tight smile. "No, but I know about *women*, and I intend to find out everything I can about this one. I came all the way from New York, and I don't intend to let anyone ruin our plans. It's not as if we will be taking anything from her. We're offering to *buy* the land—at ten times what she purchased it for."

"That makes no difference to her."

Trying to summon patience, Robert smoked more. They had never faced anything like this. He and Jacob usually chose the most viable site, built, then hired a competent person to oversee the management of the hotel while they moved on.

He wasn't certain he considered the woman's reluctance to sell a problem really. It was Jacob who irritated him. What person in her right mind would turn down such an offer? She stood to benefit, to make a sizeable profit from her land. He respected Jacob's business sense and tactics, but perhaps Jacob hadn't put the offer to the lady in the right way. Perhaps he had not made it sound inviting enough. Perhaps he hadn't made clear that she would be making a profit. After only weeks of weak effort, Jacob was giving up.

Robert *despised* the thought of giving up.

"We wanted to build another hotel in a place where people were flocking," he said. "As soon as we saw the painting of Dubuque in that gallery in New York and read reports of its rapid settlement, we decided to build here. It was—"

"Our first mistake," Jacob grumbled.

Robert folded his arms across his chest. "Why is Dubuque a mistake?"

"Because it's raw."

"So is Cleveland, but Cleveland has potential. People are coming in by the hundreds. The same thing is true of Dubuque. Of course, it's a little behind Cleveland as far as progress is concerned, but it's developing. That piece we read in the *Gazette* did not exaggerate—close to fifty people got off the boat with me. Some were coming to visit relatives and friends, but others were coming to settle. I asked. And as we were disembarking, two other ships docked at the levee with two more loads of people! To the north, there's lumber. Here, there's lead. Dubuque is situated on the banks of the largest river in the United States. One certainly cannot ignore that fact. The opening of the mines and the territory is luring people and businesses here, and people are our business, Jacob."

"All right," Jacob responded, sighing. "You're right. I . . . I can see that. But let's think about another lot. Then we won't have to . . . Well, look." He reached for a piece of paper. "This is a drawing I made of the city."

Robert gave the sketch a brief glance, a look of disgust and dismissal. "I do not take well to having to settle for anything but the lots you chose."

Jacob made a sound of exasperation deep in his throat. "Don't be stubborn! We offered, and she said no. Quite forcefully. She won't—"

"So we give up on having the most strategic site? Any farther out and we're into the hills and the mines—not the best place for a hotel. No," Robert said, smoothing his coat. "I intend to go talk to her."

Jacob stared incredulously at him, then hit the secretary with a clenched fist. "For God's sake, sometimes you're more hotheaded than I am! Well, I'll tell you something, my friend, after staring down the barrel of her rifle, you won't be so hotheaded anymore. And you won't be so determined to have those lots!"

"That is defeat," Robert said succinctly.

"No . . . No, that's having good sense."

"Good sense got us where we are. Giving up is not good sense."

"We haven't given up! We'll just choose another—"

"Not until we've exhausted every means at our disposal. How old is the lady?"

"The 'woman' is nineteen."

Robert laughed, then drew from the cigar again. "Nineteen. Unmarried, I presume? You haven't mentioned a husband."

Nodding, Jacob squinted one eye. "Unmarried. What's going on in your head? You might get just about anything you want in New York since your father is *riche*, but Robert, out here . . ."

Robert stiffened. "I've made my own way these last ten years. You've no cause to say something like that," he responded softly, as always resenting anyone who thought he relied on his father's money. Certainly he had used his trust fund to enable himself and Jacob to start building the hotels, but he had politely turned down every dollar his father had offered since. For years he had listened to whispers that all he had to do to get what he wanted was ask his father. While that was true, he would not do it anymore—he hadn't for *years*. He had wanted the dignity and the pride that came with self-reliance, and he had done a fine job of attaining those qualities.

"But Daddy is there to pick you up if things go wrong. You know that."

"I don't rely on him." Robert studied Jacob—the fire that suddenly leapt in the man's eyes. He and Jacob had been friends since their boyhood. Robert *had* always had everything he asked for, but Jacob had not exactly led a childhood filled with poverty. His father had simply refused to give him everything.

Robert tossed the remainder of his cheroot in the spittoon and stuffed his hands into his trouser pockets. "Refusing to give a son everything he requests doesn't mark a man a bad father. It says something for Richard Fletcher: that he wants his son to know how to make his way in the world. My father has always stood ready to hand me the world."

"And it's the world you've come to expect," Jacob bit out. "Yes, we built the hotels in Pittsburgh and Cleveland, but if someone had stood in our way, your Kingston mentality would have reared. Now is a fine example of that. Don't—"

"Damn!" Robert exploded. "We aren't stepping on anyone to build this hotel! Now . . . the *woman* . . . Nineteen and unmarried . . . What does she look like? Do you know anything about her likes and dislikes?"

Jacob furrowed his heavy brows and studied Robert. "What are you thinking to do?"

"I told you—go talk to her."

"Uh-huh. And you'll include a little romance in that talk, too, won't you?"

"Well, I hadn't planned to . . ."

"But it's a fine idea. You can't deny that. Nothing else has worked."

A slow grin worked its way across Robert's face. A fine idea . . . "Jacob Fletcher, your proper mother would turn over in her grave. *Now* who is prepared to go aggressively after what he wants?"

Jacob snorted. "Well, she did threaten me. I'm sore about that, but I just haven't known what to do." He ran a hand along one side of his face. "I'm sorry for those remarks about you and your father. I'm frustrated. I've been here for three weeks trying to arrange everything by the time you arrived, and I've nothing to show for my time and efforts."

"No matter. I'm glad to see you acting like yourself. I was beginning to wonder if you'd lost your ability to laugh."

Jacob rubbed a temple. "There's no denying you could charm any woman into just about anything. But you should be careful, you know. Lord knows that during the season in New York, the mothers are all looking your way. One woman nearly caught you, and it's through no fault of yours that she didn't."

Robert turned back to the window, wishing Jacob would not insist now and then on trying to make him talk about the fact that he had come close to getting married. That mock wedding day had been the most embarrassing, most humiliating day of his life.

"Tell me about the woman who holds the land title," he said.

Jacob took a deep breath. "Well it's not just her. There's her grandfather and mother, too."

"But she's the one who seems the most ferocious."

Jacob nodded. "Oh, but Clarence Watson, her grandfather, adores her. Don't forget that, whatever you do. Whatever Caroline says is how things go. Win her heart and you'll have his. Win his heart, and you'll have hers—she adores him, too. He can be stubborn. But it's little Caroline who shoots fire."

Amusement pulled at one side of Robert's mouth. "Caroline sounds very feminine. Very . . . unthreatening."

Now Jacob laughed, but not in disbelief. No, his laughter was more . . . anticipation.

Robert cast a glance over his shoulder just as Jacob leaned back in the creaking chair, folded his hands behind his head, and regarded Robert with twinkles in his eyes. Well, at least they were back, too, Robert could not help thinking.

"My friend, I have a feeling I'm about to be entertained," Jacob said, chuckling more. "Unthreatening, huh? Once you acquaint yourself with our sweet, unthreatening Miss Watson, I expect full accounts of all happenings. Is that agreed?"

Robert furrowed his brow, then composed himself, relaxed, and nodded. As if there will be happenings, he thought. There wouldn't be a lot to tell, aside from a report of how, once he presented Miss Watson with the amount of cash they stood ready to pay her and her family, she agreed quickly and politely.

Jacob grinned. "All right, then. She and her mother take in laundry and mending. Her father and grandfather were both miners, but her father died in an accident at a mine two years ago. Her grandfather is in his seventies and not in the best of health. Every other afternoon, she delivers food to the miners. They're a rough lot, but they respect her because, as I said, her father and grandfather worked alongside most of them."

Robert pulled a face in surprise. "You obviously know quite a bit about the lady."

"And you assumed I hadn't tried."

"I didn't say that, Jacob."

"No, not in so many words, but you were thinking it. You still are. Well, I have tried. Now it's your turn. We'll see if you do better. We shall see. They'll be delivering to the miners tomorrow afternoon if you're interested in taking a peek at her. But I'd use caution. She carries a pistol, not a parasol, beneath her wagon seat—and she's not afraid to use it."

"I'll manage," Robert said, tilting his head back.

Jacob snorted. "I don't know why I'm trying to warn you. I should sit back, shut my mouth, and just watch the show. Which is exactly what I think I'll do. You go right ahead. Meet Miss Caroline and offer to buy that land. Yes, sir . . . I'll just watch."

Robert did not like the smug look on his friend's face.

CHAPTER

TWO

With her usual enjoyment, Caroline listened to her mother sing "Amazing Grace" as their wagon approached Madden Hollow, located not far southwest of Dubuque. It was ironic, Caroline thought. The Watsons were such God-fearing people, yet because of their position of not wanting to give up their connecting lots on Dubuque's Main Street, they had acquired enemies, even in the Methodist congregation.

Jacob Fletcher, the man who wanted to build a hotel on their land, wasn't the only person who had knocked on the front door of the family's small cabin numerous times these past weeks; the Methodist ladies and the Reverend Brunson were becoming persistent and annoying, too, saying things like "As members of the church, you would be doing a service to God by allowing a place of worship to be constructed here. Look around at all the drinking and

13

sinning, then look into your hearts and ask yourself what would be a better place for a church than this location right here in the middle of the devil's lair?"

"Humph!" Grampa had said the last time the reverend visited. "The 'devil's lair,' is it?"

"Yes, sir, it is, Mr. Watson," Reverend Brunson had responded. "That's exactly what Dubuque has become."

"Can't rightly call miners trying to entertain themselves servants of the devil."

"Christ spoke against engaging in pleasures of the flesh. He—"

"Do you have sex with your wife?"

The Reverend Brunson went white. Then he sputtered: "Mr. Watson, I hardly think that is any of your concern! Besides, my wife and I . . . we are married!"

"An' the matter of our land ain't none of yer business. We claimed it by preemption, an' we've held onto it through speculators an' through the city's efforts to move us out. We paid for it, we're happy here, an' nobody's going to talk us into moving. Now, you'd best go on about the business of yer day," Clarence Watson said. "Business you ain't gonna find here."

The reverend stood from the seat he had taken at the family's table a half hour before, smoothed his black coat, and muttered something about how the congregation wasn't going to like Mr. Watson's attitude. It was an unseemly attitude for someone who had pretended to support the church for several years now.

That remark had really sparked Grampa's temper—he didn't pretend at anything. Instead of gripping a Bible like the reverend did, he strode over to where he kept his rifle on a rack above the door, lifted the weapon, and aimed it at Mr. Brunson. Mother gasped and said he should put it down, that he had no call to threaten a man of God, that she wouldn't be able to darken the church steps after today.

But then, she'd said nearly the same thing the afternoon

Grampa had been sleeping and the hotel man had come calling and Caroline had aimed the gun at *him*. Neither man had had the sense to realize that the rifle wasn't loaded either time. Looking down the long barrel staring at them, they'd hurried to the door. The reverend and Mr. Fletcher were welcome in the Watsons' house so long as they didn't mention the Watsons selling their lot, and both men had been told that plenty enough times.

No one had come calling to talk about the land in ... oh, at least three days now, Caroline thought as she guided the team of horses alongside the hollow where tall oaks and cottonwoods mingled with clover and colorful wild-flowers. The air was hot, but now and then a breeze cooled her, and she inhaled deeply of the earthy scents.

She loved her home—not just the cabin and farm, but the land outside of Dubuque ... the bluffs, hills, and val-ley, and the mines, despite the tragedy they'd caused her family a few years back. She'd been five years old when her parents and grandfather had brought her here, and she hardly remembered what Mother often called "the longest journey of my life."

Upon receiving a letter from Caroline's Uncle Paul about the wonderful mining prospects to be found just west of the Mississippi, the family had traveled from west-ern Virginia, from the coal mines there to the lead mines here, and they'd fared well since.

Caroline couldn't remember one winter since coming here that she hadn't had boots to wear—but she remem-bered going without during the cold season back in the Virginia hills. She couldn't remember going hungry since they'd arrived—but she'd gone hungry plenty of times be-fore. Mining was often hard, dangerous work, but it had always been a vital part of her family's existence, and though she regretted the accident that had killed her father, she still had great respect for the business that had lured her family to this territory.

Besides, the accident might very well have happened

back in the coal mines, so it had never caused Caroline or her mother and grandfather to resent the family's move to the western bank of the Mississippi. If anything, her father's death had caused them to become more attached to the land and to their home. They didn't want to move from the cabin the Watson men had built upon the family's arrival, though Mother sometimes mentioned that maybe they ought to consider the change Dubuque was going through, that a town— "soon to be a city"—was rising around them.

Grampa always silenced Ma with a glare, and Caroline was always glad. She'd never move. She wanted to pluck weeds from the garden her father had plowed every year and that she now plowed because Grampa was too feeble. He was feisty but feeble—there was no denying that. Of late he could barely ride the two miles to the mining camps to have dinner with his friends.

Caroline wanted always to sleep in the loft where her father had built her a bedstead and a chest of drawers, and where she'd lain many a night during her childhood and listened to the low hum of her parents' and grandfather's conversations. She'd never been able to decipher what they were saying, but just hearing them had brought her comfort, had made her feel safe and secure. Even now, during summer nights when the loft was often hot, she still snuggled beneath the counterpane Ma had stitched for her during the journey from Virginia, and listened for her grampa and mother's voices.

"We're being terribly stubborn, you know," Rebecca Watson said now, pausing in the middle of the third verse of the old religious tune as the wagon rattled along. She'd attended ample years of school in Richmond, Virginia, before marrying Caroline's father and moving to the western part of the state. An only child, Ma had come from a fine family, yet she'd given up what had apparently been a fancy life in Richmond. All for love, Caroline sometimes thought during reflective moments. Of course, now Ma couldn't go back if she wanted to. Unless she wanted to be alone, that was. Some four years before the Watsons had left Virginia, Ma's parents had died in a fire.

"I've been wanting to say this to someone for some time," Ma ventured, neatly folding a homespun handkerchief in her lap. That was Ma; she'd always keep her fine ways. Caroline, however . . . well, sometimes rifles and fists were the only things respected out here.

"You seem to be the only one I can talk to about the matter of late, Caroline, so I hope you will listen. God only knows Clarence won't," Rebecca said somewhat apprehensively. "And sometimes . . . sometimes I fear you're getting as cantankerous as he is. But do listen and try to be reasonable. We haven't been to service now in three weeks. Three weeks! I vowed that once the church came to Dubuque—and there was a day when I didn't think it ever would—I wouldn't miss a service. I never thought an argument about our land would keep us away. A pity it has. It's a shame, that's what it is, and maybe it's time we saw that we're being stubborn. Just plain stubborn."

Caroline sighed, then irritation slithered like a serpent under her skin. She understood Ma's reasoning and even her inner desires. Having been educated and raised a different way, Ma sometimes craved respectable social activities, the sewing circles and various causes taken up by ladies in the church. Caroline wished Ma could be a part of those things, but not at the expense of everything they cherished. Not at the expense of their cabin, which they'd watch torn down so the congregation could build another church.

"It ain't just the land, Ma," Caroline responded, always speaking her mind. "It's our home. It's the cabin Pa helped Grampa build. Why can't the reverend build the new church on another lot an' stop tryin' to make us feel guilty about not givin' ours up? We've worked hard for what we have, an' the church offers us nothin'. The Reverend Brunson ain't named a price. He just expects us to buy another lot an' move. There's nothin' right about that. When

I think of all the mendin' and launderin' you an' I've done . . . We only finished payin' the preemption last year. We've worked years for what we have, an' no one's gonna make us feel like we might not go to heaven if we don't give it all up so the congregation can build another church."

"But, Caroline, the hotel man . . . he *did* offer money, and we turned him away! We should rethink his offer."

"Ma, we all agreed we didn't wanna move. For myself an' Grampa—I believe even for you—it's become a matter of principle. We said no, an' that means *no*. That means we ain't willin' to sell. That means they oughtta leave us alone. That means they *better*."

"When I see my daughter reduced to aiming a rifle at a man—"

Caroline breathed deeply. She'd known Ma wouldn't just express shock about the incident, then forget it. She'd known something, punishment of some sort, would blow her way sooner or later. Fortunately it hadn't yet, but it was threatening, otherwise Ma wouldn't have mentioned her aiming the rifle at the man.

"It wasn't loaded. Jacob Fletcher just didn't have the brains to realize that," Caroline said.

"What a mean thing to say!"

"It's true. I reckon if a person doesn't have the sense to realize whether or not a weapon's loaded, this is the wrong place to be. I hope by now he's gone back East where he belongs. New York, I think he said."

"Just the same, I don't want to see you do that again. No—don't do it. Caroline Mae Watson, do not ever again aim a rifle at another human being."

"Oh, Ma. There're times when a person *has* to."

"Never again," Rebecca said sternly, shaking her head. "Never ever again."

Caroline fought a smile. "I'll try not to. Course, that means—"

"You will have to redeem yourself in my eyes."

Caroline thought about saying, "Oh, that's silly," but she'd had to redeem herself enough times as a child that she knew her mother wasn't trying to be silly, and she knew Ma would feel angrier and more insulted if Caroline implied she was. Rebecca Watson was really mortified that her daughter had aimed a rifle at someone.

Caroline couldn't recall how many times the persistent Mr. Fletcher had come to the cabin, offering his bundle of money in exchange for the right to tear down their precious home and build a hotel on the soil they'd worked for years.

Numerous times—more than twenty. She'd finally become exasperated that he wouldn't take her no and leave, never to return again, and she'd grabbed the rifle and softly told him she'd shoot him dead if he ever asked again, politely or rudely. She'd told him she was a good shot—which she was; Pa and Grampa had seen to that—so getting him right between the eyes would have taken little or no effort.

Fletcher had scrambled for the door like a buck fleeing a hunter, and she hadn't seen him since.

After hanging the rifle back on the rack, she'd turned to find Ma gaping at her. Soon Rebecca's mouth had snapped shut, and she'd turned back to slicing mutton for stew. Later she had expressed shock that Caroline had done such a thing, but she hadn't commented about the incident since, and Caroline had thought—hoped—she'd forgotten.

She knew better. She knew her mother would expect her to do penance.

"I ain't sorry," Caroline said stubbornly as they started down into the hollow, nearing the creek that ran through it.

"You are not sorry," Ma said, correcting her English.

Caroline often wondered why Ma bothered. It was always a temporary thing. Sure, she could clean her speech up. She'd been taught proper—Ma had seen to that. But a few minutes of being around Grampa, and Caroline's clean speech always became smudged again.

"And yes, you *are* sorry," Ma said.

"I ain't. Every day for two weeks while we delivered laundry and food to the miners, Fletcher followed. He was on our doorstep every evenin'. We offered him the hospitality of our table an' our home. We told him we didn't want to talk about the land, that we weren't willin' to sell. But he kept askin'. I won't say I'm sorry for drivin' away that nuisance of a man. An' if he comes around again, I'll—"

"Caroline, I didn't say apologize to Mr. Fletcher. I said redeem yourself in my eyes. You're going to have to do something very, very good. Something that makes you worthy of my respect again."

"Oh, Ma, I ain't a little girl anymore! I don't need discipline."

"Obviously you do."

"I'm—"

A horse whinnied nearby, then a rider broke from a line of oaks and charged toward the women, hooves pounding furiously. The gray horse had a wild look in his eyes, as if something had startled him. He tore through the brush, nearly ran smack into a lone dogwood, and all the while the man on his back held on for dear life.

The reins Caroline held jerked, and she tightened her hold on them and spoke to her horses as they tossed their heads and stamped their hooves. She wondered if the spooked animal would frighten them into running away, too.

The fool who leaned over the gray's neck was trying to talk to the horse instead of taking his chances and jumping off. He'd land in the muddy creek if he jumped, but that would be better than staying on a horse that surely would charge into one of those wide oaks near the water any minute.

"Lord!" Ma cried as she gripped the wagon seat. "He'll be killed! We have to help him!"

Reining her horses, Caroline considered what she could do to help.

She was just reaching for the pistol she kept hidden beneath the buckboard seat when the gray halted, bucking and whinnying. The man didn't have to jump. The animal *deposited* him in the creek—on his rear, lucky for him— then raced on.

Caroline gaped, then laughed.

The man looked as undignified as any man in such fine dress could possibly look, seated in the middle of the creek with water swirling around his waist and mud splattered all over his face and what had been a white linen shirt and neckcloth. He shook water from his black hair the way a wet dog might, and Caroline laughed again. If she didn't somehow restrain her mirth, she'd fall off the wagon seat!

"Caroline, stop it this instant!" her mother scolded, gathering her skirts and stepping gingerly from the wagon. "My goodness, let's help the poor man. Someone getting tossed by a horse is nothing to laugh about!"

"It was . . . the way it happened!" Caroline said, struggling to control herself. "He didn't have a choice . . . Just . . . there he went . . . plop! An' right on his backside!" She slapped a knee and began laughing all over again.

"Stop it!" Rebecca again commanded as she swept away from the wagon.

She headed for the creek, but by the time she reached its edge, the man had gained his footing and was plucking twigs and wet grass from his clothes. He cast Caroline a sour look, then flicked specks of mud from his shirt.

His gaze froze on the water flowing around his calves, and Caroline heard him mumble something about a snake.

A second later he tore out of the creek in much the same way his horse had burst from the trees, with a crazed look in his eyes.

Caroline's laughter had faded to snickers. Now it erupted again. The image of him bolting from the water, unable to scramble up the slight embankment fast enough, was the funniest thing she'd seen in a good long while. Funnier, even, than the Reverend Brunson's wide-eyed look when Grampa asked if he had sex with his wife.

The man stumbled onto a high grassy patch near the wagon and made no effort to get up. He rolled onto his back and stared up at the blue heavens, pushing dark hair from his brow and from his very nice brown eyes.

"I hate snakes," he gasped, closing his eyes and struggling to slow his breathing.

"Then you'd best not lay in that patch of grass, mister," Caroline advised, unable to resist temptation. "Snakes do like grass."

As he shot up from the ground, she thought he'd flee up the edge of the creek, deeper into the hollow, the same way his horse had. Instead he turned his gaze on her, studying her.

Something flickered in his eyes. Recognition? No . . . she didn't know the man. She was sure of that. She'd never met him.

But studying her . . . *recognizing* her seemed to calm him, though he took care to step out of and away from the high grass.

The movements put him nearly behind the wagon, and Caroline had to twist on her seat to keep watching him. She didn't know him, and she didn't like feeling as if he knew her.

For some reason she suddenly wanted Ma to get back on the wagon seat. Then she'd give a flick of the reins, and the wagon would lurch forward and leave the man behind them.

But he's not dangerous. He doesn't even have guns strapped on. Besides, if he tries anything stupid, I have the pistol I keep under the seat. One shot will flatten him.

Caroline thought of Jacob Fletcher, how he had followed her and Ma to the camps those days, and she wondered if this man was maybe one of Fletcher's men. If he was, he'd mention the hotel and their lots soon. Then she'd sure enough pull out her pistol. She, Ma, and Grampa had said no, that meant no, and she wouldn't talk about the land business anymore.

"Snakes in the grass," the man said. "That's very funny, Miss . . ."

"Caroline Watson," she responded, still studying him. Hair slipped over his forehead again, ending just below his dark brows. He pushed it away, and the sun glittered in his eyes.

Only a woman should have lashes that long and curly, Caroline thought. And no man should have such a perfect face . . . a face she could sit and look at for a good long while.

God had begun with the best stone and had chiseled that narrow forehead, the nose that was neither too small nor too large—*perfect* came to mind again—the chin that jutted forth proudly—and angrily, she thought.

She expected to glance at his mouth and find it drawn in a tight line. Instead she observed that his lower lip was slightly larger than the top one and nicely curved. His top lip was perfectly formed also, with a disruptive valley in the center of its arch.

"Caroline," he said, as if testing the name. He said it smooth as cream being poured over a batch of peaches, then he smiled a crooked smile, a *knowing* smile, and Caroline figured she'd been caught staring. Gawking was a better word. She'd been caught gawking.

And now she found that she wanted to hear him talk more, just say a few more things in that rich voice of his. It was neither too deep nor too soft. Like his nose and lips, it was right in the middle; it was perfect. She didn't even mind when she caught a whiff of the sour-smelling creek on him—mud and crawfish and minnows. The way he'd said her name—not in a drawl the way most folks said it—that did something to her. Most folks said the *C* like a harsh *K* instead of in the soft way he'd said it, and they stretched out the *-line*.

Yes, indeed, he could talk all day and she wouldn't mind. She'd even think about encouraging him by making him a batch of tea or lemonade from the fruit delivered to Dubuque by the steamers. But most of all, he could say her name a million times, and she'd love hearing it. She'd tell people to listen to the way he said it so they could learn from him and, for heaven's sake, say it like he said it. Say it in his nice, polished way. Was that too much to ask?

He inclined his head to her in greeting in a way that made her feel like . . . well, like a lady, so to speak. She suddenly thought about smoothing the wrinkles in her dress made of brown homespun, and she wondered why she hadn't worn one of her Sunday dresses, either the calico or the gingham.

But that was a silly thing to wonder—she never wore her Sunday clothes while delivering food and laundry to the miners! Doing that would be a waste, and Lord only knew she could afford just two new dresses a year. Well, now that the preemption was paid, maybe three.

Funny though . . . She'd never worried over how many new dresses she could afford. Until now. Until the man—the gentleman standing near the tail of the wagon bed had spoken softly to her and dipped his head in greeting instead of uttering a harsh "Afternoon, Miss Watson," or "Afternoon, Caroline," the way most people did.

And now he was walking around the wagon, nearing her, drawing close, and Caroline became oblivious to everything but him. The birds' chirping fell away. The low rustle of branches stopped. She couldn't even hear the brush of the man's boots on the grass; she could only stare at him as he regarded her appreciatively, gold flecks floating in his brown eyes.

He reached for and lifted her hand, bringing it to his mouth.

The feathery touch of his lips on her skin drew a gasp from her, and she jerked her hand back. "Hey! You wanna watch yourself." No man had ever been so forward! Even the rambunctious miners kept their distance.

But as Caroline cradled the hand he'd kissed in her other hand and told herself again that he shouldn't be so forward, that she'd be sorely tempted to smack him if he tried that again, she entertained the thought of *offering* him her hand, of *asking* him to do that again. The kiss had startled her, but it had felt awfully nice, too.

He smiled again, but Caroline didn't think he was silently laughing at her. No . . . she saw not a hint of mockery in his expression.

"I didn't mean to startle you, Miss Watson," he said softly, as if the words were meant for her and her alone. "It was only a greeting, extended from a gentleman to a lady. Please accept my apology for approaching you covered with mud and filth."

Her heart melted a little. He was asking for forgiveness? For doing something that had felt so wonderful? For doing it after being tossed in the creek?

Why, if he'd been covered with lead dust, if his fingers had been as gray as his horse, if he'd smelled like a privy—she wouldn't have minded.

"No need to apologize," she heard herself say. Her response sounded so lame, so unrefined, compared to his. She wanted to crawl under the wagon seat and hide until he disappeared. But wait—she didn't really want him to disappear!

His gaze drifted to her mouth, and Caroline swallowed and lowered her lashes. She told herself once again that she oughtta feel offended, that she oughtta say something smart to the man, chide him for his forwardness.

But she wasn't offended. She was only uncomfortable because no man had ever looked at her in such a way. Because no man had ever glanced at her lips as if he were contemplating kissing them.

"I didn't mind so much," she mumbled, aware that she was still cradling the hand he'd kissed. "Just . . . I've never had . . . No one's ever done that."

"No one? *Ever?*"

She forced herself to look at him. His eyes sparkled with amusement, and her cheeks began burning. Exasperated with herself, she managed a nervous laugh. "I'm bein' silly. Sorry for laughin' at you. You could've been killed or hurt real bad."

"Yes, well, fortunately only my backside is wounded. I believe I must have landed on some stones."

Her eyes widened. She couldn't help herself—she laughed again, apologizing between snickers.

He cast her a playful glare. "For a lady who keeps apologizing, you look very sorry indeed."

"You ain't angry?"

"Why should I be angry? Well, perhaps annoyed that you laughed about the snake, then teased me. Do they really hide in the grass?" he asked, looking worried. He glanced down at the ground, then back up at her.

"Yep," she answered, unable to help a smile. "Are you really afraid of 'em?"

He scowled. "They just uh . . . They make me a little nervous, yes."

"But they only hide in the tall grass," Ma said, stepping up beside him near the wagon. "I'm Rebecca Watson, and this is my daughter Caroline—"

"I've met your charming daughter," he responded, looking pleased. "I thought the day had turned sour when that horse tossed me. But now I'm in the company of two lovely women, and the outlook doesn't seem so terrible. Although . . . the walk back to Dubuque will be a long one. I think we're at least two miles from the town."

"Not to mention there'll be lots of tall grass along the way," Caroline said, unable to resist another snicker.

"Caroline!" Mother objected.

As the man leaned toward Caroline, she braced herself, thinking he might reach for her hand again. Instead he smiled up at her and asked, "Is there not one thing you're afraid of, Miss Watson? Not one little thing?"

"Why, she's afraid of men," Rebecca said. "Afraid to let one too close to her for fear she'll get caught up with taking care of him and won't have time to devote herself to me and her grandfather the way she does now. As if we need to be taken care of."

Caroline's mouth dropped open. "Ma!" Now her cheeks didn't burn just a little. They felt like they were on fire.

"It's the truth. She turns them away when they call."

"Afraid of men?" the man remarked. "Afraid to let one too close? That's a shame. That seems a complete waste."

"It ain't your concern," Caroline blurted, annoyed that her mother had shared private information about her with a stranger. He surely hadn't meant to sound rude or assuming. Her temper and the way she acted without thinking much of the time had gotten her in trouble before . . . "I'm sor—"

"Caroline Mae Watson, you've fallen more!" her mother scolded. "That's two things now. Two things you will have to redeem yourself for in my eyes. You'll begin by extending this gentleman a little kindness, a little hospitality. That will be a fine start."

Caroline's gaze fastened on the reins resting in her lap. Ma couldn't imagine how she was embarrassing her! She didn't mind the words about extending kindness and hospitality, but this business of her redeeming herself—it made her seem like a child being disciplined.

"I meant what I said as a compliment, Caroline," the man said.

She knew that, and she was sorry her temper had flared. "We'll be glad to help you find your horse, then wash your clothes an' offer you supper. That is, if you don't mind goin' with us to take food to the mines first. There's a kettle of chicken stew goin' back at the house, an' I make good biscuits—if you like biscuits, that is. Ma brews a good pot of coffee, an' Grampa tells a fine story . . ." Sighing, Caroline glanced at the man. "Guess I'm tryin' to apologize in my own way without sayin' I'm sorry over 'n' over."

He flashed her a smile. "And I ask you—how could any man look into your blue eyes and not accept?"

Caroline swallowed hard. Lord, but this man could charm her right off her feet. He could make her feel like there was no ground beneath her. He could make her feel special.

"Well, then," Ma said, looking delighted, and her blue-gray eyes shimmered. "I'll push aside some of these crates of laundry and sit in the wagon bed. I don't believe I heard your name," she told the man.

"Robert Kingston."

"Grand," she responded.

It is grand, Caroline thought. *Oh, yes, "grand" fits him perfectly.*

"Very well, Mr. Kingston . . . I offer you the seat beside my daughter."

Caroline wanted to crawl beneath the nearest rock. Ma liked Mr. Kingston, too. Very much, apparently. And maybe she'd seen the looks of interest the man had given Caroline. Maybe she had, but that was no cause to push the man her way.

Irritated, Caroline started to object about him sitting with her as he began scooting the crates closer together for Rebecca, then she thought better and clamped her mouth shut. She'd had more than enough lectures for one day about redeeming herself, and she couldn't live through more embarrassment without hiding her face. Better to sit quietly, guide the horses toward the camp, feed the men, then head back to town, wash Robert Kingston's clothes, and . . .

And all the while, Ma would be peering from under her lashes to see how things were progressing.

Caroline sighed. The remainder of the afternoon was gonna be unbearable. Absolutely unbearable.

CHAPTER

THREE

A good half hour later, they found Robert's horse wandering in the wood near the hollow. Robert tied its reins to the back of the wagon, then jumped back up onto the seat. Soon they were moving again, cutting across the dip the hollow made in the land.

As the horses splashed through the creek, he caught himself searching the water for snakes. That snake slithering through the creek toward him earlier had made him act a fool, and he could not really blame Caroline Watson for laughing at him. He was a bit embarrassed to be sitting on the buckboard seat with her, as bad as he must smell. But respect for his own mother had long ago taught him not to argue with one. If a mother said sit on the wagon seat, there was exactly where he should sit.

The wagon creaked as the horses started up the slight

embankment, and Robert wondered if they would make it. They finally did, muscles bulging as they plodded forth onto grass as lush and green as any Robert had seen. Catlin, the *Gazette* writer, was right—the land here was fertile, stretching far and wide in one direction while rolling hills rose and blended in another. The air was sweet, filled with the fragrances of flowers and tall grass and sunshine. There was something undeniably attractive about city life, but this land, this western bank of the Mississippi, Iowa Territory—it could prove captivating if a man failed to keep his goal in mind.

They rode over the gentle hills, making conversation here and there. Rebecca Watson asked how long he had been in Dubuque and where he was staying.

"I arrived two days ago," he answered. "I have a room at Mrs. Johnson's Boardinghouse on Main Street."

"Why, that's just up the street from our farm!"

"Jacob Fletcher's stayin' at that boardinghouse," Caroline commented.

Robert glanced at her and found her suddenly regarding him warily from the corners of her very nice blue eyes. Caroline Watson had a definite mischievous nature about her, and he couldn't decide whether or not he liked that. He *had* been angry when she laughed at him, then had the audacity to tease him about snakes hiding in the grass. He was about to growl at her, then he realized who she was, that the small woman grinning at him from the wagon seat was the very woman who had frightened Jacob away with a rifle. And so he calmed his ruffled temper, disregarded his appearance for a moment or two, and summoned the charm that rarely failed to work on the fairer sex.

"Mr. Fletcher was asking about our lot in Dubuque," Rebecca explained as Caroline shifted her gaze back to the horses. "He wants to buy it so he can build a hotel there. Lord knows the city could use another one. These little boardinghouses here and there just don't hold all the people who come our way anymore."

"Mr. Fletcher can build his hotel somewhere else," Caroline said tightly. "A few streets over ain't gonna hurt his business none."

"Do you know that for fact?" Robert asked, feeling his temper rise a bit. She was wrong in saying that building the hotel a few streets over wouldn't hurt business. It could.

Her eyes flashed to him. "Do *you* know whether or not it would?" she demanded as a strand of curly auburn hair blew across her face. She brushed it away, not bothering to try to tuck it back beneath the ribbon that restrained the rest of her waist-length hair. She was slender without being thin, feminine without being soft. Dark brown lashes lined her eyes. Her small nose, sprinkled with freckles, curved gently at the end, and her narrow jaw came together to form a sharp chin. She was becoming but certainly not stunning.

Robert skirted the question. "I would assume that if there are other hotels in Dubuque—and there are—location will be very important. A few streets might make all the difference."

"You know a lot about this hotel stuff," she accused, her pert chin shooting up.

"And you seem entirely hostile all of a sudden, Caroline," he responded. "I thought you were going to show me some Iowa hospitality."

He held her gaze, half expecting her to demand to know where he was from and what he was doing in Dubuque. He wouldn't lie to her. But neither would he offer information that would undoubtedly make her want to dump him off the wagon seat. One spill an afternoon was enough.

The color in her cheeks and the sprinkling of freckles across her nose caught his eye, and he could not resist a smile. If she had been a New York socialite, she would have been fluttering with manners and etiquette, and not only would she not have been sitting beside him driving a team of horses, but her skin might have resembled fragile white china. There was something unmistakably engaging about the hard edge to her.

And yet there was a delicate edge, too, one that was just as engaging, an edge he didn't think she showed many people. He'd seen it in her startled expression right after he kissed her hand. She liked being a woman, and she liked the attention he had bestowed upon her.

She was . . . fresh. He imagined she could dress in frills and lace or happily don a plain brown dress such as the one she was wearing. On any other woman it might have appeared drab. On Caroline Watson . . .

One simply watched *her*—her face, her pretty sparkling eyes, the loose curly hair frolicking on both sides of her face, the way she tipped her head to regard you. She was lively and direct, and those attributes appealed to Robert, too.

But he shouldn't be having such thoughts. He only wanted to befriend her and her family a little, then ease into a discussion about their lots.

Caroline shifted her gaze back to the reins. Startled by his reaction to her, Robert caught himself trying to breathe a sigh of relief. Behind them, Rebecca laughed low and remarked that the camp was located just over the next hill.

They soon reached it—an encampment of numerous tents held up by poles. Wooden and steel tools lay in piles beneath some of the structures. Robert jumped from the buckboard and rounded it just as Caroline was preparing to leap down.

To her objection, he handed her down. He stood about eight inches taller than she, and she gazed up at him with distrust, sparks leaping in her eyes. She looked angry enough to . . . He could almost imagine her handling a rifle, aiming it at a man.

"I could've gotten down by myself, Kingston," she told him.

"I'm sure you could have," he said calmly. "You've no

doubt managed for years. I was being polite . . . gentlemanly. Say thank you, Mr. Kingston . . . or Robert."

"If you're here about the hotel, you ain't gonna get anywhere."

"I didn't mention a hotel." He would have to remember to apologize to Rebecca later for not helping her down— she had already climbed from the wagon bed and was lifting a crate out. "Your mother mentioned it. Then you made the remark about two streets over not making a difference in the location."

"An' you acted like you knew whether or not it would."

"Perhaps I do. You've no idea what my business in Dubuque is. I hope you do not make judgments about all people a half hour after meeting them."

"You're right, Kingston. I don't know what your business is, an' I don't wanna know. All I know is that you're workin' charm on me for some reason, an' I don't like it."

Well, she had certainly changed her tune. And what was this annoying business of calling him nothing more than Kingston?

He leaned toward her, a breath away. "Now, that's odd, Miss Watson. You seemed to like it very well when I kissed your hand."

She winced, obviously knowing he spoke the truth.

"Have I offended you?" he asked, noticing the scraggly miners drawing forth from their tents. He and Caroline held their interest; their eyes certainly were not fastened on the crate of laundry Mrs. Watson handed one of them.

"I don't like what I've heard so far," Caroline said. "I do like it—your charm, that is. But don't think to talk hotels to me! I'll fill your rear full of shot. Water will freeze in hell before—" She clamped her mouth shut, then lifted a hand to cover it as if doing so would stop the flow of words.

Chuckling, Robert caught the hand, wrapped his fingers around hers, and eased them from her lips.

"W-what are you doin'?" she demanded quietly, shifting from one boot to the other.

He wasn't quite sure. He knew he didn't want her to stop the words. He was used to people weighing what they said before they said it, and he admired the fact that she didn't, even if her words so far had been barbs aimed at him, even though he suspected she could hold a fair discourse with any one of Dubuque's saloon rowdies.

But there was something more—he had reacted out of habit.

He dropped his hand and stepped back, bowing slightly. "Again, I beg forgiveness. My mother grows roses, you see, and I grew up hearing that a touch destroys the petals."

She still looked confused. Not nearly as startled, but confused. "What's that got to do with—"

"Your lips resemble her finest blooms."

She stared at him for a long moment. Then the color in her cheeks brightened. Glancing at the ground, she brought the hand back up. It hesitated an inch from her mouth as she swallowed. Then she lowered it, said, "Oh," and moved toward the wagon bed to lift a crate.

Robert stepped up beside her and lifted another one just as she walked away, unable to approach the tents fast enough.

As soon as Robert met Clarence Watson, he knew where Caroline had acquired her temper, her directness, and her feistiness. The man was thin, hunched, and rather frail-looking. But the sparks in his eyes suggested that though he would welcome you into his house, he would watch you closely, too. You could sit at his table and sup with him, but if he learned later that you had cheated him at something, he would take down the rifle stored on the rack above the thick wooden door and not think twice about ordering you to leave.

"Fished him from Madden's Creek, did ya, Car'line?"

he croaked, chuckling, as Mrs. Watson said something about checking the stew out back.

•   "Nope, Grampa. He ran out," Caroline responded, sounding weary. "If you get a good whiff of him, you'll know why he needs a bath."

Her words were a direct shot at Robert, and he knew it. He lifted a brow and gave her a look of mild annoyance just as she turned away and grabbed a bucket from the gaping hearth that occupied nearly the entire west wall.

The cabin was the most primitive dwelling Robert had ever stepped into. But it was clean, neat, and had an unmistakable air of homeyness.

It was all of four rooms, or so it appeared to Robert. One door led off to the left while another led to the right. Rebecca Watson opened yet another door in the back of the main room—behind a ladder leading up to a loft—and a beam of bright sunshine poured into the house.

There were three paned windows—a little one in the western wall beside the fireplace, and two flanking the front door. Brown curtains were tied back at each one. Logs formed the walls, and cracks between them were sealed off with what looked like a mixture of grass and dried mud. The floor was constructed of thick planks laid east to west.

The furniture was sparse—some rickety chairs, a settle near the fireplace, a thick oak table and a few cupboards nestled on either side of the door in the eastern wall. A few knitted throws hung over the backs of the chairs, and what was obviously a rather worn gray shawl hung across one arm of the settle. Pots and pans were stacked neatly on the hearth; a small kettle hung from one hook of a trammel. What appeared to be pewterware—cups, bowls, and plates—filled the cupboard shelves.

Plain but pleasant, Robert thought. If he had spent his childhood here, he would have been much more comfortable than he had been in the twenty-room mansion he'd grown up in in New York. There were no statuettes for a boy to worry about toppling, no crystal to worry about breaking, no brocade-covered settees and wing chairs to worry about dirtying—this was truly a *home*.

A home he had come to tear apart.

Robert shook the thought from his head. The cabin was simple enough. It could be rebuilt somewhere on the out-skirts of Dubuque, perhaps somewhere in those rolling hills. The hills would certainly be a better surrounding for it than the businesses surrounding it now. And his desire to build a hotel here had nothing to do with that thought; it was simply the truth. This house did not belong on Main Street. Perhaps it once had, but not anymore.

"Let's see about makin' some coffee," the old man said as he headed for the hearth. "Rebecca an' Caroline cook outside durin' the summer, but I'll jist build a small fire here to make us menfolk something to drink. Then we'll commence to talkin'." He coughed, a rattly, wet sound, and Robert remembered Jacob commenting about the man's poor health.

"I'll do it, Grampa," Caroline said, reaching for the pot.

"Naw, now, you go on'n heat water for the man to have a bath. Course, if this was '33, we'd be haulin' 'im to the river an' lettin' him take a good dip there." Clarence Watson laughed.

So did Robert, nervously. Right—the river. For that one snake he had seen in the creek, there were probably a hun-dred in the Mississippi.

Caroline glanced over at him, doubtless reading his thoughts. She grinned, the devil in her sparkling eyes again. "Couldn't do that," she drawled. "He's afraid of snakes."

Her grandfather turned lifted gray brows on Robert. "Ya don't say . . . ?"

Robert shrugged, resisting the urge to glare at the woman. She loved teasing at his expense. "I've, uh . . . I've never liked them. I think I'll avoid the river if you don't mind. Mrs. Johnson's Boardinghouse is just up the street. I'll go there and bathe. Then I'll return."

"Only way I'll stand for that," Clarence said, narrowing his eyes, "is if ya give me a promise to come back for supper. Stew's about done, I imagine, but Car'line here's still got to make biscuits. We'll hold things for ya."

"I would be honored."

"You'd be . . ." Mr. Watson lifted both brows. "Listen at that, Car'line! He's a city gentleman. Says he'd be honored." He shifted from one boot to the other, chuckling again and rubbing his jaw.

Robert couldn't help a smile. The man was not jabbing fun at him; he was truly amazed.

"Don't reckon my gran'daughter's got somethin' to do with you feelin' honored, now, does she?"

Robert looked into Caroline Watson's bright blue eyes, observed her smart chin and the curls springing around her face, and he had the unsettling thought that she *did* have something to do with why he felt honored—and intrigued. She was spunky and more than a little insulting when she wanted to be, but she was also like a dose of sunshine after years of rain; she was different. As much as he told himself to rein his interest, he knew he would not return later for the sake of business alone.

"I reckon she might, Mr. Watson," he said, unable to stop the words. He wanted to take them back as soon as he said them. But no . . . the situation so far was just as Jacob had said—Clarence adored Caroline, and Clarence seemed to like the fact that Robert was interested in her.

Caroline glanced down at the rough handle of the wooden bucket she held, then back up at Robert Kingston. Was he sincere? Or was he looking to charm her, then broach the subject of their lots? She didn't trust him—she was sure of that.

She made the mistake of looking him straight in the eye, and her will and temper melted. She oughtta avoid this man. Oh, she surely ought to . . . She oughtta tell him to get on out of here; she felt almost certain he was after their land. But Grampa, even as hard-nosed as he could be, would think that rude, because Kingston hadn't mentioned wanting to buy their lots.

I reckon she might, Mr. Watson. His response to Grampa made her foolish heart skip.

She again glanced down at the bucket handle, then back up, again meeting Robert Kingston's gaze. He *hadn't* mentioned the land, and she was wrong to condemn him without knowing for sure what he was up to. So maybe, just maybe, she'd try to be a little nice and polite to him this evening. Only time would tell if he was after her—or the land.

Yep, and maybe you're not thinking too clearly either, Caroline.

Ignoring the warning in her head, she smiled a little smile. "Stew ain't gonna keep forever, Mr. Kingston."

"No, I don't imagine it will ... Miss Watson," he responded in a thick voice. Then he turned and headed for the front door.

Just before he pulled it shut behind him, Grampa laughed and said he wished he were young again. Then Kingston was gone, and Grampa teased playfully: "I believe Car'line's got a beau. An' one she likes, at that. One she really likes."

Caroline blushed. "Don't go puttin' too much store in him, Grampa."

"Don't plan to put no store in him 'tall. Reckon I'll jist sit an' watch the developments."

"I should make the biscuits," she said, shuffling off to clear one of the cabinet tops of items so she would have a place to work.

"Gonna get fancied up?" her grandfather asked as she tied on an apron.

She grabbed a wooden bowl, placed it on the cabinet, then dipped flour from a nearby barrel and poured it into the dish. A thin puff of beige smoke rose from the bowl. "Why would I wanna do that?"

"Just thought you might, is all," he said, settling cross-legged on the floor in front of the fireplace. He lifted the coffee grinder, placed it between his folded legs, and turned the handle.

"He's got an Eastern accent, he's stayin' at the same boardin'house as Jacob Fletcher, an' he knows about hotels."

Grampa stopped grinding and glanced up just as she pulled a bowl of lard from a cupboard shelf. "So you think he's in with that feller?"

"He was in the woods near the creek when we rode by. Somethin' spooked his horse—or maybe he spooked the animal himself. Hard to tell. But I've been thinkin' 'bout all those days Fletcher followed me 'n' Ma, an' I don't like what I'm thinkin'."

Her grandfather's gray brows furrowed. "What's that?"

Caroline scooped lard from the dish with a spoon. "That maybe the looks he gives me ain't so much 'cause he likes me as much as he likes the land we're standin' on. That maybe . . . well, maybe he's gonna to try to court it out from under me."

Grampa worked his jaw, as if he were chewing something. Moving his jaw that way was a habit with him when he was thinking. "Even if he got ya to say yes, I'd still say nope."

"He won't get me to say yes," Caroline said, smiling suddenly.

Grampa studied her through narrowed eyes, his jaw still working as she began mixing the flour and lard.

"Whatever you're plannin', Car'line, it'd best not be tonight. Whatever trick or jig's goin' through that pretty head of yers, ya'd better save it for another day. Your ma ain't been none too happy with either of us since we ran Fletcher an' the rev'rend off. I git the feelin' she's 'bout to explode. A quiet woman mostly, yer ma, but I've seen her git fired up plenty enough times when me 'n' your pa stayed 'way of a night longer'n we planned. She didn't take too well to that, an' she told us, but we didn't listen. She set everything we owned outside the door one night an' bolted the both of us out, said she didn't want us around no more. Took her a coupla days a seein' we wasn't goin' nowhere an' that we were sobered up an' a mite sorry afore she finally agreed to let us sleep somewhere besides the barn. Then it was the hog pen. *Then* it was the field." Laughing, he shook his head.

Caroline laughed. "I remember her boltin' you out. I don't remember how many *days* you were bolted out."

"A good week when you sum it up, I reckon. A week spent eatin' meat from the smokeshed an' corn from the crib. Wouldn't wanna rile her too much," he cautioned, rubbing the loose skin on his neck.

"Aw, I wasn't plannin' anything too terrible, Grampa. Just a little dirt here 'n' there on my face an' arms. Thought I might don the dress I wear to muck out the barn. Then we'll see how long Mr. Robert Kingston keeps comin' around. I figure he'd get right to his business then. He'd wanna get it over with so he wouldn't have to come around anymore."

Clarence grinned. "Reckon you're right. But yer ma'd have your hide if ya did that tonight. She'd see through the jig, an' then ya might find *your*self sleepin' with the hogs."

Caroline made a face as she finished mixing the flour and lard. Grampa was right. The two of them were already in hot water with Ma, and dirtying up her face and arms and donning her mucking dress would only make things worse. The hogs were smelly—she couldn't imagine sleeping with them or even sleeping close to them.

She placed the bowl on the cabinet top, wiped her hands on her apron, and said she was going to fetch milk from the stream that ran near the barn. Every day, after milking their two cows, she and Ma stored the milk in a crate lowered into the cool stream. She'd check on Ma, too, while she was out, since her mother had gone outside some time ago—right after they'd arrived with Kingston.

Leaving Grampa with his coffee mill, she headed toward the back door.

CHAPTER

FOUR

"In the creek?"

Jacob laughed as he and Robert stood watching one of Mrs. Johnson's girls pour hot water into the tub in the washroom at the end of the downstairs hall. The girl, clad in a dark blue dress with a smock tied at her waist, withdrew from the little room just as another girl appeared from the kitchen door, located at the opposite end of the hall, with yet another bucket in hand.

Six buckets of hot water now! Jacob had counted them. The girls would add cold water soon, then Robert could sink down into the bath, lather, and hopefully not smell anymore like he'd been dunked in the muddy river.

Some ten minutes ago, just as Robert had appeared in the back doorway, probably hoping Jacob wouldn't see him, Jacob had been coming downstairs, thinking to take a walk around Dubuque because he was tired of the four walls upstairs. He'd spotted Robert, and though Jacob didn't know exactly what had happened, he had a huge suspicion that Miss Caroline Watson had a little something to do with Robert's smell and unusual disheveled appearance.

Robert's hair looked as if he'd raked his hands through it a number of times, and his clothes were splattered with dirt. When Jacob saw him, he grinned; and when Robert turned to politely ask the portly Mrs. Johnson if a bath might be had at this time of day, the sight of the mud caked on Robert's backside doubled Jacob over with laughter. It wasn't like Robert to go rollicking in the mud, so something had happened. Something.

Caroline Watson.

Mrs. Johnson had fought a smile herself; Jacob had seen it twitch the corners of her cherubic mouth. Robert looked surprised, then he twisted to have a look at his rear. He shot Jacob a scowl as he turned his back to the wall.

Apparently he was determined to stay just so until the girls finished preparing his bath.

"You *fell* in the creek?" Jacob asked again between rounds of laughter, a hand clutching his belly. "You?"

Robert scowled. "That's not what I said. The horse threw me into the creek. Miss Watson and her mother happened to be passing by."

"Well, what an ingenious way of introducing yourself to little Caroline. Not a very big thing, is she? Just ferocious. All five feet, two inches of her—if there's that much."

"I did not plan what happened. I hadn't planned to introduce myself to her at all today, and certainly not in that fashion," Robert snapped. "I only planned to have a look at her. And if I had been thinking right I would not have declined her offer of a bath. I would have stayed there instead of coming—"

"She invited you to bathe in her home?"

Mrs. Johnson passed, face aflame as she toted a bucket

of cold water. She had obviously heard the men's words; she cast Jacob and Robert a look of sharp disapproval, then hurried on.

Jacob chuckled low behind his hand. "Scandalous, Mr. Kingston. Bathing in Miss Watson's home! Absolutely—"

"Damn you—hush!" Robert whispered angrily. "What other boardinghouse are we going to reside in when Mrs. Johnson sends us packing? She runs one of the few reputable establishments in Dubuque! I've seen the others— dilapidated and filled with undesirables. The hotels are filled, and while there are rooms to be had above saloons, I would not sleep in one." He shook his head. "Keep your voice down. Caroline Watson was being polite."

"Mm . . . Yes, she can be polite. Seconds before she explodes in your face."

"I told her where I'm staying. We discussed the location for the hotel."

Sobering, Jacob stared at him. "Why did you do that? If you told her where you're staying and you discussed the hotel . . . Who brought the subject up? I thought you were going to go about this slowly. I thought you planned to romance her, *then* talk about the hotel."

"I never said I was going to romance her. That was your idea."

"It may be a bad idea now. She's probably guessed that you're working with me."

"We do not need to deceive the Watsons to get them to sell to us."

"What do you think of her?" Jacob asked.

One of the girls walked by carrying a bucket of cold water. Mrs. Johnson started back toward the kitchen, keeping her gaze straight ahead this time.

"Unusual. Refreshing. You didn't tell me she was pretty," Robert said.

"You didn't ask, my fine friend."

"When you suggested romancing her, you might have mentioned the fact."

Jacob studied Robert again, knowing most women either bored or annoyed Robert. Robert danced with them and took them on buggy rides and all that around New York when the occasion arose. He rode with them at countryside estates and attended all the socially required teas and supper parties. But there was no excitement in his actions; since his fiancée had neglected to appear at the church nearly three years ago, he merely went through the motions of what was expected of a man of his class.

If Robert called a woman "unusual" and "refreshing," that meant the woman interested him.

"You're sweet on her," Jacob blurted in disbelief, forgetting to talk low. "But she's not your type!"

"Lower your voice!" Robert whispered.

"In just a few hours, you're sweet on her," Jacob mumbled, feeling dazed.

"She appeals to me—yes. That's all. That's as far as things will go. We need her land, and I do not plan to let emotions get in the way of business."

"The bath is ready, Mr. Kingston," one of the girls said.

"Thank you."

Still in shock, Jacob rubbed a temple. "By all that's holy! She scares me with a rifle and smites you with one glance! What, did you hit your head on a stone in Madden's Creek? I suggested you romance her, not fall in love with her!"

Sighing with frustration, Robert turned away and started toward the washroom. "Kindly don't talk to me about love. I am going to bathe."

Jacob latched onto his arm. "That's all you had time for, right? Only a few glances?"

Robert twisted his limb away. "Of course that was all we had time for! Why in the name of Go—"

A cough sounded from down the hall. Robert glanced that way and found Mrs. Johnson and her girls standing near the kitchen doorway, watching him and Jacob. And what a scene they beheld: He, in all his disheveled glory, and Jacob looking stricken, as if his best friend were about to march down the aisle with a bride and kneel before the priest. If the bride appeared, that is.

"Your pardon, ladies," Robert said, dipping his head slightly. "My friend and I . . . A mild disagreement. But it's settled now. Jacob . . ." He shot his associate a look of severe warning. "I'm going to bathe. Then I plan to dress and go out again. You'll behave yourself until I return? Not give our charming hostess reason to send you to McClane's Boardinghouse up the street? I'm certain Mrs. Johnson is not hurting for customers."

"Why no, Mr. Kingston, I'm not," she said, gushing beneath his onslaught of manners.

Jacob looked positively wounded. Terribly insulted at the very least. "I was, uh, just going out myself," he stammered, pushing past Robert. His boots thudded softly on the maroon carpet runner. An instant later, he excused himself past Mrs. Johnson and her girls and pulled open the front door. The light lace curtain covering its four rectangular panes fluttered as he shut the portal.

Robert inclined his head to the women again. "Ladies, thank you for the bath."

The girls smiled nicely. Mrs. Johnson blushed to her hair roots. Robert turned and walked to the washroom, feeling their eyes on his back. Then the smiles and the blush turned into giggles.

He sighed. The mud again—the mud caked on the seat of his trousers. He felt inclined to toss the women a glare. Instead he laughed, too, weakly, thinking he might as well find some humor in the indignity.

Despite her apprehension about Robert Kingston, Caroline decided to pretty up.

She had finished the biscuit dough. Then she'd rolled and punched the biscuits and finally baked them in the fireplace oven. The bricks had been heating all morning and afternoon above the fire Grampa had built in the little area beneath the oven, so the baking hadn't taken long. After removing the biscuits and placing them in a bowl on the table, she had gone upstairs, thinking to brush her hair. And now here she stood, peering into the looking glass hanging on her west wall.

Not only was her hair mussed, but her homespun seemed awful drab compared to the calico hanging by a hook on the wall opposite the mirror. That dress looked wonderful on her. It was soft and printed with hundreds of red flowers with green stems that always seemed to bring out the highlights in her hair. She had a blue-and-white gingham, too, but it didn't seem fancy enough to wear to supper tonight and—

She never dressed up for supper.

The thought stopped her cold just as she was lifting a hand to pull the ribbon from her hair. She was about to dress for *him*—for Mr. Robert Kingston. And after she'd conceived that plan earlier to mess herself up so he wouldn't find her attractive!

But suddenly, as she remembered his soft way of looking at her, the way that made her insides tighten and her breath catch, she didn't want to mess herself up. She wanted to look as nice as possible so he might . . . maybe . . . give her another of those looks.

No man had ever looked at her like that.

So she went on and pulled the ribbon and let her curly hair flow around her face. She unfastened the buttons on her homespun, pushed the dress from her shoulders, down her arms, and stepped out of it, then took the calico from its hook and lowered the skirt over her head. Her arms found the sleeves, and she pushed them through. She pulled the dress down, smoothed it over her breasts, waist, and hips, over her plain chemise and camisole, then buttoned the many front buttons.

Taking a deep breath, wondering at her sanity in fixing up for a man she strongly suspected only wanted to charm the land from her and her family, she brushed her hair with her wooden brush, not even flinching when it got caught in a nest of tangles and she had to free it.

She drew up the sides of her hair and fixed them to the back of her head with a red ribbon, then scrubbed her face with a wet cloth until her skin shone with cleanliness. She even scrubbed away the dirt that had gathered beneath her fingernails.

She stood gazing nervously at herself in the looking glass, wondering what else she could do . . . wishing she had some of Ma's perfume made from wildflowers.

She remembered what Mary Sue Jackson had told her in service one morning a few months ago—that pinching your cheeks and lips brought color to them. Color the men couldn't resist. Caroline had laughed Mary's words away as silliness then. But now . . .

Caroline lifted her hands, pinched her cheeks until tears sprang to her eyes, then dropped her hands and smiled at the results. A few seconds later she did the same to her lips.

She stood frozen in place, frightened suddenly.

What *was* she thinking? Oh, what? She'd made herself as pretty as possible, hoping Robert Kingston would again smile at her and talk to her in his polished way. She must be going mad.

But really . . . She spun a little in the dress, then glanced at herself again in the mirror. What was wrong with wanting something that felt so nice? That made her feel flutters and tingles she'd never experienced? She was certainly entitled. She worked hard. She was a responsible person, dedicated to her mother and grandfather. She was permitted an evening of enjoyment, no matter that the enjoyment came to her from a man she shouldn't let get too close.

She'd just be careful, that was all. She'd just be real careful.

"Caroline Mae!" Her mother's voice broke through her thoughts.

Startled, Caroline jumped. "Yes, Ma?"

"Company's here."

That must mean Mr. Kingston had returned. Caroline breathed deeply, then glanced at herself in the mirror again, wondering what he would think. "Be right down!"

She couldn't believe how nervous she was. *Silly school-girl*, she scolded herself.

Nevertheless, she picked up her brush again and smoothed back a stray tendril, knowing full well that as soon as she turned her head, it would wander again. She often wished for straight hair so she could keep it in place, and she wished for it more than ever this evening.

She put the brush down on top of the chest of drawers, telling herself she couldn't wait forever. Her mother and grampa would wonder about her soon, if she'd taken ill or something. They'd call upstairs again, then Robert Kingston might just guess that she was dallying because she was nervous.

She pinched her cheeks and lips one more time, then forced herself to approach the ladder that led downstairs. Taking a deep breath, she placed a booted foot on the first step and descended.

Downstairs, Robert sat on the settle opposite Clarence Watson, drinking the finest coffee he had ever tasted. Clarence shifted in his chair, grinning, the lines around his eyes and mouth deepening in his leathery skin. Robert had arrived just as Rebecca Watson was bringing the small kettle of stew in from outside. Now she moved around the table, arranging spoons, knives, and tin cups. Four wooden bowls sat in a stack to one side of the table. Rebecca mumbled something—she wondered under her breath why Caroline hadn't set the table already. She had brushed her hair and pinned it in a fresh chignon.

"Well, whadya think?" Clarence asked.

Robert lifted a brow. "About . . . ? Oh, the coffee," he said, glancing down at his near-empty mug. "It's the best I have ever had, Mr. Wat—"

"Not the coffee. Her," Clarence said, jerking his head to the left.

Robert turned just as a woman who had to be Caroline began descending the ladder from the loft.

Her pretty calico dress just touched the toes of her boots as she moved away from the last step. The red flowers on her dress enhanced the reddish highlights in her auburn hair, the ends of which just touched her slender waist. Her curls were not the fake ringlets he had seen dangling near so many women's faces and over so many shoulders; they were real, they were natural, and they were stunning. Robert felt a sudden urge to touch them, to move them around, to watch them spill over her shoulders and her nicely curved breasts.

She turned, and her eyes locked with his. But while he looked into the wide blue pools, he drank in her entire appearance.

In front, her hair was drawn up and away from her face, allowing him to truly appreciate her slender jaw, sharp cheekbones, and finely etched brow. And even more than her hair, the dress enhanced her lips. Flushed red, they parted breathlessly like a spring bloom.

She stood stiffly, her shoulders wide, her waist tapered, the skirt flowing down over her hips and legs. There were no frills—no plumed hat on her head, no folded parasol at her side, no lace or ribbons on her dress.

He had thought her pretty earlier. But now . . . now the sight of her took his breath.

"Well, whadya think?" Clarence asked again.

Robert scrambled to his feet, hoping the little coffee remaining in the mug he held would not splash out. He had employed some charm in the hollow this afternoon, easily, confidently, even a bit arrogantly. But seeing Caroline like this . . . The sight of her disturbed him so, he had forgotten an important rule: stand in the presence of a lady. He found himself in the position of having to search around inside himself for the composure he had always thought inherent.

"Why, I . . ." Apparently he needed to find his voice, too. *Damn.*

Caroline gripped the sides of her skirt. Then, as if suddenly aware of her self-conscious act, she opened her hands and let the material fall. Her lashes drifted down to rest lightly on her cheeks. Then up. Then down and up again.

Disturbingly charmed, Robert breathed deeply. He was acting ridiculous, of course. Absolutely ridiculous.

"I think she's exquisite, Mr. Watson," he said softly, placing his mug on one arm of the settle and forcing himself to move toward Caroline.

"Ex-quisite?" Clarence said. "Now what in blazes does that mean?"

"Mr. Watson," Rebecca scolded severely from her position near the table. "Just turn your eyes to your pipe. Maybe pick up that Iowa City paper you've been reading of late."

He grumbled something just as Robert halted a distance of a mere foot before Caroline, who now blushed deeply.

"Never seen anyone stare like you do, Kingston," she said. "I've a mind to go up'n change back to like I was."

He managed a smile. "Why would you want to do that, Caroline?"

"Ain't you supposed to call me Miss Watson? That's proper, I reckon."

"I am . . . But I do not always do what's expected of me."

"I was just wonderin'. You, with manners 'n' all."

"I'll call you 'Miss Watson,' then—if you insist."

"Naw . . . On second thought, I like the way you say my name," Caroline said, aware that she was flirting. Just a little, and certainly not in the expert way she'd seen Mary Sue flirt many a time. But flirting, no less.

His eyes darkened. "Do you?"

"Yep—an' that's the truth." She tipped her head to one side and regarded him from the corner of her eye.

Grinning slightly, he folded his hands behind his back and rocked forward on the balls of his feet. "Caroline, Caroline, Caroline . . . ," he said quietly—for her ears only. "Did your mother fail to warn you that trifling with a man can be dangerous?"

Caroline's breath lodged in her throat. She stared at his parted lips, his strong jaw, the way he had tied his gray-striped neckcloth so neatly. He was fancied up in a tailored suit complete with the smoothest black waistcoat she had ever seen, and her fingers itched to touch it, to skim his broad shoulders.

She swallowed.

"Who says I'm triflin'?" she asked, then flounced past him toward the table, where she picked up the stack of bowls and glanced at him over her shoulder. "I'll dip the stew, Ma."

Robert Kingston had turned to watch her. She *had* been trifling with him, and no, Ma had never told her that doing such a thing could be dangerous. But in Mr. Kingston's case, she thought it could be. Thought it *was*. Mary had flirted then flounced off a thousand times, never seeming to be in danger. But then, she'd never encountered Robert Kingston.

Caroline trembled. What had she done? Something she might be sorry for later? What was going on in her mind today? Madness, surely, for she wasn't another Mary. She and Mary were friends, but Mary's flirting always left Caroline shaking her head in disbelief and embarrassment. She'd certainly never thought she'd ever "trifle" with a man.

As she was dipping the stew from the pot now hanging in the fireplace, Robert returned to the settle. He was there when she turned around. Just standing there. She wanted to ask, irritably, why he didn't sit down. Instead she put a bowl in his hand and told him to take it to the table.

Grampa chuckled behind his Iowa City paper. Mr. Kingston looked a little taken aback for a second or two, then he turned away and carried the bowl to the table. Ma's eyes flared at the sight, and Grampa hooted. Caroline flicked a corner of his paper.

"Caroline surely *does* have a beau," he quipped in a low voice.

"Hush now!" she scolded. Ma hurried forth to take the dish from Robert just as Caroline turned to fill another one.

Seconds later, she handed that one to Robert, too; after all, he'd walked up behind her again with no intention of planting himself on the settle. He was just *there*, right behind her. So she put him to work.

"Caroline!" Mother said, rushing toward them. "Here, Mr. Kingston, I'll take that."

"Aw, Ma. He's got an idle set of hands. Might as well give 'em somethin' to do."

"I can think of plenty for them to do," he mumbled.

Caroline gasped. Grampa chuckled again. Rebecca apparently didn't hear the remark; she hurried up to Mr. Kingston, again urging him to give her the bowl. He finally did, and Caroline filled the third one and put it in his hands before Ma could take three steps toward the table.

He grinned at Caroline. "Trying to keep me busy, are you?"

She scowled. "Washbasin's over in the corner after you put that dish on the table," she said, jerking her head to the left. "Bet your as—*self* I'm tryin' to keep you busy. We're havin' stew tonight—not me."

Grampa chortled. Caroline thought Robert would have something smart to say about that remark, too. Instead he laughed heartily, then walked off to take the bowl to the table.

Caroline flicked the corner of Grampa's paper twice more. "C'mon. Time to eat. Course, I don't imagine you'll eat much. You're too busy watchin' an' listenin'."

He lowered his paper. "I ain't been this entertained in a long time. In a dang long time!" he whispered, wiping wetness from the corner of one eye as he rose. "Imagine he's used to bein' served, an' ya jist put him to work. An' oh, what a look on his face! Lord, Caroline, I wish yer pa was still alive to see this."

"I thought you were readin'," she retorted.

He hoisted himself from the chair. "Shoo . . . I've read that paper durn near twenty times now! Havin' stew tonight, not you . . ." He slapped one knee, laughing more.

Shaking her head in exasperation, Caroline looped her arm through his.

" . . . finest set of doin's I ever seen," Grampa was saying to Robert later as Caroline and Rebecca cleared the table and washed the dishes while the men settled back near the fireplace. Grampa handed Mr. Kingston a corncob pipe. The city gentleman looked skeptically at it for a moment, then said that if it was a pipe, it was a pipe.

Clarence tapped shredded tobacco leaves into the bowl and lit the pipe for Mr. Kingston from a chunk of coal he'd placed in the brick oven. Robert looked a little odd, sitting there in his fine clothes with a corncob pipe protruding from one corner of his mouth. His dress suggested he ought to pay a visit to Mr. Dillinger's Smoke Shop on Second Street. But he seemed content, drawing from Grampa's homemade pipe, listening to Clarence Watson start in again about a county fair he had attended years ago.

"Wagons with ice cream kept froze down betwixt blocks brought from the icehouse . . . Women servin' up ribs, taters, 'n' pies . . . Ole George Tuckett from down'n Charlotte County won the turkey shoot that year. Best damn shot I've seen. Could shoot a cherry off a whore's—"

"Clarence!" Ma scolded.

Grampa chuckled, stuffing another pipe bowl with tobacco. Robert Kingston grinned. "Well, he could shoot a cherry right off anyone's head, I reckon," Clarence went on. "I took the pig that year, of course. Don't know how, though. Thought I'd never catch that thing. My friends Phillip an' Bill, they greased it with lard so thick ya made tracks in it when yer hands slipped off. I finally caught hold of its tail 'n' wrapped the other arm round under its neck. Had me some fine chitlins come winter," he said, lighting the tobacco and drawing from the pipe. Smoke made little clouds above the men's heads.

"Chitlins?" Robert looked puzzled.

"Y'know," Grampa responded—and no, Caroline didn't think the city gentleman knew at all. "Insides . . . 'testines."

Mr. Kingston's eyes widened. Caroline clapped a hand to her mouth to keep from laughing aloud. A sound squeaked out, drawing a look of annoyance from Robert.

"Ya heat a kettle of lard, y'see. Take them 'testines, unwind all ten 'n' some-odd feet of 'em an'—"

"That's quite all right, Mr. Watson. I do not need to know. So you had . . . intestines . . . 'chitlins' come winter."

"Ayah. Did some dancin', too—all night after I put that pig in a crate for safekeepin'. Played Old Dan Tucker till my feet hurt, swingin' the girls round, passin' people. Yes indeed, that was as fine a fair as I ever did see. An' lordy, did I dance a good reel! Could show ya how, if you've a mind to learn."

"To tell you the truth, I was thinking of walking outside a bit with Caroline."

"Were you now? Didja hear that, Car'line?"

Caroline, just drying the last bowl, felt her face warm. After the way she'd flirted with Robert Kingston earlier, and after the way he'd warned her about trifling, she wasn't sure she ought to venture from the cabin alone with him.

"Yep, Grampa, I heard."

"Well, whadya say?"

Her grandfather was too excited about Mr. Kingston's interest in her. He was thrilled, in fact. She knew Grampa well enough to know what the gleam in his eyes and the "whadya say" meant.

"Go ahead, Caroline," her mother said. "There's only the pot left."

"I don't know, Ma."

"Surely Mr. Kingston will be a gentleman," Rebecca Watson said, loud enough that Robert was sure to hear.

"Ma!" Caroline's objection was a harsh whisper.

"You have my word, Mrs. Watson," he responded.

Caroline thought she might die of embarrassment. She didn't need her mother to protect her anymore. She was plenty old enough to protect herself.

"Well, you said you didn't know . . .," Ma whispered. "He's been warned—in a subtle way, but warned. Now, go. It will be all right, Caroline. There's no need to be afraid of him."

Caroline opened her mouth to respond, then shut it. She couldn't tell her mother that she was more afraid of herself—how she reacted whenever Robert Kingston looked at her in a certain way, or when he said certain things, or when he just said her *name*, for heaven's sake.

"Whadya say, Car'line, honey?" Grampa pressed again from near the hearth.

"Oh, all right!" she grumbled, untying the apron she'd donned to help Ma wash dishes.

She folded it and put it in a cupboard drawer, then turned and saw that Robert had risen from his seat, put his pipe down on the hearth, and was heading this way.

She met him near the table, where he smiled and offered his arm. Caroline started to loop her arm through his, but Robert caught her hand and placed it lightly on his forearm, palm down.

She smiled back nervously. She'd seen fancy drawings of ladies being escorted by gentlemen this way, but she'd never thought ... "Ain't like we're goin' to a ball or nothin'," she grumbled.

He made a little bow, sweeping his other arm in, then out—toward the back door. "Why, Miss Watson, do you not hear the musicians?"

"Oh, don't be silly." But she laughed despite herself. Rebecca laughed, too, and Grampa lifted his Iowa City paper, probably grinning like a smart 'coon behind it.

Robert led Caroline to the door.

"It's gettin' about dusk," she said. "I wouldn't wanna stay out too long."

"Afraid of the animals? I'll protect you." He was obviously amused.

"That's what I'm afraid of," she whispered tightly.

He pulled the door open, then placed a hand on the small of her back in a familiar way to urge her outside. Caroline stepped away from him and out into the cool evening air.

CHAPTER

FIVE

The barn was located directly to the right, and that was the direction they turned. A russet-haired cat meowed and nuzzled against Caroline's leg, and she bent to scoop it into her arms.

She nuzzled the animal right back. "Hello, Henrietta. Where've you been? For days 'n' days now I haven't seen hide nor hair of you. You're heavier, that's for sure. Been off scroungin' around for woodchucks again, haven't you?"

"I thought cats ate mice," Robert said.

"Henrietta eats just about any little vermin she can get her claws on. We get a nest or two of field mice now an' then, an' Henrietta cleans 'em out, then goes searchin' for woodchucks the next day."

"Woodchucks are rather large for a cat, aren't they?"

"Yep, but jus' how do you know how big woodchucks are?"

He lifted both brows, looking rather insulted. "I go to the country now and then."

Caroline couldn't help herself—she laughed. She scratched Henrietta's head, listening to the cat's loud purr, then put the animal down gently.

"So you go to the country now 'n' then, Mr. Kingston," she said, straightening. "An' is the country a big adventure?"

He studied her. "Sometimes. It can be."

It wasn't nearly dusk; she had been lying when she said that, unnerved by the thought of walking alone with him. There was still a streak or two of red and orange in the sky, and the colors glittered in his eyes, turning the gold flecks to red shards. He took a step toward her, and Caroline began walking again.

He followed her up the grassy hill on which the gray barn perched. One of the two cows the Watsons had owned for nearly four years, a brown-and-white one Caroline had named Rose, grazed with the two horses at this end of the nearby fenced pasture. Rose's companion, Princess, was solid black except for the white streak running down her nose, and she grazed near the far fence.

Behind the pasture, on the other side of the stream, rose business buildings, many of them gaming houses and saloons, separated by an occasional dentist, apothecary, and attorney. Buildings also rose not far from the westernmost wall of the barn. A hostelry occupied land just east of the Watsons' property line.

"We'll go down by the stream," Caroline said, lifting her skirt to keep dirt from the hem. She heard barking, then Rose and one of the horses spooked, mooing and whinnying. Caroline shook her head. "That'll be Colonel. He likes to scare the cows an' horses."

"Colonel?"

"Our dog. Not but a foot tall, an' the ugliest speckled

gray you've ever seen." She pointed to the little gray form darting between Rose and the horses. "But no matter that he's ugly—he's lovable."

"He'll be trampled."

"Maybe he will. But keepin' him out of there's impossible."

"I like your grandfather," Robert said suddenly.

Slowing her steps, Caroline smiled over at him. "You like his corncob pipes an' tobacco."

"Yes, but ... No. I like *him*."

"Honest?"

He nodded. "Honest."

"He's had some adventures. Wasn't always a miner. He 'n' his friends ... when they were young, they made regular rounds of the county fairs in Virginia. He only told you about one." She laughed, remembering some of Grampa's more bawdy stories, none of which she'd relate to Robert. "They'd win the turkeys an' the pigs, some times hogsheads of vegetables and fruit, an' that's how they'd feed their families for weeks. After a while Grampa joined up with the military for a spell, until one of his legs got hurt."

"I didn't notice."

"It only pains him on days when there's lots of rain. Then he can't walk from here to the house without it bucklin'. He always says how lucky he was that the surgeon didn't have to take it. He got wounded durin' the war with the British in 1813. He hated bein' sent home. He wanted to fight more."

"I imagine he did. He's spirited."

They reached the barn. Chickens clucked, squawked, and raced out of their path. Several roosters strutted near the barn doors, contemplating a fight.

"Red'll win," Caroline observed, jerking her head toward the scarlet-colored cock. The bird ruffled his wings and tipped his head.

"Does he always?"

"Yep."

"I favor the black one myself," Robert said. "The silver on his wingtips gives him character."

Caroline laughed. "Have you ever watched a cockfight?"

He shook his head.

"It's ain't a matter of character, of appearance an' . . . charm," she said, eyeing him. "It's whoever's the fastest an' has the deadliest claws and beak."

His gaze skimmed her face, making her blush. "I've never been involved in one either."

If appearances *did* matter, and if he *were* participating in a fight for females, he would win, Caroline thought.

"No, I don't imagine you ever have to get in fights for women, Kingston. They probably jus' come saunterin' your way, an' the men know they shouldn't lift a fist 'cause they're already beat."

She wondered what she was thinking—if she was thinking. He was watching her closely, amusement making his eyes turn up at the outside corners.

"An' just you never mind. There's no one waitin' behind the barn to challenge you for me," she said softly, against her better judgment.

Was she trifling again?

He studied her, then reached for her hand. But she quickened her steps again, gripping the sides of her skirt, leading the way around the barn, stopping when he stopped, evading his touch.

She glanced over at him and found him looking around beneath a hand hooding his brow. She frowned . . . then laughed when she realized what he was doing.

"As you said—there is no one here to challenge me, Caroline," he remarked, grinning.

"Oh, c'mon, you!" She punched him lightly on the upper arm, trying to be lighthearted. She smiled shyly, a little embarrassed that she'd touched him.

He shrugged. "I had to be sure."

"What's your waistcoat made of, anyways?" she asked, watching it shimmer beneath the remaining sunset.

"Satin."

Her eyes widened. "Satin?"

"Yes, and I don't know why I wore it, except that it's the only evening wear I brought. I imagine the trousers and the shirt alone would have served as well."

"You talk finer'n anyone I've ever met," she said with admiration. "You don't stumble over words an' have to search around for 'em. You just say what you've gotta say."

"I attended school for a number of years."

"I didn't go long. Ma's taught me most everything, an' had a hard time. She's always called me difficult."

"I cannot imagine why."

"Watch yourself, Kingston," Caroline said playfully.

They started down the hillside, toward the gurgling stream. Flecks of color glittered on its surface, and rocks and patches of grass rose in places. Hickories, willows, elms, and occasional walnut trees crowded the easternmost edge, some leaning as if they might topple into the water any moment. Birds fluttered in the many branches as Henrietta darted by Caroline and disappeared into the thick undergrowth.

"Another woodchuck?" Robert asked.

"Something. She catches a lot of little animals. Sometimes she offers them to me 'n' Ma."

"*Offers* them?"

Caroline nodded. "She kills 'em, then brings 'em an' drops them at our feet. She's real friendly that way."

"I wouldn't want a cat that friendly," Robert said, pulling a face, looking taken aback.

Caroline laughed. "You ain't afraid of dead animals, too, are you? Little mice 'n' woodchucks?"

"No," he answered, too quickly.

"You are!"

"I would not want one dropped near my feet, but I'm not afraid of them."

"You are!"

A smile pulled at the corners of his mouth as he poked her ribs. "Stop teasing, Caroline-who-is-afraid-of-men."

She lifted her chin. "I'm not."

"You are. You won't let me get too close."

"That's because you keep wantin' to kiss me." She almost dropped her jaw at her boldness, at what she'd said.

He lifted a brow. "Do I?"

"Yep."

"I don't imagine you would mind as much as you think. As much as you pretend," he remarked, and his tone dropped a notch or two.

"Maybe I would," she retorted.

"Why don't you find out?"

"Because maybe I don't want to." Her skin was beginning to tingle. She wasn't sure she liked the direction this conversation had taken. Rather, she liked it, but it made her jittery. It made her nervous.

"Why are you frightened?"

"Frightened? I ain't frightened! I'm not the one who—"

"Then kiss me."

She planted both boots on the ground and came to an abrupt stop. Kiss . . . *Kiss* him? Be as bold as Mary Sue often was—or at least bragged that she was? She didn't know if she could do that.

But if she didn't, he'd keep thinking she was afraid of him.

She stared at his mouth for a few seconds, then marched over to him, raised up on the balls of her feet, and kissed him on the lips.

He grinned. "That was nice, Caroline. Now—"

She turned and walked off toward the trees. He'd gotten his kiss, her face felt like it was on fire, and now she would very much like for him to leave. Just leave.

She neared a crooked hickory just as his hand slid

around her arm, gently urging her to turn back. She did and found herself looking up into his soft brown eyes, into their gold flecks . . .

"Don't, Kingston. I—"

"I'm not going to hurt you, Caroline," he murmured in a low breathy voice. "Calm down."

His hand slid to her wrist as he stepped even closer, and she gazed up at him, startled. He smelled spicy, like Grampa smelled sometimes when he treated himself to a shave at the barber. Lines created by smiling a lot cut at angles on both sides of his nose, and a small dimple marked an area just below his lower lip. Above his right eyebrow there was a pink scar, something she'd not noticed before. As he stood staring at her, she thought again that it was a sin for any man to have eyelashes so long.

Neither of them said a word as they stood assessing each other. But his gaze soon slid to her lips, and Caroline wondered if she would ever breathe slowly and evenly again.

He took another step forward, positioning himself only a few inches from her, and she thought about bolting. But she didn't really want to—he was going to kiss her, sure as the sun would rise in the morning, and this kiss wouldn't be a peck.

"Easy," he coaxed in his thick tone. "Your hair glows like copper in the sunset, do you know that?"

Slowly reaching up, perhaps fearing she'd run away if he went too fast, he lifted a handful of her hair and draped it over her shoulder. She gasped when the outer part of his hand grazed her breast, then slipped down the length of her hair to her waist. She tipped her head back just as his other hand slid around her middle and drew her to him.

His mouth touched hers, lightly, then he lifted his head, seeming to measure her reaction.

Will he kiss me again? Caroline wondered frantically. His hand on her back felt so strong and warm . . . He was breathless, too, she noticed, not nearly as calm as he was trying to pretend. The hand that had stroked her hair came up to caress her cheek.

Closing her eyes, Caroline whispered, "What're you doin'?"

"Touching you the way I've been wanting to touch you all day."

She opened her eyes just as he lowered his head. He kissed her again, a feathery touch, and she waited, sensing there was more. Oh, there had to be. *Had* to—

His lips covered hers in a hungry caress, coaxing them farther apart. His tongue slipped into her mouth, and Caroline went limp against him. He tasted of tobacco and the herbs Ma always added to the stew, sweet and pungent like marjoram and tarragon. Her arms eased up over his shoulders and around his neck, slipping over the smooth satin, feeling the solidness of him beneath that.

He raised his head, taking his kiss away.

Caroline stared up into his heavy-lidded gaze, wondering at it. Then she licked her lips and pressed her fingertips to the back of his neck, wanting him to give the kiss back.

"Enough, Caroline," he said, shaking his head. "I promised your mother I would be a gentleman." He laughed, a throaty sound, as he glanced down at the hair covering her breast. "I think I've already broken that promise. If we continue, believe me, I'll become even less of a gentleman."

"You didn't offend me," she said, pressing again.

He ducked her arm and her hand, and moved out of her reach. "Caroline, if we continue, do you know what might happen next?"

She did. Well, she'd watched animals—especially Henrietta—a time or two, so she had a good idea. And that was the worst of it—*knowing* what might happen next but still wanting him to continue.

"We'll walk more," he said, starting off.

When she didn't follow, he stopped, then twisted

around, looking irritated. "Stop staring at me like that. The grass would make a fine bed. Right here. Right now. Don't look so wounded, Caroline."

Glancing at the stream, she touched her lips. The red and orange in the sky had burned down to pink, and the coolness of evening had set in. But she was hot all over. Her skin beneath her dress felt strange—still tingly, and it burned.

"I wanna put my feet in the water," she said.

"What?"

"My feet . . . when they get hot, I come here an' put 'em in the stream."

Surprised, Robert gave a flourish with one hand. "Then by all means put your feet in the stream."

He hadn't meant to deepen that kiss quite as much as he had. But once Caroline had been in his arms, he had not been able to resist. Her lips had tasted sweet, like sugar sprinkled on waffles, and she had passion inside her waiting to be set free. He had felt it in the way she parted her innocent mouth so eagerly beneath his, had seen it in the blue heat and curiosity of her eyes. And her reaction had set him afire. It had made him want to teach her more.

"Come on," he said, taking her hand and pulling her with him toward the water.

Once they reached the stream, he removed his waistcoat, spread it on the ground for her, and motioned her to it. Caroline gazed at him in shock.

"You'll ruin it!" she objected.

"I've a dozen more like it."

"Oh." She sat down and drew the waistcoat around her hips, touching it and petting it as if it were a precious object.

Robert sat on the grass beside her and reached to untie the laces on her boots, not failing to notice her slender ankles. His hand slid up to her calf to brace her shapely leg while he pulled the boot off.

Once he had removed both boots, he turned his back so

she could remove her stockings. Moments later he heard splashing, and when he turned around, she was in the stream. She lifted her skirt to her knees as she walked across a row of small rocks. Her smile was a force, brightening her entire face.

"You comin' in?" she called. "It feels good!"

"I'll stay here," Robert said, lying back on the embankment and folding his hands behind his head.

She nodded and went on walking on the rocks, back and forth, laughing as the water flowed between her toes, then around her ankles and calves, not fussing when it dampened part of her hem. He watched her gentle features, the haze dusk created around her. A breeze rustled the trees just as she pulled the ribbon from her hair, loosening the curls to spill around her face and shoulders, not having a care in the world. She was odd, not at all what he was used to in a woman. But despite her being so odd, there was something else about her . . .

She was free, unbound by expectations, undriven by ambition, unhampered by a need to prove something to herself. She was bright and fresh and . . . She was warm country sunshine.

He could lie like this and watch her forever.

"You wanna kiss me again?" she asked much later as they lay on the grassy bank, staring up at the moon. The noise from the saloons drifted their way—the tinkling of music, shouts, laughter, horses whickering from where they doubtless stood obediently at hitching posts in many places. The area where Caroline and Robert lay was fairly dark, but the darkness was broken by the glowing lanterns outside Dubuque's businesses, and by the light emanating from numerous windows.

Robert couldn't help a grin. "You *want* to be kissed again."

"Well . . ." He heard the amusement in her voice, the breath she expelled, almost felt the laughter she restrained.

"My dear Miss Watson, I do believe you have discovered one of the pleasures of life," he teased.

She barked laughter. "One of the *sins*, surely!"

"Do you often lie and watch the moon like this?"

"A lot. I watch the stars, all just hangin' up there. Sometimes there's more, sometimes there's less. It's pretty, ain't it? All silver in that black sky. But not really black. More a really dark blue. It's a fascinatin' world God gave us."

Robert turned to glance at her, to smile at her shadowed face, to admire her.

She felt his gaze; she turned her head and met his eyes, hers sparkling with wonderment and freshness that warmed him deep inside, in a place he thought had never been tapped. "Well, ain't it?" she whispered.

"I suppose it is, when one stops to observe it. *If* one stops."

"You've never laid an' just watched the moon and the stars?"

"No. I've had too many other things to do."

There was a pause, then: "I don't think it's s'posed to be like that. I mean, sure, God told Adam you've got to work for what you need—food an' clothes an' whatever else—and sure, he sent Adam an' Eve from that beautiful garden, but he sent 'em out into this, into a world with lots of things to see, with pretty sunshine and night skies with twinkling stars ever'where. I've never seen Eden, of course, but I can't imagine anything matchin' this. God wouldn't have put us in such a pretty place if he didn't want us to enjoy it."

"Perhaps you're right. Perhaps it's *not* supposed to be like that, Caroline," Robert responded, still smiling. "Maybe we are supposed to stop and enjoy it sometimes."

The cows lowed not far away. The dog—Colonel, if Robert remembered right—had settled near Caroline's feet, his head tucked beneath a paw.

"Guess this means you don't want to, huh?" Caroline asked.

Turning onto his side, Robert propped himself up on an arm and settled his jaw in a cupped palm. He gazed down at Caroline, who gave him a slight smile, one he returned. "Kiss you, you mean?"

She wrinkled her brow. "Well, what else would I mean?"

He reached down and worked a few of her tight ringlets around his forefinger. "You're absolutely disorderly, do you know that? Your hair is everywhere." It was true. The auburn mass partially covered her shoulders, framed her face in a harsh but alluring way, spilled onto the ground and covered a good half foot of grass around her head. There was so much of it, springing all over. He pushed his hand into it behind her ear.

"You've no idea how *badly* I want to kiss you," he murmured, dipping his head to touch his lips to her jaw. She smelled like the air, like flowers and dew and freshly cut grass. How could anyone smell so good?

Instant images of her frolicking in the stream earlier flashed in his mind—her hunching to scoop up handfuls of the cool water and splash it on her face; her not noticing that she wet the bodice of her dress, not even caring; her with bare feet and ankles and a bright face he wanted to watch and watch and watch.

"You're captivating, Caroline," he said, wanting to ease closer to her, wanting to make love to this odd but incredible woman, wanting to drink of whatever it was that made her so special. It frightened him to realize he was losing sight of his goal: He was after the land, not her.

"You mean that?" she queried, her eyes widening. "That's a fancy word . . . captivatin'."

"It's appropriate."

She turned her head, turned her face to him, her lips to his. "What I mean is," she whispered, "are you jus' sayin' that—sweet-talkin' me? Or do you mean it? Really mean it?"

"No, Caroline. I mean it." He certainly did. That was the really frightening thing—he meant it.

Her eyes searched his, deeply, thoroughly, looking for lies, he thought. He felt a flicker of shame that he and Jacob had jested about him romancing her.

But *he* was the one being romanced. He was the one admiring and wanting and wishing . . .

He was mad. He had lost his perspective.

Something small hit the elbow he'd lodged on the ground to help prop himself up, then a timid meow sounded near his head. Something cold nudged its way between his arm and Caroline's head, then fur brushed his skin. Henrietta pushed her way forth and dropped an object on Caroline's chest.

As Robert glimpsed the furry, limp thing that had been in Henrietta's mouth a second before, his brain screeched, and his body shot into action, lurching him away and up onto his shaky feet and legs.

Henrietta stood on Caroline's stomach, watching Robert with glowing eyes.

"Damnation!" he blurted without thinking. "What the—?"

Caroline winced. "I didn't tell you Henrietta gets jealous?" she asked a bit reluctantly.

"No, you didn't."

Caroline nodded. "Even when Ma or Grampa just hug me, Henrietta's got to make sure I know she's still about."

"That cat's glaring like she wants to claw me! She *pushed* her way between us!"

Caroline nodded again. "Jealousy."

"And that . . . that *thing* she dropped on you. It's . . ."

"A woodchuck."

Robert scowled. "Dead?"

"Yep."

"Well, throw it off—or something. Don't leave it there!"

"That'll hurt Henrietta's feelin's," Caroline objected, cupping the small dead animal in one hand while stroking Henrietta's head with the other. "Thank you, Henrietta. It's a very nice gift, an' I love you, too."

The cat meowed her response, then stepped almost gingerly from Caroline's stomach, nudged her furry gift, licked Caroline's hand a few times, then disappeared into the darkness of nearby trees.

"Now that she's gone, you can throw it off into the stream," Robert suggested as Caroline sat up, still cradling the corpse.

She glanced up at him wide-eyed. "Oh, no, I can't do that! Why would you even suggest such a thing? Henrietta would see it, an' her feelin's would be hurt. A gift this nice . . . He's a fairly big one, so Henrietta must be proud of herself. Can't believe she gave him to me instead of eatin' him—and she does relish woodchucks, bones 'n' all, so givin' up this one was givin' up a feast. A gift this nice can't be tossed into the stream. That's somethin' I never do anyway. I bury 'em real deep when Henrietta's not around, y'know. I wouldn't want her to get mad an' stop bringin' me gifts—"

"Heaven forbid."

"—stop lettin' me know she loves me. Why, if you come round often enough, she might jus' take a likin' to you and start bringin' *you* gifts."

"I'll do my best to make sure she dislikes me."

Caroline laughed. "Well, it could be worse," she said, getting to her feet. She leaned toward him and whispered, "She could bring *snakes*."

Robert gave her a severe look, then took a step back since she still cradled the woodchuck. "You're captivating, yes, but also eccentric and more than a little mischievous."

She shrugged. "I have fun. You don't seem to know how to, Kingston." Then she walked off to take care of her "gift."

Henrietta emerged from the shadows to toss Robert another glowing glare just before she hurried off after her mistress, apparently satisfied that she had succeeded in interrupting Robert and Caroline's passionate interlude.

It was the first time he had been thwarted by a cat.

Caroline walked up the hillside toward the barn, aware of Henrietta catching up with her, hurrying along beside her. She planned to deposit the woodchuck in a pail in the barn—Henrietta never minded that—then come back out and say good night to Robert since the hour was getting fairly late, and she always rose early to get the chores done. When she didn't get her sleep, she could be a bear.

With Henrietta trotting beside her, she entered the barn and strode to the opposite side, where more doors opened, allowing silvery moonlight to enter. Beside the doors sat the pail in which she kept Henrietta's gifts, usually until Henrietta wasn't about and she could bury them. Since Henrietta frequently wandered from the farm to explore—about every other day—her gifts never sat for too long and kicked up too much of a smell.

Thank the Lord Henrietta had become reasonable a few years back and had stopped expecting Caroline to sleep with whatever she brought her. She and Caroline had had a few disagreements about that, because although Caroline had a powerful stomach for the most part and didn't want to hurt her cat's feelings, sleeping with a dead animal was too much to expect of anybody, let alone of your best friend.

Henrietta and Caroline had had numerous arguments, with Henrietta bringing the rodents to Caroline's bed and Caroline promptly taking them back to the barn while listening to Henrietta meow, then watching her topple the pail, collect the gift, and take it back to the house.

Caroline had told Henrietta she had to stop being unreasonable, the she loved her and felt loved whenever Henrietta brought her these things, but that Henrietta had to understand that she had a number of things she cherished but didn't care to sleep with.

For the longest time, for months, Henrietta had not understood, and she'd stopped bringing gifts. She'd even pouted and avoided Caroline for a few weeks.

Then one morning while Caroline was milking the cows, she'd felt Henrietta brush against her leg and looked down to discover her friend peering up at her, wanting to be civil again. Caroline withdrew from Princess, the cow, and eagerly pulled Henrietta onto her lap, cuddling and stroking her.

The next time Henrietta brought Caroline a gift, Caroline delicately deposited it in the pail, and Henrietta didn't exactly like the idea—she'd stared at and sniffed around the pail for a good hour—but she left the woodchuck right where it was.

Caroline cradled her latest gift against her chest until she reached the pail, then she gently lowered it into the bucket. Henrietta watched, meowing once to draw Caroline's attention.

"Yep, I'm real proud of you," Caroline said. "You must've hunted an' hunted until you found one big enough to impress me special."

Henrietta meowed her agreement, then sat back on her hind legs, waiting . . .

Caroline lifted a heavy stone slab and placed it over the top of the pail, a means of preventing stray animals who smelled the woodchuck and wandered into the barn from turning the bucket over and making off with her present.

"You don't want me to go back outside, do you?" Caroline asked Henrietta, casting her a suspicious look. "It wouldn't be so hard for you to learn to like him, y'know."

Henrietta tipped her head, as if considering that.

Caroline straightened. "I've gotta go back outside. We left him by the stream. That's rude."

Henrietta meowed again.

"The hour is growing late," Robert said from the opposite door. "I thought I would say good night, then be on my way."

Henrietta rose and began circling Caroline. Stooping, Caroline picked her up and nuzzled her neck. "You don't like him much at all," she whispered in Henrietta's ear. "I've never seen you act this jealous! Are you jealous, or are you tryin' to warn me?"

As Caroline stepped toward Robert, Henrietta leapt from her arms and trotted away, halting near a wide stall, where she sat and stared at Caroline.

Caroline glanced at Robert, who turned his hands palms up and shook his head as if to say, "I don't know what I've done . . ."

"Well, good night, then," Caroline said, wondering if he'd think about kissing her again. Just once more tonight. His lips were soft and warm. She really enjoyed the feel of them. She was getting carried away, she was sure. She was being much too free with him, allowing him too many liberties. Allowing herself to believe he liked kissing and touching her.

He leaned against the barn door and looked at her thoughtfully, then straightened, said a quick good night, thanked her for an enjoyable evening, and turned away to start off.

Feeling disappointed, Caroline wanted to snort at herself. Good Lord, she'd only just met the man today, and she couldn't very well keep throwing herself at him! She was bound to end up getting her heart broken. Like she often chided Henrietta whenever male cats came around and got friendly with her: *You give him too much rein, and he'll just take what he wants, just enjoy himself for a while, then disappear.*

Henrietta never listened to her about that. She enjoyed the attention the male cats gave her, enjoyed it very much, so much so that once Caroline had threatened to paint and dress her up and deposit her in one of those saloons. "Too bad you aren't human," Caroline had said, shaking her head. (She sometimes forgot that Henrietta wasn't.)

"There's so many hungry men comin' to town lately, they could sure use help in the saloons from the likes of you."

Henrietta had been insulted; she stopped brushing against Caroline's leg and ran off with her latest beau— just to show Caroline she didn't want her advice and certainly did not plan to heed it.

Robert turned back and walked toward Caroline. Her heart leapt because she saw in his eyes that he meant to kiss her good night after all.

She smiled, encouraging him, feeling a little guilty about scolding Henrietta for encouraging those male cats with little flicks of her tail and glances over her shoulder. Here *she* stood, waiting, smiling, glancing from beneath her lashes as Robert drew near. She felt somewhat embarrassed in knowing that if she'd had a tail like Henrietta's, she'd have been flicking it, too.

Robert's smooth strides were suddenly broken. He tripped and sprawled toward Caroline. She instinctively reached out to break his fall, hearing him curse under his breath, watching from the corner of her eye as Henrietta trotted back to where she'd apparently been only seconds before—before she'd decided to take action and prevent another kiss.

"Damn cat ran between my feet!" Robert muttered, collecting himself, looking not only angry but embarrassed as he tugged at his shirtsleeves and brushed them off, as he gathered his dignity.

"Henrietta!" Caroline scolded. Then she couldn't help herself. She giggled.

"There is nothing funny about what she did!" Robert objected, his eyes flashing.

"No, no. It's you! You looked so serious, like you knew what you were doin' an' what you wanted, like a man who meant to get it . . . The funniest thing is, I've wanted to do the same thing to some of Henrietta's persistent beaus."

He stared at her, looking doubly insulted now, his brows lifting, his eyes hardening. "Good night, Caroline," he said stiffly. Then he turned and left the barn again, but this time with purpose in his steps.

Caroline thought of a rebuffed, wounded rooster, strutting one moment, gathering his feathers and pride the next. She ought to go after him and apologize. But since she'd already allowed him to become awfully sure of himself where she was concerned, she thought the indignity good for him. So she let him go.

She did muster a glare for Henrietta. "After all the times *you've* encouraged men ... Can't I do it just once?"

Henrietta had sat back down on her haunches. She reached up, licked a front paw, and indifferently began cleaning her face with smooth strokes.

"Uh-huh," Caroline huffed, snapping her hands to her hips. "We'll see how indiff'rent you are the next time one of your men comes around an' I trip him up with a broom. You'll be standin' there or hunchin' there, whatever the case may be, flippin' that tail around, just waitin' for him to do what he's come to do. He'll be wanderin' over, all confident, then fall flat on his face, maybe break his little thing right off. Won't that be a pity? Won't that just be a shame? You all set, an' him runnin' off screechin' ... And you know what, Henrietta? I won't act like nothin's happened, like I didn't do anything. I'll *laugh*."

That got Henrietta's attention. She stopped cleaning her russet face and meowed as if asking Caroline not to be angry, please—she'd only done what she'd thought best at the time.

"Oh, don't look at me like that! You're just jealous. It's not like you really care that he might only be after the land."

Caroline considered the probability that he *was* only after the land, then she approached Henrietta, grabbed a nearby milking stool, plopped down on it, leaned forward, and rested her chin in her cupped hand. It was time to think. And it was time to talk.

"Well, what do you think—*is* he only after the land?"

she asked Henrietta. "I know, I know . . . he's really after more than just that. All males are. The question is—will he stick around after he gets it? If he gets it? You know Henrietta, *your* men never do, I don't mind tellin' you. You don't seem to mind havin' a litter just about every year and takin' care of them all alone, but *I* wouldn't take kindly to that. I can understand now why you flip your tail around an' such, 'trifle' Robert called it, 'cause flirtin' is awful easy when you like the man. But I don't care to ever let any man have all the fun while I'm left to tend a brood.

"Are you even listenin' to me?" Caroline asked, annoyed as she realized Henrietta was staring worriedly at the doorway through which Robert had left. "Blazes! He ain't comin' back tonight! Stop starin' at the door!"

Henrietta walked over, nuzzled Caroline's legs, then sat down in front of her, facing her and giving her her undivided attention.

Caroline tapped her chin thoughtfully. "That's better. Y'know, you tripped him 'cause you're jealous—I'm not real happy with you about that. An' you brought that big woodchuck to hopefully impress me more than he was impressin' me. Lord only knows what else you might do in the future—if he comes around again, that is." She crossed her legs, swinging the top one, thinking more.

Thinking she hadn't been too smart tonight in acting so friendly toward Robert Kingston.

"If he wants the land bad enough, he'll keep comin' around, no matter what—no matter how mean you are to him. But then, he'll keep comin' round if he wants me, too . . . Maybe he won't complain much about whatever you do if he just wants the land, but I can't imagine a man not complainin' if he wants a woman and somethin' or someone's keepin' him from gettin' near her.

"That sounds right to me. I've seen your suitors, Henrietta. Some of 'em wouldn't care if you'd just rolled in Princess's or Rose's dung—but they'd sure have something to say about not bein' able to get the right thing in the right place, about not bein' able to even get near the right place. I've seen bulls go after Princess and Rose, too, so it ain't like I'm stupid about these things. An' I've glanced over the tops of saloon doors and around tent flaps enough to know that when a man wants what a woman's got, he doesn't always care what she looks like or if there's five other males around her at the time. He just pushes his way between 'em and gets to her. An' if he can't get to her—well, I figure that's when a fight happens.

"So maybe you just keep on with your tricks." Caroline straightened. "Yep, that's right. Keep me sensible. Trip him, bring woodchucks—if you can manage it, bring snakes," she said conspiratorially. "Along the way, we'll think of a few more things. If he just wants the land, he ain't gonna get it, an' he'll give up tryin' sooner or later. If he wants *me*, if he wants to roll in the hay with me, that is, or on a tick, he'll keep comin' around until he does. Nothin'll stop him. An' I won't let him till I'm sure.

"I don't plan to make it easy for him. I think I did tonight, Henrietta. I decided right off that I liked his kisses. Durn! You could paint me, dress me up, and put me in a saloon, the way I acted!" she said with a deep blush. "But I plan to be different from now on. I don't plan to be as free with what I have to offer. I reckon you've figured out by now that he still worries me, haven't you?"

Henrietta didn't exactly meow, but the soft sound that emerged when she opened her mouth was nevertheless one of sympathy.

"He worries you, too, a whole lot, I reckon. Well, don't you worry. I'll act better from now on." Caroline wagged a finger at her friend. "But mind you, it ain't 'cause you're jealous. It's 'cause I'm concerned about myself. It's usually real easy for me to say no to a man.

"You should be glad this happened. I understand you better now, after all. Why you act the way you do sometimes. You might be a cat, an' I might be a human, but we're not so different."

Yawning, Caroline moved from the stool to scoop Henrietta into her arms. "You can sleep with me tonight. But remember—I'm not rewardin' you for what you did, though I do thank you for makin' me see things in a sensible way again."

She thought again of Robert sauntering confidently toward her, then suddenly stumbling and having to smooth his feathers. He'd looked so startled and he'd looked indignant, like he'd wanted to break Henrietta's neck, so much so Caroline laughed again just remembering. Henrietta snuggled more deeply against her as Caroline walked out of the barn and headed for the house.

CHAPTER

SIX

When Robert came calling late the following afternoon, Caroline happened to be wearing her mucking dress.

She'd been doing chores, after all, weeding the garden, mending a fence, making butter, scrubbing laundry she and Ma had collected from the miners earlier. Ma had gone to the mercantile to buy sugar, flour, coffee, and a few other items, and Grampa was inside resting after having spent the morning walking around the farm a little, helping with a few chores, and sitting some on the front steps watching the doings up and down Main Street.

"I knocked on the front door, and when no one answered, I wondered if you were back here," Robert said, approaching Caroline where she stood some ten feet from the back of the cabin, stirring laundry in a large tub hanging over a fire. "What are you doing?"

"Laundry," she answered. "Stay around long enough, an' you'll be helpin'."

He chuckled. "I do not doubt that." He held up a small basket. "I brought food. Beef and bread. Cake. I thought we might go down to the stream and picnic."

"There's laundry to be done."

Silence.

"Very well. I don't mind helping. Doing it together, we'll finish soon."

Caroline eyed him. He was dressed like he was going to church—in some finely cut black trousers that hugged his narrow hips and in a white shirt with sleeves that caressed his upper arms and chest. Only Caroline suspected he dressed this way all the time, not just for church, and not just when he had romance in mind. She reckoned fancying up was a habit with him.

He looked fine, gazing at her with his maple-brown eyes, his dark hair combed all neatly in place. She wanted to mess it up, rumple it, and see what he'd do. He was too orderly for her peace of mind.

"I was just spoutin' words," she said. "I wouldn't really put you to work at this. The soap me 'n' Ma make'll take the hide right off your delicate hands."

His face tightened. "Delicate . . . ?"

"Yep. That's what I said. They look mighty delicate to me. Like they ain't seen a good day's work in your whole life."

"They've seen different kind of work, Caroline. I would not call them delicate."

"You didn't. I did. Don't get your feathers ruffled."

Chuckling in disbelief, he shook his head. "You are not being very friendly. You and Henrietta talked, I suppose, and you decided to take her side against me?"

Caroline removed the stick from the kettle and dropped it on the ground, then grabbed handfuls of dirt from a nearby pile and tossed them at the flames beneath the pot. The fire sparked, then began dying.

"Henrietta can't talk," Caroline finally retorted, feeling embarrassed because she *had* talked to Henrietta. Because she *always* talked to Henrietta.

"Well, you must admit that for a cat she has some very human qualities. Jealousy, wanting attention—your attention. Bringing gifts." Robert shook his head. He'd never seen a cat act the way Henrietta had acted last evening.

She shrugged. "Animals can be like people."

He studied her, wrinkling his brow slightly. "You're talkative today, too."

"No, I ain't. I—" Caroline glanced up and realized he was being sarcastic. She shut her mouth and dragged a dripping shirt from the pot. Some of the water spilled over onto the hot coals, making them sizzle. Caroline took the shirt to the board and tub she'd placed on a table not far away, and began scrubbing the garment.

"That doesn't look hard," Robert said.

"Never said it was."

"I could do it. And your hands don't look bad. So why do you think I would lose my skin if I helped you?'

"Because you ain't used to the strong soap."

"If it does not affect the skin on a woman's hands, it won't affect a man's."

Caroline made a sound in her throat, one of disgust and annoyance. She often did work enough for two or three men around the farm, work one man might not be able to do alone, depending on his sturdiness, and she didn't like the sound of what Robert Kingston had said. That a man could do just about anything, put his hands in just about anything, and come out it better than a woman. She'd seen hands burned from strong lye soap, *plenty* of hands, all kinds of hands, and she knew better. She'd nursed them— her own and a few others. He didn't know what he was talking about.

He stepped up to the kettle and reached out, meaning to stick his hand into the water. Caroline had heated it just enough that it wasn't boiling. But it was enough to burn a person if that person wasn't used to hot water.

"I wouldn't do that," she advised, but she knew by the skeptical look he gave her that he meant to anyway, especially now that she'd warned him against it.

She grunted. So he didn't believe her. That was fine. He could go on and do what his wise mind was telling him to do. He could treat her like a stupid country girl and stick his hands in that pot if he wanted to. But she knew that if he did, he'd probably get burned. Come an hour or so from now, that lye would be eating his hands raw.

According to him, she didn't know much of anything about what she was dong, no matter that she'd been doing it for years, and his attitude was downright insulting. So let him go and be smart and stick his hands in the water. She didn't care. Who was she to stop him? If he wanted to be a fool, if he wanted to ignore common sense and her warning, she'd get out of his way. That was the way she operated. She had no patience for stupidity.

She'd be fixing him later, she thought with an unhappy twist of her lips. When he came to her with sore hands, asking for something to put on them, she oughtta turn him away. Yes, sir. She surely ought to. But she didn't suppose she would. He'd look at her with his rich brown eyes, and she'd melt.

He stuck a hand in the water, and promptly jerked it out. Caroline went on with her scrubbing, working at a particular spot she didn't figure she'd get out—it was dark and looked as though it had been a part of the gray shirt for a while—but it was something to concentrate on anyways, so she wouldn't appear worried about Robert.

Still, she watched him from beneath her lashes as he picked up the stick, dipped it in the water and lifted what looked like a pair of trousers. He brought them to the table and placed them beside her tub.

"We'll take turns, shall we?" he asked.

He was trying hard to get her to be more sociable, to get

her to talk to him, to help her. He was working his charm on her again. Charm she was determined to resist today.

But resisting it was hard. She knew by looking at his nicely manicured, pale hands that he wasn't accustomed to hard work, and yet he was willing to scrub clothes so she could finish the laundry sooner than she normally would and have time to go sit by the stream and eat with him.

The way he whittled at her heart and will was irritating.

"I'll do the scrubbin' " she said, worrying about his skin again, worrying about herself. Worrying in general.

"We'll take turns," he said stubbornly. "Do you have another board and tub?"

"Hellfire! Would you stop tryin' so durn hard to help?" she snapped, slapping the shirt against the washboard. "I know for a fact that the soap on these clothes'll burn you. I've done wash like this for years. I know what I'm talkin' about!"

She suspected that the entire business she'd discussed with Henrietta last evening and mulled over most of the night was about to spill out. She was irritated, thoroughly irritated.

They were so different, she and Robert Kingston, and while he'd said some awfully sweet things to her last night, she had to keep her wits about her. He wasn't after her . . . he was after the land, she felt certain. He was just trying to go through her to get it.

She didn't like being played for a fool, and she was determined that she wouldn't be. She knew she was the backbone of her family right now. If Ma had been alone, the Methodists or Mr. Fletcher would have had the land already, and if Grampa had been alone . . . well, he had his rifle—when he could reach it. But the truth was, Grampa didn't have a lot longer to live, and if he alone were trying to keep the land, when he died in a few years, the church people and the hotel men would move in and take it then. Caroline meant to see that none of them got it—ever.

So if Robert Kingston's attempts to romance her were

so he could get the land, they might as well put the issue on the table and talk about it right now.

Tipping his head back, Robert stared down his nose at her.

She spoke softly but firmly: "Just put your head back straight, Kingston, pull that stool over"—she jerked her head toward the back of the house, where a three-legged stool sat—"sit, an' tell me what a fancy man like yourself sees in a girl like me. It ain't smarts, that's for sure. I can tell by the way you don't believe me about the lye soap burnin' you."

She shook her head. "Explain what you see in me, 'cause, y'know, I've been thinkin' about all that kissin' we did last night, about all those smooth things you said to me. Fact is, I thought about it most of the night, that it was fine but that it makes no sense. I'm not like you, you're not like me, an' honest to Pete, it just makes no sense. There we were, you kissin' me by the barn, you watchin' me from the grass by the stream, us layin' together in the moonlight. I figure by the look of your skin an' clothes— hell, just by the polished way you talk—that you've got some education an' money behind you. More money than I'll ever see in my life, that's for certain. So I can't figure it, as much as I puzzle over it. Of course, there's the matter of the hotel an' that Mr. Fletcher you work for. That's the only reason I can figure that a man with your polish would be interested in a girl like me."

"Y'see, Kingston . . . ," she began scrubbing the shirt again, pausing only to flash him a sly smile, "I've got a good head, and I'm wearin' it better today, now that the sun's shinin' real bright an' there's no one whisperin' sweet words in my ear an' comin' real close and kissin' me. Now that there's no one tryin' to romance me. So pull that stool over, put *your* head back on right, and talk. Surely Fletcher's told you we won't sell, but you can ask. I'll warn you, though—ask once, we'll say no. Ask twice, we might do more than say no. An' that's not a threat, that's just fact. We've fought the Methodists on one side and Fletcher on the other, an' by now me 'n' Grampa are damn sick of it all."

He stood watching her, one brow lifted slightly higher than the other. He looked surprised, as if he didn't quite know how to react to her verbal onslaught.

Then he did something that surprised Caroline. He threw his head back and laughed. Laughter bubbled up from his chest, deep and delightful, erupting until Caroline couldn't help but laugh a little herself.

But not in good humor. No, no, she didn't feel too amused right now. She felt pretty damned irritated if the truth be known. He still wasn't taking her seriously. He was laughing at her. She'd said no to Jacob Fletcher when he'd asked about the land, then she'd backed that no up with an unloaded rifle. Maybe she ought to make sure it was loaded when she said no to Robert Kingston. Maybe she ought to make sure and let him *know* it was loaded.

Looking confident and far too handsome, Robert folded his arms across his chest and chuckled more, then had the nerve to lean forward and say, "We both know you liked those sweet words and kisses."

"Uh-huh," she muttered. "And you prettied up again today an' came here to give me more, didn't you?"

"You're assuming I don't want to, that I'm forcing myself."

"Yep. To get our land."

"Have I mentioned land?"

"You're thinkin' it."

"You're entirely too distrusting, Caroline." He said her name in his smooth way, the way she liked it said.

She fought the warmth that began in the pit of her belly. "Just a bit wiser than you think I am," she responded, setting her jaw.

"I came to ask if you would have a picnic dinner with me. That's all. You certainly had no misgivings about walking with me near the stream last evening, about boldly asking if I wanted to kiss you again."

"Last evenin' I had Grampa and Ma needlin' me. An' when they weren't needlin' me, you were romancin' me. But today, like I said, it's brighter an' my head's clearer. I can see right through you, Mr. Robert Kingston. I ain't lived in Dubuque this long, with so many rough sorts all around me, and not figured some things out. I've watched all kinds of people come through here with all kinds of plans. You're just another one."

Slowly but surely his grin began to fade as he studied her. Finally he went after the stool, plopped it down a distance of maybe a foot from her tub, then settled on it.

Caroline wrung the shirt she'd been scrubbing, rinsed it in a large tub to her left which contained rainwater, then wrung it again and draped it over the twine strung from one corner of the cabin to a tree. She grabbed the trousers he'd brought over and began scrubbing them. In silence, he watched her work.

"Start talkin'," she said. "Get right to it, Kingston. I don't mind tellin' you that today I feel a little like a fool, lettin' you kiss an' romance me like that. Feelin' like a fool does something to my pride. Hellfire, it does something to my temper!"

"I can see that," he said, half grinning.

She wanted to smack that silly smile off his face. "Are you workin' for Fletcher?"

He leaned forward, parted his thighs, threaded his fingers together, and let them hang between his knees. He glanced up at her beneath his dark brows, and she didn't miss the sparkles in his eyes, the amusement. Like he still didn't take her seriously.

"I work with Jacob Fletcher," he finally said.

She eyed him. "Yep. But I just bet you're at the helm most of the time." He had something in his eyes Fletcher didn't have. He was sharp, cool, and he could be shrewd. He was measuring her up, but not as carefully as he ought to. Even she knew how unpredictable she could be, how quick her temper sometimes went off. A loaded flintlock, pointed at just the right place, might send him running with his tail between his legs . . .

She didn't trust him, and she durn sure didn't like him laughing at her. He obviously thought he'd get the land sooner or later if he hung around long enough, if he courted her enough.

"You ain't gonna get our lots," she said quietly, evenly. "So if that's all you're hangin' around for . . . if that's the only reason you're in Dubuque, you might as well leave."

"Are we going to picnic or not?" he asked calmly.

"After the laundry's done," she responded. "As long as you understand what I'm sayin'. You think a lot of that charm of yours—I can tell. But, Kingston, it ain't gonna work on me."

He didn't move. Well, except for the fact that his smile widened a little. Like she didn't know what she was talking about. Like he thought he had the upper hand. Like he figured he could just reach out and touch her and she'd melt.

She might have yesterday. Hell, she *had* yesterday! But not today, and not in the future. She wouldn't. She had him figured out now. Better than that, she had herself figured out.

"I bet you're used to romancin' women, ain't you?" she asked, thinking aloud. "An' gettin' 'em all, too." She bet it'd make him nuts not to get one he went after. She bet it'd hurt his male pride real bad. More than her pointing a loaded rifle at a certain part of him would.

"Caroline," he said, "would you like to go picnic by the stream?"

"What I'd like is for you to ask me outright about the land so I can tell you no. So we can have that out in the open."

"Now, that would be rude, wouldn't it? I didn't come to

talk about the land. I came to picnic with you—if Henrietta will let us. Where is Henrietta, by the way?"

"Chasin' vermin, most likely. Trippin' 'em up, like she did you last night."

He chuckled. "You're so complimentary, Caroline."

She scrubbed the trousers on the board much harder than she normally would have. "An' you're slick—or think you are. Y'know, I've got plenty of other men interested in me. You ain't so special. Why, I turn away at least two a week. Maybe I'll stop doing that."

"That's your prerogative."

She glared. "Like I said, Kingston. I've got laundry to do. An' I don't plan to do anything else until it's done."

"I asked if you had another board and tub."

She opened her mouth to warn him about the lye soap again, then snapped it shut. He'd insulted her in a roundabout way by looking so self-assured, by treating her as if she didn't know what she was talking about, by regarding her as a stupid little female, by trying to romance her just to get the land . . . So she reckoned she'd let him find out that she did know what she was talking about. She reckoned she'd let him find trouble.

She wasn't going to worry over the fact that his hands would end up raw if he helped her. Let him help her, let him try to impress her, let him go on thinking she wasn't intelligent. Let him go on looking mighty and arrogant, like he'd win in the end. He fancied that stool as being a lot higher off the ground than it was, like it was a throne or something similar, and she'd love to topple it and watch him fall. She reckoned letting him stick his hands, which surely had never seen a day of hard work, in laundry water would help tip his throne a bit.

Yep, it surely would.

Without another word, she scurried off to get the other board and tub.

Not twenty minutes after she had fetched them from the shanty attached to one side of the cabin, made room for them on her table, and he had begun working, Robert noticed that his hands were getting warm. He felt tingles at first, then heat, then a rawness that went well below the skin, burning deeply into his flesh. The soap affected more than just his hands; it burned halfway up to his elbows since water splashed up from the garments while he scrubbed.

The scrubbing itself was not as easy as Caroline made it look. Beneath the afternoon sun, Robert broke into a sweat. Perspiration gathered beneath his arms, on his back and chest, wetting his shirt and making it cling to him.

Still, he kept working. To back down now, to admit that the soap was burning him and that doing laundry was harder work than he had imagined, would do something to his pride. Too, he could only imagine the smug look Caroline would surely give him if he admitted to being burned and that he was tired. She would flash him a knowing grin, then laugh, just as she had laughed when he had been thrown by that horse and frightened by that snake.

He scrubbed four shirts and five pairs of trousers, and seethed inwardly when Caroline tossed two of the shirts back at him and said they weren't good enough, that they still had dirt on them. He wanted to throw them back at her and tell her that if she did not approve, perhaps she could scrub them more herself. But she gave him a haughty look that said, "I told you you couldn't do laundry. You're too delicate," and he went to work harder than ever on the shirts, gritting his teeth to keep from wincing, his hands burned so badly.

He took the last shirt from the pot and concentrated on scrubbing away ever small spot of dirt, trying to ignore the fact that not only did his hands burn as if being roasted, but also his shoulders and arms had begun to ache. Being raised the son of wealthy New York socialites had definite advantages, he had decided long ago, but right now he thought—no, he *knew*—one advantage was that he had never scrubbed his own clothing, let alone scrubbed it under a scathing summer sun with lye eating away at his hands.

Caroline had been right about the soap burning him. Unfortunately his extreme pride would not permit him to admit that aloud.

"Well, I reckon we won't be havin' a picnic dinner after all," Caroline said, glancing off at the sun. It was beginning to lower some to the east. "Ma must've decided to stop an' visit friends. She'll be comin' home soon, though, an' we'll start supper."

"There's still time," Robert said. He was not about to let her escape the picnic he had planned. Not now. Not when he had scrubbed clothes for several hours so she would eat with him by the stream.

Shading her eyes, she peered at him. "It ain't the time I'm talkin' about necessarily." She jerked her head to the left, indicating he should look behind him.

He did—and cursed when he saw the toppled picnic basket, its contents scattered and half-eaten, the Watsons' mangy dog wolfing down what looked like the last slice of beef.

"Get the hell— Why didn't you stop him?" Robert demanded of Caroline. "You obviously knew he'd been behind me all this time having a feast! Why didn't you stop him?"

She shrugged. "Figured you wouldn't be in any kind of shape to have a romantic picnic anyways, not with your hands an' arms lookin' so red. I reckon—"

"My hands are fine!" he virtually roared.

"Oh, don't yell," Caroline said, giving him a crooked smile. "My pa used to say my gramma used to look like a mad cloud about to bust when she got angry. Till now, I've never seen anyone look like that. If you really were a mad cloud, you'd have lightning an' thunder rippin' all around you. You sure your hands are all right? They do look awful red. You could stay for supper with us, y'know. I bet Ma'd be more than happy to have—"

"No, thank you," he responded tightly, wringing the shirt he had just washed.

"Aw, shucks. If it's a matter of smellin' like Colonel there 'cause you've been sweatin' so, we've got a washbasin. You could even go down an' take a dip in the stream. Ain't no snakes in there. Lots of other critters from time to time, though. But surely nothin' that'd scare you. You bein' such a man 'n' all."

Robert dipped the shirt in the rainwater, rinsing it, watching her, silently seething, wanting to wring her neck the way he'd wrung the shirt. Wanting to throttle her. Feeling childish and temperamental and on the verge of shouting rude words at her. She was having the time of her life.

The woman irritated him to no end.

He watched a breeze flutter messy auburn curls across her sunburned cheeks and freckled nose. He observed the way she had pushed her sleeves up past her elbows, and he took note of her glittering blue eyes and the smudges of dirt on her face. She was pretty, endearingly pretty sometimes. But how in the world he—Robert Allen Kingston—could be so attracted to the mischievous young woman, wearing a ragged gingham dress that had seen better days at least ten years ago, he didn't know.

And she smelled like a stable, at that. He had noticed the smell of manure and animal sweat on her soon after arriving earlier, and had said nothing. But truthfully—she reeked.

"I'm a gentleman, Caroline," he said with careful control. "Otherwise I would turn you over my knee."

"Hah!" She laughed. "Stretch that shirt out real good now when you drape it over the line. Sorry about your picnic. Seems a shame it's gone to waste when you worked so hard over that scrub board. I'll be doin' more laundry tomorrow if you wanna come help again."

She turned and walked off, her curls bouncing on her back, her hips swaying just enough to be provocative. She flashed him a smile over her shoulder, one that lit her entire face like a ray of sunshine.

Muttering a curse at her smug look, Robert threw the shirt on the ground, then growled at Colonel, making the dog whimper and creep away. He grabbed his basket and shot a string of curses at Caroline's back and the cabin she was just entering. He shot a string of curses at himself, too, then headed around the side of the cabin toward Main Street.

Rebecca had just arrived home with various items she'd bought at the mercantile. She had arranged the items in the bed of the wagon she'd guided carefully through Dubuque's ever-increasing traffic. Delighted to see Mr. Kingston drawing nigh, she smiled and sat more erect on the buckboard seat, preparing to greet him.

But as he came closer, her smile faded, for he looked anything but happy. His brow was creased, he was muttering what sounded, shockingly, like curses, and perspiration dampened his shirt in places.

She'd known him little more than a day, but already she knew that he took great care with his appearance—or so she had assumed. He had not seemed like a man who rolled up his shirtsleeves and actually worked. She wondered why his hands and arms were beet red to a good five or six inches beyond his wrists.

"Mr. Kingston?" she queried, grabbing the edge of the wagon seat to steady herself while climbing down. "What's happened? Why are your hands so red?"

"Your daughter," he said, breathing deeply, looking like a man on the verge of losing his temper, "is a scoundrel."

Rebecca's mouth formed an O. She lifted a hand, fingers bent, wanting to erase whatever it was Caroline had done now the way she might erase figures or letters from a slate.

"Oh . . . Caroline. You will come back, won't you?" Rebecca managed, watching him walk away. She so wanted Caroline to marry and *calm down*, and wouldn't it be nice if Caroline married someone like the mannered, obviously well-to-do and educated Robert Kingston?

But no, Caroline was undoubtedly putting him off the way she had put off so many promising young men—with her sharp, insolent tongue and atrocious manners, taught to her by none other than her grandfather, who was something of a scoundrel himself.

Caroline admired Clarence and, disturbingly, wanted to be like him in many ways. Would she never learn that she shouldn't always say exactly what was on her mind, and that if she was determined to do so she must learn to speak in a tactful manner? Dear. And for heaven's sake, behave herself! Not laugh when a horse tossed someone or when a person ran from a snake. Not aim rifles at people.

As Rebecca watched poor Mr. Kingston walk off, she could not help but shake her head. A minute or so later, she lifted her skirt and turned toward the cabin, meaning to scold Caroline good.

A few hours later, at the boardinghouse down the street, Harriet Johnson shook her head of graying curls at the sight of the hands displayed on the table before her. She wondered if any remedy she, or anyone, applied would heal the skin on them or take away Mr. Kingston's discomfort. When she glanced up, she saw pain he wouldn't admit in his tight expression and in his brown eyes, and she gave him a sympathetic yet reproving look.

"Even men feel pain, Mr. Kingston," she said softly.

He withdrew his hands and slid them beneath the small table as his associate entered the sitting room and approached. He obviously didn't want Mr. Fletcher to know that he had somehow burned his hands.

Harriet wondered how exactly Mr. Kingston had managed to find so much trouble. Yesterday he had come in smelling like the river, with dirt caked on his— Well, that certainly had been startling! And somewhat amusing. Even now, Harriet fought a smile and a blush, recalling the sight.

Mr. Kingston was a city gentleman—she had seen enough refined men and women come through Dubuque to spot one—and the incident yesterday had been an absolute affront for him, though he had managed to laugh at himself in the end. Now this . . . But she didn't suppose he would be laughing about this. He was in pain.

How in the world had he managed to burn his hands so? And why had he come to *her*, asking if she knew of anything he could put on them, looking sheepish, angry, and embarrassed all at once? She had sent one of her girls—Clarissa—off to the kitchen for some lard to rub on his hands. But they were not burned in the regular way. They weren't blistered. They were just red and raw. Harriet wondered if the salve would help.

"Good evening." Jacob Fletcher first greeted Harriet with a nod of his head, then glanced at Robert Kingston, narrowed one eye, and said suspiciously, "You look distressed, my friend."

"Mrs. Johnson and I were conversing," Mr. Kingston responded, straightening his shoulders. The fact that they had even been slumped surprised Harriet. He seemed like such a strong man, a man with purpose, with resolve. So confident. She again wondered what had happened to him, if he had had a run-in with some of the town ruffians.

She wished all the rowdies would be run out on a rail so decent folk might be left alone. She wished much success to the churches being raised here and there about the city, too, because the congregations were the ones who would take the law—what little there was—into their hands and see this place tidied up. Dubuque could certainly use more God-fearing people, individuals who were doubtless not afraid to pull down every saloon and gaming house board by board, pole by pole. People who were not afraid to lock up every ruffian, if need be.

As far as she was concerned, however, she minded her

own business. One could not be a successful proprietress in a town such as this if one did not mind one's own business. Of course, she always observed things . . .

"I don't know that this'll help, Mrs. Johnson," said Clarissa, hurrying into the room with a small bowl in hand. "If you don't mind me saying so, those look like lye burns. My sister takes in laundry from time to time, and now and then her hands get all red and raw like that. I've never seen hands like that on anybody but a laundress."

"Don't be foolish, girl," Harriet scolded, snatching the bowl from Clarissa. "Mr. Kingston does *not* do laundry. Do not compare him with a laundress."

Meekly lowering her lashes, the girl turned and rushed off.

Suddenly realizing Clarissa was right, Harriet met Mr. Kingston's gaze with curiosity. He shrugged, something flickered in his eyes, and for a few stricken seconds, she wondered if he *had* been doing laundry.

But what a foolish notion! Why would he need to? She had no way of knowing the level of his financial success, but she'd spoken to Mr. Fletcher, who often volunteered information, and she knew enough—that Robert Kingston was from a well-to-do New York family and that he and Jacob Fletcher were the owners of two prospering hotels in other cities—to know that he didn't need the pittance most laundresses earned.

"Should I apply it for you, Mr. Kingston?" Mrs. Johnson inquired. "Or do you wish to do it yourself?"

"I'll do it."

"Can you?" she had to ask.

"Someone making me feel I *could not* do something was what caused this," he muttered, exposing a hand to grab the bowl.

Or ridiculous pride, she thought, drawing back. "I didn't mean to—"

Pushing back in his chair, he inclined his head to her. "I'm grateful for your concern, Mrs. Johnson. I truly am.

But I need to know if I can manage at least one thing to-day, one simple thing, and it might as well be rubbing lard on my hands."

"And your arms," she mumbled, feeling sorry for him. "Don't forget your arms."

"They will not let me forget."

"Another encounter with Caroline Watson?" Mr. Fletcher asked, pressing forth, a silly grin twitching the corners of his mouth as he stared at Mr. Kingston's hand. "Robert, you made a promise. That I would get detailed accounts—"

"Of all happenings," Mr. Kingston finished tightly.

Jacob folded his arms. He had the nerve to grin, to actually grin at his friend's troubles! "She's a laundress . . . You've fallen for her, but she obviously hasn't taken such a liking to you. What? Did she forcibly put your hands and arms in water laced with lye soap?"

"Of course not!"

"Well . . . ?"

"I'll tell you upstairs."

"I just came from upstairs. I'm going out. Tell me now. Here. You've always been a man of your word . . ."

Mr. Kingston tipped his head so that his chin was properly lifted for a man of his class. "I asked her to picnic with me. She did not have time. She had laundry to—"

"Didn't have time?" Jacob Fletcher grunted. "Caroline would make time if she really wanted to."

"She had laundry to do," Robert Kingston continued, trying to appear undaunted. "I told her I would help, then we would eat."

"And did you enjoy your picnic?"

No answer.

"Robert . . ."

"The . . . dog enjoyed the picnic," Mr. Kingston bit out. Then, under his breath: "Last night, the cat. Today, the dog."

"I'd hate to have to start spying to get the entire story," Mr. Fletcher remarked, chuckling.

Mrs. Johnson lifted a fine brown, wondering what this was all about, suspecting she knew, horrified at thinking that a woman would put a man off in such a way, touched that Mr. Kingston had been so sweet as to offer to help the girl with her laundry so she would have time to picnic with him. She'd only met Caroline Watson once, in the mercantile, but she'd seen her plenty enough times on Dubuque's street and had often thought the girl could be better groomed and mannered.

"So apparently things are progressing well between yourself and little Caroline?" Jacob inquired.

"Progressing . . . Yes."

"Well?"

"Enough."

"Respectably?" Mrs. Johnson had to ask. Both men turned their gazes on her, Mr. Kingston's annoyed, Mr. Fletcher's amused. Shocked at herself, Harriet clapped a plump hand over her mouth, then lowered it to her throat and smiled weakly.

"Things are progressing, just as I said," Robert Kingston growled, shoving past his associate.

"Oh!" Mrs. Johnson exclaimed as Jacob rammed into the table. They both watched Robert huff from the room.

"Well," Jacob said once Mr. Kingston had disappeared. "That means Caroline has the upper hand."

"Mr. Fletcher!" Harriet gasped, appalled. "Am I to presume that this girl is . . . is tormenting Mr. Kingston in some fashion and that you are delighting in it?"

He bowed with a flourish. "Presume what you will, madam. If he didn't learn a much needed lesson the first time a woman made a fool of him, perhaps he will this time."

Leaving her with a slack jaw, he, too, exited the room.

CHAPTER

SEVEN

Caroline *had* made a fool of him, and that was exactly why Robert was so angry, why he was more determined than ever to get the land Jacob had chosen for the site of the hotel. Facing Jacob's laughter and the knowing look in the man's eyes was a humiliating enough thing. But after Caroline's scheme earlier today, Robert would not—he absolutely *refused* to—see his and Jacob's latest business venture built on anything but the lots Jacob had chosen. The day he finally left this godforsaken town, he would do so with his chin lifted proudly, knowing Caroline had not succeeded in chasing him off and that he had obtained the lots, helped oversee the building of the hotel, and wiped the smirk off of Jacob's face.

Another woman had humiliated him.

Pretty little harmless Caroline Watson had undoubtedly

laughed behind his back, all the while watching that mangy dog chomp on the picnic dinner he'd had one of Mrs. Johnson's girls prepare. He had planned the afternoon, and Caroline had destroyed his plans—and laughed while doing it!

Stewing, Robert spent the remainder of the day and most of the night nursing his hands, applying the lard Mrs. Johnson had given him. The grease didn't help to soothe the burns at all; in fact, his hands felt hotter. He awoke four times during the night to apply more lard, cursing Caroline every time.

Shortly before dawn he awoke again, to thunder and lightning and rain slashing against his room's one window so hard he expected to see and feel flying glass any minute. Saloon music, laughter, and shouts drifted in through the window. His hands were smarting again.

Some of this was his own fault, he supposed in grim retrospect as he stared down at them. Caroline had told him the lye soap would burn him, and he had chosen not to heed her warning. He had chosen to be stubborn and smart and help her scrub the clothes anyway, assuming she was wrong about the soap burning him and that laundry could not be that difficult to do. He was still angry about her letting Colonel eat their picnic dinner, but the burns on his hands and arms were his fault, not Caroline's.

Still, she was a scoundrel, he thought, stumbling from the bed to apply more lard.

Despite the thunderstorms, the sky began to lighten; the day began to dawn. Robert found that as much as he had been awake during the night, he could no longer sleep. He finally dressed and went downstairs in search of coffee.

He found a fresh pot and clean cups in the center of the large table in Mrs. Johnson's plain but comfortable and spacious dining room. Here evergreen curtains were tied back at the three tall windows, allowing dim morning light to filter in through lace panels. There was activity on Main Street, Robert observed through one window after he had poured himself a cup of coffee and settled in a chair. But wasn't there always activity on Main Street, and even the surrounding streets? How quickly he had learned that Dubuque was a town that did not sleep, that there was always shouting and carousing in the streets, that there was no quiet to be found here.

But then, the only quiet to be found in New York— home—occurred during the early morning hours, when even the ruffians there slept. Here, they didn't seem to sleep at all.

Handling the cup was difficult. His hands smarted every time he moved them the wrong way, every time he bent his fingers. But the coffee smelled good, its heady aroma twisting up from the mug along with puffs of steam, and he meant to enjoy it whether or not doing so caused him pain.

He tried bending and slipping his fingers through the cup's handle, but quickly decided that handling the cup in the usual manner was not possible this morning. The heat from the coffee made his hand smart more.

He finally ended up pulling the cup closer to him, hunching down, putting his lips on the rim, and sucking up the delicious brew. Hoping that no one would enter the room and see him slurping from the cup, he glanced around nervously.

Managing to tip the cup, he consumed nearly all the coffee he'd poured. He heard a crash, then Mrs. Johnson speaking in a sharp tone to someone in the kitchen next door. The dark portal leading to that room was partially opened, he noticed for the first time since entering the dining room. He knew there were two other entries into the kitchen, one from the hall and one from the back of the house, through which whoever was in the room might have entered. Which explained why he hadn't heard them before.

"If you would not run in here with the milk and eggs, you might not have so many accidents, you foolish boy!"

Mrs. Johnson scolded. "I've had enough of my girls and I having to clean up your messes. I'm of a mind to buy what I need from someone else, perhaps from one of the merchants here in town. How would that strike you? Not only are you late most of the time—I've told you five A.M.— you spill and break half of what I pay for!"

"D-don't fire me, Mrs. J-Johnson, p-p-please," a small voice said. "My pa'd b-be aw-aw-awful mad. I'll do better—p-p-promise!"

"I just bet he would. I hear he drinks most of what I put in your pockets! Disgraceful! And that's the other thing. Why should I contribute to a drunk's habit?"

"P-please, Mrs. J-Johnson. I kn-kn-know . . . kn-know I'm c-c-c-clumsy. I kn-know I'm l-l-l-l—"

"Oh, do spit it out, boy! You won't get sympathy from me! I've never heard anyone stutter so."

"I-I-I'm s-s-sorry. I'm . . . I'm . . . I'm . . ."

Hearing a low groan of frustration, Robert rose from his seat at the table and moved toward the kitchen door, softly, quietly. Curiously, an all too familiar feeling closed around his heart, his brow drawn with concern.

"Stop that, I said!" Mrs. Johnson shouted just as Robert peeked through the crack between the door and the frame. "No one talks like that. Take this cloth and get down and clean the floor! Don't open your mouth again today, and when you return tomorrow, I expect you to speak to me in an understandable, reasonable way. And not spill the milk and break the eggs!"

Robert watched the haughty woman toss a small towel at the boy standing before her, his face downcast, his bottom lip quivering as he dared a glance up at the creature ridiculing him. The child couldn't have been more than six years old, if his size was any indication. He snatched the towel out of the air, then stood unmoving—except for that quivering lip.

The boy's tousled black hair was fairly long, hanging wet and stringy to well past his shoulders. He was pale and thin, perhaps even bony beneath his clothing—a tattered brown shirt and baggy pantaloons. His brown eyes were like twin chocolate drops, they were so large and such a contrast to his skin.

"You heard me!" Mrs. Johnson said, waving an arm as if she would have liked to strike the lad. "To the floor with you and start cleaning!"

The stout, austere woman turned away toward a table cluttered with pots and kettles, and Robert pushed the door open all the way as the boy dropped to his knees.

"Now that I've had a moment to think," Mrs. Johnson said, turning back, "I do not care for anything about you. I do not like your speech, your appearance, your tardiness, or your clumsiness, as you call it. I want fresh milk and eggs, but I can get them elsewhere. I refuse to contribute to your father's whiskey habit. Do not return after to—"

"That's a bit harsh, don't you think, Mrs. Johnson?" Robert interrupted, startled. The woman was being an absolute ogre. "I had a brother who stuttered when he was nervous. A child should not be blamed for the actions of one parent or another, or both, whatever the case may be. As for the boy's clumsiness ... admitting a fault is the first step toward remedying it. Of course, a person needs time to work through something so difficult, and patience from those around them."

"Mr. Kingston!" Harriet Johnson flashed him an embarrassed but patronizing smile. "With all due respect ... the boy works for me, but his habit of spilling the milk and breaking the eggs—I cannot do business that way!"

"And that is your excuse for ridiculing him?" Robert demanded.

She flushed cherry red. The lad had paused in wiping at a spreading pile of milk, broken glass, and eggs to glance up with a flicker of what Robert thought was hope—mixed with fear.

"I manage the people who work for me in the best way I know how, Mr. Kingston," Mrs. Johnson said quietly, clearly shocked and insulted. "There are other boardinghouses—"

"None as respectable as yours certainly, but then, lodging at a less reputable establishment might be preferable to compromising my principles," Robert responded just as quietly. "Just as you feel you should not contribute to the boy's father's undesirable habit, I should give serious thought to contributing to what I suspect is your habit of tearing apart the character of people you feel are beneath you. I've been shocked a number of times since arriving in Dubuque. But nothing . . . *nothing* has shocked me quite as much as what I just heard and observed."

Inhaling deeply, she raised a finely etched brow, pursed her lips, then dropped her gaze to the floor.

With some effort and discomfort, Robert dug several coins, quarter dollars, from a vest pocket, and tossed them on the table cluttered with dishes. "For your trouble," he told Mrs. Johnson, having learned almost from birth that money could make most everything all right again, that people respected money.

Her brows jumped, but her lips relaxed somewhat.

Robert turned to the boy, who had gone back to wiping furiously at the mess on the floor.

He approached the lad, hunching near him. The boy glanced up, a look of gratitude softening his brown eyes. "Your name?" Robert asked.

"D-D-David, s-s-s-s-sir."

"Do you have other eggs and milk to deliver this morning, David?"

"N-n-n-n-n-no, sir."

"Then perhaps you would join me for breakfast at a restaurant up Main Street a ways."

David's eyes widened more, if possible. "I'm n-n-not dressed good. I g-g-g-got no other clothes. N-No money to b-b-buy any with. Yer r-real nice to off-ffer, b-but I'd embar-embarrass you. N-not a good th-thing."

Robert laid a smarting hand on David's arm. "You would not embarrass me."

"Y-yep I—"

"Would *you* be embarrassed?" Robert asked gently.

The boy nodded.

"Then we'll buy you new clothes."

David studied him, clearly mystified. "W-why?"

"Because you need them—and because I want to have breakfast with you."

"Y-y-yer sure?"

"I'm sure. With what I've just given Mrs. Johnson, I'm certain she won't mind finishing up here for you. So come along," Robert said, taking David by an elbow and urging him to stand.

The boy stepped right into the mess he had created, crunching a piece of eggshell and slipping in a patch of yoke. As his feet slid out from under him, Robert had the presence of mind, despite the fact that he'd had only one cup of coffee and not even all of that, to latch painfully onto David's arm and try to set the lad right.

David grappled at Robert, twisting his shirtsleeves, then his vest, before Robert was able to put him back on his feet. David brushed Robert's sleeve back into place, then tugged at his vest, making a heroic effort to tidy it, too. Robert smiled.

"S-s-s-s-s-sor-ry," David said.

"I could cook breakfast for you and the boy, Mr. Kingston," Mrs. Johnson offered, stepping forth before Robert could respond to David's apology.

"I would not think of inconveniencing you," Robert said. "Besides, David may benefit from more hospitable surroundings."

Clutching her hands in front of her, the woman shrank back.

"Shall we, David?" Robert asked the boy.

Grinning slightly, David started from the room with him.

Robert wasn't sure how David did it, but before they reached the door leading to the dining room, the boy managed to upset two pots from Mrs. Johnson's table and a pewter cup that had sat peacefully on a nearby cupboard. He tipped the latter, fumbling fruitlessly with it before it toppled over and clattered to the floor.

Mrs. Johnson spoke up, her voice containing none of its earlier harshness, only resignation and a plea: "If you would, Mr. Kingston ... please ... take him through the back door? I have silver, china, and crystal in the dining room. Not the finest, but it is all I have."

One side of David's mouth twisted grimly. "M-m-maybe a g-g-g-g-good idea," he told Robert.

Robert agreed.

Once outside, Robert and David avoided the rain by walking beneath awnings that extended from Main Street businesses. David toppled a chair situated near the swinging doors of a saloon. Righting it after several fumbling tries, he moved on, bumping into people and stumbling off the edge of a walkway, right into the mud.

As Robert helped David to his feet, he noticed an approaching lady who carried at least four packages obviously bound for the post. Slipping in the mud again, David accidently tripped her.

The lady gasped as she tumbled, clutching her little black hat to the top of her head and staring in disbelief from where she sat, her packages scattered around her. Her beady blue eyes darted in surprise from Robert, to David, to her ruined parcels.

"S-s-sorry," David said, sighing, scurrying to gather the packages. He slipped again, and down he went, splattering the lady more.

"Oh!" She shielded her face with her arms, then turned her hands over and grimaced at the mud on them.

Now Robert sighed, wondering what he had gotten himself into and wondering if he and David would ever arrive at the dry goods store where he hoped they could purchase clothing that would fit the boy.

He somehow managed to put the lady on her feet and gather her packages himself. He offered to take them to the post for her, but she scowled at him and David, then huffed away, finally disappearing in the laughing crowd that had gathered on the walkway behind them.

Looking sheepish and embarrassed, David shrugged at Robert. Robert shrugged back, trying to make light of the situation. They grinned at each other and walked on.

David followed Robert's gentle suggestion that perhaps he should put his hands in his pockets. Luckily they reached the dry goods store without further calamity.

But once inside the two-story business, whether from excitement or nervousness, or both, David pulled his hands from his pockets. Almost immediately the pieces of a toy china tea set went flying. Robert turned around and around, lunging this way and that, trying his damnedest to catch a saucer, a teapot, a sugar bowl, and a creamer.

He did manage to snatch the teapot out of the air, but everything else . . . He closed his eyes when the shattering began. It was all over in the space of seconds, he was certain. But damn if those seconds didn't seem like very long minutes.

"Here now! You young'uns get— Oh, pardon me, sir. Some of the local young ruffians come in from time to time, an' I have to shoo 'em out. What's happened here?"

Robert turned around to find a small, thin man regarding him from beneath heavy silver eyebrows. His matching mustache twitched in silent disapproval as he surveyed the damage incurred by David's errant arm.

"You're the proprietor, I presume," Robert said, smoothing his vest. It was a wonder he himself hadn't caused damage to something, the way he had swung around trying to catch the flying china.

Toy violins, a cooking set, a doll cradle, and a bureau sat on the same shelf the china had occupied, though Robert didn't think the cradle had been lying on its side and the violins had been so scattered about the shelf when he and David first started down this aisle. Brushes and combs, pipes, tobacco, and cigar cases lay in neat order on an opposite shelf. At the very end of the shelf stood a Turkish water pipe—of all things to find in a Dubuque shop—its amber glass shimmering in the morning light that spilled into the store through the open doors.

David stood a distance of a good two feet from the water pipe, but he was too close for Robert's peace of mind. Robert moved to stand between the boy and the fine, rare item.

" 'At's right, I am," the twitchy man said. "The proprietor. Mr. Fulton's the name. Now, answer my question—what's happened here? A man can't be too cautious in these parts."

"An accident, Mr. Fulton," Robert assured the merchant.

"Yeah, well, even accidents have to get accounted for."

Nodding, lowering David's right arm, Robert dug into his vest pocket. Wincing at his smarting hand, he pulled out some bills. "Name the price, Mr. Fulton, and please accept my apologies."

Mr. Fulton did exactly that. After graciously accepting Robert's money, he asked if he could help him find something.

Robert again lowered David's arm. He wondered if the boy even knew when the arm rose. "Put your hands back in your pockets, David. Yes, Mr. Fulton, there is something you could help us find. We're looking for clothes, ready-made clothes for David here, if you have anything. If not, perhaps you could direct us to another shop."

Mr. Fulton studied him. "Not from around here, are you?"

"Does that matter?"

"Can't rightly say whether it does or doesn't, or whether it will or won't. Depends a lot on you—and how you handle being in a place like Dubuque. Depends on how you treat the people. It ain't unheard of for a person to survive here," he said, ducking slightly as splintering glass sounded somewhere outside, not too far away. "We've got a town marshal, for all the good it does us. Have to say, though—we've got more law an' order now than we had, say, five years ago. Hell . . . more now than two years ago!"

"Where?" Robert couldn't help asking as two male voices rose just outside the open doors.

"Round about. Clyde tries, bless his soul. You fellers go somewheres else and quarrel!" the shopkeeper suddenly shouted toward the door.

"Yessir, Mr. Fulton," one of the men responded, and within seconds the disputers had moved on.

Mr. Fulton slanted a grin at Robert. "A'course, some things you have to handle on your own, y'see, an' hope for the best."

"I see," Robert said grimly. "Perhaps you have the secret to getting at least one good night's sleep in Dubuque, too?"

"Plug your ears," Mr. Fulton answered matter-of-factly.

"Plug your ears—"

"Yep, that's what I said. Either that or move out of town."

"Thank you for the advice, Mr. Fulton," Robert said, and despite not liking much about what he had found since coming to Dubuque, he smiled. He liked the friendly storekeeper regardless of their startling first meeting.

Mr. Fulton inclined his head, his grin widening. "Now then . . . the boy needs clothes, you said. He's your boy?"

"No, he's uh . . ." Robert glanced at David, who stood staring, shamefaced, at the ruined china set. Robert draped his arm around the lad's thin, narrow shoulders. "He's a friend."

David glanced up at him in amazement. "W-w-wh—?"

"That's nice," Mr. Fulton said. "That's real nice. We need more people making friends with each other in

Dubuque. It ain't a hopeless place. It just needs to be cleaned up a bit. It's improving. Respectable businesses going up here and there on Main. Clay, Iowa . . . other streets . . . they'll get cleaned up, wait 'n' see. Last I heard, some fellers are planning to build another hotel. Or they want to, that is. Them and the Methodists are trying to get their hands on the Watsons' land just up the street. Watsons won't budge, though—I could've told the church people and the hotel men that."

"I'm one of the hotel men," Robert said.

Mr. Fulton's heavy brows shot straight up. "Is that right?"

Robert nodded.

"Well now, we wanna make you feel real welcome then. And if this boy . . . What'd you call him—David?" At Robert's nod, Mr. Fulton continued. "If David's your friend, we wanna make him feel real welcome, too. Reckon it won't hurt none to introduce you to the committee aimed at cleaning the city up either—the mayor, aldermen . . . some of the temperance ladies, who're all in favor of closing up some of the sinful places—and movin' the Watsons outside of town. Or at least off Main Street, so it can be all business," he said in a low voice. His tone was back to normal when he finished: "Won't hurt none if I close down for a spell this morning to do just that."

"I would be glad to meet the committee members, Mr. Fulton," Robert said. "But first, I promised David clean clothes and breakfast at Mrs. Everly's Kitchen and Restaurant."

"Emmaline's Kitchen is a nice place to breakfast, if I must say so m'self," Mr. Fulton said with a wink. He lowered his voice again. "Got a little interest in the Widow Everly, if the truth be known. I'm a widower, you see, an' Emmaline's lookin' better and better to me every year. She can cook real decent, too, an' that's important."

With a grin and another nod of his head, Robert agreed.

He liked Mr. Fulton almost as much as he liked Clarence Watson. And the odd thing was, neither man was his sort.

But then, what kind of man—or woman, for that matter—was?

"The clothes . . . ," Mr. Fulton said, rubbing his mustache. "Don't have ready-made ones in the store, but I have something just as good. Have a trunk upstairs where I live. They're outdated, but the wife kept everything that had to do with our three children, an' so the trunk's full of some of my grown boys' old clothes. We could rummage through and find some things for David."

David's face lit up. Robert gripped the boy's shoulder good-naturedly.

"I-I-I'll k-keep my h-hands in my p-p-pockets," David managed.

"A barber friend of mine runs a shop at the other end of the street if you're interested in his services," Mr. Fulton offered.

"If David is agreeable to getting a haircut," Robert responded.

David nodded eagerly.

Mr. Fulton gave a small tug on one side of his mustache, then dropped his arm and started past Robert and David. "It's all set then. I'll get the broom and clean this up, then we'll close up for a time, go upstairs, and dig down into that trunk."

"Y-yessir!" David said.

CHAPTER

— ● —

EIGHT

"Well, would you look at that," Caroline said in wonder, her eyes fastened on one of the windows of Mrs. Everly's Kitchen and Restaurant. Only recently the two-story gray building had been whitewashed, and a new sign proclaiming ownership and the business to be found within had been stenciled and hung just above the green awning that sheltered the walkway.

"Where do you s'ppose those two met up?" Caroline asked no one in particular, though Mary Sue stood nearby. Caroline dodged snorting horses, creaking wagons, and conversing people as she started across the street, mumbling, "Never figured him to be one to like children."

"What are you talking about?" asked Mary Sue, catching up. Despite the overcast day, her pretty blond curls and hazel eyes shimmered in the morning light.

"That feller there." Caroline pointed to a lower front window in Mrs. Everly's establishment, where, just beyond, Robert and a boy sat across from each other at a square table.

Caroline glanced at Mary, then back at the surprising sight before them. "He's one of the hotel men. I can't seem to get him to ask me about the land outright. Figure he'll whisper the question in my ear one day soon, though, since he's romancin' up to it. That is, if he comes back courtin' after yesterday."

Mary looked baffled, her face all scrunched. "You told me about the hotel men, but you didn't say one was romancing you!"

"Tryin' to romance me. I got caught up in it at first. It ain't every day a man tells a girl she's captivatin', after all, an' talks to her in such a smooth voice. But now I—"

"Captivating?" Mary released a small squeal. "Caroline, he really told you that?"

Caroline shot her a scowl. "Sure he did! I wouldn't lie to you."

"That's pretty special. Why didn't you tell me?"

"Since he first came callin', I haven't seen you till this mornin'. Ain't had a chance to tell you. Besides, it's nothin' I'm especially proud of. He thinks I'm a stupid country girl."

Mary's eyes grew large. "He said that?"

"Naw. He wouldn't."

"Then why do you think he thinks that?"

"It's the way he's so slick half the time, I reckon. Like he always gets what he goes after, like I don't know what I'm talkin' about. He's really workin' the charm on Grampa, an' the bad thing is, I think Grampa likes him a lot."

Caroline watched the fork Robert held fall to his plate. He picked it up again, and it fell back onto the dish, landing on a pile of fluffy scrambled eggs. The biscuits looked delicious, the bacon crispy. If Caroline had that plate of food in front of her, she'd eat it up real fast.

But he sure didn't seem too enthusiastic. He picked the fork up again, but this time, doing so took effort; he couldn't seem to bend his fingers around it right. A second later it fell again.

Caroline put a hand to her mouth as she realized what was happening: The poor man couldn't hold onto the fork, his hands had been burned so bad!

Poor man?

Hellfire! He'd insisted on helping her scrub the laundry. She'd warned him, but he'd insisted.

Heaving a sigh and looking disgusted, his face taut with frustration, he managed to push the plate away from himself with the tip of a finger. Caroline felt a shiver of guilt go through her, a shiver she fought off.

"You don't like him?" Mary Sue asked.

A man came flying out of a nearby gaming house, landing in the muddy street. He scrambled to his feet and started off in a rush. Three other men charged out after him, shouting curses and waving bottles. Two deputies rode up the street, looking as scroungy as most men in Dubuque. A person wouldn't know they were deputies if the person didn't spot the stars roughly cut from tin and attached to the fronts of their dark shirts. One pulled a pistol, turned it upward, and shot a bullet into the air. The men who'd charged from the gaming house paused, glanced off after the man who had come flying out of the building and who was now running up the middle of the street, then glanced back at the deputies and finally turned back, grumbling, to the gaming house.

Mary and Caroline went on talking, undeterred by the everyday occurrence. "I like some things about him," Caroline admitted. "But I know what he's really after, an' that sticks in my craw. Why not just ask for the land? Why try to charm me 'n' Grandpa an' Ma? Clyde must've hired himself more deputies," she mumbled, watching the two lawmen ride by. She didn't recognize them. They tipped their heads to her and Mary. Fights and drinking and rollicking really were a common occurrence in Dubuque, but there was something different about what she and Mary had just witnessed. Fights weren't usually broken up, because there weren't usually lawmen around to break them up.

"Clyde did," Mary said. "That one . . . that dark-haired one. Isn't he so fine? So handsome?" Mary gripped the sides of her skirt and swung it back and forth while glancing at the man from the corner of her eye. The deputy gawked, gripped his saddle, then grinned and tipped his head again.

Caroline laughed. "Mary, he's gonna fall off his horse! You think just about every man's fine. That's why you're not married yet. You can't decide. You flirt with one one day an' another the next."

Mary giggled. "Well, the world is so full of men. How can I possibly choose?"

They turned back to the restaurant window. "You like some things about the man in there, you say?" Mary asked.

Caroline shrugged. "Some things."

Her friend leaned close. "The way he kisses?"

Caroline gave Mary a light shove. "Now, that ain't none of your business."

"Is too. We're best friends. What happened to his hands? They're so red!"

Caroline watched him wince when he tried to lift a mug. Looking down at its contents, he ran his tongue across his bottom lip. The boy seated opposite him said something, and Robert glanced up and gave him a hopeless shrug and a sigh, then made a show of slowly pushing the mug to the center of the table. The boy shook his head, obviously feeling sorry for Robert, then commenced to shoveling food into his mouth.

Robert's sleeves were unrolled today, but Caroline knew

that halfway up to his elbows, his arms were just as red and raw-looking as his hands.

She wondered if he'd seen one of the doctors in town, if anyone had given him anything to help relieve some of the pain he must be feeling. Most likely they'd given him butter or lard or some sort of ointment. But that wasn't what really worked on a burn. Those things wouldn't take away the pain—only cider would. She'd learned that from Grampa a long time ago when she'd burned her fingers on a hot kettle.

She'd walked away from Robert yesterday because his stubbornness had made her angry. If he was so determined to help her scrub clothes, who was she to stop him? she'd thought.

Now she wished she *had* stopped him somehow.

She squared her shoulders and again told herself that she shouldn't be feeling sorry for him. He'd chosen to ignore her warning. He'd acted as if she didn't know what she was talking about. He'd put his hands in the strong lye soap water, insisting on helping her. She hadn't forced him to help her, so she shouldn't feel bad about his discomfort.

She wasn't far from home, where a jug of cider sat near the cupboard. . . .

"*Has* he kissed you?" Mary Sue asked.

"Oh, what does it matter?" Caroline retorted more sharply than she had intended. "What matters is that he wants the land, not me."

"He said that?"

"No. But, Mary, look at him. There's somethin' fine about him. An' you should hear him talk! He's educated an' polished . . . Even if he was after me and not the land, I'd have to think twice. We ain't nothin' alike."

"You like him a lot. I can see that in your eyes, Caroline."

"That doesn't mean he's for me."

"Why couldn't he be?"

Caroline frowned. "You're talkin' nonsense."

Mary sighed. "It wouldn't be the first time a fancy man got caught by a plain girl."

"I ain't out to catch him. An' I ain't plain," Caroline objected, self-consciously touching her hair. She wasn't. She had bright blue eyes and pretty auburn hair. Leastwise, that's what Grampa always told her.

"How do you know?" Mary taunted. "You don't peer into a looking glass often enough to find out. Only long enough to put your hair back in a ribbon and make sure you're dressed."

"I pretty up for church!"

"You ain't been to church in a month. Besides, it's one thing to pretty up for church. It's another thing to pretty up for a man."

"I prettied up for *him*!" Caroline blurted before thinking.

She groaned at herself. She didn't want anyone to know just how much she liked the way Kingston looked at her, just how much she wanted him to look at her in his soft way again and talk to her in his polished voice. She didn't want anyone outside of Grampa and Ma to know that she'd dressed up for him the other evening. She didn't know what had gotten into her head then! Some fool nonsense about enjoying his attention.

"You did?"

"Yep," Caroline answered, real low. "But only once, an' only once it'll stay, you hear? Who is that boy? Where did he get him?" she asked no one in particular as she watched Robert smile and talk to the boy seated opposite him. For some reason, Robert looked more at ease than Caroline had seen him, more at ease than when he conversed with Grampa. His eyes were real bright, too. Whoever the boy was, Robert liked his company a lot.

"Why don't you go in and find out?" Mary asked. "Find out what happened to his hands, too. They look bad. They look like they hurt."

"It's his own fault." Sniffing, Caroline turned away. She

started down the walkway. "If he hadn't been so durn stubborn . . . if he'd listened to me instead of thinkin' I don't know anything . . . if he hadn't been thinkin' whatever a woman can do a man can do . . . I ain't gonna feel sorry for him. He burned his hands, an' that's his fault, not mine. He ain't my responsibility. Lord knows, I have *enough* responsibility. He's seen a doctor by now, I bet. He's had somethin' put on his hands."

But not cider, surely, 'cause she hadn't heard too many people other than Grampa talk about putting cider on a burn. And why weren't his hands wrapped? Why was he letting the air get at them? That didn't help none. That probably made them smart worse.

"Sounds like you know what happened to his hands and just aren't telling," Mary Sue said, falling into step beside her. "Do you have something to do with them looking that way?"

Caroline put her hands on her hips. "No, I don't! An' just don't you accuse me of that again!"

"Criminy, Caroline," Mary responded in a small voice. "I didn't accuse you. I just asked."

"Well, I didn't have nothin' to do with 'em gettin' burned! I told Kingston he shouldn't oughtta help with the laundry, an' he did anyway! So he can nurse his own hands!"

"He helped you with the laundry?"

"That's what I said." A man staggered in front of Caroline. She caught a strong odor of sour whiskey and glared at him. He nodded his head, considering her with what must have been blurry vision, then staggered off. On the walkway just ahead, the Reverend Brunson accosted the man with a shake of his Good Book, and began telling him to repent, to give up the evils of the bottle and follow him to the house of the Lord.

"Ya got whiskey there?" the man asked, grinning, showing all of two teeth.

The Reverend Brunson forced a stiff smile. "The ladies

of the congregation have made the finest brew you can imagine, and cakes to go with it."

"Ya don't . . . ," he hiccupped, ". . . don't say?"

"Oh, but I do, sir."

"Wife hasn't made cake in a long while," the drunk said. "Haven't seen her in a long while, really." He leaned close to the reverend, who jerked back the slightest bit, and who Caroline could tell fought to keep from reeling back. "She's in Pennsylvany. Had to leave her there while I come here to scout the possibil'ties. Been sleepin' out at the mines unner the stars of a night."

"We have beds set up in the basement of the Lord's house."

"Now, don't—"

"Come along then. Have some brew and some cake and a warm bed tonight. All are welcome in God's house." The Reverend Brunson looped his arm around the man's shoulder. The clergyman met Caroline's gaze, and his head immediately tilted up and back.

"Hypocrite," Caroline muttered, brushing by him. She wheeled around and faced the drunk. "You wanna watch that church brew. I bet the congregation ladies spiked it with scriptures they don't necessarily live by." She looked at the reverend, all proper-looking in his clerical black and white. " 'Do unto others as you'd have them do unto you,' huh?"

She was tired of people not being what they seemed. She was damn tired of it.

"Reverend Brunson, maybe you oughtta think about buildin' that church over one of *your* loved ones' restin' place," she said. "Maybe you oughtta think about givin' up everything you have, everything your family has. The Lord says be compassionate—an' 'thou shalt not lie.' So why don't you be a real decent man of God if you're gonna claim to be a man of God at all, an' tell this feller the truth, that that 'brew' ain't nothin' more than punch and that you're out to save his drunk soul, not just give him food an' a warm bed."

"Miss Watson! Out of our way!" the minister exploded. The drunk looked altogether surprised. His eyes had grown large in his wobbly head.

"Reverend Brunson. Reckon I'll do just that," Caroline said. "A mighty good day to you." She dipped her head, then walked on.

Mary had to catch up to her again. "My goodness, Caroline. You certainly told him! But he's only trying to help. If drunks aren't bumping into you on the street and men aren't flying out of saloons—"

"Uppity hypocritical church people are tryin' to save souls when they oughtta take a good look at their own."

Mary Sue looked flustered. Her face had turned pink, and she was eyeing Caroline in a strange way.

"Well, but . . . well, you're right, I guess. But you're living in the middle of it all, Caroline. Don't you and your family get tired of it? Now, don't fly off in another temper," Mary said when Caroline shot her a glare. "I'm just asking. I know I'd get tired of it. Thank goodness Pa decided to move us outside of town a few years back. From what he's said, Dubuque is this way day and night."

"A body gets used to it," Caroline responded stubbornly.

"Really? You should come and stay a night with me, Caroline, and see how quiet it is once you're away from it all. I think you've forgotten."

Maybe I have, Caroline thought. But maybe the solution was to run them all out of Dubuque—the drunks, the church people, everyone, so she, Ma, and Grampa could have their quiet again. Or pick the town up and move it. A crazy idea, but one she wished she could make happen.

"I'm going home, Mary. You can come along if you want—"

"But you'd rather I didn't."

Caroline sighed. "I've been in a temper off and on now

for two days. You're right—I like Robert Kingston a whole lot. So much, I wish he'd pack his things an' head back East where he came from. No matter what he says or how he kisses me, it ain't me he wants."

"He couldn't even pick up his cup. Did you see that?" Mary asked, shaking her head.

"I saw," Caroline said gloomily. "I don't wanna be reminded."

"He looks like a nice feller, Caroline. Any man who looks at a child like he was lookin' at that boy must have some good in him."

Yep, Caroline thought, and that's what had her upset more than anything this morning—the fact that Kingston just might have some good in him.

Robert leaned toward David and whispered, "Is she gone?"

Grinning, David nodded.

"Good. Now I'll eat."

Robert pulled his plate back toward him. The food would be a bit cold now, but he didn't mind eating cold food in exchange for making Caroline feel terrible about his burned hands and arms—even if the burns weren't her fault.

He still couldn't manage a coffee cup very well, but the fork fit nicely in the crook between his thumb and forefinger. The utensil contained no heat, and the smell of the biscuits and fried bacon made his mouth water and his stomach growl. The cup was hot and made him wince with discomfort every time he put his hands near it, but he could handle the fork and plate.

"Th-thank you," David said. "F-for the clothes, hair, f-food . . ."

Robert glanced up to find the boy regarding him with glassy eyes, as if he were about to cry. His hair had been cut to up around his ears and forehead in front, and to just above his shoulders in back. It was combed neatly, his face and hands were clean, and now and then Robert caught a whiff of the barber's spicy but pleasant tonic. David's eyes seemed even wider now with the hair cut away from them.

The brown vest Mr. Fulton had dug out of the trunk was a little oversized and hung loosely on David's thin shoulders, over a slightly crumpled beige shirt. The dark brown trousers the shopkeeper had pulled out of a different trunk fit David nicely, however, and Mr. Fulton had even succeeded in finding the boy a pair of old but sturdy boots—which were far better than his tattered ones.

Robert had always been fond of children, but he felt a particular tug at his heart as he sat looking at David. The boy reminded him of a smaller version of someone he'd lost long ago. Of someone he'd always wanted back.

He swallowed hard. "There is ... there is no need to thank me, David," he said softly. If it was possible to give the boy some hours of enjoyment, he meant to do exactly that.

"Do you live here in Dubuque?" Robert asked in a lighter tone. He picked up his fork.

"Out-out a ways," David answered, chewing a piece of biscuit. "N-near C-Catfish Creek." He carefully reached to the middle of the table for the pepper shaker, watching his slightly trembling hand the entire time. He lifted the shaker, not daring to take his gaze from it until he held it safely over his plate. Then he smiled up at Robert and shook pepper on his remaining eggs.

He was a nervous child, for whatever reason. Perhaps he'd had encounters with too many impatient people—like Mrs. Johnson, and perhaps his father.

Surprisingly, since Robert and David had entered the restaurant, there had been no calamities. No broken glasses or overturned cups, no spilled milk, no toppled chairs, not even so much as a piece of egg in David's lap as far as Robert could tell. Since entering the establishment with Robert, the boy had calmed down somewhat.

There were no other people in the restaurant at the moment except for Mrs. Everly, a thin owlish woman with reddish-brown hair and rapidly blinking brown eyes. She was washing tables over in a far corner of the large open room, and Robert had noticed that every time she drew close, whether to replace napkins on tables or to check the level of salt and pepper in the shaker sets, David grew more fidgety and stuttered more. Back in the barbershop, he had been the same way, swinging his arm around and accidently knocking over a bottle of cologne water, and later crashing into the barber as he stepped from the man's chair. While the boy seemed fairly at ease with Robert, he obviously was not at ease around most people.

"Catfish Creek," Robert said. "Is that north, south, west ... ?"

"S-south and w-west a ways. N-n-not far. I b-bring M-M-M-Mrs. J-Johnson's m-milk and eggs, and the m-milk's still cold w-when I get th-th-there."

David had not stuttered so much since right after the collision with the lady and her packages. Perhaps the reason he did so now was his mention of Mrs. Johnson.

"I g-get th-them there. Then ... then sp-sp-spill them," David said with a weak smile. He shrugged. "I d-d-d-don't kn-know why. Always t-t-take m-more than n-needed."

Robert smiled back. "Where near Catfish Creek, David?"

The boy paled more, if that were possible. His hands began to tremble more, too. He tried putting them around the pepper shaker to bring it safely down to the table, but it spouted out of his hands and went flying, landing right in Robert's plate.

"S-s-s-sorry," David said, grimacing.

Robert lifted the shaker and placed it upright beside the salt container in the center of the table. "It's all right. Where do you live near Catfish Creek?"

"A-a big c-c-c-curve. M-mile past. Y-you're not from D-Dubuque."

Robert shook his head. "No. You're right. I'm from New York."

David took another bite of biscuit. "L-long way. I-I go to the l-l-levee sometimes. L-listen to talk. L-listen to ship whistles and w-watch everything. S-someday, I'll g-go on one."

"On a ship?"

David nodded.

"The kind that bring passengers?"

Another nod, an eager one this time. "Fun," David said. "I-I want t-to work on o-one, go up and d-down the river. H-have adventure. L-l-l-leave for g-good." His eyes darted to the window through which Caroline and her friend had been looking, then to the door, then back to Robert.

"Are you afraid someone might have heard you say that?" Robert asked quietly.

David's head bobbed.

"Your father?"

"Y-y-y-yep," David whispered.

"What about your mother?"

"N-no ma. Sh-she died."

"Do you have brothers or sisters?"

David shook his head as he reached for the second biscuit on his plate.

"You live alone with your father?"

Another nod. Wide, glassy eyes.

"You're afraid of him?" Robert pressed. Perhaps he shouldn't pry, but his concern was growing. He did not know how he would let

David's half-filled glass of milk toppled, crashing into Robert's coffee mug. Milk and coffee splattered everywhere—on the checkered tablecloth, on David's vest and face, on Robert's shirtsleeve . . .

With a sharp scrape of his chair across the wooden floor, David shot up and patted the spreading wetness with his white napkin. The salt and pepper shakers went flying.

The overturned mug clattered against Robert's plate, and a pool of coffee joined his eggs, bacon, and biscuits.

"S-s-sorry!" David groaned. He groaned again, louder this time, and made a desperate attempt to gather everything he'd knocked over in a pile in the center of the table. He succeeded only in making a worse mess—and in shoving his own plate onto the floor. As it shattered, he bunched his fists and emitted another groan, one of severe frustration, which reddened his face and made his eyes water.

"D-d-d-dis-*aster*!" he shouted. Then he turned and ran toward the door, upsetting chairs along the way, darting between tables and nearly crashing into Mrs. Everly. She fairly leapt out of the way, then put a hand to her mouth in surprise and watched him flee.

Robert was halfway across the room himself, having jumped up from his seat the second he realized David meant to flee.

"David? David, come back! It's not a disaster. It's not your fault! We'll order more food and continue—"

David had flung the door open and raced outside.

Robert followed. He ran up the street after the boy, observing him plunge into a crowd of men gathered to watch others throw dice near a street corner. When Robert reached the other side of the crowd, David had disappeared.

Robert spent an hour asking after the boy in and around a nearby hardware store, a blacksmith's shop, and an insurance office.

Having no luck locating David, he finally stuffed his hands into his pockets and trudged back to the restaurant, where he paid a grateful Mrs. Everly for his and David's breakfast.

CHAPTER

---◆---

NINE

Caroline twisted her lips and dropped her gaze to the leaf designs on Mrs. Johnson's nice carpet, spread beneath daintily scrolled, tufted, and carved parlor furnishings. Anything was better than watching those gold flecks dance in Robert's eyes while she said she hoped the cider she'd brought would take away some of the pain in his hands and arms.

She shifted from one boot to the other, her nervousness growing as Robert stood watching her, not saying anything, not responding.

Durn it all! She didn't belong in a fancy place such as this. And coming here to help him this afternoon had been hard enough. Did he have to stand there just looking at her as she held the jug of cider trying to sell him on the fact that putting his hands in some of it would help him? He oughtta at least say something! Even telling her he didn't want her help and ordering her to leave would be better than silence.

"I was six the first time I ever burned m'self," she said. "Grampa was right there, tellin' Ma 'no, no lard on her hands, 'Becca. Cider works best. Cider so strong it's almost turned to vinegar.' I brought some that's almost like what Grampa had me stick my finger in that day. Cider so strong it's almost turned to vinegar. You put some in a—"

"Mr. Kingston, Clarissa told me . . . Oh! Heavens! What in the world . . . ?" The plump Mrs. Johnson stood in the doorway, a hand to her throat near where her prim bodice ended. She gazed with increasing disbelief at the mud prints that trailed in from the hall, tracked across her pretty carpet, and ended near where Caroline stood. Caroline hadn't noticed them before, but now . . . Mrs. Johnson's sharp, accusing eyes landed square on her.

Caroline fought a wince. She hoisted up in front of her the brown jug she'd toted all the way here. "Sorry about your nice carpet, ma'am. I brought cider for Mr. Kingston here's hands. It's the best thing for burns, y'know. Or maybe you don't know. Y'see I burned a finger for the first time when I was six, an' Grampa told Ma—"

"Do you think I give a fig what your grandfather told your mother, girl?" Mrs. Johnson scolded. "It will take a day's scrubbing to get this carpet clean!"

Caroline took a deep breath, fighting her flaring temper. "My name's Caroline, not 'girl.' An' I said I'm sorry. I'll be glad to scrub it m'self in a bit."

"I don't remember employing you."

"You didn't. I offered. But if you wanna be snooty about—"

"Caroline," Robert intervened. "We were just off to the kitchen, if you don't mind, Mrs. Johnson, where Miss Watson intends to help me soak my hands and arms. I'll pay Clarissa or the other girl's wages for the day if you have one of them scrub the carpet."

Caroline turned a disbelieving gaze on him. "I don't intend no such thing! An' I can clean up my own mess, thank you. I—"

He gripped her elbow. "Come along, Caroline. Surely we can find a large bowl in the kitchen. Surely Mrs. Johnson will allow us to use one."

Caroline twisted her arm away. "Hellfire! You wanna watch touchin' me," she warned him. "I came to offer cider in a neighborly way. I didn't come to let you put your hands all over me the way you did the other night! That ain't gonna happen again."

Mrs. Johnson gasped.

"He did, too," Caroline said smartly, enjoying the shock dancing across the woman's face. "All over me. He's some romancer."

A door opened and closed out in the hall. Footsteps sounded. "Mrs. Johnson . . . ??"

"Oh, heavens! It's Parson Whitefield," Mrs. Johnson whispered, glancing about frantically. "Quickly now, off with both of you! To the kitchen then. And, girl . . . Caroline . . . do mind your mouth when you pass him in the hall!"

Caroline's jaw dropped open. "Mind my . . . ?"

"Come along," Robert said, in a stern voice this time as he again took Caroline's elbow.

Caroline was just lifting a foot to stomp his when she looked up into his face and saw a grin twitching the corners of his mouth. Then he grimaced and pulled his hand back, cradling it in his other.

"Please, Caroline," he said. "If you're certain that cider will work, let's go try it."

The way his face was twisted did something to her heart. So did the way he said her name. The way he'd grabbed hold of her, though . . . she was inclined to think he was faking. But his hands were still pretty red and puffy in places.

"Show me where the kitchen is," she said. "I'll pour the cider, an' you can soak."

They passed the parson out in the hall. The man gave her and Robert a curious look as Mrs. Johnson scurried up behind them, saying some crazy thing about Mr. Kingston escorting the unruly, unmannered kitchen girl out of the boardinghouse for her—*out*, as in dismissing her.

Caroline started to turn around and tell the parson what was really going on, that she wasn't a kitchen girl, that Mr. Kingston had burned his hands and so she'd brought cider 'cause lard or butter never really worked. But Robert quickened his steps behind her, urging her to keep walking, and for some insane reason, she kept her mouth shut and went.

"I felt a storm brewing," he said, chuckling, easing around her to shoulder open what she guessed was the kitchen door.

"I coulda opened the door by m'self," she told him.

He grinned. "Gentlemen open doors for ladies, Caroline." With a flourish of his arm, he ushered her into the kitchen.

"Don't accuse me of bein' such a thing," she retorted. "Ain't got no airs about me an' never plan to get any neither."

"I'm delighted to hear that. I like you just the way you are."

She approached the large oak table situated in the center of the room, running her fingers along a dark vein in the wood. "You . . . you do?" her fool mouth couldn't help asking. It wasn't like she cared whether or not he did. It wasn't like she even wanted to know.

Robert pushed the door shut with the toe of his boot. "I do, Caroline. Scoundrel though you can be."

She jerked a nod. "That's me—a scoundrel. An' just don't you forget it."

"I don't think you plan to let me."

She tipped her head. "What if I turned into a lady?"

"I like ladies," he said, approaching her. "In fact, I have an affinity for women in general."

Caroline snorted. "Reckon I know that. It's written all over you."

He was coming a little too close for her peace of mind, and those gold flecks were dancing again. They always did when he looked at her that way, as though he'd like to take her to the nearest bed and—

"Course, there's some women who might not have such an affinity for you," she said, stepping back. "You wanna keep that in mind." She oughtta drop the jug of cider and run out of here. But then he'd know how nervous he made her. "But I bet you like ladies more'n you like a girl like me. I just bet . . . I bet they're the kind of women around you mostly."

"Mostly."

He took two more steps forward. She took two backward, and glanced around when she felt the hard table edge touch her waist. Thinking she ought to move up the table a ways, but not wanting to run scared from him, she reached back and gripped the edge with her one free hand.

"Yep, cider's real good for burns," she said, trying to keep her voice low and steady. "Let it sit an' sit an' it concentrates just right, an' then you put whatever's burned in it, if it's a finger or a whole hand, maybe an elbow you can dip down into it. It's real coolin', an' pretty soon you can't tell by feel that you've even been . . ."

He was two small steps from her now, his head cocked, his full lips curved into a grin, his shirt opened some down his chest . . . hair curling there. Her breath had quickened, and her heart was bumping around in her chest something awful.

". . . that you've even been . . . burned."

"I really did want to have a picnic with you yesterday," he said in a disturbingly low tone.

Caroline swallowed.

"But even doing laundry with you . . . ," he continued. "You were right about the soap. I'm sorry for doubting you. But, Caroline, I would do it again to be near you."

"To be near . . . ?" Her eyes opened wide. Her heart did a flip as she glanced at his mouth, as she felt his warm breath on her face, as he lifted a hand to touch one side of her neck. She couldn't let this continue. He'd be kissing her in a minute, and she didn't want that. She surely did not. That would be terrible. Real . . . terri . . . wonderful.

Awful!

Nice.

Nope. There was no way on God's green earth she was gonna let him kiss her again.

She started to step away, out of his reach. He reached around her, in the direction she intended to flee, stopping her. His lips were a breath away from her forehead, his body too close for her comfort. Too warm and right there . . . easy to touch. Her eyes fastened on the wiry black hairs curling on his chest.

It wasn't as if she'd never seen a—

He stepped back, a large wooden bowl in his hand. "Is this what you were about to go looking for?"

About to go looking for . . . ?

Regaining her senses, Caroline snatched the bowl from his hand. "You ain't hurtin' too bad, if you can hold a bowl like that!"

"When a man is distracted by other things . . ." He stepped back, his eyes glowing.

She noticed that his breath had become faster, too. She lowered her gaze, meaning to fix it on the puncheons, but the front of his trousers caught her eye. She was reminded of the center pole of a tent.

She spun toward the table, her face ablaze. A pretty fool thing since she'd seen plenty of animals mate and had a mighty good idea of what went on between men and women! She wasn't stupid. But somehow, knowing what went on and seeing a man's body get ready—no, seeing it respond to her, get ready for *her*—that did something to her.

It made her feel light-headed and . . . and proud, almost. Like she wanted to turn back, face him, and see what else might come of—

With shaking hands, she plopped the bowl and then the jug onto the table. She popped the cork from the jug, then, still trembling, poured a good amount of cider into the bowl, watching some of it splash over the sides. She glanced around the kitchen for a chair, caught sight of one near a door across the way, and hurried over to fetch it.

"Have a seat, Kingston," she said roughly after she'd brought the chair to the table. "Have a seat, put your hands in the cider, an' your mind on makin' yourself feel better."

"My mind is on making myself feel better," he replied, and she could feel his grin—she didn't need to see it.

"Yeah, well, you wanna watch yourself." She met his gaze, sharply, angrily. "You wanna watch yourself real close. You try to get so friendly again, I might just knock your tent right down."

Puzzlement wrinkled his brow. A few seconds later, he glanced down at the front of his trousers, then back up at her. A chuckle rose in his chest. "Caroline, Caroline, Caroline . . . You're the damnedest woman I've ever met. You say exactly what's—"

"I'm sure you're wishin' by now that you hadn't met me."

He shook his head slowly. "No. Perhaps I should be wishing that. But no, I'm rather glad I met you."

Well, I'll have to see that you get unglad, Caroline thought.

He sat in the chair and lifted his hands, giving them up to her care. She shoved them down into the cider hard enough that liquid splashed up at him and all around the bowl.

"Be forewarned, Caroline," he said, tipping his head to gaze up at her. "You will not scare me away."

He irritated her more than anyone ever had. His smugness, his arrogance and self-assurance—she wanted to pour the rest of the cider over his head and watch him sputter.

Lifting her jug, she corked it, then jerked her head toward one of the doors "That one leads outside?"

"It does."

"Keep your rear on that seat an' your hands in thât cider for a good hour," she advised. "Splash some up on your arms every now an' then. Do what I'm tellin' you 'cause I won't be back to help you again. Keep what's there an' soak your hands in it again tomorrow."

"Could I get an invitation to supper, Caroline?" he asked.

He was only teasing, she knew, but the question irritated her.

"I'm afraid not, Kingston. Not unless you get one from Ma or Grampa." She flashed him a crooked smile. "Y'see, Marshal Clyde Butterworth's been trying to catch my eye for some time now. I always said no before about going to socials, to any kind of socials, mind you, whether they were church suppers or barn dances. But he stopped me on the way here, asked me to a barn dance tonight, an' I said yes. Can't resist him anymore. Not when he smiles and looks so nice. Smells nice, too."

She watched something flicker in Robert's eyes and knew her dart had hit its mark. Oh, well. It was time he realized he wasn't the only man in the world, in Iowa Territory, who could make her heart beat in that funny way.

Flashing him what she knew was another brilliant smile and giving him another word or two of advice—"Coat your hands with a flour paste an' wrap them in cotton while you sleep."—she sauntered across the room, around the table and then the big iron stove, feeling his eyes on her until she pulled the door shut behind her.

*   *   *

I am not jealous, Robert thought later as he walked toward the Watsons' farm, the latest Iowa City newspaper tucked beneath an arm. His hands and forearms felt considerably better, but he had only ventured out, he told himself, to get a new paper for Clarence. He'd take it to Clarence, say hello to Rebecca—and perhaps even say hello to Caroline if she happened to be about.

If she hadn't gone off to the barn dance with Marshal Clyde Butterworth, Robert thought, tipping his head to watch the line of gray clouds that was slowly but surely transforming what had been a beautiful blue sky. He could almost feel the moisture in the hot air and smell its coming freshness.

What kind of name was that anyway? Clyde Butterworth. Put the title Marshal in front of it, and it sounded truly ridiculous! As if anyone with the last name Butterworth should be taken seriously. The man was probably either an oaf or a fumbling fool who could not even kiss a woman right.

Marshal Butterworth.

Robert almost laughed aloud.

That Caroline had refused his attention, then topped that by telling him she was going to a dance with the marshal did not wound his pride a bit. It did not touch something inside of him that still hurt. It did not play havoc with his pride. It did not make him any less sure of himself.

It did not make him jealous.

He would take the newspaper to Clarence and spend the evening conversing with the man. Clarence often talked about things that were foreign to Robert—chitlins and county fairs and fishing and traveling up and down the Mississippi River in something called a flatboat—but things that intrigued Robert, no less. Robert would ask Clarence if he knew of a boy named David, a boy who was the size of a six-year-old but who claimed to be eight.

A boy who was frightened nearly to death of his father, and nervous around most people.

He had a lot with which to concern himself this evening, and he would not give any thought at all to Caroline having gone to a barn dance with Marshal Clyde Butterworth.

Moments later, he was shown into the Watsons' home by Rebecca, who wore a bright yellow-and-white-gingham dress, her hair pinned back in a proper chignon. The cabin, as always, smelled of drying onions, herbs, a recently cooked meal—perhaps a roast with juicy carrots and a mouth-watering sauce—and, of course, Clarence's sweet tobacco.

"I'm waiting for Rufus Pennsberry to come for me in his gig," Rebecca told Robert, smiling as she dipped her head and turned a becoming shade of pink.

Robert could not help a smile himself. Nor could he help leaning forward to say covertly, "Mr. Pennsberry will be utterly flustered by your beauty. He will be a gentleman—won't he?" Forget the fact that he himself wasn't always one, that he hadn't minded the rules of propriety the evening he had gone walking with Caroline near the stream—and after he had promised Rebecca that he would be the perfect gentleman.

She giggled like a schoolgirl.

"Didn't come to see Car'line, didja?" Clarence asked from where he sat on the settle near the fireplace. He ran a hand down over his eyes, looking as if he had just awakened. "I'm sorry to say she ain't here. She perttied all up in that nice calico dress of hers, the one with the—"

"Red flowers," Robert said, surprising himself. Caroline looked breathtaking in that dress, prettier than she knew.

"Ayah," Clarence responded, squinting one eye suspiciously. "That'un. Looks a mite perty on her, wouldn't you say?"

Robert nodded in agreement, but not eagerly. He did not want Clarence to misinterpret his reason for being here.

He pulled the newspaper out from under his arm. "I brought—"

"Had her hair all caught up, pulled back fancy like—y'know, like it was the first night you met her. All curly round her face, the way it looks so perty. Her face was scrubbed mighty clean, an' her eyes were jist a-shinin' when the marshal came, puttin' up a right nice-lookin' appearance hisself. Way they looked at each other, Clyde 'n' Car'line," Clarence said around the corncob pipe he now held between the teeth to one side of his mouth, "well, I wouldn't bc su'prised to hear one day soon they wanted to get hitched. He was mighty dudded-up. Showed up here in . . ."

Hitched? What a crude way of saying that this Clyde person and Caroline might want to get married one day soon. Hitched . . . when a person talked about two people—a man and a woman—getting *hitched* . . . well, using *hitched* while talking about a man and a woman getting together . . . A person might imagine that man and woman *connecting* in some fashion. And the image that appeared in Robert's head when he thought of a man and woman connecting certainly had nothing to do with mere hand holding.

Disgruntled, Robert tugged at his cuffs, then ran a hand down his waistcoat to smooth it. He needn't have gotten so dressed up to call on Clarence. He might have left the waistcoat in the boardinghouse room.

But then, he needn't have waited most of the afternoon and part of the evening to bring Clarence his newspaper either.

Subconsciously he had hoped to arrive before Caroline left. Actually he had hoped to run into Caroline and her oaf of a beau.

Surely the man was just that—an oaf. A bumbling, oversized man who towered over her, who stepped on her feet while dancing with her, who fell off his horse now and then becausc he did not know how to ride; a man who knew nothing about bringing a smile to a woman's face and light to her eyes.

Clarence was still talking: ". . . sturdy boots fine for dancin' a reel or two. Car'line, she stood up 'n' gave him a peck on the cheek right afore they headed for the door. Right in plain sight. Didn't she, 'Becca?" Clarence asked, looking to his daughter-in-law for confirmation.

Robert looked at her, too, hoping she would say, "No, Clarence, she didn't kiss him. Caroline doesn't like any man well enough to kiss him on the cheek right in front of us. Any man that is, but Rob—"

"She sure did," Rebecca said nervously instead, a hand fluttering to her stomach. "My goodness, I was never so shocked. Clyde was never so shocked either. He— Oh, I just bet that's Rufus pulling up near the door." She turned away to grab a knitted shawl off the back of a chair, then turned back. "If you care to join us later, Mr. Kingston . . . this barn is very large—large enough to hold hundreds of people. It's out near—"

"That's quite all right, Mrs. Watson," Robert replied, drawing himself as erect as possible. "My associate and I plan to spend the evening at other entertainments."

"Oh." She fingered the tasseled edge of her shawl. "Well, then, have a nice evening," she said just as a knock sounded on the door. She hurried over to open it and seconds later disappeared outside, pulling the door shut behind her.

"Should be a mighty fine evenin'," Clarence said. "All that dancin' 'n' frolickin' . . . Car'line lookin' so pertty."

"I came to bring you a new Iowa City newspaper, Mr. Watson," Robert responded, hoping the man did not plan to talk endlessly about how pretty Caroline looked, and that she had kissed Marshal Clyde Butterworth on the cheek. *I received better than a peck from her*, Robert thought smugly, and his next thought was that he was not acting very mature. He was acting like a sixteen-year-old boy who had been rejected by his girl and who was now unhappily, gloomily, watching her go off on the arm of another boy.

Acting so, when the last thing he wanted to do in Dubuque—or anywhere on the earth for that matter—was seriously involve himself with another woman. No more emotional involvement—that had become his motto.

"Ya don't say?" Clarence said as Robert approached him. "A new Iowa City paper?"

Robert handed him the newspaper, then took the seat across from him. "If you do not mind me asking, Mr. Watson, why the *Iowa City News*? It's not easy to locate in Dubuque. Why do you not read one, or both, of the two newspapers printed in Dubuque?"

"What, so I can read 'bout all the bickerin' goin' on between the church folk 'n' the saloon owners, an' the aldermen 'n' merchants 'bout silly things like whether hogs oughtta be 'llowed to run the streets? News comin' outta Iowa City might be a lot of high political bus'ness, but it makes a helluva lot more sense'n fussin' 'bout what this or that alderman sees as a 'nuisance.' Damn pompous people sit in the churches an' that city hall they built, expectin' us to pay 'em for arguin' 'bout how fast a horse oughtta be allowed to go in the streets an' whether or not a man oughtta be able to bet on a good cockfight—an' whether or not a man oughtta be allowed a drink when the urge hits him! Hellfire, a whole lot of us was here afore the righteous came, an' we were jist fine! Caroline says Clyde's finally been 'llowed to hire hisself some more help. Well, we'll see.   We'll just keep a watch on things," Clarence said, leaving the newspaper on the settle while he moved to the hearth to light his pipe with a coal glowing in the fireplace.

He laughed, a raspy, throaty sound. "I'm feelin' a bit cantak'rous, t'day, as 'Becca sometimes calls me. I sat out on the porch 'n' watched a group of temp'rance ladies go up 'n' down Main this afternoon, arguin' with the saloongoers an' owners. This town needs some cleanin' up—

there's no doubt 'bout it—but there ain't nothin' right 'bout gettin' in men's faces an' tellin' 'em what they can or cain't drink or whether they can or cain't put bets on a cockfight. We'll see how Clyde fares. We'll see."

He chuckled, then faced Robert. "Reckon you didn't figure on gettin' all that when ya asked me 'bout why I read the Iowa City paper instead of the ones here in Dubuque. Reckon I just got a hankerin' for that paper. Get on over here now. I know you're wantin' a pipe an' some of my fine tobaccer."

Robert was grinning. He had never met anyone like Clarence. He had never met anyone who spoke his mind without even the slightest hint of reservation; he had never met anyone who let a man know exactly where he stood with him.

Except Caroline.

"I'll get ya a pipe," Clarence said. "Then you 'n' me, we'll sit 'n' mull over what's in this here paper. Dubuque ain't s'bad, if the aldermen'd get their heads outta their asses 'n' stop squabblin'. I bet ya ain't had a good impression of our town. Like I said—I know it needs some cleanin' up. But it ain't bad, not really. Only the crust is. There's some good people when ya scrape away what's on top. When ya take away the do-gooders an' those that fight all the time. We'll smoke, then take a walk 'n' see some sights."

"Mr. Watson, I don't think—"

"Aw, hell, boy! Dubuque ain't gonna grow on ya if ya don't get out in it. I bet ya ain't been nowhere but here 'n' at that boardin'house. Well, it's time ya saw some sights— more than Car'line, I mean—an' I'm feelin' spry an' rested up this evenin' so I plan to take ya. Women 'n' their dandies've gone off for some fun. Reckon we'll find some fun ourselves. Fun like you ain't never seen. So c'mon over here an' take this pipe," Clarence said, stuffing another pipe bowl with tobacco, not giving Robert a choice.

"Then we'll venture out into the better part of Dubuque. Yep. I'm feelin' jist full of . . . well, somethin' t'night."

Robert stepped forward, feeling charmed but uneasy, knowing without doubt that he and Clarence had different ideas of what constituted the "better part of Dubuque." The mood in which he had found Clarence made him uneasy, too.

The man had a devilish gleam in his eyes.

CHAPTER

— ◆ —

TEN

"I thought I should let you know, Marshal," the meek-looking deputy said, drawing Clyde away from Caroline and the dancing. The two men stepped a distance of several feet away and began talking in low voices, casting occasional worried glances at her. Every time Caroline eased toward them, they stepped farther away, until they stood a good one hundred feet from where everyone was gathered. They turned and faced some bales of hay that were stacked at least ten high.

Caroline shuffled her feet, wondering what was going on, wishing she could hear above the fiddling and all the talking and laughing. Clyde stood nearly a foot taller than his deputy, and was as sturdily packed as the bluffs overlooking Dubuque. Men didn't cross him. When he stepped into your path and leveled his dark gaze on you, you either looked away or you asked him in a nice respectful voice what you could do to fix the situation. Clyde didn't often look nervous, and when he did, you got nervous.

Right now, Clyde looked real nervous. His face had grown red, and he kept putting his hand on his hip, taking it off, putting it on again ...

"Why the hell'd you *arrest* him?" Clyde suddenly exploded at the deputy, causing the man to shrink back. "Didn't you know who he was ... ? Don't you think you shoulda checked before you put him in jail, Belmont? You've gone and put me in a damned bad situation with ..." He glanced worriedly over his shoulder at Caroline again. She couldn't imagine who Belmont had arrested and why Clyde was frowning at her while hollering at his deputy about arresting whoever he'd arrested.

"I'm goin' for punch, Clyde," she said, yelling to be heard over all the noise.

He nodded, looking relieved—but only a little. Then he and Deputy Belmont turned back to face the bales and talk more.

Caroline walked off, around the stacked bales on the other side, watching Clyde and Belmont from the corner of her eye to make sure they weren't watching her. She eased around to the far corner of the bales, where she could hear the two men, but where they couldn't see her.

"... supposed to do? He and his friend had too much liquor," the deputy was saying. "They were unhitching all the horses on Clay Street and they got a cockfight going at the corner of Iowa and Fifth, right in front of the Bissells' home."

"Good—! Lord Almighty! If that's not all we need!" Clyde uttered some choice curse words, none of which shocked Caroline, none of which made her think any more or less of him. She'd grown up with that sort of language. "Mrs. Bissell heads the Temperance Society!" he blurted near the end of the curse words.

Caroline knew the woman. She'd seen her at church a

time or two and had thought she resembled a brick wall with a painted-on face, all ruddy, with no emotion.

"What was Clarence thinking?" Clyde said.

Grampa? Grampa had been arrested for drinking, releasing horses, and running a cockfight? Caroline put her hand to her mouth to stifle a giggle. A few seconds later, she sobered. Oh, Ma was going to be angry. Spitting angry. Grandpa might end up in the hog pen again.

"The bottle was thinking for him, Marshal," the deputy said.

"What about his friend? Where was he while Clarence was running that cockfight in front of the Bissells' home?"

"He was there. Just as drunk, whooping it up right alongside Clarence. This ain't good, sir. He's one of the men come to build that hotel. The committee ain't going to be very happy. They had hopes, but they won't put up with harboring another drunk in Dubuque."

"To hell with the committee! A man having an occasional drink shouldn't mark him a—"

"He's drunk, sir. Passed-out-in-the-jail drunk."

Robert . . . drunk? Caroline didn't doubt that her eyes were as wide as twin saucers. Polished, refined, mannered Robert Kingston, the city gentleman, drunk?

What in the world had happened? How had he and Grampa managed to get in so much trouble? Never mind Grampa—she knew he had a mischievous streak in him, and it all made sense come to think of it; Grampa had been in something of a temper earlier this evening before she'd left the cabin with Clyde to come here. He'd apparently sat out on the front porch for a while this afternoon and witnessed the Temperance ladies at work. And lo! when Grampa was in a temper, you either joined him or got out of the way. Obviously Kingston had joined him.

But Robert . . . drunk? Somehow Caroline couldn't picture the refined man tipping a bottle of whiskey. Maybe sipping at a glass of wine or some such thing, but not slugging back whiskey.

Course, he might not have had to drink much to get tipsy. Anyone who wasn't used to drinking the raw spirits that could be found here shouldn't drink them at all. If Robert had gotten drunk on Dubuque whiskey or rum or brandy, he was going to feel mighty bad tomorrow.

"We can't hold them, Belmont!" Clyde sputtered. "Do you realize what this could do to my chances with Caroline? You arrested her grandpa and charged him with disturbing the peace. Caroline's temper is well known. You hightail it back to that jail and let both men out—Clarence and his friend!'

"That wouldn't be a wise thing to do, Marshal," the deputy advised. "I mean, I know you're telling me to and all, and I will if you won't change your mind. But it was Mr. and Mrs. Bissell who sent someone to fetch the law. They'll make a stir in Dubuque if we just let those men go without having them charged before the justice. The stir might mean our jobs, too, when people see we're willing to play favorites."

"Damn it all, Belmont, I said—"

"He's right, Clyde," Caroline said, walking around the bales to face the two lawmen. They both gawked at her, then tried to compose themselves, unscrewing their faces and glancing around nervously to see if anyone had noticed their odd behavior.

"Don't worry," Caroline continued. "I ain't mad, just worried about Grampa drinkin' so at his age . . . But Deputy Belmont's right, Clyde—if you let Grampa and Kingston go without chargin' 'em, you might as well set your sights on marshalin' in another town. The Bissells an' plenty others wanna see Dubuque cleaned up. They won't take kindly to you lettin' troublemakers go."

Clyde ran a hand through his hair in frustration. "You shouldn't have been listening, Caroline. That's not nice."

"I know, but I figured you were talkin' about somethin' that had to do with me, an' you looked nervous. I tell you, though—Ma's the one who's gonna be fired up. Bad enough they were arrested for disturbin' the peace, but drunk, too! We'd best go sober 'em up before Ma gets wind of all this an' pays 'em a call at the jail.

"I ain't so concerned about Kingston, mind you," Caroline said, starting off. "I'm concerned about Grampa. Angry at him myself. I've a mind to leave him there! Lettin' horses go an' runnin a cockfight—he oughtta be ashamed.

"I hope he had fun," she said, smirking a little as Clyde and Deputy Belmont caught up to her. "More fun than he's had in years."

As large as the two men's strides were, when Caroline slipped out between the barn doors and headed for the wagon she and Clyde had ridden there in, the marshal and his deputy had trouble keeping up with her.

Whoever was manhandling him ought to be shot, Robert thought as large hands propped him up against what felt like a concrete wall. He felt as if he'd been run over by a team of horses, very large horses. When he could not stop his head from lolling back and hitting the wall, he groaned at the pain that shot through it.

"Thank you, Clyde," said a soft voice.

Someone grabbed hold of his head, and if he had had the strength, he would have smacked the hands away, even though they felt smaller than the previous ones. They did not feel more gentle, that was certain. They felt impatient and harsh—but feminine.

Where had Clarence dragged him now? he wondered.

First they had gone up and down Main Street, as Clarence had insisted on introducing him to this and that person. Robert had found that the majority of the people were exactly as Clarence had said they were—warm. In fact, they were just as friendly and approachable as Mr. Fulton at the dry goods store. Some had been closing up their businesses for the day; others had already closed and were going to their respective homes. But none had been too busy to stop and sit on stoops and smoke and talk with

Robert and Clarence. And to Robert's great surprise, Clarence had introduced him repeatedly as one of the men who wanted to build a nice hotel in Dubuque.

Then, later, Clarence had suggested they make the rounds of a few saloons. Robert had strongly objected, but Clarence had ignored him and started off, and soon Robert had followed. Having no idea what he was getting himself into, of course. Having never been inside a saloon—he had only viewed them with distaste from the outside, where their drifting music and laughter often sounded so bawdy he didn't care to take even a peek inside—he imagined half-naked people copulating on the doors, men swigging whiskey from bottles and staggering about, if not losing money hand over fist at cards.

When he and Clarence first stepped into one of the disreputable establishments, he almost closed his eyes.

Almost.

"Chin up an' don't walk with airs," Clarence had warned under his breath. "Wouldn't want them thinkin' you're too green or too good. You can get along with these fellers s'long as you handle yourself right."

"I'll follow your example, Mr. Watson," Robert had replied.

"Naw, now, it's Clarence from here on. Remember that."

Some friends of Clarence's had spotted them right off and urged them to join them at a nearby table. The air was so thick with smoke, Robert could barely make out the figures of men and women on the other side of the large, open room. The women were painted and wore frills and satin dresses in loud colors, but at least they were dressed—no matter that they were spilling out of their bodices. A large bar harbored every conceivable shape and size of bottle, and all were filled with one sort of liquor or another. Shelves behind the bar were lined with glasses, and the walls were papered with paintings of more painted and loudly dressed women.

Drinks were shoved toward Clarence and Robert soon after they were seated. Robert politely started to refuse, but Clarence stopped him with a narrow glance. Robert picked up the small glass and, following Clarence's example, tossed back its amber contents, coughing and sputtering as the liquid burned its way down to his stomach.

The table of men had a good laugh. Several whacked him on the shoulders and boasted how there was nothing like the whiskey brewed in these parts. A still-coughing Robert told them they were right, they sure as hell were right, and the lot of them erupted with laughter, refilling his glass twice more and urging him to drink up. The warning in Clarence's eyes did, too, so he drank.

What seemed moments later, he felt the whiskey start to warm him—then it took over. Clarence suggested that the group of them take Harold Drury's fighting roosters, find a quiet corner—maybe the corner of Fifth and Iowa—and liven it up real nice with a cockfight. He'd never been against men having fun, he said, s'long as things weren't broken and people weren't hurt, and it seemed to him that there were a few people in Dubuque who needed to be shown a cockfight first hand so they could see that men bettin' on one were men only trying to have fun. A harmless sort of fun.

Sluggishly Robert had thought then that he ought to go back to the boardinghouse and not tag along with Clarence. But Clarence had said something about how he'd almost come to realize that the town had grown too much for him to feel at peace about Rebecca and Caroline staying on in it once he passed on, that he'd like to see them find a nice few acres outside the city. There were too many men like himself roaming the streets for his peace of mind, he'd said with a cackle. "B'sides," he remarked, "I'd rather put the land in your hands than in the hands of the goddamned righteous."

So Robert had followed Clarence and his group. But the whiskey had hit him very hard shortly after he and the other men stepped outside the saloon, and he remembered only bits and pieces of what had followed. He remembered someone objecting strenuously to the cockfight, and the image of a stately, ornately decorated home kept popping into his head.

He also remembered having the most fun he had ever had. The most incredible, outrageous, shocking sort of fun.

"C'mon, up with you!" someone growled at him. A feminine voice. Not too soft, but with a definite tone of authority. "Hellfire!" it said. "Hold your head straight so I can pour this coffee down your throat. I'd like to choke you, Kingston. But no, here I am, tryin' to sober you b'fore Ma gets a look at you. At least Grampa can hold his liquor. You . . . you're a pitiful sight!"

Caroline.

"Who the hell . . . else would has . . . have shuch a time insultin' me?" he managed, his tongue feeling thick.

"That's right, Kingston, it's me. Now drink this coffee. Marshal's off to rouse the justice so we can get this over with," she mumbled, pressing a cup to his lips. It was warm, but Robert's stomach was doing flips, and he had no desire to drink anything, not even coffee.

"What . . . ?" Robert said. His head wobbled again, and he jerked it upright, managing to crack open an eye.

Caroline sat on her heels in front of him, holding forth a cup, looking furious and looking beautiful, lamplight dancing on her skin and making her auburn hair glow. Her blue eyes flashed.

"What . . . Marshal? Jussice?" he asked, unable to form the questions that came to mind.

"You're in jail, in case you ain't noticed," she snapped, waving her free hand. "You 'n' Grampa got yourselves in a passel of trouble with all your drinkin' an'—"

Robert forced his other eye open. "J-jail?"

"That's right, Mr. Gentleman. Jail. You're sittin' behind bars, locked in a cell, looking pitiful. Marshal Butterworth's gone for the justice so you can have a hearin' right quick an' so I can get Grampa home right quick. That way Ma may never know. Except she'll ask about the money," Caroline said softly, regretfully, as if to herself, as if she had just realized something. "Oh, no. There'll be fines for sure! But not so much, surely, since this is Grampa's, an' I hope your, first time bein' arrested in Dubuque. But little or not, what am I gonna tell her?" she fretted. "She never liked Pa an' Grampa drinkin', an' now—"

"Get Ja . . . Jacob," Robert stuttered, trying to lift a hand to the cup. He finally did, though shakily. He lifted the other hand, too, and wrapped them both around hers on the cup, then tried to focus.

She was right—he was in jail, surrounded by cold gray walls and tall bars on one side. He had never seen anything but the outside of such a place.

He glanced back at her. "You're beautiful, Caroline. Like sunshine . . . You're so beautiful . . ."

"Oh, don't get sappy. Don't go tryin' to flatter me! Course I'm pretty in this settin'! But I'm still mad. I wouldn't be here, except for Grampa. Here, the coffee's hot. You're gonna spill it on yourself." She pushed his hands away and brought the cup to his lips again.

He smiled what he knew was a silly smile. "You shay— say you don't care . . . You care."

"I don't, so just don't go imaginin' me havin' feelin's I ain't havin'. If I don't sober you up right along with Grampa, Ma'll be real mad 'cause she likes you. Can't for the life of me figure why, but she does."

"Get Jacob."

"Fletcher?" She withdrew. "Is that who you're talkin' about? Jacob Fletcher?"

"Has money. He'll pay . . . fines. No need to spend your . . . money."

Her fist went to her hips. "Oh, so you want me to get him to pay your fines, an' Grampa can just sit here?"

"No. He'll pay both. Tell him to bring money. Give me . . . give me . . . coffee."

She hesitated. He reached for the cup.

"No. Lemme help you," she said, speaking more gently now. She brought the cup to his lips, tipped it slightly, and Robert sipped the warm brew. He put his hand over hers and turned the cup more so he would get a larger drink. Not that he was thirsty. He had to become sober fast, or at least get in much better shape, for when Jacob came. Jacob was going to be shocked, to put it mildly.

"What makes you think Jacob Fletcher'll believe me or come with me?" Caroline asked. "I threatened to shoot him, y'know."

Robert grinned. "Cannot imagine you doing . . . such a thing," he said sarcastically, then drank more from the cup.

"Course, he didn't have the sense to realize the rifle wasn't loaded."

Robert sputtered coffee.

"Hey, watch that!" Caroline said, brushing droplets from her cheek.

" 'Wasn't loaded'?"

"That's right. Like I told Ma, if a man ain't got the sense to know whether or not a rifle's loaded, he ain't got no business bein' in Dubuque."

Despite feeling terrible—his head was pounding, and his stomach was churning—Robert laughed. "Go get . . . Jacob, Caroline," he said, taking another big drink of coffee.

He drained the cup as she studied him.

"I'll go," she said finally, "but I'm payin' Grampa's fines. You wanna remember that. I don't want you—"

"I'll pay them."

"Like hell you will! *I'll* pay them. Answerin' to Ma about where the money's gone is a whole lot better'n owin' you."

"Caroline . . ." Robert reached for her just as she grabbed the cup from him and rose. He weakly caught a handful of her skirt. She jerked it away, glaring at him.

"You just sit there 'n' behave. I'm goin' for more coffee."

"Where's Clarence?"

"He's Mr. Watson to you!"

"He told me . . . told me to call him Clarence."

"You're that friendly with him now, are you?" Her glare deepened, became more fiery.

"Where is he?" Robert asked.

"Two cells down. They thought separatin' you two would make for less trouble. You sang at the top of your lungs all the way here, that's what the deputy said."

Robert started to shake his head in disbelief at himself, then a sharp pain reminded him that he had better not. There were more sharp pains when Caroline rapped on the cell door. Moments later, a man with a pale silver star hanging unenthusiastically on his dark shirt appeared with a jangling set of keys in hand. The keys created too much noise for Robert, who closed his eyes momentarily, trying to block the noise.

When he opened them, Caroline was gone, and the ridiculous notion that she might not ever return—that he might have lost her—popped into his head.

It was absurd, of course, because he could not lose someone he did not have.

Pay the fines . . . He'd pay the fines? All of them? *Why?*

The man was out of his mind. He was drunk. He was crazy, Caroline thought, as she trudged across Third Street toward Main and Mrs. Johnson's Boardinghouse. She ought to be walking faster, but she didn't relish the fact that it was almost the middle of the night—the moon was high, almost full—and she was going to have to rap real hard on the boardinghouse door and try to convince what she bet would be a grumpy Mrs. Johnson to wake Jacob Fletcher.

Oh, Lord . . . She was about to wake the woman and ask

her to do something for her after the tracks she'd made on
Mrs. Johnson's carpet, after the sharp words she'd flung at
the woman.

She didn't want to do this.

But if she didn't, Robert would sit in jail, 'cause she
sure couldn't manage Grampa's fines and his, too. After
hearing what the fines were, she knew she didn't have
enough money to get both men out. After getting Grampa
out, she and Ma were really going to have to work to have
enough money for the property taxes.

She didn't know why she cared about Robert's comfort,
why something deep inside her didn't want him sitting in
that cold, damp, gray jail. She didn't care to think much
about it either, she was so tired. All she knew was that
Mrs. Johnson would just have to wake Jacob Fletcher.
Would just have to . . .

"Mr. Watson, for disturbing the peace," Justice Porter
had boomed not an hour ago, "I'm finin' you fifty dollars.
Same to you, Mr. Kingston," he'd grumbled. "Don't know
why you people had to wake me in the middle of the night
for foolery such as this."

Upon hearing the maximum fine leveled on both men,
Caroline had jumped up from her seat near the marshal's
office door, where she'd sat watching Grampa and Kingston's backs. Foolery was right—why two respectable men
such as themselves—course, Grampa had never been all
that respectable—had gone out and done such a thing . . .
If they'd had to drink, why hadn't they bought a bottle and
taken it back to the cabin?

"That's too much!" Caroline had yelled at the justice.
She'd run to his large desk, pushing her way between
Grampa and Kingston, and leaned toward the frowsy man.
"Hellfire! It's the first time Grampa's been drunk in—"

"Take your seat, li'l lady, before I charge you with
abatin' and fine you, too," the justice growled.

"Car'line honey, go sit down," Grampa advised softly,
and Caroline turned and trudged back to her seat.

"For public cockfightin', ten dollars each."

"One hundred and twenty dollars!" She jumped up and flew at the desk again, then something occurred to her, and she turned to Clyde and Belmont where they stood against one wall, their hands folded in front of them as they watched the proceeding. "Why wasn't anyone else arrested, Belmont? Grampa said there was a crowd of men. So why just Grampa an' Kingston here? Why not anyone else?"

Deputy Belmont flinched. "The two of them . . . they were firing a pistol into the air to try to get the cocks more riled—and to annoy Mrs. Bissell, Clarence said."

"How many times did they fire?" Justice Porter demanded.

"Wha . . . ? Uh, at least three, your honorable . . . uh, sir."

Caroline had known what was coming before the justice opened his mouth again: "Five dollars for each shot! They can split the third one. And li'l lady, it's ten for you, for getting out of your seat again—and for demandin' things in my court that you ain't got the right to demand. These men were charged with crimes, and I've found 'em guilty. Now, if you want both of 'em out of jail, you can pay the fines. If you don't want to end up in jail yourself, you pay your fine by mornin'. If I can't sleep, nobody will! Adjourned!"

The man lowered a fist to the table, stood, yawned, and stomped from the marshal's office.

"I'm sorry, Caroline," Clyde said, drawing forth to put a hand on her shoulder. The rest of them—Grampa, Robert, and Henry Belmont—turned to stare at her. That was when Caroline realized that tears were falling down her cheeks and dripping off her jaw.

She and Ma . . . they only had about one hundred and fifty dollars saved from all the laundry and food they did for the miners. Grampa's fines alone were gonna take nearly half of that! Not to mention the embarrassing, infuriating fact that Justice Porter had slapped her with a ten-dollar fine. She'd like to kick the shins of everyone in the room!

"It ain't your fault, Clyde," she said. Then she turned a hot glare on Grampa and Kingston. "It's theirs!" After wiping her face with two quick swipes of her hands, she told the two of them: "I'm goin' to get the money to get you out, Grampa. An' I'm gonna rouse Jacob Fletcher to get you out, Kingston. After you're both out, I don't wanna see either one of you, y'hear? I don't wanna see either one of you!"

With that, she ran from the marshal's office and jail, and went off to sit and cry in the shadows of some trees in the nearby town square. She wouldn't go home crying, and she couldn't tell Ma just yet that she was about to take half of their money to pay Grampa's fines 'cause he'd gotten drunk, let loose people's horses in the streets, found some roosters somewhere—she wondered if they were theirs—fired a pistol to rile them, and held the cockfight right in front of the Bissell's home, just to irritate the Temperance Society leader!

And, of course, there was her own ten-dollar fine for not being able to keep her mouth shut.

She might oughtta start learning to watch what she said and when she said it. Just a little. Maybe just think about it first, turn it over in her head a bit, and change it some before she let it go—if she let it go. She sure had a knack for offending people with her mouth sometimes.

She'd sat there and cried and cried, finally deciding that tears weren't going to fix anything. She'd stood straight up, smoothed her skirt, wiped her face for what seemed like the hundredth time tonight, and marched forward, still not quite sure how she was going to face Mrs. Johnson. If the woman took her I-smell-like-flowers-and-you-don't attitude with her again, she was going to get riled. She just knew it.

Hell, facing an irate Mrs. Johnson in the middle of the

night might be a fine lesson in learning to control her temper and her mouth.

So here she was, headed for the boardinghouse, hoping for the best, practicing what she was going to say: "Mrs. Johnson, Mr. Kingston's been in an accident, an' he's asked that Mr. Fletcher come . . ." It wasn't exactly the truth, but what the hell? Mrs. Johnson didn't know that. And when the sun rose, Kingston could do his own explaining.

The boardinghouse came into view. It was dark and foreboding, all three stories of it. Dark, foreboding, and intimidating. Caroline thought about turning away, but knew she couldn't. As angry as she was with Grampa and Kingston, she wouldn't let either of them sit in jail. She just wouldn't. She couldn't. She loved them both too much.

Well, she loved Grampa. She didn't love Kingston. How could she love a man who was so different from her? Who ran from snakes and who didn't like Henrietta or Colonel, not really—a man who surely didn't know how to dance a reel or bait a fishing line and who didn't care to walk across the rocks in her stream? How could she care even a little about a man who was only romancing her to get her family's land? Who had probably only gone along with Grampa tonight to humor the man and get more on his good side?

She didn't even like Robert Kingston. No, she did not.

Taking a deep breath, she stepped up onto Mrs. Johnson's porch and lifted her fist to beat hard on the door, not giving herself time for second thoughts. A minute or so passed, and she beat on the door again and called Mrs. Johnson's name.

She heard grumbling on the other side of the door, then it creaked open a crack. "I do not take in boarders in the middle of the night," Mrs. Johnson's voice said. It was thick with sleep.

"It's Caroline Watson, Mrs. Johnson. Mr. Kingston's in

a whole lot of troub— Mr. Kingston's had an accident, an' he needs Mr. Fletcher."

"Caroline Watson?" Caroline couldn't see much of the woman, only a glistening eye, but she could sure hear Mrs. Johnson drawing herself up, proper-like, haughty-like, preparing to get all pompous.

"Now, Mrs. Johnson, b'fore you slam that door in my face, you oughtta know Mr. Kingston won't be happy if you don't fetch Mr. Fletcher for him. B'lieve me, ma'am, he won't be happy at all. He's cold and he's miserable right now. His surroundin's ain't the best. He'd be more comfortable in your boardin'house, where he could drink your fine coffee, eat your fine food, an' sleep in one of your fine beds. It ain't myself I'm concerned about, Mrs. Johnson, it's Mr. Kingston. So if you slam that door, you might as well be slammin' it in his face."

Another long minute passed. A heavy sigh sounded, then the door creaked open, a little more, then a little more, until Mrs. Johnson stood full in the doorway, clutching her white nightrail at her throat.

"Mr. Fletcher has not come in yet," the woman said stiffly. "Neither of them . . . well! They're not the gentlemen I thought they were. Mr. Kingston is far better than Mr. Fletcher, but . . . Well, Jacob Fletcher is not here either. He has not been here all night, so if you want him, you'll have to find him yourself. Though I would not suggest conducting a search. When a man does not come home at night, that usually means he's . . . preoccupied. I do not expect you to know what that means, Miss Watson. But heed my words—he's undoubtedly engaged in shocking activities. My husband, you see . . ."

"I heard your husband ran off some years back, ma'am. I'm real sorry. You sure he—"

"It's hardly your concern, girl!"

"No, ma'am, you're right," Caroline said, feeling her temper flare. "My concern right now is findin' Mr. Fletcher. You sure he ain't here?"

"I don't lie," the woman said with a sniff.

"Didn't mean to say that, Mrs. Johnson. Thank you kindly. Sorry I woke you."

Caroline turned and started off the porch, letting her boots hit the steps heavily. What was she going to do? She didn't want to leave either man in jail. But the fines were one hundred forty-five dollars in all—five dollars less than all the money she and Ma had saved!

"Miss Watson," Mrs. Johnson called softly.

Caroline turned back, hoping the woman was about to tell her that Jacob Fletcher was in, that she'd been cruel and lied.

"Tell Mr. Kingston . . . and when you find Mr. Fletcher, tell him, too . . . they're welcome. I . . . I do make a fine cup of coffee and I don't mean to be . . . Oh, never mind."

Caroline managed a smile, albeit a weak one. "I'll tell 'em you want 'em to come back."

"Yes . . . Yes, please do."

Nodding, Caroline shuffled off.

CHAPTER

ELEVEN

"Clarence, please come out of the cell and let me walk you home," Robert pleaded much later. He had been at this for hours, it seemed. "Caroline would not have paid the fines if she didn't want you to go home."

"That's jist it," Clarence responded stubbornly from where he at on the edge of a cot, bent over, holding his head in his hands. "She paid the fines. She shouldn't oughtta have done that. I don't have the best mind no more, but I can still beat anybody in Dubuque County at cipherin', an' the way I've got it summed up in my achin' head don't sit right. Can't show my face round the farm anymore. Reckon it took all but 'bout five dollars of their money to bust us loose. They'll be workin' theirselves half to death to pay the property taxes. I'll just go off'n live down'n the minin' camps with the boys so I won't be no more trouble for Car'line an' 'Becca. You neither. I got ya in the most trouble you've prob'bly ever been in in all yer life an' all 'cause I had a itch to make some trouble with the Temp'rance ladies."

"Clarence, I had a good time," Robert said quietly.

Clarence glanced up, disbelief in his bloodshot eyes. "What're ya sayin'?"

Robert leaned against a cell bar and shrugged. "That I've never met a friendlier, more unstuffy bunch of people—and that includes your friends in the saloon. Hell, I've never been in a saloon, but the camaraderie I found—"

"Now, watch yerself," Clarence warned. "It ain't always so friendly. Fact is, half the time—"

"No, but last night it was. You showed me something about myself, Clarence. That I've been a pretty unfriendly, stuffy person myself, and that I don't want to be that way anymore. You and Caroline . . . ever since I came to Dubuque, you've been showing me how to have fun. How to just have fun. Last night showed me that I need to take off my boots, roll up my trouser legs, and walk across those rocks in Caroline's stream. I've spent the last ten years or so doing very little but working, and when not working, trying to associate with people with whom I don't really belong. With whom I've never belonged."

"You're talkin' mighty strange," Clarence said, raising both brows.

Robert shook his head. "I've never seen a family that survived almost solely on its members caring so much for each other. You see, Clarence," he said, stepping into the gray cell, "I was raised to believe that the basis of everything is money. That if you hand someone a roll of it, they'll do almost anything you ask them to do. My father always handed me money, because it was there to hand out, because he could bribe me with it. If I wasn't doing exactly what my nursemaid told me to do, if I was not pleasing my mother, the promise of money or something material would make me mind. But in your family and among your acquaintances, it's not money that matters. It's love and friendship. You have so little . . . and yet you're so happy.

"Caroline paid your fines so you could go home. You said it yourself a few moments ago—she'll be working herself half to death during the next six months or so in order to pay the taxes on your family's property. But she loves you, Clarence, and that is why she's willing to work so hard."

At length, Clarence said, "Aw, hell, I reckon you're right." He slumped back against the stone wall. "But how can I go home an' face the women after the jig I pulled?"

"Rebecca might be angry, but she'll cool off. Caroline . . . she didn't mean that, Clarence—that she didn't want to see you anymore. She wouldn't have paid your fines if she had meant that."

Clarence grumbled around for several more minutes, then said, "She cares 'bout ya, too, y'know. Otherwise she'da left yer hide in yonder cell. You'da sat right there till yer buddy was found."

"Which reminds me," Robert said. "I need to take you home then go look for my buddy. I hope Jacob hasn't found trouble himself."

Clarence snorted. "Out all night? Yep—trouble with two long, smooth legs, a nice patch betwixt, two mounds of—"

Robert coughed. "Clarence!" he teased. "You embarrass me!"

"Thund'ration!" Clarence chuckled as he stood and scampered toward the cell door. "Say, ya know *you* were the one doin' all the shootin' las' night. Ya got so riled at them roosters jist standin' there lookin' at each other an' not doin' anything, ya jerked ole Telford's pistol outta its holster an' commenced to ashootin'. We grabbed the gun, 'cause we wasn't sure but ya might shoot ole lady Bissell's parlor winder out or somethin'. I tell ya, I never seen a wilder feller. Shoo! An' settin' those horses loose! Hell!

That whiskey did somethin' to ya, Kingston. Turned ya into a diff'rent person. I don't care what Car'line says . . ." He glanced over his shoulder at Robert and grinned his crooked grin. "I like ya.

"But," he said, shaking his head and laughing, scampering on with Robert following, "ya ain't got to worry about me passin' ya another bottle. I ain't plannin' on doin' it—ever! Ooh, lawdy, no!"

"Stop making me laugh, Clarence," Robert cautioned, still chuckling, trying to imagine himself drunk and wild. "My head still hurts. Say, Clarence." He caught up to the man and laid a hand on his bony shoulder as they stepped beyond the gloomy hall leading to the cells and into the marshal's office, where the justice had had his say from behind Marshal Butterworth's large oak desk—and where the marshal sat now, tapping his fingers on the desk and watching the two of them with a squinted eye. *As if he's afraid one of us might pull another bottle from the inside of a shirt,* Robert thought, amused. He didn't like the man, if for no other reason than that Caroline had gone to that barn dance with him—but also because he didn't appear to be the oaf of a creature Robert had hoped he was. He appeared composed—too sure of himself.

"You sit watching Main Street a lot," Robert told Clarence. "Do you perhaps know a boy named David? Eight years old, black hair, thin, small, pale, stutters, is rather clumsy? He doesn't mean to be, but he is."

"Little David Perkins," Marshal Butterworth spoke up. "Delivers milk and eggs to some of the business folk in town."

Nodding, Robert paused before the desk with Clarence. "That's right. He delivers every morning to Mrs. Johnson's Boardinghouse."

"Can't say I know the sprite," Clarence said.

"I know him." Clyde scowled. "Leastwise, I know his pa. Too well, I know his pa. He's snoring away on a cot in the back cell right now. If I had my way, I'd toss him in the pile of offals, heads, and shanks the butcher down the street always throws out. That's where the man belongs—in a pile of rubbish. Let someone pound on him a bit, and he might not pound on David so much."

"He beats David," Robert grated, gripping the edge of the desk. "I knew it! The mere mention of David's father upset the boy. I knew something was wrong!"

"Hal Perkins pounds on David every time David forgets to bring drinking money home. Hal somehow manages to keep track of how many jugs of milk and how many eggs David takes into town to sell, and if the boy doesn't come back with the right amount of money for Hal to drink up, Hal starts in on him. David doesn't have to be so careful this morning—like I said, Hal's snoring away in the back cell, sleeping off what he drank last night. He's always got money in his pockets to pay his way out, though, and the first thing he usually does is go looking for David to collect from the boy."

"Man oughtta be shot!" Clarence grumbled.

"Or left in jail to rot," Robert muttered.

"I don't know," the marshal drawled, lazing back in his chair. "I think the butcher's rubbage pile sounds like a good place for him. He'd surely get some disease."

Robert withdrew from the desk and paced before it. "He's already sick." He stopped. "I would like to see the man, Marshal Butterworth."

Clyde sat up straight again. "Now, look here. The justice wasn't the only person who lost a night's sleep over you two," he said, his eyes shifting between Robert and Clarence. "Ain't going to be no more trouble this morning. Besides, Hal's in no condition to see or talk to anyone. Just go on home and see him another day—outside the jail. I'm warning you, though. None of us likes him, that's for damn sure, but if you do anything to him, if you beat him up the way he does David, I'll have to toss you boys back in those cells. Clarence, that means you, too, Caroline or no Caroline."

"Arrest us for beating up a man who 'pounds' his son?" Robert asked, a brow twitching. "Something does not sound right about that, Marshal."

"Ain't nothing right about it, but it's the law here," Clyde warned.

"The law stinks—not that I plan to beat any man."

Slowly Clyde stood behind the desk, unfolding every bit of himself, what amounted to at least a six-foot, five-inch frame. He was muscled, and the night's growth of beard that peppered his jaw made him look a lot more rugged than Robert knew his made him look. His eyes were dark and sinister, suddenly staring at Robert and Clarence with an iciness that made Robert nervous. If anyone could tame Dubuque, Clyde Butterworth could. Robert suddenly had no doubt about that.

"I'm the law," Clyde growled low. "Have been for four months now. The citizens of Dubuque put me where I am, and I plan to make their votes worthwhile. So if you see Hal Perkins on the street, Kingston, you'd better keep walking and not lay a hand on him. Course, drunk or not, Hal'd beat your scrawny ass to a pulp if you challenged him. Just let me worry about letting him rot in that cell, or shooting him, or putting him on that rubbage pile."

"You will decide what to do with him before he kills David someday if the boy is a penny short?" Robert responded coolly, refusing to look away, refusing to let the giant of a man intimidate him—though Clyde did. His dark gaze alone would intimidate anyone.

"Watch your mouth, Kingston," the marshal warned. "I'll toss your fancy New York ass back in that cell so fast—"

"Oh? And charge me with . . . ?"

Clarence latched onto Robert's elbow. "Robert, maybe we'd better—"

"That's right, Clarence. You'd better get him out of here."

Robert somehow mustered the nerve to reach across the

desk and tap Clyde's chest with a forefinger. "The town elected you, yes, but if David is found dead in a culvert some night because you couldn't decide what to do about his father, I will not be averse to using my family's influence and money to bring Washington down on this city. I don't imagine the mayor and aldermen would care for that, Mr. Butterworth. You would be shipped downriver on your ... ass, as you say, as quickly as the mayor and aldermen could get you out. Political men are, after all, political men."

"It's Marshal Butterworth," Clyde growled, shoving Robert's finger away. *"Clarence!"*

"Robert, c'mon now," Clarence urged.

"Yes, I did momentarily forget that you're the law in this town," Robert said softly, making his point.

"Get out of here!" Clyde exploded.

"I'm going, I'm going."

Robert gave the man a nice, patronizing smile, then let Clarence give him a good shove toward the door leading outside.

Moments later, Robert and Clarence stopped in another saloon, this time to convince a grinning, good-natured proprietor to let them clean up in a back room. Their clothes were still dirty and even torn in places, but at least they were able to shave, comb their hair, and wash their faces and hands.

Clarence had suggested they stop—the sight of them looking a little clean might cool Rebecca some. Robert couldn't imagine Caroline's nice, mild-mannered mother losing her temper, but Clarence assured him that oh, yes, Rebecca could. Rebecca most certainly could. And when she did, you wanted to get out of her path, Clarence said, then he began telling how she had locked him and Caroline's father outside one time, how they'd kept company with the livestock for days.

They left the saloon, walked down Main Street, and approached the Watsons' cabin. Just as Robert reached out to quietly open the cabin door—Clarence hung back hesitantly behind him—it flew open, and things began raining out: corncob pipes, tobacco pouches, tin cups, a strop, a sheathed razor, shirts, trousers, stockings, boots, a small metal safe, three leather pouches, a tin coffeepot, Clarence's coffee grinder, a lantern, a rifle, a powder horn, a pair of gloves . . . Each item went in a different direction as Robert shielded his head to protect it from flying objects.

"Don't you come back for . . . days, Clarence!" Rebecca shouted breathlessly, throwing more things.

Glimpsing the small pile of objects she had yet to throw, Robert grimaced. "Mrs. Watson, please . . . ."

"I don't care what . . . your health . . . is like! You took that nice Mr. Kingston out . . . got him drunk and cost us darn near all . . . Oh Lord, oh my Lord . . ."

She stopped throwing things to stare at Robert in shock, then horror.

"'Becca, now, you've gotta simmer down," Clarence said gently behind Robert. Behind Clarence, a small, early morning crowd had gathered on this section of the street to point, talk, and laugh about what was going on at the Watsons' cabin; about the fact that Clarence was being thrown out.

Rebecca grabbed more items, one in each hand, darted around Robert, who wouldn't move for fear that she might go for Clarence's throat, and threw them straight at Clarence. Robert grabbed her around the waist and hauled her, kicking, back inside the cabin, away from the pointing fingers and the laughter.

"Mrs. Watson, please! They're laughing at you."

"All the money Caroline and I have worked so hard to—"

"I'll replace the money, Mrs. Watson," Robert said. "All of it. Please don't embarrass yourself. You'll have to go out among those people again soon and—"

She kicked wildly at the pile of Clarence's belongings

she had gathered. "I'm selling the lots, Clarence! Do you hear me? I'm selling the land. I don't care anymore. I do not care to stay—"

"The people in the street are laughing at you," Robert said, straight into her ear.

That sobered her. She went still in his arms, sniffed twice, jerked herself away from his hold, squared her shoulders, straightened her dress, pointed to the door, and said, "Out."

"I plan to replace the money you and Caroline spent to get Clarence and me out of jail," Robert said. Then he stepped back outside, pulling the cabin door shut as he went.

He raked a hand through his hair. "I suppose we should collect these things," he told Clarence, motioning to the items scattered everywhere.

"I told ya I shouldn't oughtta come home," Clarence said, shaking his head.

"That's not like Mrs. Watson. It's not like her at all."

"Oh, yep, it is. Once 'bout every five years she gets enough an' goes off that way. Somethin' like what's happened is enough to make her do it. Can't say I blame her. That was a fool thing I pulled last night."

Robert began filling his arms with Clarence's belongings. "You didn't do it alone, Clarence. You said I was setting the horses loose and firing the pistol."

"But I got the cockfight together out front of ole lady Bissell's."

"You can come and stay with me at the boardinghouse," Robert offered. "I'll ask Mrs. Johnson."

"Don't reckon I'd better do that. Nope, best thin'd be to stay out'n the barn, where 'Becca can see I'm takin' my punishment. Give her a coupla days, an' she'll be a mite sorry she pushed me out. She'll come an' apologize, an' that'll be the end of it till I pull another trick—which I ain't likely to do. Course," Clarence said, rubbing his thigh where he'd been hit by one of the flying objects, "I always say that after she explodes."

Robert helped him pick everything up and take it all to the barn. Rebecca had thrown so many things out that they had to make two trips each. During one trip, Robert spotted Caroline walking near the stream just downhill from the barn, and felt the urge to go to her and apologize. But no. Being quiet and giving both Watson women several days to cool their tempers was the best thing he and Clarence could do.

"What about food?" Robert asked Clarence once they had piled the last of his belongings on the barn floor.

"I'll manage," Clarence responded. "Who knows, maybe Henrietta there'll fin'lly decide she likes me an' bring me a woodchuck or two."

Robert turned and spotted Henrietta perched on a stall rail, watching him and Clarence with her slitted green eyes. "She doesn't like you either?" Robert asked Clarence, not wanting to take his eyes off of the russet cat, not knowing what she might have planned. The last time he had been in this barn with her, she had tripped him.

"Nope, she sure don't. Henrietta's kinda partic'lar."

"She, uh, she won't do anything to you, will she? She won't hurt you?"

"Naw. She knows Car'line an' 'Becca'd be mad."

Caroline ... Rebecca ... the money. Robert planned to go to the boardinghouse, get the proper amount from the small safe he kept in his room there, bring it to the cabin, and slip it beneath the door if Rebecca wouldn't open the door to him. He had never been so exhausted, but he meant to return Caroline and Rebecca's money to them.

And bring Clarence decent food. And find Jacob. And collect David and hide him away ...

Grampa likes him, Caroline thought as she sat near the stream staring into the water. *Grampa really, really likes him.*

Grampa was also getting tired of fighting about the land. She could tell by some of the things he'd said lately: "Dubuque ain't goin' anywhere. It's gettin' bigger 'n' bigger all the time. The mayor an' aldermen are passin' new ordinances all the time, too, an' since an awful lot of people'd like to see us take our farm somewhere b'sides Main Street, they just might pass somethin' that says no farms allowed on Main. Maybe we oughtta beat 'em to their guns."

Grampa durn sure didn't mean they ought to pull the mayor and aldermen's guns and shoot them before they passed such an ordinance. What Grampa meant was that maybe they oughtta look at land outside of town and think about peacefully moving before they were forcibly moved.

Caroline pulled her knees to her chest and stared into the stream, trying to block the noise that came from nearby saloons and other businesses. The clear water trickled and gurgled over the stones, sparkling and turning a million different shades in the early morning sunlight. Ribbons of red, pink, and purple waved, curled, disappeared, and reappeared. In the distance Rose and Princess lowed, probably wanting to be milked. One of the roosters greeted the day for about the tenth time in the last hour. Most likely he was trying to impress the hens.

The grass was still damp with dew, but Caroline didn't care. Morning freshness had lightened the air and brought forth earthy smells—sweet grass, minty pine, and fragrant wildflowers that grew in patches along the banks. Caroline plucked a small white one, brought it to her nose, closed her eyes, and inhaled its perfume.

She lay back on the damp grass, staring up at the blue, blue sky, wishing, wanting things to be like they had been. If she could just go back some and freeze time, to that happy period before Dubuque's growth had started getting out of control and before Pa had died . . .

She'd help Ma pack Pa and Grampa's dinners, then she'd watch the two men ride off to the mines together in the buckboard, laughing and joking. She'd come here, sit near the stream, and look in all directions at the miles of land rolling and dipping, uncluttered by buildings.

She couldn't go back.

She didn't want to go forward.

She sat up, drew her knees to her chest again, and stared into the water.

By and by, she rose and walked off. She entered the cluster of trees not far from the stream and walked between the white pines, the oak, and the black walnut. Trees were getting pretty scarce in Dubuque. That would have made Pa shake his head; that would have made Pa sad.

Caroline's boots snapped twigs and rustled through leaves remaining from last fall. She plucked a handful of blackberries from a bush and popped a few into her mouth, biting down on them, enjoying their slightly sour juice. She loved jam, and the bush was full of berries now. If she'd been wearing an apron, she'd have plucked a lot more, dropped them into her pockets, taken them back to the house, and cooked them.

She pushed a few vines out of her path, then came to an open area in the middle of all the trees and dropped down before a roughly chiseled, upright stone. Grampa had made it, and while his spelling was pretty awful, the thought behind the stone had been sweet and touching. It was his last gift to her pa, his son.

Caroline touched the crooked, uneven letters, feeling the rough stone beneath her fingertips. There was a *J* and up a ways an *E*. Up a little more there was more, an *S* without curves, only those crazy, broken lines, and another *S*, this one half the size of the last. Another *E* finished the name.

"Jesse," Caroline whispered, feeling tears burn the backs of her eyes. Then she read what Grampa had carved beneath the name:

"Husbun. Pa. Good man. Good sun."

Grampa had spent weeks carving those words. Caroline remembered him sitting in the shade of these trees, right near where they'd buried Pa amid the trees he loved. Caroline had seen Grampa's eyes all misted up sometimes, and she'd come and sit near him while he worked, not talking, just watching him carefully chip away. They had both missed pa so much, yet neither of them had talked about it.

She still missed Pa. But she didn't think Grampa did so much anymore. Leastwise, not so much that he thought about what it would be like to leave Pa here and move on.

"I ain't gonna let anybody cut down your trees, Pa. I promise," Caroline whispered. "They ain't gonna tear down our cabin an' run us off the land you worked either. I'll fight 'em till the day I die. Then somebody better bury me right b'side you. Right here in these trees."

She glanced up and around, listening to the birds chirp and sing. She inhaled the heady fragrance of the pines, and heard a breeze sough through the boughs.

"Nope. Ain't nobody gonna cut down your trees."

She sat just so for a long time, touching the stone, listening to the sounds, smelling the smells, being near her pa. When she finally rose, thinking to go change her dress and do the morning chores, he realized her face was wet with tears.

Henrietta meowed close by, and Caroline glanced to the right in time to watch her friend trot over and drop a gift near her hand. Managing a smile, Caroline thanked her, straightened her legs, then lifted Henrietta and pulled her onto her lap.

"I made Pa a promise I'm not sure I can keep, girl," Caroline confided, nuzzling Henrietta. "But I'll *die* tryin', an' that's the truth. Someday people might come with axes 'n' saws to cut down these trees an' clear the land. I'll stand here with a gun an' get a few of them before they topple anything, before they mark a single branch . . . before they touch that stone."

She surely would.

Henrietta meowed again, low and sweet, understanding perfectly. Standing, Caroline lifted Henrietta's gift and walked from the trees toward the barn. She'd take the woodchuck there, but she wouldn't dare look at Grampa again yet—she knew he was in there because she'd seen him enter with Kingston, then Kingston come out a bit later. She was still too angry and hurt to look at or talk to Grampa. And to think she'd hoped, shortly after hearing that Deputy Belmont had arrested Grampa and Kingston, that Grampa had had a good time. Course, that was before all the maximum fines had been given by the justice.

In the barn Grampa was quietly sleeping on a pile of hay in a corner stall. After depositing Henrietta's gift in the usual place, Caroline couldn't help herself—she crept over to the stall, just to make certain everything was all right with Grampa. Not that she wanted to talk to him, not that she wanted to look him in the eye just yet. He was up in age and had had no business drinking all that whiskey, and she just wanted to make sure he hadn't lain there and died.

He was fine, breathing nice and steady.

Releasing a sigh of relief, Caroline left the barn and went to the house.

Inside the cabin, she found Robert Kingston standing in the open front doorway, handing Ma a small bundle.

"We don't want your—" Caroline stopped because Ma turned a glare on her. She didn't want to cause Ma any more grief today. Between her, Grampa, and Kingston, Ma had had enough.

Stuffing his hands in his pockets, Kingston glanced down at his shuffling feet, then back at Ma, then back at his feet. "It's all there," he said quietly. "I'm sorry, Mrs. Watson. Clarence was taking me to meet friends. He wanted to show me that Dubuque wasn't all bad. Things got out of control, however, and I . . . I did most of the disturbing the peace . . . freeing the horses, firing the pistol . . . I . . . At any rate, I'm very sorry, and that amount should replace what Caroline spent in fines. This was all very untypical of me, Mrs. Watson, but I must say in all fairness to Clarence that I caused all the trouble. I don't know why Caroline came to my aid, but I'm grateful that she did."

Robert glanced up—at Caroline this time. She was still angry and she strongly suspected him of looking so sheepish, embarrassed, and guilty to gain more sympathy, to creep into her and Ma's hearts a little more.

He had no way of knowing, and she wouldn't admit it aloud, but he was already into hers so far that pushing him out was going to hurt something awful. But push him out she would. He wanted the land they were standing on, but the sooner he realized that all his attempts at romancing her and all the soft looks he gave her weren't going to sway her, the better off all of them would be.

She desperately wanted him to leave town. She wanted him out of Dubuque, out of their lives. She told herself she never wanted to see him again, no matter how much pain not ever seeing him again might cause her.

No, she didn't want to cause Ma more grief, but just like having a tooth pulled hurt like hell, yanking Kingston out of their lives was going to hurt like hell. Sometimes pain eventually made a person feel better. Caroline had heard enough war stories from Grampa to know that amputations were awful—painful and bloody—but in the end, the infection and the hurt would disappear, and the person might be healthy again.

She reckoned she and Ma were both in for more grief, whether or not they liked the idea. Obviously Kingston still hadn't given up.

He shuffled his feet more just as Ma turned to look at her, silently imploring her to be kind and polite. Caroline thought of the white pines, oaks, black walnuts, and Pa's stone again, and she turned away, not wanting to meet Ma's gaze for long. She'd get all weak inside when she couldn't afford to.

Ma and Grampa were ready to hand Kingston their land, and Caroline now saw herself as the only resistance he faced.

CHAPTER

TWELVE

After handing Rebecca Watson the money and offering her the apology—which she graciously and calmly accepted—Robert walked back to the boardinghouse and gladly ate the breakfast of eggs, ham, and biscuits Mrs. Johnson offered. After his meal he went upstairs, intent on sleeping.

He was shocked that Mrs. Johnson had not tossed her nose in the air and demanded to know where he had been all night. He couldn't have answered her in an intelligent manner anyway; he was exhausted, his head still hurt, and his brain was heavy with thoughts and concerns.

He wondered where Jacob was, if he'd come in yet, and he trudged back downstairs to ask Mrs. Johnson about him.

"I have not seen him," she replied, blinking rapidly and not meeting Robert's gaze.

"Well, where could he be?" Robert wondered aloud.

"I've no idea, Mr. Kingston," she answered, dusting the tables in the parlor. She glanced at him. "But we will keep it quiet, wherever he is, and whenever he returns."

The mischievous thought of telling the proper woman what Clarence had said about Jacob probably having busied himself with a woman—"long, smooth legs, a nice patch betwixt, two mounds"—made Robert fight a grin. He shook his head, remembering. Clarence had no sense of propriety—and Robert loved the man's frankness, though sometimes Clarence shocked him.

"Yes, of course," Robert responded. He turned to leave the room, then turned back. "Mrs. Johnson . . . the milk boy . . . David. Did he deliver this morning?"

"He did, and on time—imagine that!"

"And he looked well?"

"Normal. Dressed in tattered, dirty clothes." Turning from a table, Harriet Johnson faced Robert, a curious look on her cherubic face. "But his hair has been neatly cut, and it was combed, too. I was never so shocked. He only broke two eggs instead of his usual half dozen, and he concentrated hard on not spilling a drop of milk. As soon as he sat everything down on the table, he put his hands in his pockets and refused to pull them out for anything— not even to collect what I owed him. He said 'put it on the table please,' which I did. He grabbed it, stuffed his hand back in his pocket, and opened the kitchen door by turning about and bumping it with his bottom. Nothing knocked over, nothing broken."

She folded her hands before her. "I do not mind telling you that I am pleased, Mr. Kingston. It is an improvement. If you had something to do with—"

"Why in tattered clothes?" Robert asked himself aloud.

"I've no idea, Mr.—"

"Why dirty?"

"I'm certain I do not know, Mr. Kingston."

"He was clean when he ran out yesterday. Clean and groomed," Robert said, wrinkling his brow.

"His boots were more atrocious than I've ever seen them. Ripped, stitched in places, poorly patched, and certainly not by a—"

"Mr. Fulton gave him new boots."

"Did he? Mr. Fulton?"

"Yes, he did. Well, not new. But they were in fine condition. David was embarrassed to go have breakfast with me dressed as he was, so we went to Mr. Fulton's—"

"The boy has some sense of his wretched appearance?" Robert narrowed his eyes at her.

She sighed. "I'm sorry, Mr. Kingston, but I've known David for some time now, and he's never seemed to care how he looks. He must take very good care of his animals, though—the eggs and milk he delivers are the best I've tasted. Lord knows his father takes care of nothing."

"Did you ever stop to think that David's appearance might be his father's fault?" Robert asked, more sharply than he had intended.

"Do calm down, Mr. Kingston. I'm not insulting the boy. I'm only stating fact."

"But have you?"

"Well . . . no."

"Mr. Fulton gave him a complete set of fine clothes yesterday, Mrs. Johnson. Fine but old. He was proud of everything, so proud I cannot imagine why he would have changed back into a set of old clothes."

"I see."

Scratching a temple, Robert started off again, then turned back. "Where does he live, Mrs. Johnson, do you know? He said near Catfish Creek."

"Oh, no. He's never lived near Catfish Creek. For years he and his father have lived on acreage near Pleasant Hill. That's just west of Dubuque."

"Now, why would he lie to me?"

"He does not want you to know where he lives?"

"Obviously not." Robert scratched his temple more, then rubbed his rough jaw. "I'm going to sleep, Mrs. Johnson. Disturb me only for Mr. Fletcher, please. Or for one of the Watsons. Especially Caroline."

He watched the woman's eyebrows shoot up in disapproval, but he merely exited the room.

Upstairs, Robert couldn't sleep, despite being so tired. He thought about Caroline, how she had stood this morning in the cabin, while he had apologized to Rebecca, and looked at him as if he were the worst blackguard in the world. She didn't trust him. She didn't believe anything he said—and that bothered him. Teasing her was easy, watching her react was fun, and listening to her and watching her ramble when she became nervous or flustered was almost . . . endearing.

He was beginning to care for her.

The faster he wrapped up the sale of the Watsons' land, the better.

Why not another piece of property? he asked himself.

Because Jacob would never let him forget that he had lost, that once again a woman had made an absolute fool of him.

He could not stomach that—a woman making a fool of him.

So he would keep on with what he was doing, and sooner or later Caroline would surely give in. Caroline would sell him the land. If he made the sell look very, very good, very, very enticing, Caroline would agree.

Surprisingly a rather meek Rebecca called that evening to offer *him* an apology. But Clarence had to be taught a lesson, she insisted. Robert cautiously asked about Clarence's meals—if he was receiving anything to eat—and Rebecca said Caroline had taken him a late breakfast and then supper only a short time ago. That relieved Robert.

Obviously Caroline was cooling off, too.

Early the next morning, Caroline rose, dressed, then stepped out onto the front porch to have a good stretch before she went to milk the cows. Henrietta was prowling around in the tall grass to the left, apparently stalking some small animal. The sky wasn't even pink yet, but it had lightened up some.

Caroline yawned and stretched, then watched a little boy come tearing up Main Street in a rattling buckboard, his one horse working for all it was worth—which didn't look like much—kicking up clouds of dust. The animal was scrawny and scarred in places, but looked well otherwise. And it was sure as hell hauling that wagon, in which milk was splashing from buckets and eggs were popping up right and left and splattered either on the ground or on the edge of the bed *then* on the ground. Some drunks across the street were whooping it up, pointing and laughing at the frantic boy.

Caroline wondered what the wide-eyed, white-faced child was running from. If somebody were after him, why didn't he jump off the wagon and go on foot? His chances of escape sure would be better. If he was worried about losing all the milk and eggs, well, there was no chance for them now anyway, no matter how safe he'd packed them.

Caroline had brought a lantern out with her, and the light from it together with the light from the saloons across the way—the saloons that never slept, as Ma called them—allowed her to see the boy's face better as the buckboard drew nigh to the cabin.

He was silently crying, big tears streaming down his face.

"Hey!" Caroline called, stepping off the porch. "Come—"

Two more boys, perhaps fifteen or sixteen years old, tore up the street on horseback, hooting and hollering that they'd have his hide—what there was of it—and that they were going to take all his milk and eggs, mix them all together in the nearest watering trough, and dunk him in them.

"Skinny, mangy riffraff!" one boy called, laughing.

"Your pa ain't sober but a second ever' day, an' ain't you just sweet, deliverin' eggs an' milk like a good young'un!"

To Caroline's horror, one of the pursuers pulled a pistol from a coat pocket and fired at the boy's wagon. Milk began trickling out of the hole left in the back of the buckboard, and the boy squealed as if he'd been hit.

He hadn't—he'd ducked, which had put him off balance. He tumbled from the wagon and had the good sense to keep rolling. He scrambled to his feet, obviously now forced to try to outrun the bullies on foot. They were racing down the street on their horses, however, and they'd catch him real soon, no matter where he went.

Caroline darted to the cabin's front door, threw it open, and reached up and grabbed Grampa's old rifle from where it hung. Unlike when she'd taken it down to point at Jacob Fletcher, she loaded it, pushing the ball down and pouring a good amount of gunpowder into the barrel, enough to blast the backside off of one, if not both, of those hellions. She wasn't thinking, not really. She was reacting.

Outside she went, running up the street to where the bullies had reined in front of the druggist's. One had the milk-and-eggs boy by the scruff, pounding him; the other was waving the pistol around.

"An' a damn dinky one it is, too," Caroline muttered. She took aim and fired, durn near blasting a crater in the ground near where the one bully was holding the boy.

Both bullies drew up short, staring at her in shock.

"You wanna let him go—right now!" Caroline grated.

The bully did. The milk-and-eggs boy went sprawling on the ground.

"Now then," Caroline said, still aiming the rifle. She hoped the boys didn't know or wouldn't realize that it held only one shot—and that that shot was gone. Other makes of rifles held more, but hopefully the boys were too shocked and scared to realize that this was one hell of an old one, that it would only hold one ball and one load of gunpowder at a time. After that, it had to be reloaded.

"The law ain't about at the moment," she continued. "Leastwise, I don't see 'em, so I'm takin' matters into my own hands—as you can see. You two turn around an' march up Main Street, same direction you were headed. Cut over on Fifth 'n' go to the jail. Lucky for you, nobody'll have to wake the justice. It'll be daylight b'fore long. If you get any notions about runnin' off, you wanna remember that I'm a fine shot, that my Grampa taught me to aim a little off, so a bullet'll veer an' go pretty much where it's suppose to go. I could take the cloth off your backside without touchin' your skin, or I could take off your backside, whatever you want. Fact is, runnin' would be a bad idea."

The two boys looked at each other as if considering that. Then they looked down at their boots.

"You there," Caroline said to the milk-and-eggs boy. "You have a name?"

"D-D-D-D-David," he answered, dusting himself off. He swiped at his face, smearing it with dirt, then he sniffed.

"David," she repeated. "Go after your wagon if you want, or go to that cabin over yonder an' wait. When I get back from puttin' these hellions where they oughtta be, I'll help you locate your horse an' wagon. Either way, go to the cabin in a bit, an' I'll replace some of those eggs an' that milk. What I can."

He gazed at her, wide-eyed, as if he didn't believe her.

"It ain't often I tell a lie," she said gently. "I mean what I said."

Nodding, he went shuffling off in the direction of the cabin.

Caroline gave one of the bullies—the one who had fired the pistol—a shove in the back with the barrel of Grampa's rifle. The boy was still holding the pistol, obviously in too much shock to think about turning and firing it at her. Or too scared she might blast him clear across the Mississippi if he did.

"Drop it," she ordered, and he did, lickety-split.

"Now walk," she told both boys.

They did. When laughter sounded from outside a gaming house across the street and Caroline turned the nose of the rifle that way, the gawking men there sobered up real quick. Caroline gave her attention back to the boys as they marched up Main Street.

She realized they were about to pass Mrs. Johnson's Boardinghouse.

The rifle blast jolted Robert from a sound sleep.

He sat up, rubbed his eyes, realized just *what* had so rudely interrupted him, tossed back the counterpane, and flew to the window.

An assortment of lanterns dangling outside establishments up and down the street winked up at him. He saw men lingering outside of gaming houses and saloons—other businesses were still closed up tight—and he saw two boys being led up the middle of the street by a woman who pointed a rifle at their backs.

Caroline!

"What the hell is she *doing*?" he muttered, suddenly wide awake. "Oh, Caroline, what are you doing now?"

His movements became frenzied. He tore across the room, grabbed a pair of neatly folded trousers from atop a chest of drawers, and yanked them on. Realizing he had them on backward, he pushed them off, turned them around, and yanked them on again. He threw open the doors of a small wardrobe, grabbed a shirt, any shirt, not caring about the color or the design, and pushed his arms into the sleeves. He grabbed his boots—to hell with stockings right now—fumbled one of them, and snatched it back up before it could hit the floor.

He raced to the room's door, pulled it open, and tore out into the hall, not bothering to comb his hair or wash his face—the only thing that mattered right now was his concern that Caroline was about to get in trouble. For all Dubuque's rowdiness, discharging a firearm in the city was against the law—and that law was enforced. Robert knew that firsthand.

She knew that, too, so what was she thinking? She must have discharged the blast that had awakened him—she held a rifle.

Mrs. Johnson was awake and working in the dining room; she appeared in the doorway just as Robert hopped by the room, intent on the front door, trying to put his bare foot into a boot as he went.

She gasped. "What, pray tell, was . . . ?"

"It's Caroline, Mrs. Johnson," he said breathlessly. "Forgive my appearance. I'm afraid she may shoot someone."

"Oh . . . Shoot? Why, no . . . Heavens! Have mercy! Where is she?"

Another hop. Another attempt to fit the boot on. Robert grabbed for the front doorknob. "Out there. Marching several young men down Main Street."

He managed to open the door, but finally ended up tossing the boots aside.

Jacob was just coming up onto the porch, making his first appearance at the boardinghouse in two days. He wore brown trousers and a beige shirt and collar, and his reddish-brown hair was neatly combed—despite the fact that he hadn't been here to tidy up. Holding his belly, he laughed and pointed Caroline's way. "You should have seen her! Mrs. Johnson's milk boy came tearing up the street in his wagon with two bullies after him. They took a shot at him, then Caroline tore off after them with her rifle! You should see the hole she blasted in the street! Little Caroline—nothing she does surprises me. She's taking them to the jail.

"Look at you!" he said, sizing up Robert. "You look like you just crawled out of bed, my friend. A hero on his way to rescue a damsel in distress? She's hardly that. I wouldn't get in the way of her shotgun. But if you insist on being a knight, at least button your shirt. You're looking slovenly these days."

"Out of my way," Robert growled, starting around his associate. "She'll end up in jail if—"

"You've fallen in love with her. But don't think about marrying her," Jacob warned, still grinning, his green eyes sparkling. "Has it occurred to you that she's merely playing the same game you are? That she's trying to charm you so you'll do what she wants—look elsewhere for a site on which to build the hotel?"

Robert stopped dead in his tracks, then turned back. "Did it occur to you that that rifle was not loaded when she aimed it at you?"

Jacob's grin faded. "It was!"

"It was not. She told me it wasn't."

"She . . . she lied!"

"Caroline has not lied since I met her. She told me the laundry water would burn my hands, and it did!"

"We're accomplishing nothing in Dubuque!" Jacob exploded. "Nothing but laundry, that is. And I'll tell you something else—I plan to go home soon. Home, where everyone will ask about our latest venture. I'll have to tell them that it failed. That I failed. That you failed. *That we failed.* I'm not even enthusiastic about choosing another site on which to build anymore. After I told you of the resistance I met, we should have packed our bags and left!"

"I don't give up," Robert said tightly, turning to start off again.

Jacob grabbed his arm. "Perhaps you ought to, just this once. Perhaps you should stop trying so damn hard to show your father that you can be as good and prosperous a businessman as he is—without his help."

"She'll kill them," Mrs. Johnson said behind the men, gasping as Caroline bumped one of the boys in the back with her rifle. "What you see in her, Mr. Kingston, I don't know. She's uncouth and ill-mannered and—"

"Not afraid to be what she wants to be, live how she wants to live, and to hell with what everyone thinks or says," Robert responded, jerking his arm free of Jacob's hold. "She's unlike anyone I've ever met."

Jacob snorted. "That's for certain."

Robert shook his head. "So she went after some bullies who were tormenting David . . ."

"My milk-and-eggs boy!" Mrs. Johnson remarked.

Robert smiled. "She'll be in the barn with Clarence before the morning is over."

"Clarence? Caroline's grandfather?"

Mrs. Johnson sniffed. "Indeed. The very man with whom Mr. Kingston became inebriated and spent the night in Marshal Butterworth's jail."

"What?"

"Oh never mind, Jacob. Of course, you've never deviated from the righteous path in your life, Mrs. Johnson," Robert growled, uncertain of how the woman had learned of his and Clarence's activities. "I have to stop Caroline before she hurts someone."

"She defended him from bullies," Mrs. Johnson said in a tone of wonder, giving a little clap. "Oh, that's marvelous!"

Robert turned a half-grin on her, reminding her, "You don't like David or Caroline."

She lowered her hands, straightened her face, and erased the sparkles of admiration from her eyes. "The boy can be an annoyance, and she . . . well, she's . . . shocking."

Robert nodded. "That she is, Mrs. Johnson. But there's something redeeming about her, I'm sure you will agree."

She answered with another sniff and stepped carefully from the porch. "I suppose I will go along. She may need a respectable witness, after all. Someone who will verify that those boys were bullying our David."

"You didn't witness a thing!" Jacob objected.

Her chin shot up. "Certainly I did! I had come outside to, uh, to pluck a tomato from the vine over there"—she pointed to a large vegetable plant—"when the ruckus broke out. I glanced up in time to see those bullies punching him."

"Your front door was shut, and the house was dark!"

"Nonsense. The house might have been dark, Mr. Fletcher, but I know more about what goes on in this town than people think I do. I'm observant."

"Come alone, then," Robert said, pleased that she meant to defend Caroline. "When Caroline goes before the justice for firing that rifle, she'll need whatever help she can get."

Mrs. Johnson said "oh" when he took her hand and pulled her along with him. She grumbled and complained about being yanked about so, then she quickened her steps, briefly wondering aloud if one of the kitchen girls would arrive in time to prepare breakfast for the other patrons. She quieted as they caught up with Caroline.

"What do you want, Kingston?" Caroline demanded.

"To help you, if I can."

"I don't need help."

"No, I'd say you don't. But Mrs. Johnson and I would like to help anyway. The justice will not be happy with you—you know that."

Caroline was quiet as the small group turned the corner and walked on. She wore her mucking dress, as if she had been preparing to do the morning chores. Her cheeks were flushed with determination which had no doubt been anger a short time ago, and wispy auburn curls that had escaped the ribbon tied at her nape blew gently around her face.

"Don't reckon I thought about it," she said. "But I don't care. They were mean to that boy, an' I'm not settin' 'em loose."

Robert smiled. "I don't think you should, but you'll need help when you go before the justice for firing that rifle."

"I was just bein' a good citizen. They were gonna whup him good. Made him lose a lot of his eggs 'n' milk, an' they shot a hole in his wagon for good measure."

"The justice will remember you from yesterday, and he will not be happy—"

"He'll remember you a lot more."

"Perhaps he will," Robert said thoughtfully. "I'll wait near the jail while you and Mrs. Johnson go inside."

"Justice might not show up for a while."

"Perhaps Mrs. Johnson telling Marshal Butterworth what happened will discourage the marshal from holding you."

She gave a short laugh. "Hell, Clyde would love to hold me!"

Robert wanted to say, "So would I, if you would calm down for a moment." Life since he had arrived in Dubuque had been entirely too eventful, mostly where Caroline was concerned. Instead he said, "In jail. Put you in jail. Perhaps Mrs. Johnson's testimony will discourage Marshal Butterworth from doing that."

"Clyde wouldn't . . ." Caroline grimaced. "Clyde might have to." She gave Mrs. Johnson a questioning look from the corner of her eye. "You'd do that for me?"

Harriet Johnson lifted a finely plucked brow. "Of course, girl! Do you think I would be walking down this street right now if I did not mean to do it for you?"

Caroline lightly punched the woman's arm. "Aw, that's mighty nice of you. An' after I woke you up the other night."

Mrs. Johnson's eyes flared. She pursed her lips until they resembled a bow and straightened her sleeves like a hen smoothing its feathers.

"Kingston, don't think to gain anything with this," Caroline warned, narrowing her eyes at him. "No land, no kiss, no nothin'."

"I would not dream of making such a presumption, Miss Watson," he said, fighting a grin.

"Don't use that slick talk on me neither. I'm wise to you, y'know," she said as they reached the jail. "You can go on now. Me 'n' Mrs. Johnson can manage from here."

"I do not plan to go anywhere, Caroline," he replied. "Out of concern for you, I plan to stay right out here, waiting for your safe release."

She made a sound in her throat, probably more objection to his "slick talk," then she ushered her prisoners inside the marshal's office.

A good half hour passed before the two women—such opposites, Robert thought, grinning again—emerged.

"She's a good talker," Caroline said, grinning herself as she eyed Mrs. Johnson. "Thanks a bunch, ma'am."

Very properly, Mrs. Johnson inclined her head.

Propping herself against her upturned rifle, Caroline said, "I owe you. I can cook real good. I'd be glad to cook a coupla meals for the people stayin' at your place. I'd stay outta sight of the parson, too, if he came callin'. I could do it, say, day after tomorrow. I have mornin' chores—Ma helps an' sometimes Grampa does, too, but he's too feeble to handle the hogs an' cows. They get stubborn sometimes, y'know, as hogs and cows do, an' a body has to force 'em to go where they're s'ppose to go. Right now I've got to get back to the cabin 'cause David's waitin' there. I told him I'd replace some of his milk an' eggs. Of course, if you don't want me, I could just—"

"Do stop rattling so, girl," Mrs. Johnson scolded lightly. "The day after tomorrow will be fine. But, mind you, I do not take kindly to my employees speaking out the way you do. And you must watch your words. No vulgarity."

"No, ma'am. No vulgarity," Caroline said, starting off alongside the woman. "I'll remember that. I'll even keep to the kitchen if you'd like."

"Mm."

"Aw, you ain't gonna hurt my feelin's, Mrs. Johnson. I know I ain't of the class you an' your customers are. I'll keep to myself in the kitchen an' cook you the finest batch of food you've ever tasted. Y'know, I thought you were pretty uppity. Turns out, you ain't half-bad . . ."

His arms folded, Robert watched them as they walked off, Caroline's word trailing. He chuckled, then started off after them, planning to hang back a bit. He stepped on a twig and winced at the pain in the arch of his foot.

His foot . . . How long since he had walked on dirt, barefooted? he wondered.

He couldn't remember.

He wriggled his toes, tucked them under, rubbed them in the cool dirt. He looked at the smudges on them and laughed. Then, shaking his head in disbelief at himself, he followed the women.

CHAPTER

THIRTEEN

Caroline went straight home and found David sitting crossed-legged in the grass near one side of the cabin, Henrietta curled lazily in his lap. He was stroking her russet coat from head to tail, and when he paused to scratch the back of her neck, she turned her throat up to him and twisted over, belly up.

"Now, how'd you manage that?" Caroline asked, approaching. She sat beside him, still watching Henrietta. "She ain't friends with nobody but me 'n' Ma. She don't even like Grampa."

"C-c-cats l-like m-me," David said, grinning.

He was a pretty cute kid. Scrawny and pale, but cute, his brown eyes sparkling, a smattering of freckles across the bridge of his nose, his black hair mussed from his earlier escape. She wondered what was wrong with him that he couldn't talk right. But she wouldn't ask—that would be rude.

"Why were those boys chasin' you?" Caroline asked.

David shrugged. "S-s-sometimes th-they do."

"They shoot at you a lot?"

"N-not a lot. F-first time in weeks."

"Weeks!? Why, m'self, I keep a loaded pistol under the buckboard seat just to blast at anyone who gets a fool notion to bother me 'n' Ma when we're takin' food an' laundry to the camps. You oughtta think about doin' that. How old are you?"

"Ei-eight."

"Y'know how to shoot a rifle or pistol?"

"N-n-no," he answered, his eyes growing as big as moons. "D-d-d-d-on't wanna learn."

"Now, don't go lookin' all scared," she said gently, noticing that he stuttered more when he grew nervous. She wanted to ask him why he didn't want to learn to shoot a gun, but she didn't like to be questioned a lot herself, and maybe he didn't either. Besides, if he wanted to tell her, he'd tell her. "Pet Henrietta there more if that'll help calm you. That's her name—did she tell you?"

He shook his head as a slow smile spread across his face.

Caroline grinned. "Oh, I know. She can't talk. But sometimes it seems like she can. When I'm uncomfortable talkin' to somebody or about something, I just talk to Henrietta. She's a real good listener. When she's not flippin' her tail around some . . . Well, I shouldn't oughtta tell you that. Henrietta likes the boy cats, that's all."

"Sh-sh-she has k-kittens," David said.

Caroline's eyebrows shot up. "She did. We gave away the last bunch pretty quick—they were lookers. People are always wantin' cats around here to scare away critters, so they—"

"Sw-swollen." David point to one of Henrietta's nipples. The area around it did look larger than normal. And, come to notice, even her belly looked larger.

"You're right, I reckon," Caroline said with a sigh. "She's gone an' done it again. Henrietta—"

"C-c-can I h-have o-one?"

"What—a kitten?"

David nodded, scratching Henrietta's neck.

"Sure you can."

"I cannot for the life of me figure out why anyone would want one of her kittens," Robert said, stepping around the corner. "The kittens will probably have her disposition."

Caroline jumped to her feet. "Henrietta's disposition's just fine. Just because she doesn't like you . . . You been spyin' on us, Kingston?"

A sly grin was her answer.

She propped her hands on her hips. "I don't take kindly to—"

"Wh-wh-why d-doesn't H-Henrietta like you?" the boy said, gazing up at Robert.

"She's smart, that's why," Caroline said.

"She's jealous," Robert responded. "She thinks I'll take her mistress away from her."

"She doesn't think that! She knows—"

"How do you know what she thinks?" Robert asked Caroline.

" 'Cause I know Henrietta!"

"D-d-d-don't f-fight!" David said, struggling to get to his feet. His eyes had grown huge again. "Pl-pl-please d-don't f-fight. F-f-f-fights are sc-sc-scary." His voice became a whisper with the last sentence.

Caroline and Robert glanced at each other. Robert's grin had faded. Apparently the fearful look on David's face had hit him in the gut as hard as it had hit her. Someone in David's life must fight a lot.

"Aw, we don't mean nothin' by it," she heard herself saying. "We just kinda—"

"Have differences of opinions sometimes," Robert said gently.

"Yep. That's right. Diff'rences of opinion. We get along for the most part." She saw surprise and shock flicker in Robert's eyes, and she narrowed her own at him. If he disagreed with her, she'd get him later. Maybe she'd take after him with her rifle.

"We certainly do," he said. "We have picnics ... We sometimes have supper at Mrs. Everly's Kitchen. Caroline wears her pretty calico dress and minds her manners. Why, the other night we even went to the barn dance together!"

"Shoo! You're dream—I mean, that's right."

Ooh, she was going to do something awful to him when she got him alone again! Something real awful. He knew she wouldn't disagree with him in front of David, not when their hot words frightened the boy.

"Only yesterday we were planning another supper for tomorrow evening," Robert said. "Would you like to join us, David?"

"N-n-n-no," David said quickly. Then he dipped his head in shame. "S-s-sorry. I c-can't."

"Why not?" Robert asked.

"Don't bully him into it," Caroline objected, peeved that Robert was using David to try to force her to have supper with him. The man couldn't seem to stoop low enough.

"I'm not bullying him. The next evening then, David?"

"N-n-no. C-can't." Staring down at the ground, David held Henrietta close to his chest.

Robert hunched to his level. "Where are your clothes, David?"

"He's wearin' clothes," Caroline snapped.

"D-d-d-on't f-fight!" David's normally pale face had reddened.

"All right, David, we won't fight," Robert promised. He glared up at Caroline. "We'll both be pleasant—and polite."

She stepped back, recognizing how fiercely protective

David was of Robert. She realized that David was the boy she'd seen Robert having breakfast with that morning. Obviously he cared a lot about the boy. So did she, already.

"We won't fight," she promised, too.

"The clothes and boots Mr. Fulton gave you," Robert pressed David. "Where are they?" Caroline knew Mr. Fulton—he owned the dry goods store just up the street. So Mr. Fulton had an interest in David, too?

"Y-y-you said y-you c-could give me m-m-milk and eggs," David said, glancing around Robert at Caroline.

"Sure! I meant it, too."

"Th-thank y-you. I-I n-n-need m-milk and e-eggs." He blinked rapidly, struggling. "Can't go h-h-h-h-h-h-h-h-h—"

"Home," Robert said. "Without money in your pockets."

"How much milk an' eggs do you need?" Caroline asked softly.

"S-s-s-six b-buckets. F-five d-d-dozen."

Her jaw dropped open. "You deliver that every morning?"

David nodded.

"You collect it yourself?"

Another nod.

"From all your own cows an' chickens?"

"Y-y-yep. I t-t-take g-good care of th-them."

"Why, you must! An' spend half the night milkin' an' gatherin', too. You must make a good penny off all of it. But why's it so important that you go home with your pockets full of money? A person can be happy without so much money."

"M-m-milk and e-eggs. Pl-pl-please!" David looked desperate and scared again. "Mrs. J-Johnson w-will f-f-f-ire me if I d-d-don't b-bring th-them! Other p-people will b-be angry. I'm already l-late! C-can't be fired!"

"My cows don't give six buckets of milk a mornin',"

Caroline said. "An' the hens—the most we get from our hens is a couple dozen."

Closing his eyes and looking white again, David sank to the ground.

Robert put a hand on the boy's shoulder. "We'll get Mrs. Johnson's milk and eggs, David. Other people will just have to understand. Don't worry about the money. I have money to give you, but you're not going home. I'll find a place for you—a place where you can stay without being frightened."

"What're you so afraid of?" Caroline asked David.

The boy silently stared at his ragged boots.

"His father," Robert said. "Isn't that right, David?"

David's face turned pink.

Home . . . Without money in your pockets, Robert had said. And David was afraid of his father.

"Your pa hurts you if you don't bring money home?" Caroline blurted in disbelief. "Why the low-lying ba—"

"Caroline!" Robert snapped.

She clapped a hand over her mouth. "That beats all I ever heard! What's he doin' while you're milkin' an' gatherin? Lazin' in bed?"

"P-p-passed out," David said, not looking at either Robert or Caroline. "B-but h-h-he knows how m-much. H-he expects."

"I'd run away," she said. "I'd take all the money one mornin' an' run off."

"I tr-tried."

"Aw, David." Sighing and shaking her head, she plopped down on the grass beside him. "You can stay here with me 'n' Ma an' Grampa. You'd like Grampa. He still does a li'l fishin' from time to time."

"P-pa w-w-would c-come. H-he'd b-be real an-angry. I-I-I've g-got animals . . . Th-they'd d-die."

A window shattered across the street, and David ducked his head under an arm. The movement startled Henrietta, who leapt out of his lap.

Caroline moved closer to David, wrapped her arms around him, bent her head to rest on the top of his, and closed her eyes. The world could be a mighty bad place sometimes.

"Honey, you ain't goin' home. I know you love your animals, an' that's real nice, but what makes you think your pa won't beat you someday till you're dead? Then there won't be anyone to take care of the animals anyway. You can't go back there. Think about it. Now, here. Let's go see Grampa in the barn. I'll milk the cows while we tell him how things are. He's got lots of friends all around an' outside of Dubuque. I bet he knows a place where you can stay where your pa won't think to look. Damn fool man . . . I'll blast him to—"

"Caroline," Robert admonished gently.

He drew close and ran a hand across her shoulders. Her eyes flew open. She thought about jerking away, but the movement would have scared David, and she didn't want him scared any more than he already was.

"Caroline," Robert said again, but this time in a different way. His voice was all soft and full of emotion. "Caroline, I . . . I . . . care for you."

Her eyes flared. She scowled at him. Now, what kind of fool thing was that to say? She wanted to shout that at him: *What kind of fool thing is that to say, Kingston?* But she didn't. And she didn't know if she would have even if she hadn't been holding David.

She saw tenderness in Robert's eyes, tenderness and caring that made her heart leap, flip over, stop beating for a second or two, then start again.

Could she believe him? Should she believe him? Should she take a chance and—

He leaned forward and kissed her cheek. Real sweet like. Real tender. Like he really did care about her.

"Let's go talk to Clarence," he murmured, withdrawing, still holding her gaze. She knew that if they were alone right now . . . if he took her in his arms . . . she wouldn't fight him. She'd like for him to look at her so hard and tender for a long time. She'd also like for him to kiss her again.

Suddenly the kisses they'd shared out between the barn and the stream that first evening came flooding back to her. His mouth had tasted good, all spicy, and his tongue had—

"Yep," she said real quick. "That's what we'll do. We'll go an' . . . go an' talk to Grampa. Find you a place to stay, David. That is, if you wanna stay somewhere else."

Robert looked startled. "What do you mean—if he wants to stay somewhere else?"

"You can't force a person into somethin' he don't wanna do," Caroline said smartly, happy to be collecting her senses again.

"Finding him another place to stay is in David's best interest."

"I reckon David's got a good enough head on his shoulders to know what's in his best interest."

"I don't doubt that, but—"

"D-d-d-on't f-fight!" David's voice was muffled beneath his arm.

Caroline took a deep breath. Robert withdrew more and stood, raking a hand through his hair. With surprise, Caroline noticed his bare feet. Hellfire, she'd never seen his feet! Not that she'd been interested in seeing them. She'd just assumed he never took his boots or his clothes off.

Dirt had gathered between his toes. The hems of his black trouser legs were gray from brushing the ground. His shirt was collarless and not buttoned right—the first button was in the third hole, the next two weren't buttoned at all, the fourth was in the sixth hole . . .

Robert caught her tipping her head, looking at his shirt, and he looked down at it himself. His brows shot up in surprise, then he glanced back at her and grinned.

She'd expected him to get all indignant and start fixing

the shirt, undoing and redoing buttons in the right holes. She couldn't help but grin back.

"Next thing I know, Kingston, you'll be swimmin' in the creek."

"No." He shook his head—adamantly. "No. I'll never do that."

"Grampa says a person shouldn't say never. Never say never."

"I will never, ever swim in any creek or river—or in any other body of water. Now ... David, would you like to go meet Caroline's grandfather? I've never met a more delightful person. He'll tell you stories that will have you holding your aching stomach. When you get older, he'll offer you a corncob pipe. For now, perhaps he has a friend you could stay with. Someone who is just as delightful as he is, though I cannot imagine anyone being more delightful than Clarence Watson."

"That's true," Caroline said proudly.

David moved out of her arms and got to his feet. "I-I-I wanna meet h-him," he said, hanging his head.

Caroline and Robert breathed a sigh of relief at the same time.

In the barn, Grampa was just beginning to stir. Caroline walked over and roused him gently with a hand on his shoulder. He turned over in the pile of hay on which he was sleeping and stared up at her.

"Me 'n' Rob—I mean, Kingston brought somebody to meet you," she told him.

"Didja?"

"Yep. A boy named David." Caroline cocked a thumb over her shoulder to indicate that he should look behind her.

Grampa sat up, rubbing his eyes. Soft morning sunlight trickled through the open barn doors, creating a haze around him. The hay smelled dry and sweet. "Well, outta the way so I can see 'im," Grampa grumbled.

"Now, you be real nice. He's upset enough as it is, an' I

know what a grouch you can be in the mornin'. Watch what comes outta your mouth, too. Yours is a mite worse than mine, an' mine's bad enough around a kid. Kingston'll bring 'im over," she said louder, waving Robert and David this way, "while I go get one of the cows an' start milkin'. I broke up a little somethin' earlier, an' now David needs milk an' eggs to deliver to Mrs. Johnson. Kingston can tell you about it. David needs a place to stay, a place to hide. I said you have enough friends, so we oughtta be able to find him a place."

"Well, hell if that ain't right! But why's he gotta hide, Car'line?"

She stood and waved Robert and David over again. They approached Grampa—David still hanging his head and Robert with a hand on the boy's shoulder—while she went to lead one of the cows in from the pasture.

Princess came nice enough when Caroline traipsed through the grass and gave her leather collar a slight tug. The bell beneath the cow's neck jingled as she lifted her head, mooed, then began walking toward the barn. Rose was always the stubborn one; she'd go on grazing usually even after Caroline yanked on her collar a good five times. The tenth time and a few shouts at her to mind and get to the barn always finally drove her there. But some mornings Caroline was so impatient she whacked her on the rump after about four shouts to get her to go.

She settled Princess in a stall, drew up a small stool, splashed water up on the cow's teats and udders to wash them clean, then began milking. She heard Robert and David talking low now and then, and Grampa talking normal—except he stopped himself whenever a curse word started out of his mouth.

"I'll still need to talk to his father," Robert said from nearby, after Caroline had milked Princess, taken her back outside, rounded up Rose, and brought her in for milking.

Caroline tossed a handful of hay into the feeding trough, then settled herself on the stool. She'd collected two buckets of milk from Princess, and they sat nearby, covered with clean clothes to keep bugs and dirt out. "Somebody needs to talk to him," she said, cleaning Rose. "But I ain't sure you're the one who ought to."

"Why not?" Robert asked, his arms folded on the uppermost rail of the stall, near Rose's head.

"'Cause you have no idea what you might be gettin' into. He could be one mean son of— sucker, an' flatten you with one punch. Bam! There you'd be, flat on the ground an' us havin' to doctor you up, if there was anything left to doctor. I've seen men sashay into town, thinkin' nothin' can hurt them, nothin' can touch them. Next thing y'know, they're seein' stars—and not 'cause it's nighttime either. It's 'cause they got in the way of someone they shouldn't have gotten in the way of."

"I'll take a pistol," Robert said, getting a little indignant; she heard his tone change, could almost imagine him smoothing the wrinkles from his shirt. Smoothing the wrinkles in his pride.

"You know how to shoot?" she asked, point-blank.

"Of course I know how to shoot!"

"Oh, don't get riled." She turned to put the wash bucket aside and draw forth an empty tin bucket for the milking. Amused and a little irritated, she glanced at Robert before turning back. "I was just askin'. If you take a pistol along, you'd better have a durn good reason for shootin' the man. If you shoot him, that is. Around here, they hang people for killin' others for fun or to get 'em outta their way."

"I would not kill a man to get him out of my way," he retorted, enunciating each word, each syllable.

Caroline laughed. "Pull out your drawers, Kingston. I'm not insultin' you. I'm tellin' you the truth. Believe me, there's plenty enough men who kill others to get 'em out of their way. All I'm sayin' is, you might wanna take someone along with you when you go talk to David's pa. Y'know, as witness if the man gets mad and comes at you. You'd have someone to say you shot him in defense."

"And of course I'm not bright enough to figure all of that out."

"Did you have coffee an' breakfast?" Caroline asked, grunting in frustration as she began milking.

"When has there been time?"

"Just like Grampa. If you ain't had your coffee an' breakfast, nobody oughtta try to talk to you."

"I plan to talk calmly and sensibly to the man. He'll have no reason to come at me."

"Oh, so why take a pistol along, then?" she asked smartly. "He'll get plenty enough riled when you tell him you've got David an' that if he wants drinkin' money he'll have to work for it himself. Don't think your looks an' pretty appearance'll get you—"

" 'Pretty appearance'?"

She tossed him a crooked grin. "Well, I gotta admit you don't look too pretty right now. Those bare feet and that messed up shirt 'n' hair don't rightly go with those creased trousers. How'd you get such sharp creases, anyway?"

"I'm certain I do not know."

"Believe me, Kingston, if you go callin' on David's pa alone, you'll take a quick tumble in a creek again, an' you might not fair s'well this time around. A snake might get you this time."

He was stubbornly silent for a minute. "Are you willing to go with me, Caroline?" he asked, and not very loudly either.

"What's that you said?" she responded, craning her neck. She was teasing, of course. She'd heard him.

"I asked if you would be willing to go with me."

She went back to milking. "I might."

"Caroline," he said sternly, "will you?"

"We'll get David tucked away, outta sight 'n' danger, then we'll go another day."

His pride would have taken another blow if he'd known she heard his sigh of relief. "Thank you, Caroline." He spoke low and sincerely, and she turned her head to have another look at him, wondering at him.

"You known David since you came to Dubuque?" she asked, her voice softer now, too.

"I've only known him a few days."

"The way you wanna protect him is sweet, Kingston. It's nice an' a real good thing to wanna do, but don't go gettin' all attached to him. Folks here . . . well, we're plain an' rough for the likes of you, I don't care how many times you walk around without your shoes. An' Lord only knows you couldn't take one of us—even a boy like David—to a place like New York and expect us to feel at home. I ain't been to the big city, but we get enough people landin' at our levees for me to know it ain't the right place for folks who're used to eatin' chitlins an' livin' with wide open land all around 'em. You wanna remember that. You've got a good heart in your chest about David, but you wanna remember what I'm sayin'."

He stared at her for at least half a minute, emotion going between them. She could feel it, and it showed in his eyes so she knew he was feeling it—and it was a downright dangerous thing, all the tenderness suddenly in the air.

"I ain't for you, an' you ain't for me, Kingston," she mumbled, still holding his gaze. "We ain't nothin' alike, an' you'd stop calling lickety-split as soon as I said yes about givin' you the land. *If* I said yes. Since that ain't gonna happen, why don't you just stop callin' now? Well, we've got David to worry together over now, I reckon, an' you know I'll help with him anyway I can, but after that . . . Oh, stop lookin' at me all soft. Scat. G'on . . . scat! I've gotta finish this milkin' so Mrs. Johnson has milk for her boarders."

Truth to tell, her heart was bumping about in the odd way it sometimes did, whenever he came a bit too close or looked affectionately at her.

He chuckled. "I'll scat . . . for now."

"Someday soon I'm gonna see that you scat for good," she warned.

"Be nice, Caroline. You would not want to upset your mother again so soon."

"Go on with you! Whether or not I upset her is me 'n' Ma's business."

He withdrew from the rail, still chuckling, his laughter circling around her head as he turned and walked off.

She felt so many different things whenever he drew nigh, so many things she'd never felt when any other man came close. She'd never thought a man being close could make her feel as if she might not be able to catch her breath ever again—but it was a pleasant feeling in an odd sort of way. She'd never felt her skin tingle so much except during the winter when she stayed outside a long time, then went inside to warm her hands and toes before a fire.

But this was a different kind of tingle. This was a good tingle, one that held a promise of more to come—if she ever cared to investigate it, follow it, on what she instinctively knew would be the most natural path in the world to follow. She'd never felt her breasts get so heavy and ache to be touched either . . .

Her face warming, she went back to milking quickly and steadily. She had to do something to make Robert stop coming around, something besides giving up the lot, and she had to do it soon, otherwise she and Robert would wind up in the bushes or on a tick somewhere. Then she'd be giving up a whole lot more than the land.

CHAPTER

FOURTEEN

Robert's hands had hardly smarted since he soaked them in the cider Caroline had brought to the boardinghouse. He had saved the liquid, just as she had advised, storing it in an empty corner of the kitchen—with Mrs. Johnson's permission, of course. He'd soaked his hands four times now because, surprisingly enough, doing so helped. The cider soothed his burns.

In fact, it seemed to speed up the process of healing. A week after he'd scrubbed laundry with Caroline, his hands were almost as good as new; they were almost their normal color instead of the red they had been. And—thank goodness—they were no longer raw and cracked in places.

He met the committee members determined to clean up Dubuque, and the meeting was pleasant for neither side. The Bissels had apparently spread the word among

Dubuque's finer people that he had taken part in the recent cockfight outside their home, and the committee members were shocked. He apologized profusely, spending days calling on various people, and finally decided that actions rather than words were the only way to clean his muddied reputation enough that no one would fight to keep him and Jacob from building the hotel when the time came to build it. No more drinking inside saloons with Clarence and carousing on the streets.

David was hidden away in the home of one of Clarence's friends, who lived just beyond a crop of trees along Catfish Creek. The crude shanty was not the place Robert would have most liked David to stay, but it couldn't be seen unless a person knew it was there, and Clarence's friend, Ben Carrol, was at least as friendly as Clarence.

Hunch backed and silver-haired, with kind, pale blue eyes and a stout, grandmotherly wife Robert did not see unaproned once in the three times he visited during the upcoming two weeks, Ben sported corncob pipes himself, played a captivating fiddle, and told his own share of old-timer's stories—his about his early days in Illinois.

Louisa Carrol was half-French, and both her father and grandfather had been trappers and traders. She and Ben had met when her father had taken her on a journey with him up the Mississippi River more than forty years before. She had few black hairs left on her head—most were gray—she spoke with a slight French accent, she was constantly busy in the shanty cleaning, cooking, and fussing over her three cats, and when outside, she spoke to her chickens while she gathered eggs and tossed the birds grain. She took an immediate liking to David, and he to her, and the two were together almost every time Robert visited.

Nearly a week after they had settled David with the Carrols, Caroline was disgruntled when Ma again invited Kingston to supper. His interest in David was sweet and endearing, and if he hadn't won all of Ma's heart before, he had now. He'd already won over Grampa, who had moved back into the cabin the day after she and Robert delivered David to the Carrols—but Caroline had tried to build steel walls around her heart. She was determined not to let Robert Kingston into her heart any more than he'd already succeeded in getting in, no matter what he said, what he did, how he talked, if he kissed her. If she couldn't resist his touches and kisses, well, maybe she'd just enjoy them. Until she scared him off for good, that was.

After supper, he and Grampa sat on the porch together and puffed on corncob pipes while Grampa told about some of his adventures in the late war with the British. He'd blown a few of those red coats to tatters, he reckoned, he said at one point, as Caroline did as Ma told her and stepped out onto the porch to ask the menfolk if they wanted coffee.

"Feller aimed his musket, but I got the first shot off, an' there he went. Couldn't tell what was the coat 'n' what was—"

"Grampa, you shouldn't tell Mr. Kingston things like that," Caroline chided, fighting a grin as she watched Robert pale a little. Not far away, shouts and laughter drifted from a tent that served as a gaming house. Rowdies mingled in the street, strutting, bumping, strolling, cajoling . . . Piano music tinkled from a saloon just across the way. Horses whickered where they stood at hitching posts.

"He's got a delicate stomach—among other things," Caroline said, unable to help a little wickedness. "Henrietta dropped a dead woodchuck on me the first night he was here, an' I tell you I've never seen anyone jump away so fast. Before I knew what had happened, there went Mr. Kingston, lookin' like he might faint dead away. So war stories are the last thing you oughtta be tellin' him, Grampa. He'd fit right in with the church ladies, though.

He might not lose his color if the conversation was about sewin' and plannin' the next social."

Rumbling with laughter, Grampa slapped one knee, apologizing to Robert between snickers.

Expecting to receive a glare, Caroline was surprised when she looked straight at Robert and found his expression one of cool tolerance. His gaze held hers, then dropped lazily to her lips, down to her breasts, slowly skimmed the rest of her, then lifted to her eyes again, proving he was anything but a church lady.

Caroline gasped and stepped back, warming and immediately growing angry with herself for responding to the man. Her heart had quickened; her breath had lodged in her chest. He'd looked at her a lot since coming to Dubuque. He'd touched and kissed her. But none of those looks and touches had held the heat this one did. It scalded her, burned her the way she knew the lye soap had burned him.

Her hands had lifted to clutch at the front of the gingham dress she'd donned after Ma had told her to change from her mucking dress, to pretty up for the evening.

She now wished she hadn't changed. The worse she looked, the less Robert would gaze at her as though he'd like to drag her off somewhere and do what healthy men were inclined to do. What Henrietta's males always came around to do.

Hellfire! The dress covered her pretty good. It wasn't like she was spilling out over the top of it. Its square-cut neckline didn't reveal so much as a glimpse of the upper parts of her breasts. And yet she felt like Kingston could see them, like he could see all of her. Like she had no clothes on.

Durn! How did a look from him make her feel this way? She was acting foolish, wanting to go inside, grab a blanket, and wrap it around herself. She was dressed, for heaven's sake! And not like some saloon girl. She was dressed respectably.

He had no cause to look at her in such a way.

"I came to offer coffee, Kingston," she bit out. "But maybe what you need is a bit of time in a back room with one of Dubuque's more friendly women. You're beatin' up an empty tree, lookin' at me that way."

Ma would've been horrified to hear her talking this way, but Grampa hooted, slapping his other knee.

Robert chuckled along with him. "Ah, Caroline. You have such a way of putting things." His gaze went to her hands, which were still clutching the top part of her bodice. "Did something come loose? Or is something threatening to come loose?"

Grampa hooted all the harder. Caroline shot him a glare. *You devil,* she thought. *You're my kin. You oughtta be defending my honor or something like that. Instead, you're encouraging the man!* She wanted to march over and stomp Grampa's booted foot nearly as much as she wanted to stomp Kingston's.

"Ain't got enough to come loose," she retorted, and immediately wished she hadn't. Robert tipped his head, squinted one eye, and looked as though he were considering whether or not she did.

"I'd say you do," he remarked finally. "I'd say you do not know exactly what you have."

Her cheeks burned. He knew it, too, durn it all! "I didn't ask your opinion! Do you two want coffee?"

Grampa's face had grown red with laughter. Instead of answering her, Robert continued looking at her in his bothersome way, not flinching, annoying her all the more.

"I reckon you don't, then," she said, spinning away. "I'll go about my business while you two smoke your pipes an' watch the doin's on Main Street."

"There's nothing more entertaining than watching you, Caroline," Robert responded.

"Shoo! Ain't that the truth!" Grampa croaked between cackles.

Caroline wanted to smack them both.

Robert spent the rest of the evening with Grampa, while Caroline helped Ma clean up from supper. Afterward Ma went to bed, and Caroline settled in a chair near the fireplace and dozed.

Rather, she pretended to doze. She couldn't seem to stop herself from straining to hear the voices drifting through an open front window of the cabin, from trying to hear what Grampa and Robert were talking about.

Grampa liked Kingston a lot, and Caroline didn't know if she liked him liking the man. She felt the way Henrietta must have felt that first night, wanting to drop a gift on Grampa's lap to get his attention, wanted to warn Grampa about Kingston—that he had as much as admitted he wanted to get their land. He was trying to charm Grampa as much as he'd tried to charm her. Only Grampa was succumbing.

Besides, she'd already warned Grampa. Plenty of times.

"He's got a plan," she tried to caution him again later, after Kingston had gone back to Mrs. Johnson's Boardinghouse. "An' he's been workin' it on us ever since he came to town. You think he really liked drinkin' with you an' hootin' it up durin' that cockfight? Look at him, Grampa. That ain't his way. Nothin' about it was his way. He's playin' all of us. What don't work on one of us one day might work on the other the next. When one of us is bein' cold, chances are the other will be warm. He's got us figured out, Grampa. He's got *you* figured out, that you like to tell about your county fair 'n' war adventures, and that you like a good drink of whiskey an' a good cockfight now an' then. If I didn't know what he was up to, I might like the way he listens to you an' smokes one of those simple pipes you hand him like he really enjoys it an'—"

"Ya do like watchin' us together, Car'line, an' that's the truth," Grampa snapped. "An' ya like the feller, too, no matter what ya say or pretend."

"Go on with you! Grampa, listen to me! Please listen! I like him about as much as I like rabbits in the garden, which ain't at all!" She felt desperate; she hated the feeling of being alone in a corner with the enemy closing in.

"I'll tell ya somethin' else," Grampa continued, undaunted. "Fancy Mr. Kingston likes you, too. Neither one of ya'll admit that ya like each other, though, 'cause you're both workin' on pride 'n' stubbornness."

She shook her head. "You're wrong, Grampa. He likes our lots. He wants to tear down our cabin an' build a hotel here. He wants to tear down the barn, maybe fill in the stream—he wants to ruin our home. Well it ain't just our home. It's Princess's, Rose's, Henrietta's, and Colonel's home, too. An' just don't you forget Pa's buried down near that stream, in the woods! Don't you forget all those days I sat beside you while you whittled at his stone!"

Grampa set his teeth and gave her a hard look, the likes of which he'd not given her in a long time. "I made your pa a promise—that once we got land for the family, I'd help hold onto it. But things've changed, Car'line Mae."

"So you're just gonna give it to him?" she blurted. "You're gonna let him build his hotel right over the top of Pa? You can't do that!"

"I've already been talkin' to him about what he might pay us, Car'line."

She stopped cold, feeling a rush of rage and desperation, feeling totally deserted, feeling her eyes burn. "You can't do that! I can't believe you're tryin' to sell our lot! You like him. He's your friend. But only on the surface, Grampa! You think he'll still come around after he gets our land? He won't care!"

"Don't shout, girl. You're gonna wake your ma."

She sniffed. "You have a mighty fine time when Kingston comes around. So did I, that first night. Then I stepped back an' found my perspective. With Henrietta's help, of course. She made me realize he was playin' me for a fool, just like he's playin' you for a fool. Don't do this, Grampa! Do you think he really likes the pipes you loan him? He's a city gentleman, an' he's had better, an' you can bet he'd rather go visit Mr. Dillinger's shop and get him a fancy one!"

Clarence Watson's jaw jutted out. "He likes 'em. He surely does. There ain't none better!"

"He knows the way to you is through me an' the way to me is through you. He's charmin' you, Grampa!" Caroline said, shaking her head and sniffing again. She couldn't remember the last time she and Grampa had argued this way, and it made her sad and more angry all at the same time. "He's in the middle of us, too, can't you see that?" she cried.

"Reckon I can see an' decide things for myself," Grampa grumbled, walking off. "Git yourself to bed soon, girl. Maybe sleep'll help clear your head."

"My head's already clear! Yours ain't! Yours an' Ma's!"

Caroline twisted around and went to look out a nearby window, not liking being surrounded by a town, not liking the men she saw staggering out of buildings and tents. She wished she could erase them all, brush the toe of her boot over them the way she brushed it over words she sometimes spelled in the dirt when she was deep in thought. Why couldn't she, Ma, and Grampa be left alone? Why had a town had to rise around their farm?

"I ain't ever leavin' you, Pa," she whispered, glancing off in the direction of the stream, her eyes tearing up more, an ache knotting her chest. "Nope. I ain't ever leavin' you. An' I durn sure ain't gonna let no one build a hotel or church over the top of you. You're buried deep enough as it is."

Turning away from the panes, she brushed the fallen tears off of her cheeks, knowing she had to be strong. She was the only one with any sense in this family anymore.

Moments later she climbed the loft ladder, feeling tired, more tired than she'd felt in a long while.

She was gonna get rid of Kingston once and for all.

* * *

Robert showed up at the Watsons' farm the following afternoon, offering to help take food and laundry to the miners. Rebecca took ill suddenly, holding her stomach, saying how she must have eaten something bad and that she was most thankful Robert was here; otherwise poor Caroline would be delivering the food and laundry alone because Rebecca could not possibly make the journey today.

"You make it sound like a long way," Caroline said, fighting a glare. She knew what Ma was up to. Ma would like nothing better than to see her marry a polished gentleman, a nice man like sweet Mr. Robert Kingston.

The cheery, eager look Ma gave her made her think sleeping in the barn wasn't going to be so bad—not so bad at all. Right now she was peeved with both Grampa and Ma, and she planned to spend the afternoon having fun at Kingston's expense, scaring him off. Then she'd spend some nights in the barn with Rose and Princess. Henrietta would keep her company, too, and they could talk and laugh about what she'd done, about the look on the grand Mr. Kingston's face.

"I've got some things to tend, then I'll be ready," Caroline grumbled, as if she weren't looking forward to the afternoon. She'd have Kingston all to herself. Ma wouldn't be about to glare at her and insist that she redeem herself. (Though she would later, Caroline had no doubt.) And Grampa wouldn't be stuffing a pipe bowl and nicely handing it to the man.

"I'll gather some food, and perhaps you can stop in the hollow and eat together," Ma said. "It's such a nice area out there. Lots of trees, unlike here in town, where people keep chopping them down. You could take a walk through the forest."

"That sounds like a wonderful idea, Mrs. Watson," Robert said.

Caroline mocked him beneath her breath as she climbed

the ladder to the loft, where she planned to really pretty herself up this time.

She shed her relatively new gingham dress and replaced it with her mucking dress. She washed the thing only once every two or three weeks, not seeing the sense in washing it more often. She let her hair go, wild and free, about her shoulders and down her back, messing it with her fingers to make it look all the more unruly. Then she hung her good dress on the hook in the loft and started down the ladder.

"Caroline, dear," Ma said, sounding a little alarmed—as well she oughtta be, Caroline thought. "Honey, why did you change your dress? You looked pretty in the one you were wearing."

"Rose ate something she shouldn't've an' got sick in the barn last night," Caroline responded. "I've gotta clean it up before we end up with maggots crawlin' all over the place."

She saw Robert flinch slightly and she shot him a grin. He tipped his head and narrowed his eyes, obviously knowing she was up to something.

"Well . . . all right," Ma said. "But you'll change back before you leave?"

"You bring the food out soon," Caroline told Robert. "Heaven knows Ma's too sick to manage it. You bein' a man 'n' all, you oughtta be able to."

He inhaled deeply at her jab.

"Course, if you can't . . ."

"I might be able to lift a basket," he retorted.

Grampa was sitting on the settle, but Caroline knew he was listening behind his Iowa City paper. But probably not with a grin after the argument they'd had last night. "We'll stop at the general store an' see if they have a new paper in, Grampa," she said smartly. "That way you can really read the thing."

She was irritated with all three of them, and they all knew it. Even Ma looked apprehensive, one hand twisting part of her skirt, her eyebrows twitching. Grampa peeked over the top edge of his paper, and Caroline shot him a scowl. *You old 'coon,* she thought. *If you ain't got the gumption to run him off, I will.*

"Caroline, honey, you will behave this afternoon—won't you?" Ma asked sweetly.

"I'll do my best," Caroline promised. But she wasn't talking about behaving. No sirree, she was not. She was talking about doing her best at anything but behaving. She was talking about doing her best at getting rid of Robert Kingston. At least Jacob Fletcher hadn't tried to romance her and win Grampa's love and trust. At least Fletcher had just asked outright if he could buy their land.

"And ... and you'll come back in and change your dress before you leave with Mr. Kingston?"

"Aw shucks, Ma. We're goin' to do work. We're not goin' courtin'."

Rebecca squared her shoulders. "Caroline—I will not—"

"Caroline would look pretty in any dress," Robert spoke up. "No matter how smelly or worn."

Rebecca turned her gaze to him, suddenly looking as if she might melt. "Why, Mr. Kingston, I've never heard anyone say such a sweet thing."

"It's true," he said, glancing at Caroline.

Yep, well, we'll see if you're still singing the same tune in a little while. We'll see just how much patience and charm you have, Caroline thought.

"Don't forget the food, Kingston," she grumbled again, as if he'd gotten the better of her. Then she stepped outside and pulled the door shut behind her.

The barn didn't need cleaning out at all, but then she wasn't headed there. She went straight for the pasture, where, as she worked at rubbing her skirt in fresh dung, she kindly thanked Princess and Rose for their help in dissuading Kingston from getting too close to her this afternoon and in running him off. He'd think twice, maybe a hundred times, maybe forever . . . Maybe he wouldn't even consider trying to get close.

But just in case he thought to despite the way she smelled, she headed for the tall grass to search for a surprise to put in her dress pocket. Colonel approached while she was searching. He sniffed around her, whining low and jumping back when she reached out to pet him. If the scraggly, speckled, mud-loving mutt wanted nothing to do with her as long as she smelled so, surely Robert wouldn't either.

Caroline laughed, then went on with her search, finally finding what she wanted. Dropping it into her pocket, she turned and walked back to the cabin, scarcely able to hide her devilish smile.

She'd left the already hitched horses and loaded wagon outside the barn earlier. Now she hoisted herself up onto the buckboard seat and led the team toward the cabin. Near one side of the house, she hollered that she was ready to go.

Ma appeared outside first, her brow wrinkled, her head tipped. "Caroline, what is the meaning of this? Would it be too much to expect you to come inside and— Oh!" She cupped a hand over her nose and mouth. "Oh, you smell like—"

"Cow dung," Grampa finished behind her, sunlight making his hooked nose shimmer. "Car'line Mae, ya get yer—"

"You're ready?" Robert said, rounding Ma and Grandpa, not one wrinkle on his straight nose. His expression was fine—there wasn't one hint that the smell bothered him. He toted another durn picnic basket, looking as ready to greet the world as he probably had the day he'd been born, with a grin on his face.

"Get over here then an' let's go," Caroline snapped.

He climbed up beside her on the wagon seat. She watched him for a minute, as Grampa and Ma watched both of them, then she snapped the reins and the wagon jolted forward.

As the force jerked Kingston backward, Caroline grinned. "Better hang on there. We wouldn't want anything to happen to *this* picnic."

He laughed, a sharp bark. "No, we certainly would not."

If we even have an appetite by the time we reach the hollow, Robert thought grimly. He thought he was doing a good job of hiding the wave of nausea he felt each time a whiff of cow dung breezed his way. He didn't know how he was going to endure the afternoon. But endure he would. The little vixen would not win. She would not put him off. He would sit beside her the entire journey to the mines and act as if he were breathing nothing but the finest country air.

CHAPTER

---◆---

FIFTEEN

She took the roughest path she knew, Robert felt certain. He had never been bounced and jostled so much. Landing on those stones in Madden's Creek the first day he had met her had not made his backside as sore as he knew it would be after today.

It had rained heavily during the night, but there was decent land on which they might travel. Caroline elected to take a difficult route, however. Three times she guided the wagon through deep ruts, then grumbled when it became mired and they had to climb down and struggle to get it out.

She ordered him to the back of the wagon to push while she pulled on the bridles to urge the horses forward. Each time they succeeded in unmiring the buckboard, Robert glanced down and saw that more mud had splattered his gray trousers. After the third time of pushing and heaving the wagon forward, he was a sight—filthy nearly up to his knees.

"The ground gets mushy in places sometimes," she remarked.

"And in some places it looks dry," he said. "We might not get mired if we lead the horses through those places."

She shrugged. "Can't always tell where the dry places are."

"That's odd. Your eyesight seems to have gone bad just since I saw you two days ago."

"Reckon so. Maybe I'd better stop by Dr. Gilbert's an' see about gettin' spectacles. They'd make me look mighty fine."

"You don't look as drab as you would like to, Caroline."

"Who says I'd like to?" she queried as he reached to hand her back up. She pushed his hand away. "I can do it."

"Where is your calico dress?"

"Hanging up in the loft, where it stays unless there's a special occasion—like a barn dance with Clyde."

"What about your other dresses?" he asked, rounding the wagon.

"They're up there, too. Like I said, I couldn't see changin' just 'cause we were goin' to deliver laundry an' food to the miners. A lot of 'em are Grampa's friends, an' they've seen me look pretty bad 'n' smell pretty awful. Smell's gettin' to you, huh? Guess I shoulda washed an' changed before ridin' out with you."

"Funny. You didn't think of doing so then."

She flashed him a grin as he climbed up onto the seat and settled beside her. "I'm so stupid, y'know . . . Some things just don't occur to me. Why, I can't even always tell the diff'rence between a man who's gettin' sweet on a girl an' one who's only *pretendin'* to get sweet on a girl. Some I can, though." She shook the reins, and the horses dipped their heads, then pulled the wagon forth.

"Take Clyde. He's been sweet on me for some time, always approachin' me on the street, askin' me to go ridin' with him or to some frolic goin' on in town. Of course, there's lots of frolics that go on in Dubuque, so a person has to be careful what she finds herself goin' to."

The wagon began dipping down into the hollow, swaying and creaking as it passed through the tall green grass.

"Clyde, though . . . he always goes to the decent frolics, the ones held at farms an' such, not the ones that get goin' in saloons. The diff'rence is all the drinkin' an' carousin', the clothes the women wear, the games that're played. In the saloons, y'know, you've got poker an' all manner of drinkin' an' other things goin' on. At the farms we just clear the barn, serve up some punch, good food, an' fiddlin'.

"I went to a few things with Clyde this past week. The church ladies don't approve, but even Ma goes to a frolic now 'n' then an' has a good time. Clyde, he's a dancer. He's tall, an' when he dips to . . ."

She kept talking, chatting about Clyde and the various dances done at frolics.

"He's kissed me some, y'know. Clyde, that is," she informed Robert, her pert chin lifted.

"Really?" he responded, annoyed at the flicker of jealousy that went through him. Ridiculous—that he should be jealous! He didn't care who or how many men had kissed her, or where they had kissed her, or how they had kissed her!

But he suspected he had been the first to kiss her. After the kisses they had shared that first night, he and Caroline had joked about her making a discovery.

"He does a good job, too. Has this way of movin' his tongue that's real nice. Better than any man I've ever kissed—an' I've kissed a lot. Y'know, most of those that come by the farm from time to time until I decided recently I only wanted Clyde callin'."

"I thought your mother said you always turned male callers away."

"She was just tryin' to get your interest. Wanna know how you compare?"

If he said no, she would know that she had succeeded in bothering him, in poking holes in his male pride. So he said yes, and found that he was genuinely curious—though he knew what he was going to say. What else would Caroline say? She disliked him so much, she was not capable of responding any other way.

"Right down at the bottom of the barrel. Y'see, it's the way you turn your head, I figure."

Robert snorted. "You love my kisses, Caroline. I'd even venture to say that I was the first man to kiss you."

He hated that he was getting snared in her game, but he couldn't seem to help himself. The woman irritated him. She insulted him, foiled his attempts to romance her, then smirked about what she had done. He admired her spunkiness and her directness, but damn if she didn't frustrate and exasperate him to hell. Knowing exactly what she was doing, of course.

And the damnedest thing was . . . he didn't act like himself when he was around her. If someone had told him weeks ago that once he arrived in Dubuque he would spend an afternoon scrubbing laundry, or that he would walk barefoot down a main street with his shirt buttoned all wrong and his hair uncombed, he would have told him he was mad. If someone had told him he would be trying to court a woman dressed in a sloppy, smelly dress, a woman who looked as though she had just stepped out of an unkempt hostelry, he would have laughed in disbelief.

He glanced off at the trees and rolling hills ahead, trying not to wrinkle his nose when another whiff of dung drifted his way.

"Guess it's the way you move your tongue, too. Clyde, he moves his all around mine, really opens his mouth wide. He wraps his arms all around me an' pulls me real close. You . . . you just sorta touch yours to mine a little an' don't make me feel so warm as Clyde makes me feel."

"I don't—" Robert stopped himself, not wanting to be snared in her trap. She looked entirely serious, but he knew Caroline well enough by now to know that this was another of her tricks, another of her attempts to irritate him.

"You don't what?" she asked.

"Nothing," he answered, fighting to keep a sullen tone from his voice. *This is utterly ridiculous,* he thought. *I'm sitting here, letting the woman insult me so. She smells horrible, she has nothing nice to say today, and I'm sitting here, enduring it all!*

She began talking about Clyde again, how he was coming to supper later, how he had picked an entire bunch of wildflowers for her last week, that he had gone to a field just north of Dubuque, plucked them, and brought them to her. Knowing flowers—his mother grew roses and loved gardening in general—Robert wanted to ask how wilted the flowers had been by the time Clyde delivered them.

But he held his tongue, even while she talked about the wonderful picnic she and Clyde had shared the afternoon he had brought the flowers. Clyde had brought chicken, fresh bread, and peach preserves . . .

Robert wanted to turn her over his knee. The day he had helped her scrub laundry, *he* had brought beef, fresh bread, and preserves. Where was Colonel when Clyde came? he wanted to ask, and this time he almost had to bite his tongue to keep from talking.

He suddenly found himself gazing at Caroline with surprise, wondering why she was chattering so. Trying to annoy him, yes, and unfortunately she was doing it. But something else . . . Something was bothering him. Something about Caroline prattling on and on . . .

She had chatted nervously at great length that first evening near the barn after he had dared her to kiss him. She always talked, droning on and on, whenever she was nervous, or flustered, or angry. Her angry talk was always just that—angry talk. Her nervous talk was rambling chitchat about anything that popped into her head at the moment, anything that would divert his attention.

She was trying to irritate him, yes, but, not trusting Caroline, he had to wonder if she were planning something, if she were trying to keep his attention where she wanted it because she was plotting mischief.

He noticed that they were drawing near to a shallow part of the creek, preparing to cross it. He noticed that one of her hands had deserted the reins in favor of the pocket stitched to her dress.

The horses began trudging through the creek, splashing water up around their legs.

"Caroline, what are you . . . *Snake!*" he whispered, suddenly paralyzed with fear as she slowly pulled her hand—and the snake—from her pocket.

Why the hell did he hate the creeping, slithering things so? Why the hell did they make him feel like he wanted to jump out of his skin? He'd *never* liked them, even as a boy.

He sat very still, watching the green thing slither toward him, its flickering tongue darting in and out of its mouth.

He wouldn't run this time . . . He would not. He would not give Caroline the satisfaction of watching him tear off in his haste to escape the snake. Not that there was anywhere to run but through the creek. If he ran, she would love it. She would love watching him make a fool of himself. She would cackle to no end.

"Ain't you just a brave soul t'day," she taunted softly. She picked the snake up and held it out toward him. It curled around her hand but poked its head at Robert, still flickering its tongue.

"I want you outta Dubuque, Kingston," she said. "I want you packin' to leave tomorrow. If you don't, I'm gonna collect a whole hogshead of these sweet little things an' pile them all over you."

Robert leaned back, to the side, unable to help himself. Damn woman! He wasn't about to let that tongue touch him. He wasn't about to let that thing slither over any part of him!

Caroline thrust the creature at him. Oblivious to all but the serpent in front of him, Robert scooted over the side of the wagon and went tumbling into the creek.

Caroline laughed.

Robert couldn't have been more outraged if he'd again been standing in the church vestibule long past time for the scheduled ceremony, waiting for the woman he was supposed to marry, feeling sympathetic and laughing eyes on him. An iciness uncoiled in his gut and began spreading to every part of his body. For long moments he was so furious he couldn't move, he could only sit and watch as Caroline clicked her tongue and began leading the horses out of the creek.

"Where do you think you're going?" he suddenly roared. She was not going to just drive that team and wagon out of the creek, nonchalantly leaving him where she had forced him. He wouldn't let her.

He sprang into action, jumping up, fighting the dirty water gathered around his knees, pushing his way through it, raising and lowering his legs against the heaviness of his soaked trousers.

Caroline glanced over her shoulder, her eyes widening as she realized he was coming after her. She stood and shook the reins, shouting at the horses, urging them on. They quickened their pace, but not before Robert reached the wagon, where he managed to grab Caroline around the waist and pull her down toward him.

She held tight to the reins while the horses screeched objections. "Let them go, Caroline!" Robert warned. "They'll rear up and upset the wagon. Think of all that laundry and food. Let them go!"

"Tarnation! You let *me* go!" she yelled, kicking and flailing.

He was booted in the stomach, elbowed in the chest, scratched on the arm. But he held on, and when she finally released the reins, he pushed her straight down into the shallow water, pushing her head into it to make certain he soaked every inch of her.

There!

She came up sputtering, cursing him in ways he had never been cursed, kicking and flailing more, swearing she'd get him for this, more or less telling him his mother had not been married when she gave birth to him. The sight of her, twigs hanging in her wet hair, her eyes wide and glittering with rage, did his heart good.

Robert tossed his head back and laughed, feeling victorious, feeling better than he had felt in days. Hell—better than he'd felt in weeks!

He underestimated her. He shouldn't have taken his eyes off of her.

She let go of the hold she had on one of his upper arms and on the front of his shirt. He felt her hands slip down the outsides of his legs. He looked down and saw her provocative, sly smile, and despite the fact that she resembled a drowned rat and that he knew her well enough by now to know that Caroline never, ever changed moods so quickly unless she had trickery on the mind, he felt himself becoming aroused instead of suspicious—as he should have been.

She jerked his legs out from under him, plopping him on his rear amid a splash of water. He got a mouthful of creek, some of which he swallowed, the rest of which he tried his damnedest to spit out—he wouldn't allow himself to think of what he might have swallowed along with the water, or what and how many tiny creatures might be swimming around in his mouth.

He tasted grit and his own string of curse words, but only the first one got beyond his lips before Caroline bounded up and away from him, obviously meaning to escape. He heard the horses whinny, as if all the commotion were frightening them, then he began trying to make his way from the creek.

Caroline scrambled toward the wagon and grappled for something under the seat just as Robert reached her. She turned around, brandishing a hefty pistol and aiming it at his crotch.

Jacob had warned him about that gun, and he had ignored the warning. Cockily. Hastily. Arrogantly.

Robert heeled back a full four steps, then stopped. He would not act frightened of her, of that deadly-looking weapon and of where she had it aimed. Caroline would like seeing him frightened. She would relish it.

The pistol surely wasn't loaded. Besides, even if it were, she wouldn't shoot him. She would not.

"You know the diff'rence between a rooster an' a hen?" Caroline asked, somewhat breathlessly, pushing wet hair from one eye.

Robert laughed, trying to keep the nervousness out of his chuckle. "Caroline, you planned that snake. What was I supposed to do? *Not* come after you? Put the gun down. We're even now. We'll climb back on the wagon seat and take the food and laundry to the miners. Perhaps we might even reach some sort of truce during the ride back to Dubuque."

"Like hell we will!" She waved the pistol around, turning the barrel up, then down, then making a circle with it. "You're stayin' right here while I ride off. You can walk back to town! An' after t'day me 'n' Ma an' Grampa better not see you again!"

"You're the moodiest . . . You know that's not what they want. The pistol is not loaded, Caroline," he said, stepping forward, hoping she would put the gun back under the wagon seat and cool off.

"You wanna stay back, Kingston," she warned, her eyes narrowing and flashing. He remembered Jacob saying "You didn't see her eyes" the morning after he had arrived in town, but he took another step forward anyway, not letting himself dwell on the words. If he kept walking toward her, she would lower her weapon soon or later.

He felt the shot whiz past his earlobe before he heard the crack. His heart did a fearful flip. He froze.

A minute or so later, he realized the horses were running away. The shot had scared them; they had screeched, reared, and raced off up the embankment. The wagon tipped and bounced its way up the hill as the animals dashed ahead of it. Laundry flew here and there, some pieces catching on tree branches. Brown loaves of bread came rolling down the hillside, skittering to a halt near the water's edge.

Shouting, Caroline tore out of the creek after the horses. Robert watched as she raised her skirt high, scurried up the embankment, then disappeared over the crest.

A minute later she reappeared, brandishing her pistol again, breathing hard. She had apparently had little luck in trying to chase the team and wagon down.

"I oughtta shoot you dead, you . . . you critter, you!" she yelled at him.

Robert raised his arms at his sides, let them fall, then made his way out of the creek. "Caroline, we have a long walk back to Dubuque, perhaps three miles," he said wearily, starting up the embankment. "And you . . ." Feeling somewhat smug, he pointed to the branches, then to the ground. "You have laundry to gather. After all, it was you who spooked the horses. And don't forget—you mentioned that Clyde the kisser is coming for supper later. You certainly do not want to miss Marshal Butterworth."

She twisted her lips. Her expression changed from rage to lightheartedness to cheerfulness—and Robert grew suspicious again.

"Yep, Clyde's comin' over, an' I wouldn't wanna miss him. You're right about that. There's no man in the world who can compare to Clyde. Not any man—an' that means you, too, Mr. Charmer."

"Well, Caroline," he said, despite telling himself not to

become indignant. He reached the hilltop to stand beside her. "Your mother invited me to supper again, too, you see." *Ridiculous—this is ridiculous!* he thought again. *She's driving me into acting jealous!*

She turned red. "You just watch how you say my name! Just don't say it at all! Just forget about supper! Don't come back to the cabin no more!"

"Your grandfather would be appalled at your hospitality."

"All right, you! I've had enough, durn it all!" She lifted her pistol, aimed it at his crotch again, and cocked the trigger.

Snapping his eyes shut, Robert clapped his hands to his ears. He heard a click, then her peals of delighted laughter—no blast—and he realized with exasperation and more anger that he'd been tricked again, that she had known there had been only one bullet in the gun.

Enraged, he marched right up to her, snatched the pistol from her hand, and threw it down into the creek. It hit with a splash and a spray of water, and Caroline stood gawking down at the place where it had landed.

"Now, what'd you wanna go 'n' do that for?" she demanded, looking truly mystified. Furious again, too. "You don't know a good pistol when you see one, do you? That was a—"

He took her by the arm and twisted her around. "Oh, would you shut up!" He watched the heavy rise and fall of her breasts, seeing the outline of hardened nipples through the wet gingham and whatever undergarments she wore—if any. "Sometimes you talk too damn much, Caroline."

"Well, sometimes there ain't nothin' else to do but talk!" she said, trying to maneuver her arm free. "Let go of me, durn it! You don't know—I might be hidin' another pistol. An' maybe I won't try to miss next time! Maybe I'll make sure there's two bullets instead of one!" She twisted and turned and tried to pry his fingers off of her arm. "I'm gonna . . . Like you said, we got a long walk back, an' there's laundry t'be gathered, so just let go. Ma 'n' Grampa'll be—"

"I can think of plenty else to do," he murmured, and bent to kiss her lips.

She tried harder to twist away—just as he had expected she would. She still smelled horrible. That dip in the water had washed away little of the manure on her dress, and on top of it now lay the thick, muddy aroma of the creek.

He had kissed her to shut her up because he was tired of her threats and of the fact that she always seemed to get the better of him. And because—he didn't like admitting this—he was jealous about her relationship with Clyde. He knew he could outdance, outromance, outcharm, outcourt, and outkiss the man! But something still irritated him about Caroline's attention toward Clyde. How dare she tease him about Clyde being the better kisser!

He had never reacted to a woman in such an immature manner. And to think he was kissing one of the most uncouth, unrefined, and *dirtiest* women he'd ever laid eyes on! Or smelled.

For the first time, he wondered if Jacob were right, if perhaps all the trouble Caroline wreaked was worth *their* trouble, if perhaps they should look closely around the city for a different lot on which to build the hotel.

He couldn't even speak the words. Jacob would be unbearable. He would laugh. Caroline would laugh—Robert would be unable to live with the humiliation.

Despite her filthy appearance—after that splash in the creek, he didn't suppose his was much better—she tasted sweet. She tasted fresh. If only he could manage to draw her close. If only she would open her mouth and welcome him.

He ought to let her go. Not only had he never forced himself on a woman, but also Caroline just might box his ears or stomp his foot in a moment. No other woman would think of doing such a thing—but she would.

Despite his thoughts, his mouth kept seeking hers, his tongue kept trying to part her lips, and his hand still gripped her arm.

He finally realized she wasn't fighting as much as he had expected her to fight, and that she was fighting less and less with each passing second.

"Caroline," he murmured against her lips, "let me kiss you—please." He had never, *ever* pleaded with a woman. The situation astounded him, with her smelling and looking so awful, him asking her to please let him kiss her.

The instant she surrendered, stopped struggling, and swayed toward him, his heart began beating faster. He expected to feel like the victor again. He expected to want to stand over her with a smug look on his face. He expected to want to say, in the most immature fashion, "See? I'm better than Clyde—or any man who might have kissed you."

Instead he felt such an incredible sense of relief; he felt a thrill, a surge of gratefulness that she meant to let him kiss her the way he wanted to kiss her—deeply and without reservation. With sheer enjoyment. With blossoming passion and desire.

She opened her mouth beneath his, sighing against him, closing her eyes, and letting him take control. A headiness went through him, perhaps because she was so strong-willed, yet in this she would let him guide her.

He traced her lips with his tongue, tasting the creek, but tasting Caroline, too. She was as sweet as honeysuckle in the summertime, as tender inside as a hard-shelled fruit—and well worth all he had endured to get here. She tipped her head up, welcoming him, inviting him, tempting him further. As he eased his tongue into her mouth, her arms slid up over his shoulders and around his neck.

He had never wanted to know anything as much as he wanted to know her mouth, to know her. Wanting her family's land on Dubuque's Main Street was not driving him at the moment; lots or no lots, having Caroline in his arms was most important to him now. Despite all the grief she had forced him to endure. Despite the fact that she had let Colonel eat their picnic food that day. Despite the fact that she had tormented him with that snake and virtually pushed him into the creek.

He told himself he was still reacting to her goading him with all her talk about Clyde and other men's kisses. He told himself this was only physical need on his part, a desire to prove that he stirred her a lot more than she admitted. He told himself there was nothing emotional about his response—that it was purely a man wanting a woman.

He could live with that.

He caressed her tongue with his, probed the tender flesh between her teeth and cheeks, then slipped his tongue beneath hers. He slid a hand around her waist and urged her closer and closer, feeling a lot more comfortable seducing a disarmed woman than he did fending off one brandishing a snake. Her fingers crawled their way up to the back of his neck, then pushed into the hair at his nape and pressed his head—and mouth—more tightly against hers. He stroked her waist, then eased his hand up to caress the underside of one of her breasts.

She inhaled a sharp breath, and her breast swelled in his hand.

"Shh, Caroline," he murmured, touching her pebbled nipple. He rubbed two fingertips back and forth over it, drawing a soft moan from her. She wasn't nearly as experienced as she would like him to believe. But then, he had known that.

He stroked her entire breast, then began unbuttoning her bodice.

Caroline knew she ought to withdraw. She knew she ought to push his hands away, make him quit touching her in this way she'd never been touched. And now . . . he was unbuttoning her dress, pushing the wet material aside!

She couldn't seem to stop him. She didn't have the power to stop him. In truth, she didn't want to stop him.

She'd told herself time after time that she didn't like this man, that Robert Kingston was after her family's lots, that he didn't care what he had to do to get them, and that once he had them, he'd think nothing of building his hotel right on her pa's grave, right on Princess's and Rose's grazing grounds. That he wouldn't give a second thought to tearing down the cabin Pa and Grampa had built, the home in which she'd been raised most of her life.

But just like on that first evening, when she'd enjoyed his kisses so much near the barn and stream, something a lot more than not liking this man's tactics was going on here. The truth was she *hated* his tactics, but she liked his expert lips and hands.

She wanted him.

But it wasn't right. It was good, but it wasn't. She'd lured him out here to scare him off from Dubuque once and for all—and she'd failed. Now her pride was wounded. Hellfire! Her pride was shredded!

With all her might, Caroline pushed away from him, kicking him in the shin just as he lifted his hands to reach for her again.

Fists propped on her hips, she watched him grimace and reach down to nurse his leg.

"Blame it all!" she said. "You just don't listen. I told you not to stick your hands in that laundry water that day, an' you did it anyway. I told you to let me go, an' you didn't! You make your own trouble, mister."

"Sometimes I wonder what the hell I see in you!" he shot back, scowling.

"You see land you want real bad, that's what you see. Well, I tell you—you're not gonna get my family's land. The answer is no. No, *no*. My folks spent a lot of years doin' without back in Virginia. We came here, where the government made it possible for us to have a new start. I remember bein' hungry back in the Virginia hills. I remember havin' no shoes in the wintertime. For all Grampa's jestin, I remember him an' Pa playin' the fairs an' turkey shoots just so we could eat. I bet you've never been hungry a day of your life, Kingston! I bet you've never gone without shoes an' warm clothes in the winter. I bet no one's ever threatened to build a damn hotel or church over one of your relative's graves!"

Tears of frustration began burning the backs of her eyes. Why wouldn't he just leave? Oh, why wouldn't he just leave!

He lowered his leg and stared at her, appearing shocked, his brow suddenly furrowed, his eyes flickering with some sort of emotion she'd not seen in them before when he gazed at her. Compassion sprang to mind. But that was a foolish thought—men like Robert Kingston didn't feel compassion. They just barreled over you to get what they wanted.

"Like you said," she mumbled, turning away so he wouldn't see her cry, "I've got laundry to gather. You just go on back to town an' don't come back to the cabin!"

She walked off, fighting the sudden urge to sit down and cry. She felt threatened and frustrated and scared—and downright angry that Grampa would give in so easily after he'd run the Reverend Brunson and the Methodists off. Ma didn't care whether or not they held onto the land anymore either; she just wanted to be accepted back into the Methodist congregation and Dubuque's finer social circles.

Caroline felt alone. She felt abandoned—by the people she loved the most.

She began gathering the laundry that had flown out of the wagon bed, snatching up shirts and underclothes, stockings and trousers. She scowled at the dirt on a number of them. Some of it could be brushed off, but the mud . . . A lot of the clothes would have to be rewashed. She couldn't expect to be paid for delivering dirty laundry.

She wished Pa were here. He was tough. He wouldn't give up. He wouldn't let anyone who shared conversation, a few smokes, and some glasses of whiskey with him talk him into selling their land. He wasn't a big man, but his cool blue eyes and fierce expressions could scare anyone.

From the corner of her eye, she glimpsed Kingston gathering laundry, too. He even picked up a few loaves of bread, though she couldn't imagine why. They couldn't sell them to anyone now that they'd rolled all over the ground.

He spotted her watching him, and he straightened and shrugged. His sheepish look tugged at her heart some, though she knew she shouldn't let it. Still, he looked sorry right now. His eyes were soft and kind and filled with understanding.

She snorted. "I said go on back to town."

He shrugged like a naughty, remorseful little boy might. "As you said . . . I don't listen. I'm sorry, Caroline. I had no idea your father was buried there. I . . . perhaps I'll look for other land."

He went on picking up laundry, shaking out the clothes before he draped them over his forearm.

She stared at him for a long time, wondering if he was serious about what he'd said.

CHAPTER

SIXTEEN

After her plan to get rid of him once and for all backfired, and after he said that about maybe looking for other land, Caroline settled down. She cried a lot 'cause she still didn't trust him and she was afraid he had lied. She cried at night, when no one knew—though she thought Grampa suspected. She caught him staring at her sometimes with sympathy in his eyes, and she turned away, not wanting to talk to him.

She cried mostly because she knew she was in love.

Robert called a lot in the evenings, saying nothing more about looking for other land, and Caroline took her meals out back rather than sit inside at the table and try to be civil. When she went back inside, he and Grampa usually had their heads together, talking in low tones, and she figured she, Ma, and Grampa might be moving soon. But she didn't know where and she didn't ask.

She spent a lot of time at Pa's grave, sitting by it, talking to him, telling him how they'd all deserted her—she hadn't even seen Henrietta for days now.

One morning Ma reminded her that she'd promised Robert she would go with him to talk to David's pa, and she grudgingly agreed. Caroline Mae Watson had never gone back on a promise, after all.

Robert and Caroline tried to call on David's father. They obtained directions to Hal Perkins's farm from Mrs. Johnson, and when they arrived, Hal was passed out on the ground near the front steps. Caroline insisted on taking him inside. "No telling how much he's drunk an' when he'll wake up," she said.

Robert grumbled that they ought to leave him right where he was. If he died right there, David would be fortunate.

But leaving the man out in the elements and out where a wild animal might have no trouble getting to him went against Caroline's principles. She scowled, then told Robert to hook his arms beneath Hal's and help her get him into the house.

If it could be called a house, Robert thought sorely, doing as ordered. The roof was halfway gone, the steps were rotted and crumbling—he cursed when Caroline's booted foot went through one—and holes gaped like wide black mouths in most of the walls. The place reeked of urine and the sour odor of whiskey, and nothing in sight even resembled a bed. Browning corn husks had been spread on the floor in one area, and Robert assumed that Hal slept on them. Several tossed aside, wide-mouthed bottles which had obviously contained food now produced an abundance of green, fuzzy mold which made Robert fight nausea. His and Caroline's footprints—and others— were clearly outlined in the thick coat of dirt on the planked floor.

"This place ain't fit for hogs to live in!" Caroline said in disbelief. She had taken Hal's feet to help him into the house. Now she dropped them and put her hands over her nose. Her next words were muffled. "Stinks. Can't believe it! David lived here?"

But no, David had not lived in the house, or so they discovered when they went to investigate the shabby barn, which had obviously been patched in places over the years. The barn was where David had lived.

Boards had been nailed over the original ones without thought of appearance. They lay north and south, east and west, diagonal, and the wood was less worn than the original wood used to build the barn; it was dark gray as compared to the lighter, weather- and time-worn original wood.

Chickens were clucking around, scratching the ground outside the barn, foraging for food. Inside, Caroline found a burlap bag filled with dried corn, and she scattered the contents about the ground outside. The cows were mooing and giving her long looks, needing to be milked.

But there was no time for that, so Caroline and Robert set them free outside the fenced area in which they were obviously kept, hoping some newcomer would drift through the forest near the place, find the cows, and decide to take one or two with them as stock. People passed through all the time on their way farther west, foraging for food, Caroline said. For anything that would make life easier. Livestock was valued.

"Isn't there something illegal about letting them go?" Robert asked.

"Yep, but they've got a better chance outside that fence than inside. Hal's milked 'em some—otherwise they'd be screamin'—but by the looks of 'em, he hasn't milked 'em for days or fed 'em much more than the pitiful grass inside that fence."

"What about the chickens?"

"They'll eventually get hungry enough to go off into the woods lookin' for food."

"Thank you for coming with me, Caroline. I'm glad you know about these things."

Caroline glanced up from where she stood near the barn doors and saw Robert's eyes glowing gratefully. She was still so angry and hurt that Grampa and Ma had given in to him. And she'd never been so scared, she thought.

But he was mighty handsome, standing there in his white shirt and dark trousers, the morning sun glowing all around him, his black hair not so neatly combed as it usually was. Some of it fell over his brow, it was thick, and it had grown a good inch since he'd been in Dubuque. His skin wasn't as lightly colored as it had been; he'd spent some time outdoors, getting browned up.

"Don't go gettin' all soft on me, Kingston," she heard herself mumble. It was her defense. Every time he got that look in his eye and that tone to his voice—a thickness—like he was thinking of kissing her again, she made her words sound as rough as possible. Doing that would put any normal man off, she thought. But damn if she didn't now realize that he wasn't any normal man.

"Heaven forbid," he said, unfolding his arms.

"You ain't got no reason to court me anymore. There's no use pretendin'. I know you've got the land, just like you wanted."

She didn't step back when he approached. She didn't flinch when he cradled her jaw in his hands. She didn't object when he raised her chin, lowered his head, and kissed her tenderly on one corner of her mouth. All she could think was that she wanted this, that no matter what she said and how she acted, she wanted him to kiss her. His hands were large and warm, and her jaw fit them perfectly.

But why? Why was he doing this? He didn't have to. It was over. She'd been outgunned, so to speak.

He kissed the other side of her mouth. He kissed the tip of her nose. He kissed her lips again, and she parted them for him, welcoming his gently probing tongue. She slid her hands up his smooth, cool silk shirt, up over his slightly muscled arms and across his broad shoulders and chest. There'd be a lot more to him if he had been raised in these parts, on a farm or something, doing work in fields and tending animals morning and night.

But she didn't mind that he wasn't as muscled and sturdy as most men she knew, or that he hadn't been raised like she'd been raised. Hell, she didn't even really know exactly how he'd been raised except that he'd most certainly never gone hungry, never had to think of how he could use a yard of cloth or garment until it was falling apart thread by thread, that he'd surely never gone without boots in the wintertime and cried while trying to warm his burning, stinging feet before an open fire.

All she thought and felt at the moment was him touching, caressing, warming . . . looking at her in a way no man ever had. All the physical sensations rushing through her blurred everything else—all thoughts of why he'd come to Dubuque and taken an interest in her.

She felt herself being pressed against the barn door, felt his hard body brush hers, then settle in, molding against hers, finding all the right curves and valleys, fitting together with hers as if it were the missing piece of a puzzle.

She realized she was crying.

He kissed her deeply and thoroughly, swirling his tongue around hers, tasting and drinking. Like her, he was unable to get enough. He passed a hand over her breast, cupping it lightly, and she gasped. But she didn't stop him this time when she felt him begin working at her bodice buttons.

His warm hand slid beneath the material of her dress, touched her plain cotton camisole, and slid beneath it to caress her breast. She moaned softly, arching into the touch, loving it, wanting more . . .

"Ouch!" He leapt back.

Blinking, she stared at him, unable to imagine what had

happened. Had he hurt himself somehow? Strained himself maybe? She never held her dresses together with pins while wearing them; she made sure to keep them mended.

"Damnation!" he growled, kicking at something on the ground. "Get away, you hear?"

He was kicking at a hen who obviously had decided she liked his calf.

The chicken pecked and pecked, trying to get a nibble. Robert kicked at the bird and grumbled more curse words. But nothing he did or said would make the hen change her mind. She was hungry, and he tasted good, and she was determined to get more of him.

"Damn chicken pecked right through my trousers!" he said, raising his knee, then lifting his trouser leg to show Caroline.

She saw the broken skin and the blood on his calf, and she knew the wound must smart. But when the hen closed in again, pecking at his other calf, making him dance a jig, she couldn't seem to do anything more than put her hands over her mouth and giggle behind them.

"Oh, it's funny, is it?" he demanded lightheartedly. "I wonder if you would laugh if she were trying to have you for breakfast! I've never heard of chickens eating meat. What—are all the animals in Iowa jealous?"

Caroline giggled more. He was getting indignant again, the way he often did. "You're tasty!"

"I'm honored that you think so, but would you help me?" The bird now had him backed up against the opposite barn door. Two more were closing in on the left.

"Maybe you should run to the wagon," she suggested, grabbing a spade from just inside the barn. She turned it so that the pole was facing the birds, and she swung it at them, lightly hitting the one who'd been pecking at Robert.

The bird squawked but persisted. Caroline whacked her again, and she stood, looking dazed while Caroline went after the other two, driving them back. At least they were smart enough to realize she meant to put them in a kettle if they didn't back off.

The first bird closed in again, and Caroline swung the spade. The hen fluttered off in a flurry of squawks and flapping wings. Caroline hoped she hadn't hurt it too bad.

Robert was smoothing his cuffs and trying to gather the shreds of his composure. Caroline couldn't help herself— she laughed again.

"Saved from aggressive hens," he grumbled, but she thought she saw a smile twitch one side of his mouth.

She propped the spade against the barn door and began buttoning her bodice.

"Could I help?" he asked, his voice thick and raspy suddenly.

She turned away, out of his sight, and walked into the barn, buttoning as she went. Her face was flushed cherry red, she was sure. She'd never had her bare skin, her breast, caressed like that!

He followed her; she felt him come up behind her. A second later he placed his hands on her shoulders.

"Caroline."

She shook his hands off. "Even if I was gonna let you ... y'know, this ain't the place for it, Kingston. If we've got time for that, we've got time to milk those cows we set loose. Look—over there."

She really wasn't just trying to distract him.

In a stall strewn with hay sat a small old chest of drawers, faded with age, over which lay a tattered, crumpled, pale orange blanket. Atop the chest sat a small brown wooden box, several old readers and other books, a slate, and a beat-up tin. Near the chest of drawers was a stool.

Robert walked into the open stall and up to the chest. He lifted the slate and stared down at it, at David's name scrawled there—and something else. Something that jolted him inside.

He was glad his back was to Caroline. So much emotion welled in him, he wondered if he would ever breathe right again. He was assailed with memories so sharp they were painful: Stephen, huddled in an area of the stable, clutching his slate to his breast, crying, huge tears rolling down his deformed face. When Robert had approached him—that awful day that seemed forever ago—Stephen had refused to try to speak. He had instead slammed his slate onto his lap, clutched his pencil in a trembling hand, and written, *I am a freak. I hate myself.*

What David had written was not nearly so bad: *Weird. David is weird. I don't like David.* But it was damn sure enough to create the same flood of emotions Robert had felt the day he'd found Stephen in the stable—compassion and love for Stephen, for David, and blind rage at the people, in this case, person, inside the house—shanty.

Robert fought for air. The barn spun so wildly that he almost could not remember where he was until he felt Caroline touch his back, until he heard her voice: "What's the matter? It's only a slate."

"Get me out of here," he rasped. "Otherwise I'll kill Hal Perkins. Take me to David."

He was thankful she asked no more questions. She led him from the barn and to the wagon and horses they had left near the shanty. He climbed up to the buckboard seat, still in shock, still trembling.

He felt a stab of embarrassment that she must have felt him quaking, but he sat straight while she climbed up, settled herself, and gave a gentle shake of the reins, setting the horses and wagon into motion.

The ride from Pleasant Hill to Catfish Creek took only half an hour at the most, and another ten minutes passed, surely, while they made their way up the bank of the creek to the wide path that wound back into the forest and led to the Carrols'. It was flanked by trees and foliage, and twigs cracked beneath the horses' hooves, but Robert was scarcely aware because he was thinking of Stephen and David, and David and Stephen, of slates and barns and little boys who loved so much but who were afraid and ashamed . . .

He spotted the Carrols' cabin and Louisa standing in the doorway, aproned, always aproned and prepared to greet guests, and David running out, alive and well, his coloring better than it had been. He even looked as if he had gained weight.

Robert nearly fell scrambling off the wagon seat. He raced toward David and caught the boy in his arms.

David felt small compared to Stephen, but then Robert had been a boy himself back then, back when Stephen was alive, and children always felt small to him now. He had known only that he loved his brother, that people stared and made fun of his brother, and that Stephen hurt inside. So much so . . .

"Oh, David," Robert whispered, tears blurring his vision. He buried his face in the lad's hair. "Oh, David, David. I found your slate. Do you remember what you last wrote on it?"

David drew his head back to look at him. He nodded silently, wide-eyed.

"You are not weird, do you hear me? You are not weird. You are not a freak. You sometimes cannot speak right, but that's because you've been mistreated and you get nervous. That doesn't mean . . . Oh, David, don't ever do anything to hurt yourself. There are people who love you."

He pressed David's head against his chest and held the boy tight. Moments later, Caroline was touching his arm, softly urging him to let the boy go— he was scaring David.

Robert placed David on his feet, as gently as he could with hands and arms that still trembled.

"What do you suppose is the matter with him?" Louisa asked Caroline in her light French accent. The women sat at a table behind the Carrols' cabin, snapping beans and watching Robert and David play in the grass with one of the cats. Louisa called the cat Rainbow, and when Caroline had asked why—the cat was all black—Louisa explained that a young granddaughter had named her.

Robert and David each had a long piece of yarn with which he was teasing Rainbow. She playfully lunged one way, then the next, leaping and twisting in the air near a patch of orange and red flowers. Once she mistook her tail for the yarn and grabbed it. Everyone laughed, especially Robert and David.

"The matter with . . . ?" Caroline asked, snapping a thick bean in two.

"With Robert. The monsieur seemed troubled when he arrived. I have never seen him embrace the boy so."

"He didn't wanna let him go," Caroline agreed under her breath, glancing up to watch Robert and David again. "At the Perkins' barn he picked up David's slate, an' then it was like he was somewhere else, someplace else. I reckon he worries that David doesn't like himself, that David might hurt himself."

"David has been happy since coming here. The first day, no, but he was not so much unhappy as worried, I think. He would not hurt himself. He loves life, and now it is happier for him. He looks better."

"He sure does," Caroline agreed. Color always flushed David's cheeks now, his skinny frame was filling out, and he laughed a lot. She didn't think he had before.

"Sometimes . . . some things make us remember things that happened before," Louisa said wisely. "I wonder if the monsieur had a child, perhaps a son. I wonder if something happened to the son."

Caroline squinted her eyes against the reddish-orange evening sun. Behind Robert and David, trees whispered, brushing together. She watched Robert scoop David up and spin him around, saw the love in Robert's eyes, and wondered if Louisa was right. It made sense. His obvious love for David, his powerful need to protect the boy, his desire to attack Hal for beating up on David whenever he didn't bring home the right amount of milk-and-egg money so Hal could go buy up Dubuque's supply of whiskey for the day . . . Caroline had never seen anyone form such a strong attachment to a child who wasn't even his.

She and Louisa finished snapping the beans, then washed them and boiled them in a kettle dangling over a fire near the back of the house.

After a supper of smoked ham, yams, beans, and corn dodgers, David, the Carrols, Robert, and Caroline sat outside under the moon and stars and listened to Ben play his fiddle.

Lanterns and the small fire Ben had built in the center of the clearing cast the cabin, its surroundings, and the people in a warm orange glow. Robert sat smiling as he listened to and watched Caroline and David sing the lyrics and tap their feet to Ben's spry tunes, then finally jump up and begin dancing to them.

Caroline lifted her skirts well above her ankles, kicking up her heels like her partner, laughing along with him, her eyes sparkling, her face beaming.

Robert found himself clapping his hands and tapping his own feet, keeping time with the rhythm she and David shuffled and stomped out in the grass. Louisa soon joined the two, and soon after she pulled Robert into the dancing, and he did his best to mimic their movements. He laughed and clapped along with them, despite the fact that he would have been much more confident in a ballroom waltzing than trying to do a country dance in a clearing in the forest.

Caroline danced circles around him at one point, her hands on her hips, her eyes laughing at him, her heels kicking up, her skirts swishing, her curls bouncing on her shoulders and down her back. He turned around and around, watching her, mesmerized, feeling himself drawn in—caught in her spell.

He was still sometimes surprised by his strong attraction to a woman who was so different from the women who had surrounded him most of his life. But attracted to her he was, and he wanted her in his arms more at this moment than he had since meeting her.

Firelight flickered in her eyes, taunting him, tempting him, luring him. The music and the laughter became a dull blur. There was only Caroline, gaily dancing around him in a way he had never danced before tonight, in a way that fascinated him but kept her just out of reach of his touch.

Warmth flooded him. The fire and his efforts to keep up with her had something to do with the heat. But most of the warmth had settled in his groin; he knew desire when he felt it.

He longed to catch her, to pull her against him, to stare down into those fascinating eyes and watch the firelight flicker in them. He longed to feel her soft but not delicate skin, to touch her silky, bouncy hair, to taste her sweet, dark mouth. She might be innocent—he felt almost certain she had never lain with a man—but right now she was purposely teasing him.

And yet her teasing didn't irritate him, because he suspected that if there were a way—right now—she would come willingly into his arms.

Sweet, tempting, sensual Caroline . . . He didn't think she was aware of how seductive she could be.

As if by magic, the strokes of Ben's fiddle slowed, then changed to what sounded like, in the midst of all the gaiety, a drab tune. But Robert quickly recognized it as a waltz.

Surprised, he tore his eyes from a now still Caroline and fastened them on Ben, who grinned slyly, conspiratorially, and dipped his head in acknowledgment. His gaze darted between Caroline and Robert twice. Robert suppressed a laugh, grinning instead, and stepped toward Caroline.

"Ben Carrol, what the hell is—?"

"Shh, Caroline," Robert said thickly from behind her. He slid a hand from her shoulder down to her hand and turned her to him. "It's a waltz."

Her eyes flared. "I don't know nothin' about—"

"I'll teach you, just as you and David taught me. Loosen your elbow," he advised, extending her arm. He dropped a hand to her waist and let it rest there lightly, feeling the curve of her hip and the rise and fall of her body with her rapid breath. "Close your eyes for a moment and listen."

She stared at him for a second, then her eyelids fluttered shut.

"Three notes at a time . . . Do you hear them?" he whispered. David and Louisa had withdrawn into the shadows. Robert's attention was so focused on Caroline he didn't know where they had gone exactly, and he didn't care to search right now. Ben was giving him the chance to be close to Caroline, which was something he wanted more than anything at the moment. To be very close to her . . .

She nodded, the firelight creating a bronze glow around her hair. The air, now damp with dew, smelled of hickory.

"You follow the music . . . You follow me. Three notes, swaying and dipping. Ready?"

Nodding again, she smiled her charming smile.

She stumbled through the first few rounds, but she was a quick learner and she followed him just as he had told her to. She allowed him to take the lead, just as she had allowed him to take the lead this afternoon when he'd kissed her in the doorway of Hal Perkins's barn.

He swallowed, feeling her warmth, hearing her breath, which had slowed somewhat, and the swish of her skirts as he and Caroline whirled around and around in the clearing. The fire crackled, the stars twinkled above, the nearly full moon peered down. The soft notes of the waltz captured them in its magical spell.

Her eyes were now open and wide, and she gazed up at him with awe and fascination, with desire, her breath catching now and then, her palm growing damp against his. Her eyes had grown smoky, more hazed with passion than they had been this afternoon, and he knew that if there were a way . . .

He wanted to crush her against him, bury his face in her hair, and another part of him between her open thighs.

They were no longer playing a game with each other, she either teasing him with sly smiles or dressing in an atrocious manner to try to frighten him away, he trying to romance her into selling her family's land. Things had changed, his goal had changed, and though something in the back of his mind warned that he should allow this acute attraction between them to go no further, that she would invariably be hurt in the end, his desire for Caroline was so intense at the moment . . .

If they were alone and she were willing—and she *was*—he would make love to her. Oh, yes . . . quickly at first, then slowly, watching surprise and pleasure dance in her eyes, feeling her press up against him.

Caroline couldn't tear her gaze from his, his was so hot and powerful, burning a path beneath her skin, searing a trail to the secret place between her legs, making it throb and want to press against him, feel his touch. She wavered between embarrassment and boldness, wanting to tear away from him one second, wanting to strip away their clothes and be skin to skin with him the next.

If David and the Carrols hadn't been seated nearby, watching them, she and Robert surely would have been writhing on the ground right now. The man might be a little prissy in his speech sometimes, he might be afraid of snakes and woodchucks and who knew what else, he might not be able to hold whiskey well, but he sure as hell knew how to handle a woman. He knew how to touch her, kiss her, dance with her—in ways that made her want to just give herself up to him. No woman in her right mind would pass him by.

He knew it, too; when the tune ended, he withdrew, cocked his head, slanted her a grin, and bowed like a prince to his princess. Grandly. Elegantly. Smoothly. And that's exactly what she felt like—a princess. No, a queen. She stood staring at him real stupid-like, in a daze, unable to tear her gaze from his face. His hair was mussed from all the dancing. It fell over his brow, partially hiding one eye, making him look dark and dangerous, like a man who'd snatch her heart and have it for breakfast right alongside his eggs.

She was still scared, she realized. But she'd always faced danger head-on. She'd never run from anything. And she always came out of bad situations—a snake rearing its head, a lone wolf trotting her way—just fine.

Clapping began behind her. More applause sounded, then Louisa's soft voice touched her ears: "Oh, that was wonderful! *Étonnant*. Like being home! Oh, again. Again! Ben?"

Robert turned toward her, giving her a bow, too. "*Merci, madame*. The hour grows late."

"Must you leave?"

Robert glanced at Caroline, who had stepped up beside him. Desire now burned low in his gaze. "I'm afraid we must."

She wondered at the drive home, if anything more would develop along the way. She felt her face grow hot again, with both want and embarrassment. "You wanna stop with the slick business, Kingston," she grated.

He laughed, glanced at Ben, said another *merci*, then turned back to take her hand in his. Ben was nodding his head and chuckling, the glint of mischievousness lighting his eyes. Thinking he was as bad as Grampa in a roundabout way, Caroline laughed softly.

She and Robert gratefully accepted the lanterns Ben and Louisa offered to light the way back to town, and this time when Robert took her arm to hand her up, Caroline didn't push him away.

She was still angry about the fact that Grampa had decided to sell him their land, but more and more she liked the way Robert looked at her.

Did she! She liked his touches, the way he sometimes spoke her name so softly. She had decided that at some point before he started building his hotel she would ask if he'd please not build over Pa's grave, if he'd fence the area or something and, please, out of respect for her and her family, leave it be. There was surely plenty of land where the cabin and barn sat. It, combined with the pastures, surely ought to be enough for him.

She'd also decided to force herself to start looking for land outside of Dubuque. She'd have to hire men to help her build another cabin. Maybe she could talk some of the miners into helping before the cold season set in.

She was shocked when Robert took the reins from her, indicating with a silent glance that he'd like to guide the horses this evening. She was so used to doing it herself, so used to taking control, that she almost grabbed them from him. She started to say that no one but her ever led her horses—not even Grampa and Ma—and that she wasn't even sure he knew how to lead them. But just like before the waltz, the warm look in his eyes made her settle back on the seat and let him have a try at it.

There're times, she thought, smoothing her skirt in her lap, when the man wants to take a little control and the woman oughtta let him.

She reckoned she was sometimes man enough for the both of them, being so temperamental and always taking the bull by the horns. After Pa's death and after Grampa had become more and more feeble, she'd felt that since there were no sons in the family, taking care of everyone and everything was her responsibility. And she wasn't one who took responsibility lightly.

She almost told Robert, "Well, if you need help . . ." But she didn't. She shut her mouth, mostly out of respect for the man that he was, and hoped that if he hadn't learned how to lead the team by watching her, he'd ask for her advice. Unless he did, or unless she suspected that they were in trouble—the horses were spooked or going the wrong way—she'd keep quiet.

They waved good-bye to David and the Carrols, then

headed off down the path Ben had cut through the darkening forest.

The birds had grown quiet, but the crickets had picked up where they'd left off, and their chirps filled the night. An owl hooted twice, something scampered through the brush up ahead, and a gentle breeze rustled the branches. Almost unconsciously, Caroline scooted closer to Robert, feeling his warm thigh touch hers. He smiled down at her.

"Evenin's are gettin' cold," she said, watching the glow of his eyes as the horses snorted and dipped their heads.

"You wore the dress I like," he said, and his voice was so soft she barely heard it above the trees' whispers.

She nervously smoothed the calico again. "I didn't know you liked it so." But she did, and that was the truth.

"You look pretty wearing it. It enhances your hair and your face. You look captivating, Caroline."

She couldn't help a shy smile. Captivating ... that's what he'd called her that first evening. But he'd only been after the land then. Now he had the land, and he could be after only her.

He smiled again, and her own smile increased just as a rut in the path forced her against him more. His breath touched her face, warm and smelling of the coffee he'd drunk with Ben after the meal earlier.

She reached up and skimmed his jaw with a finger, feeling the rough whiskers that had formed on his face.

Sobering, he stared down at her. She thought she ought to say something—words might ease the awkwardness.

Words might also embarrass her again, because what she wanted to say to him was "Touch me again like you did at the Perkins' place. Touch me an' hold me an' kiss me an' ...."

She didn't know why she was so afraid inside, why she feared all the things he made her feel. She knew they were natural. She knew that when a man and a woman liked each other a whole lot, they were inclined to do what God had put them on his green earth to do. She was just experiencing all the feelings that must go along with the act, and there was nothing she ought to be afraid of.

But she was afraid, as if she were headed down a dark path with no lanterns to guide the way. Without even a horse and a wagon. She was stumbling around on foot, wondering what to do next, wondering if what she wanted to say was the right thing to say, wondering if he'd like her touch if she dared touch him more. Wondering if he'd stick around . . . afterward.

She'd faced a lot of scary things in her life, but this was about the worst.

"I want to take you somewhere," he said. "To a home I recently purchased."

She swallowed hard. "Plannin' on stayin' in Dubuque . . . afterward?" she couldn't help but ask.

"Perhaps." Leaving one hand on the reins, he stroked her cheek, then touched her bottom lip. He tipped her chin and kissed her in his tender way, a way that was totally unlike Clyde's rough way. She wanted to melt like a burning candle in his arms, against him, all over him.

Why did he want to take her to the home he'd bought? She wondered. The question flitted back and forth in her head.

"Why'd you buy a house?" she asked.

"To make someone happy," he answered.

Her heart began to pound so she thought it might jump right out of her chest. *To make someone happy?*

Her?

Who else? He was inviting her there, so who else could he mean?

She wondered how soon he'd ask her to marry him, and her heart stopped for a second or two at that thought. She was sure he'd said "perhaps" about staying in Dubuque because he wasn't sure she'd accept his proposal.

Despite all their past differences and her wanting him so badly to leave town, she now wanted him to stay. Oh, yes! She did. She'd marry him. Gladly.

That was why he'd bought a house—surely. He planned to marry her, and he'd bought the house for them to live in afterward. He was so excited about it, he couldn't wait to show her.

"Ma an' Grampa'll worry about me if we go there tonight," she said, staring into his eyes. Luckily the horses were on their best behavior tonight, 'cause neither she nor Robert was concentrating on them anymore.

He kissed her again. "They know you're with me."

His voice was turning husky and thick again, and his eyes had changed. They didn't glow so much anymore. Caroline bet that if she lifted one of the lanterns dangling from hooks on either side of the buckboard, she'd see that his eyes were smoky. Smoky and filled with want.

She swallowed, glancing down at her lap, smoothing her skirt again. She'd grown breathless in that odd way, like she had during the waltz. "What, uh . . . what are we gonna do there? At the house, I mean? You've got chairs an' all that? Tables an' a stove or fireplace an' . . ."

"It's furnished, Caroline. In a way I think you'll like. Of course, you can change anything you want to change once you move in. It will be your home. As far as what we'll do once we get there tonight . . . That is entirely up to you."

She swallowed again. Entirely up to . . . Oh, no, he couldn't leave what they were going to do up to her! She had an idea, but . . . well, she needed his help. He obviously knew how to go about this, and she did, too, but, well, not exactly.

He put both hands back on the reins once the team emerged from the trees. Not far away lay the creek, sparkling in the moonlight.

"I suppose I owe you an explanation for my behavior at Hal Perkins's farm this afternoon," he said, and her ears pricked.

"I wanna know why what David wrote on that slate upset you so much, but you ain't gotta tell me. I mean, if it's something that hurts real bad inside, like my pa dyin' has always hurt me, an' you don't wanna talk about it . . . I can live with that."

"You really loved your father, didn't you?" he asked.

She nodded. "I still can't believe he's dead."

"I don't plan to build my hotel over the top of him, Caroline."

She stared at his profile, so handsome, so fine. "Y-you don't?"

"No."

"Where do you plan t'build your hotel, then?"

"Across Main Street, on the opposite side. Telling Jacob was hard, very hard. I thought he'd never stop teasing me. We bought four saloons there. We plan to tear them down and build the hotel on the land they're sitting on."

"Really? But what about our farm? You bought us a house. We ain't stayin' there, on Main, now. Not after tonight, that is," she added quietly.

"Don't be angry about what I'm about to say, Caroline," he said hesitantly. "Your grandfather did what he thought was best. You've apparently worn the trousers in the family for a while, almost since your father died and—"

" 'Worn the trousers'?" she couldn't help blurting.

"You've been the man in the family."

"I ain't no man! You know that, Kingston!"

"Calm down, Caroline."

"I've taken care of ever'body when they couldn't seem to take care of theirselves! Grampa and Ma woulda laid down an' died after Pa died if it hadn't been for me tryin' to keep them in good spirits. Is that what Grampa said, that I've 'worn the trousers'?"

"Caroline, think about it. You have."

As the horses began splashing through the creek, Caroline huffed back against the buckboard seat and folded her arms.

She reckoned she had done most everything, said how most everything was going to be, since Pa died. She'd gotten her and Ma the jobs doing laundry and delivering food to the miners at the camps—to Grampa's objection 'cause he didn't want the Watson women traveling back and forth alone to the camps every day. Caroline had assumed the jobs anyway, and when Ma had seen the money she was bringing in, she had begun helping. Grampa hadn't objected more, possibly because he knew Caroline had his and her pa's stubbornness and she wouldn't change her mind, and because he, too, saw the money coming in. He saw that the money paid the preemption, and that they wouldn't lose their land the way they'd feared they might since they now had to live without Pa's mining pay. His pay hadn't been a lot, but then the Watsons had never needed a lot of money to survive, to be content.

And when the land thing had started with the Methodists calling about every other day, then Jacob Fletcher showing up in time, then Robert, she'd pretty much taken the bull by the horns, too. She'd "worn the trousers," telling everyone how it was going to be. Grampa had gone along with her at first, probably because he loved and adored her as much as she loved and adored him. But reality had finally hit him in the face, and he had decided to take over as the man of the house.

"He ain't mad at me, is he?" Caroline asked. "Y'know . . . Grampa. For wearin' the trousers. I was only doin' what I thought was best. I was tryin' to help my family survive."

Wincing, she remembered the heated argument she'd had with Grampa—their first in years—the night she had become jealous of his and Robert's friendship and had realized that Grampa was giving in to him. "I ain't acted very good, I guess."

"You did what you felt you had to do, Caroline," Robert responded. "He understands that. I understand that."

"You're not still sore that I scared you into the creek with that snake? That I shot at you?"

He chuckled as the horses climbed the embankment, heaving and blowing air. They reached the crest, their bridles jingling, and walked on. Robert turned them in the opposite direction to the way that led to Dubuque. "No. But I promise you that if you ever attempt such things again, I'll turn you over my knee. I don't like snakes. Just the thought of them gives me shivers. Do not intentionally scare me with one."

"I thought you were real prissy at first because of that. I'd never seen a full-grown man run from a snake. Then you looked at me an' you kissed my hand, an' I knew there wasn't nothin' prissy about you. Nothin' at all."

"I'm certainly glad you realized that," he said dryly. "Prissy? Hah! Anyway, Clarence is arranging to sell the lot to a dentist who plans to move to Dubuque."

"But what'll happen to Pa's grave?"

"Clarence and I have discussed . . . Caroline, there are plenty of oaks and black walnuts out near the new house. We thought we might . . . We thought we might . . . move the grave," he finally managed, looking straight ahead.

Her jaw dropped open. "You mean, dig Pa's coffin up and *move* it?"

He flinched, as if expecting to be hit. "That was the thought, yes."

"I don't . . . I don't like the idea of diggin' him up!"

"I knew you wouldn't. But, Caroline, it's a lone grave, and there is no guarantee that the dentist will honor Clarence's request to leave it alone, or that the dentist will be there forever. You've no idea whose hands the land may fall into once it's sold out of the family. Think, Caroline. Think hard and long."

He was right, and she knew that without giving the matter much thought. The only place for Pa was where she, Ma, and Grampa were, where the Watsons were, and if that meant moving his coffin, she reckoned they'd move his coffin.

"All right," she said, real quick. "But I'm not sure I can help."

"I don't expect you to."

"What's the house look like—tell me!" she said, latching onto his arm excitedly, wanting to change the subject. She sat straight again.

Glancing over at her, Robert laughed. His eyes sparkled again. "You're delighted, aren't you?"

"I am, I am!" She could hardly keep from bouncing up and down on the seat.

"Calm down, you'll frighten the horses," he advised.

She eyed him. "You know a lot about them, for a city feller."

"Everyone knows about horses, Caroline, even city people."

She laughed at herself. "Well, I reckon you're right. Now, tell me about the house."

"Very well."

He told her how the house was constructed of whitewashed clapboard, that it had three bedrooms, a small parlor, a sitting room, and a kitchen with a brick floor.

"A parlor?" she said breathlessly. "We ain't never had a parlor. I hope it ain't too fancy."

Robert heard the excitement and awe in her voice, and he laughed. "Not too."

" 'Cause, y'know, if it's too fancy, I'll have to simmer it down some. Oh, Ma'll be thrilled!" she said, clapping her hands. "We'll have to bring the settle from the cabin for Grampa, though. He's mighty fond of it."

"I know. And we mustn't forget his corncob pipes."

"Oh, no, he'd make himself more if we forgot them."

"There's a smoke shed and a barn, of course," Robert continued. "And, Caroline, there's even a stream."

She smiled, thinking she'd never been happier, that she couldn't be happier if they were already married and expecting their first young 'un. The house sounded wonderful. He was wonderful. Life would once again be wonderful.

CHAPTER

---◆---

SEVENTEEN

The nearly full moon cast a silver glow on the frame house as Robert and Caroline approached in the wagon. She couldn't help herself—she grabbed one of the lanterns and held it up in front of her, trying to get a better view.

The outside was just like he had said—built of cut and whitewashed wood. It was more spread out than the Watsons' cabin, and windows peeked down from the second floors. A porch wrapped itself nearly all the way around the house. A white rail extended halfway up, and poles, evenly spaced, connected the rail with the overhanging roof. Two tall chimneys extended up on either end of the house.

Caroline whistled low. "Sure wish Pa was here to see this—an' to see how nice my feller's treatin' me," she said, grinning at Robert.

He grinned back. Then he turned and climbed down from the wagon. She started to jump down herself, she was so excited. But just as she grabbed the back of the seat and crouched a little, getting ready, he was there, in front of her, reaching for her waist.

Smiling, she enjoyed being lifted and lowered like a lady. Hellfire, if she was gonna be his wife soon, the wife of a hotel owner, if she was gonna live in a house such as the one before her, she'd better start learning to act like a lady! She'd better start learning to talk like one, too.

"Reckon we oughtta . . ." She smoothed her skirt. "Is there a barn? If we mean to stay for a while, maybe we should unhitch . . . unbridle the horses. They've been in those reins nearly all day."

He nodded. "There's a barn. And I agree—I reckon we oughtta unhitch the horses." He grinned, and she wanted to lightly punch him on the upper arm for mocking her.

"Now, don't you be laughin' at me, Kingston," she warned. "If I'm gonna live in this here house, I've gotta learn to act like a lady. Only ladies live in houses like that." She cocked a thumb at it.

"Come along, Caroline," he said, chuckling.

He took one of the horses by its bridle and led the way around the house to the barn. There, he and Caroline worked together at unhitching them. A speculator had owned the house, Robert said, and luckily the man's "staff" had left some things in the barn: three bales of hay for the horses to munch on, some blankets, and several combs. Robert took one, Caroline took the other, and they worked at brushing the animals.

"You sure know how to treat a woman right, Kingston," Caroline teased. "I knew that about you right off."

"I'm glad you've learned to appreciate me," he teased right back.

"Shoo! What woman wouldn't?"

"I've known a few, including you. I still cannot believe you rolled in cow dung that day just to get rid of me."

"Didn't roll in it. I smeared it on myself."

"Smeared it . . . ?" He peeked around his horse. She was working on her animal's neck, and she glanced at Robert from underneath. "You mean you picked it up in your hands and—"

"What else would I smear it with?" she asked smartly.

Laughing again, he shook his head. "Caroline, sometimes you're a gem. Other times . . . I don't know. I just don't know. Certainly no one can predict what you'll do next."

"You like that—not bein' able to predict me?"

He nodded slowly, his eyes going to her lips. "I do. I certainly do. Like when you marched those bullies to the jail. And like tonight when you kicked up your heels and began dancing to Ben's music."

She scowled. "Those boys belonged in jail. And ain't that what music is for? For dancing to?"

"Well, yes, but I've never seen anyone dance like that. I've never seen a woman lift her skirts so high and just . . . dance. Without a care in the world, without a thought for propriety. Without reserve. Your smile and your laughter . . . your ways . . . They're infectious, Caroline. God, but you light up the entire territory."

She winced. "Infectious. Well, I hope that don't mean they're something bad."

"Oh no," he responded, laughing. "Infectious means you make other people smile and laugh, too."

"That's good," she said, breathing a sigh of relief.

"Yes, it is. It's very, very good."

He stared at her a moment more, looking all tender-eyed again.

"Well, you've got a house to show me, Kingston, so we'd better finish up."

Nodding, he went back to brushing. So did she.

They soon finished. Feeling certain the horses were comfortable—they were warm and brushed and nibbling on hay—Caroline and Robert took the lanterns and headed for the house.

"You planned this, didn't you?" she asked as he took a key from his pocket and unlocked a back door. "Bringin' me here."

"I did. If at all possible, I meant to bring you here soon. I didn't know if you would be agreeable today or not, but I dropped the key in my pocket anyway, hoping you would be."

He pushed the door open. Then with a flourish of his hand, he ushered her inside.

Smiling, she went, lantern first, glancing around along the way, feeling Robert's presence behind her.

They entered the kitchen, their boots tapping lightly on the brick floor. To her right was a fireplace, wide opened, with two trammels on which hung pots and kettles. An assortment of iron cooking utensils lay on the hearth—a bread toaster, a rotary broiler, a waffle iron, a trivet, and a number of other things. Open cabinets held dishes, some pottery, some china.

No pewterware in sight.

Caroline looked away from the cabinets real quick, wanting to see the china but not wanting to see the china. She didn't know if she could ever even eat off one of those plates or out of one of those bowls. She just didn't know.

She moved on through the room, silently trying to calm her stomach, hoping things wouldn't get too much better—or worse, depending on the view of the person looking at things. Ma would love it here. It would feel like old times to her, no doubt. But if conditions improved much more, Caroline was going to feel downright uncomfortable. Downright out of place.

She already did.

She'd just have to get used to it all. She wasn't about to let her simple ways and life keep her from marrying the man she'd fallen in love with, a man who had the biggest heart of any man she knew. He'd bought her this house, and he'd furnished it with things he thought she would like, and, by God, she'd learn to like them. She'd learn to eat off of those plates.

A door from the kitchen led into a room furnished with what looked like a chest on legs and a large table—like the one in Mrs. Johnson's boardinghouse. Honest to Pete, there'd only be the four of them once they all settled—her, Robert, Grampa, and Ma—and why they needed a table that would seat ten people, Caroline couldn't figure. Unless Robert wanted to have people over for supper sometimes, in which case she'd better learn to cook more food at a time if she'd be feeding six extra folks some evenings.

Of course, Robert could be planning on having a slew of children, too, and that would suit her just fine. She hadn't enjoyed growing up being the only child in her family, and she'd already decided that when she married and had children, she'd have a litter. A durn litter. She'd have little girls with bouncy hair and little boys with sly grins. So all those chairs would surely come in handy one day.

The dining room led off into a wide hall furnished with little tables with funny-shaped legs and clawed feet and vases and a set of four leather-bound books looking all dignified beneath a painting of ships sailing up and down the Mississippi River. It was too wide and wild looking to be any other river, that was for sure. Caroline held her lantern up closer and gasped when the gold-colored frame winked at her.

"That ain't . . ." She swallowed, not wanting to seem foolish or simple. Still, she had to ask. "It ain't real gold, is it?" If it was real gold, she might give serious thought to fleeing outside.

"It is. I bought the house already furnished, except for a few family heirlooms Mr. Livingston took with him. You might have heard of him—he's just built a new home near Iowa Street and—"

"I've heard of him. He's bought up a lot of land around here an' he sells it for more than he should. The man doesn't think twice about chargin' a person their last penny. You ain't gonna expect me to feed him supper, are you?" she had to ask.

He gave her a queer look. "Who you invite for supper is your business, Caroline."

"Well, that's good," she said, releasing a breath of relief. " 'Cause I oughtta have some say, y'know, in my own home."

He nodded, agreeing, then walked ahead to open a set of double doors at the back of the hall. The sweet perfume of hundreds of flowers immediately assaulted her, and she closed her eyes, inhaling their fragrance.

"Oh, Robert! It smells like spring. Just like spring!"

"You can't see it right now—it's too dark because of all the trees and shrubbery—but there's a garden there. A garden with paths and flowers," he said softly. "Near the end of one path is a cluster of black walnut and oak. That's where we'll bury your father, Caroline. Beyond is the stream. Your stream."

She for sure felt like a queen now. Her own garden, and flowers and shrubs and trees and a stream . . .

She blinked back tears. She'd never thought she would be willing to leave the cabin in Dubuque, but here she was, dreaming about living in a house that wasn't really for her but that she'd learn to live comfortably in. She loved the man who stood in the doorway before her, watching her as if waiting for some indication that she didn't like the house he'd bought for them to live in once they were married. For him, she'd do just about anything.

If the downstairs was this furnished, she reckoned the upstairs was, too, as much as any loft might be, with bedsteads and ticks and maybe chests to keep folded clothes and other things in. And he'd more or less said that once they got to the house, what they did after that was up to her.

She was scared nearly senseless. But she'd never wanted to be with a man more.

"Robert," she said, holding out her hand, "let's go up-stairs."

She watched the bob in his throat, watched his nostrils flare like a stallion sniffing out the mare, and she laughed nervously.

"Course, I'd say, 'let's go up to the loft,' but there ain't a ladder to climb, an' if the rest of this place is any indication, upstairs sure ain't a loft."

"No . . . no, there's no loft upstairs, Caroline," he said slowly. "There are three bedrooms, and you can take your pick."

Now she swallowed, running a forefinger along the nearby stair rail. "Kingston, you're gonna make me all skittish with that kind of talk, an' I'm gonna take back that invitation I more or less just made an' find my way back through that dinin' room 'n' kitchen, where I hope there's a drink of water somewhere since my throat's all the sudden gone so dry. After havin' a drink, I'm gonna flee just like a nervous mare 'cause you're sayin' all the right things instead of just doin' 'em. You're talkin' about those bedrooms, but you sure ain't leadin' the way up there. I don't mind tellin' you that the day's . . ."

Grinning, he stepped away from the door, approaching her.

". . . made me all nervous, all jumpy. That you have. Kissin' me like that out at Perkins's farm, then dancin' . . . waltzin' with me so that I felt like some lady in a fancy dress. Sittin' all close to me on the buckboard seat an' . . ."

"You sat close to me, Caroline," he said in a low, thick voice as he stood gazing down at her.

His eyes had gone all smoky again. He buried a hand in the hair at her nape, tipped her head back, and stared straight down at her. Then he kissed her, lightly, teasingly, nipping his way to her ear. There he whispered, "I believe my talking is about finished. Hold tight to your lantern, love, my dose of sunshine. When I undress you, I want to see you. Every inch of you."

She gasped, but held tight, just as he had said, as he scooped her up into his arms and headed for the staircase, which twisted up to her right, up into what she suspected was heaven.

It was, surely. What other place but heaven had gold curtains with pretty tassels, a lush green-and-gold carpet on which had been stitched rambling vines, such a huge bed with dark, carved posts that nearly touched the ceiling, and such a frilly white counterpane? She didn't think she'd ever seen anything so white. Even the powdery, deep-winter snows when they fell fast and blew against doors and the cabin in drifts weren't this white!

A tall cabinet sat near one of the two windows, a little table with a chair before it nestled not far from that, and a fancy chair with what looked like shoulders or wings rested comfortably before the fireplace.

"Do you like it?' Robert asked, his voice a vibration in his chest. She felt warm and secure snuggled against him.

"I do . . . I . . . I just need some time to get used to it, that's all."

"You will."

With you, I can get used to about anything, she thought dreamily.

He approached the bed and laid her upon it.

He kissed her again, sweetly and tenderly, and she opened her mouth beneath his, wanting to feel his tongue touch hers, then explore her. Her heart had begun racing in the downstairs hall; now it bumped about crazily, and she couldn't seem to catch her breath well enough.

She might have suspected she was suffocating, but she knew better. She'd felt this same breathlessness the first night he'd kissed her, and it had increased by slow degrees since then whenever he came close. It had been increasing in intensity for days and days, and now she felt as if she might burn up inside if he didn't do something about it, help her, give her relief.

He eased a knee between hers, gently pushing her legs apart and settling in somewhat. One hand caressed her hair, her ear, her neck and shoulder on one side, while the other stroked her cheek.

She was still scared of what she didn't know—how, exactly, joining with him was going to feel. But, honest to Pete, her body wasn't going to let her get away with not knowing. If she were a female cat like Henrietta, she'd be hugging and clawing at the ground right now, flipping her tail around, getting it out of the way so her man could make his way in. No skittishness, no resistance. Just get that tail out of the way.

Which was exactly what she was doing in a sense by parting her legs for Robert, by letting his knee come up and touch her woman's place. She gasped at its touch, but she sure didn't snap her legs back together. She sure didn't push him away. She arched up to him, feeling as though he'd lit little fires all inside of her.

His kisses became more intense, more demanding by measures; a tentative touch with his tongue at first, then a little exploration to one side and on the roof of her mouth, then prodding all over, his mouth forcing hers wider, demanding more access—as if he couldn't get enough of her.

She felt she couldn't get enough of *him*, no matter how close she scooted, no matter how wide she opened beneath him.

His groin pressed against her hip, and a moan escaped her, rising from deep inside. It was shock and need all wrapped together in one package; an urge to shrink away from his hardened length, yet an urge to reach down, touch it, caress it, unbutton his trousers and coax it to her damp place. Push her drawers down and open in desperate invitation. She'd never acted like a wanton. But, oh, she couldn't help herself right now. She just couldn't.

She moved a hand down along his arm, to his hip, then between their bodies, finding the outline of the organ seeking her. She'd seen enough animals do what they were about to do, and she knew this hard part of him would push its way inside of her sooner or later. Well, the sooner, the better as far as she was concerned.

Now he gasped. "God, Caroline, what are you doing?"

Wincing, she withdrew her hand and shrank away. "I figured if you could touch me, Kingston, I could touch you. I—"

"Damn if you don't always do the unexpected," he grated. "Of course you can touch me. I didn't expect it, that's all. I feel like a volcano about to erupt. Here," he said, drawing her hand back. "But carefully, Caroline, and slowly. Very slowly."

"You ain't gonna break, are you?" she asked and immediately felt stupid. She wanted to hide her head under the soft pillows when he grinned such a silly grin.

"No. I won't break. But if you're not careful, I *will* erupt, and this will be over before it's really begun."

She thought about how when she brought in males to breed with Princess and Rose and the hogs, the males hid that part of themselves away until they got a good whiff of the female. Then they couldn't help themselves. They were up on the female, and it was all over, lickety-split— what needed to be spilled had been spilled just like that— and the males wandered around for a while looking as though they felt pretty good. But the females, it wasn't much to them at all, and they went back to grazing or rolling in the slop or whatever they'd been doing before the bull or boar had come along.

Henrietta always took her time, however, doing a lot to lead up to things, flicking her tail around but also leading her men around by the nose for a while. And when the time came and things were done, Henrietta rolled around on her back and purred and meowed. Henrietta always looked satisfied.

So Caroline reckoned Robert was right. Going slow was best. Not letting the volcano erupt for a while . . . that was smart.

She touched him with her fingertips, tracing the outline of his length, its curved end, its ridges, and the soft sac beneath. She watched her fingers, excited even more by the thick, hard feel of him. When he groaned and tossed his head back, she glanced up at his face.

His jaw had hardened. His eyes were squeezed shut. His mouth had fallen open. He looked like he was in heaven.

"Ah, Caroline, you have no idea how good that feels," he murmured.

"Hell if I don't," she murmured right back. "I'm touching it."

He managed to laugh. Then he breathed deeply.

"But I sure ain't gonna try to wear the trousers tonight," she said, withdrawing her hand and lying back against the pillows. "They fit you too good. A mite too good, I'd say. Tell me what else to do."

"Anything you want, Caroline," he said smoothly.

"What if I tease you too much?"

"Then you'll know it. Your skirt will go over your head so fast you won't know what's happening until you feel me where I want to be."

Her eyes widened, then settled.

He shrugged one shoulder. "You asked."

She sat up against the head of the bed and began unbuttoning her bodice buttons, knowing he was watching. She worked the buttons slowly and deliberately and with purpose. After about every second button, she glanced up at him from beneath her lashes, feeling herself growing wetter between her legs, wondering how much more she herself could stand.

She reached her waist, undid the buttons there, and began pushing the dress off of her shoulders, over her plain cotton camisole.

He'd seen finer, she suddenly realized, glancing around

at the lavish furnishings, and who was she to think he might think she was pretty in it?

She jerked the dress back up over her shoulders and crossed her arms over her swollen breasts, her courage suddenly gone.

"What's the matter?" he asked, concern edging his voice.

"You've . . . you've seen a lot better'n me, Kingston. I . . . I've seen some of those lace and ribbon things in the stores in town an' I . . . Well, we ain't never had the money for 'em. Truth is, it's gonna take me a real long time to get used to this fancy stuff, y'know, 'cause I ain't never had it an' I sure ain't never had one of those lace 'n' ribbon camisoles. Mine are all made of plain ole rough cotton, mostly what Ma an' I spun ourselves from what we bought from other farmers, an' they ain't much to see."

She was surprised to feel tears burning the backs of her eyes. She felt ashamed. Here she'd thought to undress slowly for him, to make things real nice. Then she'd remembered her shabby underthings. Shabby compared to the ones in the Dubuque stores.

He sat up and came close.

She dropped her gaze to the counterpane, unable to look him in the eye right now. She blinked hard and breathed slowly and evenly, trying to get rid of the stupid, irritating, embarrassing tears. She hated tears! She suddenly wanted to flee. For the first time in her life, she wanted to run from something—from someone.

His fingers lifted her chin. She turned her face away, keeping her gaze on the counterpane, and she started off of the tick.

His touch alighted on the inside of her elbow, a highly sensitive place, and his fingertips rubbed gently back and forth. Gasping, she dropped her head back against his shoulder.

"Caroline Watson, do you think I give a damn that your camisole is not trimmed with ribbons and lace?" he asked huskily. "It's you I want. I plan to make love to you, not your undergarments."

She really wanted to cry now. She didn't bother to blink back the tears anymore. Trying to blink them back wouldn't have worked anyway. She felt a river of them, and a second later they flooded the banks.

With a cry of relief, she twisted around and flung herself at him, wrapping her arms around his chest and hugging him tight.

"Here we are in this big, fancy house, an' I was undressin' for you an' then I thought 'Oh, no, what's under my dress? Nothin' fancy to go along with everything.' I couldn't stand that thought 'cause I know you like fancy things!"

"This is your house, Caroline," he said, stroking her hair. "If it bothers you, we'll sell it and buy another. We'll look until you're satisfied, until you're comfortable. I knew you were overwhelmed but wouldn't admit it. I knew . . . You have so much pride. Here now," he said, lifting her face from his chest and bending to kiss her lips. "I'm going to undress you, and I don't care a fig what your undergarments look like. You felt me . . . You know what you do to me, how much I want you, and no camisole lacking lace and ribbons is going to change that. Do you understand?"

She nodded. How could she not? No one had ever said anything so sweet. No one in the world.

He positioned her in front of him and untied her boots, slipping them off first. He pushed her skirts up, found the ties that held her ragged stockings and pulled them loose, then rolled her stockings down and off one at a time. When he rolled the second one down, he slowed his pace, taking time to admire her slender legs and smiling up at her so she would be sure to see that he liked what he was discovering.

He tossed the last stocking to the floor, and scooted

closer, unbuttoning more buttons at her waist—the last of them.

"You don't need frivolous things to look pretty, Caroline . . . Sunshine. To look beautiful," he said, pushing her dress from her shoulders. "Your smile and your bright face do that for you." He bent to press a kiss on her bare skin at the point where her shoulder and arm connected, and she inhaled deeply, wondering what he would do next.

"Up," he commanded softly, and she rose to her knees so he could push the dress down over her waist, hips, and thighs. She sat back, pulled her legs out from under her, and the dress quickly joined her stockings and boots on the floor.

His eyes surveyed her for several long moments, her sitting before him in what she considered her worn, plain undergarments. She looked at the counterpane again. He ran his knuckles over one side of her camisole, from shoulder to waist, over the swollen mound of one breast. She drew a sharp breath and whispered his name.

"Caroline . . . sweet," he murmured. "As I thought. Unadorned and . . ."

She waited, holding her breath now, certain she wasn't good enough for him, certain he'd change his mind, snatch up her clothing, toss it at her, and tell her to get out.

". . . beautiful."

She closed her eyes, releasing her breath.

He admired her more, circling the outside of her breast with his fingertips, skimming the back of his hands up and down her bare arms and up her neck, burying them in her thick hair; he brought his lips so close she felt his hot breath on her skin, then pulled away.

She began squirming, but each time he told her to sit still, she did—but only for seconds. His fingertips swirled their way to one of her nipples, pinching lightly, and she eased closer to him.

He stayed her with a hand on her hip.

There's a God in heaven, she thought, and this sweet torture's gonna end soon. Surely.

He caressed her waist, her hip, her thigh. Watching her with an intensity that threatened to set her afire, he moved to one side of her, slipped his hand between her thighs, and urged her back against the pillows just as his fingers touched her secret place.

She arched up to him, panting, her body pleading, needing him to feed the fire he'd begun. It burned, it ached, it was almost painful, but she wanted more of it. She needed more of it.

He pushed her chemise up and kissed the inside of her knee, then kissed the inside of her thigh through her drawers. She didn't think he'd keep going . . . But he did, and she found that she shamelessly longed to have the drawers slipped away so he could kiss her flesh, so he could part her lips there and discover her most intimate place. Really discover it.

"You smell delicious, Caroline," he said, and she wanted to sit up, grab him, pull him atop her, and feel him buried inside her. No, she hadn't wanted this over quickly, she hadn't wanted him to spill himself in a rush then swagger off. But this was ridiculous!

"Stop teasin'!" she whispered desperately. "Robert, please . . ."

"Not teasing, Caroline. Preparing you."

"What . . . ?" She didn't understand. Preparing her?

"I'll explain later. For now, believe that I know what I'm doing, that I'll know when the moment is right, when you're ready."

She nodded. He must know . . . He'd done this before, no telling how many times—charmer that he was, she thought with a slight grin—and he must know what he was doing.

He pulled loose the ten ties on her camisole one by one, parting it and pushing it off her shoulders. He untied the front stays on her worn corset and let it fall open. Then he worked at the drawstring on her chemise, finally freeing the material and pushing it down over her shoulders and upper arms.

Groaning at the sight of her naked breasts, he buried his face between them, then kissed his way to the tip of one mound, and finally covered it with his mouth.

Caroline was so startled and shocked she grabbed his shoulders and tried to push him away. But only for a few seconds, for his mouth was hot and it brought pleasure like she'd never known; it shot fire through her body, building the flames that had settled between her thighs.

He suckled and suckled, teasing her other nipple with a thumb and forefinger. He found the drawstring that held her drawers, untied it, and slipped his hand beneath the material. His fingers crawled along her skin, creeping down, down, finally playing in her secret curls, slipping between them and caressing her swollen flesh.

She cried his name, lifted to him, began unbuttoning his shirt frantically, popping several buttons. Now situated between her legs, he pressed against her, rocking to and fro, setting an unnerving rhythm, making the same movements with his hips that she instinctively knew he would make once he was inside of her.

She'd go mad, feeling him, the outline of him, yet not really feeling him. His trousers were in the way.

"Take 'em off," she said boldly, frantically. "Robert, would you take 'em off!"

His hands came up to cradle her head, and he began kissing her again, still rocking, still grinding, still torturing. She found the buttons on the side of his trousers, and her fingers trembled so much that she almost couldn't undo them. She tossed her head, escaping his lips.

"Please, Robert ... The clothes ... I want you inside me."

He withdrew, sitting back on his heels between her knees, and removed his shirt, tossing it aside. His eyes were ablaze, the gold flecks brighter than she'd ever seen them, despite the dim flickering light of the lantern. Black hair swirled on his chest, tapering just below his ribs and disappearing in a thin line below the band of his trousers.

She'd never seen anyone undress so fast. He tossed his boots to the floor and pushed his trousers down over his narrow hips. His stockings went with them, dropping quickly into a pile beside the bedstead. And there he was, naked before her. Naked as the day he was born. But looking a lot better, she bet silently, wickedly.

He didn't give her time to look him over good. He stripped her of the rest of her clothing almost as quickly as he'd gotten rid of his, and he settled between her legs again, his belly resting against the thatch of hair at the joining of her thighs.

"Are you sure, Caroline?" he asked, refusing to let her look anywhere but into his eyes. "I don't want you to be sorry tomorrow."

"Hell, yes, I'm sure," she barely managed. "I'da said no before we left the Carrols' if I wasn't. An' the way you treat me . . . so sweet, like I'm somethin' special . . . You don't think I'm gonna let you get away now, do you, Kingston? C'mere."

He moved up slowly, and she opened her legs wider, welcoming him. He raised up, brushing his length back and forth against her private place, wetting its smooth end. Then he gave an expert thrust and buried himself inside her.

She nearly bit her bottom lip in two, it hurt so. He began moving, whispering her name and that he was sorry he'd had to hurt her to please her. She didn't quite understand, and it was still uncomfortable, more uncomfortable than she'd ever thought it might be.

But by and by the pain eased off, changing into pleasure. Perspiration beaded his brow, and the muscles and veins stood out on his neck, shoulders, and arms. He groaned, and his eyes became slits; what he was doing obviously felt so good to him.

It felt good to her, too. Wonderful. Incredible. Like nothing she'd ever felt ... She couldn't find the words to describe its intensity, its heat, the pleasure that rippled through her. She arched up to him, meeting his thrusts, groaning, moaning, crying his name.

An explosion took her among the stars. They floated around her, a million beautiful colors in a heavenly bed.

Not long afterward, the volcano erupted. But it wasn't like any volcano she'd heard or read about. It was hot all right, but it was sweet and strong deep inside of her, and just watching pleasure dance across Robert's face and contort his features made her willing to endure the beginning pain all over again. Again and again and again ...

She smoothed the wet hair from his brow and brought his head to rest on the pillow of her breast.

CHAPTER

EIGHTEEN

Perfume . . . she smelled the perfume of a hundred flowers. No, a million flowers—roses and orchids and azaleas . . . Their sweet essence made her smile, made her tingle. The dewdrops on their petals dampened the sheets and wet her skin.

This was a sweet dream, she realized, stirring a little. Sweet and unlikely. No one had ever dropped flowers on her. No one.

She stirred and realized it wasn't a dream. They were all there—the flowers, white, red, pink, blue, yellow—in abundance, so many she had to push them aside to glance around the room.

Flowers . . . all over the bed. All over her. Sticking to her skin where it wasn't covered by the light counterpane. Dewdrops clung to petals, and the soft morning sunshine

274

beaconing into the room from an open window made some of them wink at her.

Her imagination, surely, she thought, sleepily trying to figure out where she was.

In a bed in Robert Kingston's house. In their bed.

In their house.

Birds sang outside the window, greeting the day. Caroline sat up and wrapped her arms around herself, wondering if she ought to be as eager to greet it, wondering how Robert felt this morning.

If he came along soon and said they'd made a mistake, that he'd made a mistake and had changed his mind . . . She propped her chin on her knees.

The distinct scent of roses drifted up to her, and she reached down, lifted a plump white rose from the sheet, and brought it to her nose, inhaling its sweet scent.

It was too good to be true. It was all too good to be true. This house, the night, the way he'd kissed her and made love to her for hours . . . It was just all too much to be true.

She closed her eyes, squeezing back tears. Were they for the perfect rose and all the flowers and because he'd made love to her and she'd loved his attention, or because she doubted . . . because she feared?

Too good, too much . . . Everything was too perfect. Robert was too wonderful for a girl like her, too refined for a girl who lost her temper so quick and so often, for a girl who had been mean to him to try to get him to leave Dubuque.

She was too, too plain and simple to live in this house, to be married to him. He deserved better.

"I knew you would look beautiful sitting in the middle of all those flowers," he said softly.

Her eyes flew open. She glimpsed him standing in the doorway, leaning against the frame, his arms folded, his shirt unbuttoned and hanging open, his feet bare, his hair mussed. She recalled him glowing in last night's lamplight, touching her, kissing her, caressing her, hovering over her, burying himself in her. She remembered the pleasure that had danced on his face.

Shyly she glanced down at the flower-covered counterpane, feeling her face heat. Had she really done *that* with him?

The dull ache between her thighs and the wetness there indicated she had.

Had he really enjoyed it as much as she remembered?

"Caroline."

She couldn't bring herself to glance up. So many doubts and fears this morning. And she was different . . . changed from yesterday. Changed from weeks ago. He'd taught her how to enjoy being a woman.

But she was embarrassed now at how bold she'd been, touching him, tracing his . . . like that, begging him to put it inside her. She wondered if Henrietta ever felt embarrassed afterward.

Hell! Henrietta? Never!

His feet whispered across the carpet. The tick dipped on one side. Outside the window, a robin rejoiced.

"A white rose," Robert said, wrapping his hand around Caroline's. "It suits you, Caroline. So innocent . . . so sweet. So fresh."

He lifted her chin with two fingers. She twisted her lips, still staring down at the flowers. This was a dream. She just knew it. A wonderful, awful dream, teasing her, so real she smelled and felt and saw . . .

He chuckled. "The morning after . . ."

Her temper flared a little. He was laughing at her. She was too innocent for his taste.

"Talk to me, Caroline," he said, and his tone indicated he'd sobered. "Let me know that you're not sorry."

Not sorry? Had he really said that?

"Please, Caroline."

He had.

"It . . . it really happened?" was all she could say.

"It really happened."

She cleared her throat a little. "Don't tease me, Kingston."

"Not about this, Sunshine."

"I couldn't stand that, y'know. That'd get me all riled, an' I don't always have control of my temper when I'm riled. I do an' say the first thing that comes to mind an' take time to think about it later. So if you're teasin', Kingston, you wanna watch that 'cause I'm feelin' strange enough already."

He touched the back of a hand to one side of her jaw and slowly ran it down to her chin. "How well I know that, Caroline—that you say the first thing that comes to mind. I'm not teasing. I ask you—why else would you be naked underneath the coverlet?"

Her heart skipped. She tamped down the urge to lift the counterpane and have a look. But she already knew what she'd see. She was naked underneath the cover, all right.

"Where'd all these bloomin' flowers come from anyway?" she asked nervously. "Looks like somebody raided a meadow or somethin'. An' to have 'em piled all over me . . . shoo! This is the craziest thing I've ever seen!"

She felt his grin. "Not at all wilted like the ones Clyde brought you that day?"

"Clyde never brought me flowers! He doesn't know the first thing about—" She glanced up at him, remembering the lie she'd told him about Clyde bringing her flowers. "I was just tryin' to make you mad the day I told you that."

His eyes sparkled, the gold flecks dancing. "And you did. I was so jealous I couldn't see straight. So I brought you a few flowers."

"Hellfire, Kingston!" she said, lifting her chin up and away. "You brought the whole garden!"

He laughed. "Some from the garden, some from a meadow."

"I've gotta get home," she mumbled, not believing she was sitting in the middle of this fancy bed. "Cows to milk, hogs to slop." She tried fighting her way through all the blooms to the other side of the tick. There had to be a way out of here without crushing so many—

Then she remembered: she was naked. Stark naked, same as the day she was born. Not a stitch on anywhere.

On second thought, maybe she'd just stay underneath all the flowers.

She lay back, pulled the counterpane clear up to her chin and gave it a good tuck, being careful not to crush her rose.

"Soon as you leave the room, I'll get dressed," she said.

Grinning, a gleam in his eyes, Robert tugged on the coverlet.

"Watch that!" she snapped, tugging back.

"Why are you hiding from me, Caroline? I made sure to see every inch of you last night. But I'd like to see you again," he added.

"Ain't no one seen me in my birthday doin's 'cept Ma an' Pa an' Grampa when I was younger!"

"You didn't seem to mind last evening. I'm coming under there," he warned.

Her eyes widened. "You're not!"

"Oh, yes, I am."

"I've gotta go, Kingston, dream or no dream. Princess an' Rose—"

He sobered again. "For once let someone else manage, Caroline. For once don't be so damn responsible. Take care of yourself today, not anyone else."

"Kingston, you—"

He jerked up one side of the coverlet and poked his head underneath it. "Ummm . . ."

At his touch on her naked thigh, she scooted away. "You wanna watch that!"

"I smell us, you know." His voice was now low, deep, thick. "We're all over the sheets. Even the flowers cannot hide our smell."

What? Her breath quickened. His hands ran from her

knees up over her thighs and hips. His lips felt hot against her side. They kissed their way up, pushing her weakening hands aside, then closed around a nipple. Caroline groaned.

"Now here's a fine bud," he murmured, his head still half-covered.

She couldn't help herself. Instead of fighting—which had been her first inclination—she arched up to him and her hands went to his hair, pressing his head down.

She coaxed him, fed him, loved him. Her hips rocked up, and she heard herself groan. He wouldn't be doing this again, surely, if he didn't care . . . if he wanted her gone. If he'd changed his mind about marrying her.

His hand touched her thigh, then slid around and up to her woman's flesh, to the bud that tingled and began throbbing for him. His fingers moved up and down, making her writhe, making her part her thighs wider and wider. Her hand found his arm and squeezed. What was he doing to her—*what*?

"Sweet Caroline," he whispered. "Go with it, love. Don't fight your feelings. I'm here. I'll take care of you."

She didn't like feeling vulnerable. She always had control. She was the strong one, the one who led everyone around, the one who took care of people. But last night she hadn't led. He'd led her; he'd taken care of her. And she was willing to let him do it again. In this, Robert knew best.

His fingers increased their pace. So hot, so insistent, so tender, so thrilling. They drove her nearly crazy, going fast, then slow, then fast again, taking her closer and closer to some sweet peak, then lowering her back to the meadow of wildflowers, then lifting her again.

She cried his name, squeezed his arm, tossed her head . . .

Finally she went up and up, panting, as colorful rainbows filled the world and exploded in a million brilliant colors.

She fell limp against the clouds, his warm, comforting hand resting fully between her legs.

She felt him move around, and a minute later he eased atop her; he had removed his trousers and shirt. He settled himself between her legs, and she braced herself for the pain she knew was coming. It was so beautiful, this loving, and she wouldn't stop him. She couldn't. So she opened wide for him, embracing him with her thighs.

He pressed, and she pursed her lips, waiting . . .

He filled her, burying himself deep inside her with sweetness and fire. Her eyes snapped open in surprise. She felt her body adjust around his length and she felt so full she thought she might burst. But there was no pain.

"Rob—"

"Shh," he whispered against her cheek. "I'll go slow, Caroline. Promise. Don't move away. Please."

He sounded so desperate, she couldn't help but reach up and smooth the hair from his brow. She couldn't help but kiss him. She couldn't help but murmur, "I won't. I couldn't. It just feels so different today . . . so much better. I was shocked, that's all."

The fit was still awkward, but he settled in, and she adjusted more around him. The way they conformed was almost scary. *It's meant to be,* she thought, and she began meeting his slow movements in and out.

"God . . . oh, Caroline . . ." A groan rose from deep in his throat. His eyes shut for a second, then opened. "Oh, God. Damn, you feel good. Ah . . ."

They kept up the slow rhythm, a mating dance, rocking back and forth on the bed, their hips parting, then coming together, parting, then coming together again. His breath grew ragged, and she began panting.

He rose above her, bracing himself with his hands on the tick, his fiery gaze capturing and holding hers.

"Look, Sunshine," he whispered. "Look at us. God . . ."

His excitement was contagious. It made her bold enough to glance down and watch in fascination as he slid in and out of her. He pulled out for a second, resting his slick, swollen length against her thigh, and she thought she might die, she wanted him back inside her so bad. The thick crop of dark hair might have hidden him if he hadn't been so excited for her.

He touched himself, stroked himself; he urged her hand down to touch him. Then he helped her guide him back into her.

"Ah, Caroline. Mm . . ." He whispered "Sunshine" again and quickened the rhythm, becoming urgent and desperate, clutching at her hips, driving them up to his, burying himself deep, withdrawing, then burying himself deep again.

He inhaled sharply, and she felt something inside . . . pumping, an intense pleasure that made her moan and arch, that made her want as much of him as she could get, as much as he could give her.

When she was sure she had it all, she tossed her head back on the pillow.

Moments later, with effort, he shifted his weight to his side, pulling her with him, keeping their bodies joined. The sound of their breathing filled the room, overpowering the bird's chirps outside the window.

Caroline lay watching him, admiring his finely sculpted brow, nose, and jaw, his long eyelashes as he lay with his eyes closed, trying to catch his breath. She reached up and touched the wiry hair on his chest and thought she might die of embarrassment when his eyes opened and he grinned at her.

"Curious?" he asked.

Scowling, she pulled her hand back. "I was just wonderin', is all."

His grin widened. "Curious." He returned her hand to his chest. "Your touch feels nice, Caroline. We'll spend the day discovering each other."

"The day?" she blurted. "I can't do that. I've got chores and—"

"Caroline, what do you think would happen to your mother and grandfather if you met with an accident and died unexpectedly?"

"If I . . . Why, I don't know. I don't wanna think about that!"

"You should. They would survive, Caroline. Your mother has taken an extreme liking to Rufus Pennsberry—I know that from hearing Clarence talk—and Clarence still knows how to take care of his family."

"I didn't say he didn't!"

"Let him do it, then, Caroline. Don't do everything yourself. Give him some of his dignity back. Trust him. Him getting drunk with me was a rarity, I think."

"It was," she agreed.

"Your mother would marry Rufus if he asked," Robert remarked.

Caroline's eyes flared. "She wouldn't. She couldn't!"

Robert lifted a brow. "Why not?"

"She just couldn't, is all! She's Pa's wife. My ma. She just couldn't."

"She's only thirty-seven years old, Caroline. And I hate to say this, but your father has been dead for more than two years."

"That doesn't change anything," she said, pulling away from him. "She's still Pa's wife." He slipped out of her, and she rolled onto her side, resting her back against him. Ma marry somebody else? Like hell she would! "A lot's changed, but that's one thing that ain't ever gonna change—she'll always be Pa's wife," Caroline mumbled stubbornly.

Robert moved up behind her, propped himself up slightly, and rested his head on her right shoulder. "I didn't mean to upset you, Caroline. I've wanted to talk to you about a lot of things because I care about you and your family. I knew you wouldn't like the idea of moving your father's grave, and I've wondered how you would feel if Rufus proposed to your mother. Clarence feels that might happen someday soon. I thought you were oblivious. Caroline, she's still a relatively young woman, and I'm sure she experiences the same needs and desires any woman does. I don't think she enjoys being alone."

"She's not alone!"

"She is, in a sense. Do you think she's not lonely at night?"

"She has me 'n' Grampa!"

"It's not the same, Caroline."

He needs to mind his own business, Caroline thought smartly. But a second later she realized that soon—when they married—her business would always be his business, the same as his would be hers.

"Promise me you'll give the matter some thought, Caroline," Robert said softly. "That you'll try to see your mother's side of the coin. I don't want you to explode in her face. Your mother is quite a lady."

"Kingston, your sweetness is too much sometimes," she muttered, scooting from the bed. It was. It was too darn much. One minute she was angry with him; the next she was thinking he was about the most thoughtful man she'd ever known, worrying about people so.

Shyly she crossed her arms over her breasts, wishing she had more arms to hide herself with since Robert was having one hell of a time staring at her nakedness. She searched around for her dress, finally spotted it where it lay in a crumpled heap near the foot of the bed, and snatched it up.

"Put your eyes back in your blasted head, Kingston," she warned.

He chuckled and lay back on the pillows, an arm tossed back under his head.

"You look like a lazy cat who just finished feastin' on a fat mouse."

"Or a woodchuck," he joked.

She snorted. "You wouldn't go near a woodchuck."

"Or a mouse, for that matter."

"I figured that," she said, finding the rest of her clothes scattered around the area where her dress had been. A breeze flowed in through the open window, cooling her skin. "Reckon I'll be the one havin' to keep 'em out of the pantry an' such."

"Damn, but you look wonderful," he said, preoccupied with her nakedness. The counterpane just covered his narrow hips.

Blushing, she pulled on her drawers. "You wanna stop that, Kingston. You're embarrassin' me."

"It's true, Caroline. And believe me—I know what I'm talking about."

She blushed more deeply, tied the drawstring at her waist, then grabbed her corset. "You're what the Methodists call worldly, I reckon."

He laughed. "I reckon."

She tossed him a playful glare. "You've got a smart mouth, too."

"Muffins for breakfast," he said, his gaze fastened on her breasts.

She wasn't small in that area by any means. She wasn't huge either. She was happy with herself, however, and apparently so was he.

She'd never stopped to think about her figure before, but now she paused for a few seconds to consider it. It was fine, she thought. A little on the round side about the hips but—

"The woman discovers herself," he teased softly.

She threw her corset at him.

He caught the garment in midair, grinning still, and dangled it in front of his face. "Ah, yes. A little feminine fluff to play with."

She turned away, snatched up her camisole, slipped it on, and began trying ribbons. Sometimes his smugness was too damn much.

"She's angry with me, I think," he said. "I didn't want

her to put this silly thing back on anyway. Corsets can be . . . difficult."

She knew what he meant. They could be hard to get on and off. "You didn't have any trouble, Kingston," she retorted, grinning now herself.

"No, I didn't, did I?"

"Conceited cock," she muttered.

He laughed, deep and rich. "Caroline! I might be a gentleman—well bred, educated, and all that—but men are often exposed to things most women aren't exposed to. I wonder if you really know what you just said."

Her eyes grew as wide as twin saucers all of a sudden. She figured she knew—and she figured it wasn't anything nice. "I've hung around saloons a time or two," she said, finishing up the ribbons. She turned a glare on him, hands on her hips. "There ain't much I don't know. I compared you to a struttin' rooster, that's all!"

He tossed the corset aside and started from the bed. "There's a lot you don't know, Caroline. A lot that I plan to teach you."

"Now, wait," she said, backing off. "You bought a house. Are we gonna stay in this bedroom all day? You talked me into letting' Ma an' Grampa manage alone for the day, but there's lots more to discover around here than just you, Kingston, an' the sooner we get dressed and . . ." God, but didn't he look good naked! All slender and a little muscled in the right places. Wide shoulders, a solid chest covered with curly black hair, a taut stomach, and firm thighs. Not to mention that . . . that his private area looked awfully good, too. He wasn't erect anymore. What he was was obscene—not the least bit embarrassed that she was gawking at him.

"Yes?" he asked, stretching. "Lots more to discover, you were saying?"

Hellfire! The man was bolder than she'd figured him to be!

"Th-the garden," she stuttered. "An' the stream an' oaks

and black walnuts ... An' the meadow I know has no flowers left in it."

"But first," he said, "breakfast is waiting downstairs. I was not joking about muffins."

She continued staring at him. She'd never imagined a man could look so good. She'd never ever imagined.

"Caroline?"

"Wha—? Huh?" Her eyes whipped to his face. She wanted to fan herself, she was so hot suddenly.

"Get dressed before I accost you again."

"Acco—? Oh."

She turned away, her dress in hand. Trembling, she somehow managed to lower it over her head. Then she began fastening the buttons. She had no shame. Absolutely no shame. She couldn't believe she'd stared at him like that!

Her fumbling fingers were doing the last button when he stepped past her and to the door moments later. He wore his trousers and shirt again, only this time the shirt was buttoned and tucked in, though it lay open at his throat. She ran her fingers through her hair, trying to comb out the tangles, and he approached her and gently pulled her arm down.

"Leave it," he said. "I like it wild."

"Bet I look like I've been rollin' in the hay," she mumbled, dropping her gaze.

"You do. That's what I like about it."

"Kingston, you're, uh—" She shifted her weight from one foot to the other. "You're a strange man."

He took her chin in hand and lifted it. She looked into his eyes, finding them all tender and soft suddenly.

"Do you love me, Caroline?" he asked. His brow wrinkled, as if he were surprised at himself.

She nodded. She surely did. Oh, how she loved him!

"That's ... that's ... reassuring," he said in an odd tone. "I—I love you, too, Caroline. I want you to know that. But I ..." He withdrew and raked a hand through his hair, looking shaken suddenly. "I . . . Oh, hell. Breakfast really is waiting downstairs. Cold muffins, smoked ham, and some wild strawberries. I hope you don't mind. Louisa gave them to me yesterday when I told her I'd bought the house. She worries about me, you know. She likes to mother."

Caroline smiled. "I know."

His hand slid down into hers and pulled her gently from the room. Caroline went, feeling a glow in her heart.

CHAPTER

NINETEEN

They ate breakfast in the kitchen, seated side by side at the plain table. But Robert had never felt more comfortable in his life.

He started to reach for several china plates, but Caroline said, "Oh, no, we can just eat from the basket—no need to dirty those." He smiled and turned around, agreeing with her. He liked feeling unpretentious, stripped of his neck-cloth and shoes, eating from a brown basket instead of from beautiful china plates. He couldn't remember now why he'd thought she would like the plates. He supposed he had a habit of trying to impress people—and it was a habit he doubtless would have a difficult time breaking.

She loved the ham, muffins, and strawberries, and he loved *her*. He really did.

He wondered how he was going to bear leaving her—

and Clarence and Rebecca and David—when his business in Dubuque was done. She loved the house, though it overwhelmed her a little, and he still breathed sighs of relief now and then that he was almost certain she could be happy here.

With a few changes, of course. If the furnishings and the china made her uncomfortable, it was her house, and she was welcome to get rid of them. She wouldn't hurt his feelings; he wanted her to be happy. More than anything in the world, he wanted to make Caroline smile and laugh. If she asked for carpeting, he'd buy it. If she asked for new horses and a wagon, he'd buy those. If she asked for a different barn, a different stove, new dresses, shoes, stockings, undergarments with lace and frills—anything she wanted, he would scramble to get.

He loved her too much, he thought—and that scared him.

He refused to think about it more. She'd promised him a day together. They'd eat, explore, make love, explore some more, maybe eat some more. They would while away the sweet summer day wherever she wanted to while it away—in the bedroom upstairs, in the garden, in the meadow he had raided.

"Good," she said, smiling, the word muffled around the bite of muffin in her mouth. "Hungry."

He grinned. "Caroline, Caroline . . . Have you no manners?" He lifted a napkin from the table and wiped one side of her mouth.

"Never."

"I know. Tsk, tsk. So unruly."

"Eat, Kingston," she said, ducking her head. "Stop tryin' to take care of me. You've gotta be hungry."

"After all that activity last night, you mean?"

She nodded.

"I'll have you looking at me boldly all the time before the day's over," he remarked. "But on second thought, perhaps not. I rather like your shy, embarrassed looks."

"You're the scoundrel," she accused. "Ma told me you called me that, y'know."

"No, I didn't know."

"Yep. She told me all right. I thought she'd never stop hollerin' at me that day you helped with the laundry. She told me to go invite you back to supper, to be nice to you. But by then I'd planted my feet about you and wouldn't budge."

"I know. How stubborn you can be, Caroline."

"I did have a conversation with Henrietta, y'know," she said, taking a bite of ham.

"I assumed you had." Robert chuckled. "I've never met a cat with human characteristics. Henrietta is entirely too human."

Caroline laughed, covering her mouth and swallowing. "She's really a very nice cat. She'll like it out here—as long as there're male cats around. She likes to, uh, well, y'know . . ."

"No, I don't know. Tell me" He loved watching her eyes sparkle in the soft morning sunlight, loved watching the bronze highlights in her hair. He loved the way she ducked her head when she became embarrassed.

"She likes to do what we did, you 'n' me," Caroline said, her voice lower than it had been a moment ago. " 'Cept Henrietta . . . she does it with just about every male that comes around."

"How like an animal."

She laughed again, and he propped his elbow on the table, his chin in his cupped palm, and just watched her. "You plan to keep remindin' me of that—that she's an animal—don't you?" she asked.

"As much as possible."

"Someday you 'n' Henrietta'll learn to like each other. I know it."

"Perhaps. When the Atlantic Ocean freezes entirely."

She coughed as if choking. "That ain't gonna happen, Kingston!"

He shrugged. "My point exactly."

"Aw, you 'n' Henrietta'll do better than that. Here, have some muffin," she said, breaking off a piece.

He let her feed it to him. He enjoyed her feeding it to him, relished the touch of her fingers on his lips.

"Apple 'n' cinnamon," she said. "Louisa's a good cook."

"Mm. She is," Robert agreed heartily. Caroline fed him another bite, and he nipped at her fingertips.

She caught her breath. "Watch yourself, Kingston. I'm not for breakfast, the muffins are."

He grinned. "What about the strawberries?"

She shrugged. "You suddenly can't feed yourself?"

"I'll feed you," he said, reaching into the basket in search of a strawberry.

She lurched back a little. "I don't need to be fed."

"Neither do I, but it's fun." He eyed her as he drew a berry from the basket. "Settle down, Caroline. You really do have difficulty with laying back and letting someone do something for you. It's admirable, the way you take care of people. But sometimes you should let people take care of you."

Uncertainty flickered in her eyes.

He scooted his chair so that he could sit facing her. He gently placed one hand on one side of her jaw and lifted the strawberry to her pink, slightly parted lips. "Sweet Caroline," he whispered, "close your eyes."

She hesitated, then did as she was told.

"Now, love, a taste of strawberry."

She nipped at it, biting off a small piece and chewing. Juice oozed from the fruit, and Robert touched the berry to her mouth, watching the red liquid gather on her bottom lip. She drew the lip in, licked the juice off, swallowed, then took another bite. As she chewed, he stroked the corner of her mouth with his thumb.

She laughed a little. "I don't think you're just interested in feedin' me the strawberry!"

"Hm." He grinned. "Now, I wonder why she thinks that."

"Can't figure."

She took another bite, then another. She licked her lips, drew the bottom one in again, looking more seductive than she could imagine—if she'd ever imagined. As innocent as she was, Robert didn't think she had.

When she finally ate the last of the strawberry, he was glad—and sorry he'd volunteered to feed it to her. He was fully aroused—again—but determined to take her outside to show her the garden and grounds. At this rate they might never get there.

She opened her eyes and smiled at him. "You're somethin', Kingston. Y'know? Really somethin'."

He cleared his throat. "Yes, well, suddenly I'm hungry."

"I know," she said, running her hand up his arm.

"For food," he said, turning back to the basket.

Giggling like a girl, she slumped back in her chair. A minute later, while he was working on a piece of ham, she sighed dreamily. "I ain't never had such a grand time, Robert. Never. I can't believe a girl like me got a man like you."

He smiled over at her. "What kind of girl is that?"

"Plain. Livin' in a cabin with two good dresses to her name. A girl who talks to a cat an' takes woodchucks as gifts. A girl who was mean to you an awful lot."

"We should clear the air of something," he said, and she frowned.

"What?"

"You're not plain—and you're not a girl."

She watched him silently.

"You're beautiful on the outside and, more importantly, on the inside. And, oh, Caroline, you're damn sure not a girl. A girl could not have responded the way you did last night and this morning."

Blushing, she averted her gaze, to the cupboard filled

with china, to the floor, to the table. She looked at anything but him.

He finished the ham, then stood and draped the brown cloth they had removed earlier back over the basket. "What if we eat more outside?"

"Outside?"

"Mm-hm. In the garden."

"You really wanna get me to that garden, don't you?" she asked, smiling.

"Actually," he said, lifting the basket, then turning to take her hand, "I want to get you to that stream."

She took his hand and let him pull her up gently and lead the way to the kitchen door.

A stone path flanked by low-lying white, pink, and purple flowers led straight from the hall door to the garden entrance—an arch of willow branches. The garden wasn't huge—perhaps only half the size of the house—but it was beautiful, lush, and colorful with all sorts of flowers and vines and herbs exuding sweet and pungent fragrances.

"It's rather overgrown," Robert said. "But that's what I find attractive about it." He pointed to the path they'd just traveled. "Viola back there. And here"—he stooped to pluck a deep yellow blossom marked with maroon, mahogany, and chestnut—"Nuttall's weed." He pressed the bloom into Caroline's hand, then moved on.

She followed, smiling, wondering if heaven looked like this place, like this incredible garden.

Down a small dirt path they passed lilac-pink, red, gold, cream-colored, and yellow flowers, some standing a good three feet tall, some maybe only two, and some creeping along the ground, invading the path so that Caroline nearly stepped on them at times.

"Ah, summer lilac," Robert said, plucking another flower—a violet-and-white blossom. He turned, tucked its stem just above one of Caroline's ears, grinned, then walked on again. Caroline hurried after him as he touched and spoke. "Sage, parsley, and basil ... And up there, painted lady."

"What?"

"Painted lady." Another six steps put him in front of a patch of deep pink-and-white flowers which stood tall on thin green stems. He bent to inhale their scent. "Mm. Painted lady."

"How do you know what all these flowers are?" Caroline couldn't help but ask.

"My mother likes more than just roses," he responded. "I was raised in gardens. Have a cough? Have some hollyhock." He started to pick another flower, but Caroline stopped him, laughing.

"That's enough!" she objected.

He grinned sheepishly. "Sorry. I get a little carried away where flowers are concerned. Look—canterbury bells, known in England as coventry bells," he said, stepping up to a patch of violet-blue blooms. "Perhaps named for the shape of the small harness bells worn by the horses of the Canterbury pilgrims."

Caroline shook her head. "I'm lost. I never knew anyone who knew so much about flowers! Now, how did you learn that—that they were named after the harness bells worn by the horses of the Canterbury pilgrims?"

"My mother, of course. Canterbury is a place in England."

"I figured that."

"Canterbury bells are part of a family of flowers—tussock bells, bellflower, chimney bell, and throatwort. The chimney bell grows up to six feet. You've heard the tale of Rapunzel?"

"Not unless it's told in western Virginia an' around here."

Smiling, he lowered the basket, approached her, and pushed both hands into the hair at her nape. "One very unlucky expectant father went foraging for a species of campanula—the rampion. The roots are edible, and his wife had a craving for them. The father invaded a witch's garden to get some and got caught. Needless to say, the witch was angry. She took his child when it was born, locked her in a tower, and permitted her to let down her long hair when the witch and only the witch wanted to climb up to the tower."

"That's awful!" Caroline said as his fingers caressed lightly.

"It does have a happy ending. Rapunzel is eventually rescued by a lover."

Caroline smiled. "Well, thank goodness! I'd hate to spend my life in a tower all alone. That's sweet."

"As sweet as the flower."

He kissed her, withdrew smiling, then took her hand and led her on.

They walked more paths, past sweet scabious and love in a mist and sweet sultan . . . They walked near a brick wall where vines grew rampant—scarlett runner beans, canary bird vines with yellow flowers, night-blooming moonflowers, and love in a puff. Hay had been strewn on the ground around a crop of cupid's dart, and Robert tugged Caroline down to sit beside him on it.

"A beautiful garden . . . ," he said, sighing. "But, oh, how it brings back memories." He looked distant suddenly, his eyes glancing off to the right, then all around. He drew a knee up and rested his elbow on it.

"Good memories?" Caroline asked hesitantly because she wasn't sure.

"Some." He rolled a piece of straw between his thumb and forefinger. "I told you I would explain what happened in the Perkins' barn."

"You never did though, an' I didn't think I should ask. I think it must be somethin' that's hard for you to talk about, like my pa's death is hard for me to talk about."

He inhaled and exhaled deeply. "My mother has a rose garden, and then she has a garden like this. Overgrown and wild. It's beautiful. It made a good hiding place for two brothers when they wanted to escape an overwhelming estate house. My family's estate house is rather . . . elegant. My parents do nothing halfway."

"You have a brother?"

He glanced down at the piece of straw, then back up at her. "I had a brother. Stephen." He said the name more softly: "Stephen."

"We used to hide behind the taller flowers and the shubbery borders. I'd hide from him, he'd hide from me—that is, until Mother caught us and ran us out. She would put Stephen in his room—out of sight, as always—and send me off for an afternoon with my schoolmaster. Stephen was . . . He was deformed, and my parents were horribly ashamed of him. They didn't seem to realize that all he asked of them was love. Or perhaps they realized but couldn't give it."

Caroline's eyes had grown wide. She wondered how parents could *not* love their own flesh and blood. But then, she wasn't experienced in that area—she didn't have any children of her own, so she couldn't judge.

"Stephen often had difficulty talking," Robert continued. "He stuttered a lot, and he knew our parents were ashamed of him. He knew. Sometimes he was so embarrassed by his appearance he used to hide even from me—in the stable because he knew I would look in the garden. He . . . he came to hate himself, despite me telling him over and over that I loved him, that I loved the fun we had together, that I didn't care what he looked like and that he shouldn't either.

"I couldn't find him one day—not in his room, not in the garden. So I went to the stable. Stephen had killed himself."

"Oh, God," Caroline whispered.

She wanted to cry for him, for the pain she saw in his face, in his eyes.

"No wonder you got so upset when you saw what David wrote on that slate!"

He nodded. "I love my parents and I think people tolerate situations differently. In some ways I think they were trying to protect Stephen by not allowing him to leave the grounds, by keeping him locked away much of the time. I've told myself that over the years because otherwise I think I'd still blame them and hate them. They're really loving, respectable people. At least they never sent him away from our home. I almost didn't buy this house because of this garden."

"But you did. Why, if it makes you have bad memories?"

"It doesn't, that's why. When I first saw the garden, I remembered Stephen with painful intensity. Then after a moment I recalled him running along the paths, hiding behind the pheasant-eyed pink, peeking from between the honesty, and I almost couldn't turn away."

"We'll keep it nice," Caroline said, slipping an arm around his shoulders. "I promise. We'll keep it real nice. You know all about the flowers. You can teach me, an' after we're married we'll just be sure to keep the garden real good. You'll have to show me the pheasant-eyed pink an' the honesty 'cause I don't know one flower from another. Why, I just call them all . . . What's wrong?" He was looking at her funny all of a sudden, surprise and something like fear in his eyes.

"Caroline, I didn't say anything about marriage," he said quietly. She thought his heart must be beating two hundred times a minute, he looked so stunned. He'd gone pale, too. Ashen.

And now she felt herself pale. She'd thought . . . He'd said . . . The house and all . . . He'd bought them a house. He'd asked her to come here with him. He'd told her he loved her. They'd spent the night together.

"No, you haven't yet. But I thought . . ." She swallowed. "I thought you were just havin' a little trouble askin'. I thought . . . the house an' all . . . A man doesn't build or buy a woman a house unless he plans to marry her. You don't think I'm gonna live with you without marryin' you, do you?"

He glanced off at a patch of purple flowers. "Oh, Caroline," he said, exhaling deeply. "I'm sorry. I bought the house for you, your mother, and your grandfather. Jacob and I plan to build our hotel soon, then go back home for a while. Then build another one somewhere else, I think. I'd like to come and visit you sometimes. I—"

"Like some kept woman?" she blurted, unable to help herself. The magic of the time they'd shared together was slipping away very fast. It had been so nice, so beautiful, but she'd known it was too good to be true. She'd known. Still, she was shocked.

"It won't be like that, Caroline."

"Nope, it sure as hell won't." She got to her feet, trying not to tremble. "Why'd you bring me here, Kingston? Just to do what all animals do, then leave? Well, I ain't like that. I ain't like Henrietta. I'd like my man to stick around afterward, help me raise any young 'uns that come along. I'd like my man to marry me. March straight up to an altar 'n' marry me."

He stood, too. He tried to caress her arm, but she jerked it away. "Caroline, please. Don't ask marriage of me. I've stood near an altar, and it was not a pleasant place to be. I cannot do it again. Snakes scare me, Caroline. Committing myself to getting married . . . that . . . that terrifies me."

She was on the verge of crying, she thought. He didn't know how he was breaking her heart, and she wasn't going to let him know either. She was so hurt! She couldn't believe he'd made love to her like that, brought her all those flowers, made love to her again, shared breakfast and this garden—and that was all.

That was all.

She'd given him more attention, more time, more of herself than she'd ever even thought of giving another man. Despite that, he meant to build his hotel, then walk away. Make sure she was nice and cozy in the house he'd bought to "keep" her and her family in, then leave Dubuque—to return whenever he needed some physical relief, of course!

"To hell with you, Kingston," she muttered, stomping by him and the patch of purple flowers. She hurried beyond the wall of vines, walking fast, restraining herself from running. She had to get out of here and away from him before she burst into tears.

"You're a damn coward, being so scared of things!" she hollered over her shoulder. "I don't need a man like that anyway. An' the house is too fancy for me. Keep it! Me 'n' Ma an' Grampa, we'll look for our own house!" She was being mean, but she couldn't seem to stop herself. She didn't want to stop herself.

By the time she reached the willow branch entrance, her feet were moving fast, seemingly with a mind of their own. And once beyond the entrance, she broke into a run to the right, toward the stable. She dreaded the time she knew it would take her to harness the horses. Robert could come into the stable and try to talk to her again, and the last thing on earth she wanted right now was to talk to him.

Half of the hurt was her own fault, she reckoned as she shoved tears off of her cheeks. Stupid tears! She wasn't going to cry like a baby. She just wasn't. She was stronger than that. She'd damn sure endured a lot worse things in her life so far than a little heartache over a man.

"Caroline!" he called.

"You wanna leave me alone, Kingston," she mumbled, knowing he couldn't hear her. She didn't care. Saying it made her feel a little better somehow. Putting on her tough front always made her feel better. It made her feel protected.

"Caroline, don't run away! I'll explain. I'll try."

"Leave me alone, Kingston!"

She stomped into the barn and over to the stalls where

they'd settled the horses. She grabbed a bridle and approached one of the animals, who glanced up innocently with large eyes. Caroline began working the harness on the horse, trying to calm her trembling hands. Seconds later, Robert approached the stall, folded his arms on the topmost rail, and sighed heavily. She watched him from the corner of her eye.

"Caroline, I was almost married once," he said softly. "I . . . Lord, but I hate to tell this. Saying it aloud is like being there again. Thinking about marrying does frighten me. I'm sorry you can't understand that. It's . . . I was there, waiting to be married, willing to be married, wanting to be married. The church was full—my family is a somewhat important family in New York. She never arrived for the ceremony, and later I learned it had been a cruel joke all along, that she and a group of her friends had decided that someone needed to show me that I shouldn't think so much of myself. I loved her one minute and wanted to strangle her the next. Thinking about getting married is frightening for me, Caroline. I'm sorry."

She'd probably be scared, too, if something like that had happened to her. She'd think about standing there waiting for the person she was supposed to marry and she'd be wondering if he was going to decide not to show up, too, if he was just playing a joke, too.

One part of her wanted to take a gun and shoot Robert for hurting her, for not making her understand the situation before he brought her here. For not giving her a choice as to whether or not she wanted to make love with him regardless of the fact that he didn't want to marry her. Another part of her understood why he was scared, and it wanted to hold him and kiss him, no matter what.

"What'd she look like, Kingston?"

He frowned. "What?"

"I said, what'd she look like? Hair color, eye color, how tall."

"Blond hair, green eyes. She was perhaps five feet, six inches."

"How'd she dress? Fancy, I bet, swishy petticoats under her skirt and all that. Lots of lace and ribbons. Twirling one of those things to keep the sun off."

"Yes. She's from a wealthy family herself. She wore silks and satins most of the time."

Caroline laughed, a short bark. "Have you seen me wear silk an' satin?"

"No, Caroline, I—"

"Seen me with lace and ribbons hanging all over?"

He shook his head. "And I've never seen you twirl a parasol. You're right, Caroline, but—"

"I don't have blond hair and green eyes, Kingston, so there shouldn't be a 'but.' You're scared, and I can understand that. I imagine if I'd been through the embarrassment you must have felt, I'd feel the same way you do—that I never again wanted to think about getting married. I think I'd take a good look at the people around me, though, a good long, fair look, and ask myself if they were all so mean. I take care of people I love, Kingston. I take care of them real well, I think you'll agree. I don't leave them standing anywhere. That's what you oughtta be thinking about."

He inhaled and exhaled deeply. "Caroline, I thought she was a good person, too."

"I've said my piece. Grab that other bridle and get to work. I'll take you back to town. Me 'n' Grampa an' Ma'll look for a place outside Dubuque, and you'll build your hotel. I imagine that'll take some time, maybe weeks, maybe months. You think about what I said. I don't imagine I'll be fallin' in love again anytime soon, so if you decide to trust me, just come an' knock on the cabin door. If not . . . don't come callin' again."

He was staring at her, watching her in a tender, frightened, confused way that made her long to rush over to him and draw his head to her breast. But no. She wouldn't do that. The only way to make him get through his fear and mistrust was to be hard with him, make him understand how she felt—that the best way to beat fear was to face it head-on.

She finished harnessing the horse, then sank back against a nearby rail. "I used to be afraid of the dark, Robert. Did I ever tell you that?"

"No."

"Yep. My pa told me too many spooky tales, I imagine. Ma used to get real mad at him about that, but he'd do it anyway 'cause he liked watching my eyes get all big. He liked me cuddling real close to him, too. Well, he ain't around to cuddle close to anymore. I was scared nearly to death of that when he died—that he wasn't around to cuddle next to anymore when I was scared in the dark. I don't like to admit bein' scared, so for the sake of my pride, I decided I had to stop bein' a child about it an' face the dark. Sometimes noises in the dark still scare me, an' some are things to be afraid of. But I never know that until I try to find out what the noises are about. Just like you're never gonna know if all women are like that woman you almost married until you try to find out. But first I reckon you have to want to find out."

He stared at her in silence, a muscle tensing in his jaw, his eyes glassy. Finally he said, "Please, Caroline. Stay the day here with me."

She shook her head. "Nope. Not knowin' what I know now. That'd be easy for you, Kingston, an' real hard for me. I understand why you feel like you do. I'm askin' you to understand me. I can't stay."

He raked a hand through his hair, then turned away and grabbed the other harness.

The ride back to town was spent mostly in silence. Robert wanted to say something, anything, to ease the tension of the situation. Caroline was right—he was afraid. Very afraid. But he wasn't sure he was ready to face his fear; he

wasn't sure he would ever again be willing to stand before
an altar and wait for a bride to come walking up and stand
beside him. He had never taken humiliation well, and just
the thought of possibly being humiliated again . . .

He shuddered.

In Dubuque, nearly as soon as Robert and Caroline
turned up Main Street, Clyde approached on his horse. He
looked stern, almost alarmed, and Caroline wondered if
Ma and Grampa might have been worried about her after
all.

"Kingston," he said, reining his mount near the buckboard.

Robert urged the team to slow, then stop. "Yes, Marshal?"

"Hi, Clyde," Caroline greeted, wondering what was on
his mind.

Clyde tipped his head to her. "You're looking pretty this
morning, Caroline. Interesting, though—neither one of
you've been in town all night."

"Do your duties entail making sure people are safely
tucked in at night?" Robert asked, unable to bite back the
retort.

Clyde's eyes narrowed slightly. "Kingston, you've got a
smart-ass attitude I'd like to fix."

"What can we do for you, Clyde?" Caroline queried
nicely, obviously trying to maintain some peace.

"I'm sure you would," Robert said under his breath.

"I was checking on the two of you for good reason,"
Clyde responded. "You've both taken an interest in little
David Perkins. Night before last, Hal told him his boy was
missing, and he swore he hadn't done nothing with him.
He was upset, understandably upset."

"We don't know where he is," Caroline lied, and too
quickly, Robert thought. Clyde was now looking suspiciously at her.

"Is that right?" the marshal asked, nerves jumping
around his eyes.

Caroline's chin tilted. "That's right, Clyde."

He glanced off at some nearby saloons, then back at her as he worked his jaw. "Caroline, I reckon you know I favor you a lot."

"Reckon I do, Clyde."

"And that I don't like thinking you might be guilty of snatching David from his pa."

She was silent.

"Did you, Caroline?"

"What, snatch David from his pa?" She licked her bottom lip. "Now, that'd be a terrible crime, wouldn't it, Clyde?"

His eyes narrowed more.

"Are you accusing her, Marshal?" Robert queried. "Because if you are, she has a right to counsel."

"Kingston, you and your big city ways can just shut up," Clyde growled. "I'm the marshal here, and while this might be the United States of America, it's also Iowa Territory, and I'm here to help clean up a town. So unless you've got something to admit yourself, just sit there and shut up."

"Clyde!" Caroline clicked her tongue. "Now, what kind of manners are those?"

"You're right," Robert said, looking Clyde in the eye. "It is the United States of America, and she's protected by the—"

"Kingston, I'll have you know Hal Perkins was found shot in the back last night! Shot clean through! I'm not interested in protecting anyone. I'm interested in finding out who killed him. If you want the truth, I'm thinking you might be more guilty than Caroline, 'cause you've been wanting to rough him up for weeks now. She might like to tote a rifle, but you as much as threatened Hal in front of me!"

Beside Robert, Caroline gasped. Robert felt his eyes widen. He blinked. "Shot?"

"David's pa's dead?" Caroline blurted.

"Yeah," Clyde said, shifting in his saddle. "Hal's been cold for hours. And I've been wondering all night where you two might be. I've given a lot of thought to tossing Clarence and Rebecca in jail—I've been so angry that they wouldn't tell me where you'd gone, Caroline. And you, Kingston, where've you been? Both of you want to start talking real quick. Not many people liked Hal, but no one takes kindly to someone shooting someone else in the back. I need to talk to David, too, so if you two know where he is, you'd better tell."

"You think one of us might've shot Hal Perkins?" Caroline snapped. She shook her head. "Craziest thing I've ever heard!" She'd gone rigid on the seat, and when Robert glanced over, he saw that she was gripping the edge so fiercely her knuckles had turned white.

"What else am I supposed to think?" Clyde demanded. "Couldn't find you for nothing. I've ridden all over town at least ten times during the night. I've banged on your cabin door a good twenty times, Caroline, so much I know your mother's sick of me. And Kingston, you haven't been at the boardinghouse. The two of you were seen heading out of town yesterday afternoon, and as far as I can tell, you haven't been back since. Until now. Had some business to tend, did you? Maybe out at the Perkins' farm?"

Caroline huffed. "Hellfire, Clyde! You're accusing the wrong people. We were at the Perkins' farm yesterday, but Hal was alive! Drunk and passed out and laying in a mess, but alive. After that, we left. We spent the evening and the night—"

"Caroline," Robert said in a harsh tone.

She glared at him. "Well. We were there—and Hal was still alive. This is hanging business, an' I ain't gonna lie!"

"David is staying with Ben and Louisa Carrol near Catfish Creek," Robert admitted.

Clyde nodded slowly. "I know their place. Reckon I'll take a ride out there and see for myself."

Robert lifted a brow. "You do that."

"I plan to. Where'd you spend the night, Caroline?"

"In a house Robert just bought from that Livingston speculator."

The nerves around Clyde's eyes jumped more. "Is that right?"

"That's right," she said, lifting her chin another notch.

"With Kingston here?"

"With Robert, yes. I wouldn't shoot anyone in the back, Clyde. You know I wouldn't. I don't like you thinkin' that about me."

"All the while you've been flashing those eyes at me, you've been beddin' him," the marshal growled under his breath.

Robert felt more anger rise inside him. Outrage, too. "No, she hasn't." His voice contained a dangerous edge. He heard it, and apparently Clyde heard it, too; the marshal's seering gaze whipped back to him.

"You wanna watch your mouth, Clyde," Caroline warned.

"We were with the Carrols from afternoon until late evening," Robert said. "Ben and Louisa will tell you that. Afterward, we went to what was the Livingston home. Until an hour ago, that's where we were. Do you have any more questions pertinent to David's disappearance and Hal Perkins's murder, Marshal?"

Clyde gave his jaw a quick rub. "If I ask around and find out you were seen other places . . ."

"You won't, unless you pay someone to say we were. In which case, I believe I could pay them more."

"Robert!" Caroline objected. "We don't have to pay anyone to say anything! You wouldn't do that either, would you, Clyde?"

Clyde thought for a moment, then heaved a sigh. "I wouldn't, Caroline. But I'd damn sure like to get someone to say Kingston was there. I can't believe you took up with him."

She winced. "Sorry, Clyde. I led you on, I know, an' I shouldn't—"

"I don't believe who she takes up with is your business," Robert retorted.

"Lord! You two get away from each other's throats!" Caroline objected. "Give me those reins." She jerked them from Robert's hands. He reached to grab them back, but she gave them a little shake, and the wagon jolted forward. "Clyde, go talk to the Carrols an' David. I'm takin' you to the boardin'house, Kingston, an' that's the last I want to see of you for a while. Pay somebody . . . ," she muttered as they left the marshal behind. "Pay somebody! Now, don't that beat all! You think a lot of that money of yours, don't you? Buy me a house an' fix it up real fancy with china 'n' gold frames an' pretty carpets an' I'll just stay there and wait for you anytime you want to come visitin'. An' now you're accusin' Clyde of *payin'* somebody to say we weren't where we said we were—an' threatenin' to pay that same person to change their mind! Is your world all money, Kingston? Money, money, money! I was right when I told Mary Sue it'd never work between us—you ain't right for me an' I ain't right for you. We're too different. Hell, Kingston, you have a whole different way of thinkin' than I do."

"I believe we were being accused of murder," Robert said stiffly. "I was trying to defend us. You're naive if you think people don't pay other people to say what they want them to say."

"An' the words you use! What's that mean—naive?"

"It means you're too innocent sometimes."

"I'm too innocent, an' you're too caught up in your money."

"I didn't buy the house to 'keep' you there," Robert objected. "If you don't want the china, throw it out! Give the gold frame in the hall to some church people or a society and let them sell it and further their cause. Strip the house clean and start over. Furnish it or don't furnish it—I don't care! Pardon me for trying to make people I care about happy and comfortable in the way I've been taught will make them happy and comfortable!"

"Don't shout at me."

"Don't accuse me of waving my money beneath people's noses. You see, Caroline, I know politics. My father happens to be involved in them in New York. I know how political men think."

"This ain't New York—and Clyde wouldn't pay anyone to accuse us of something we didn't do!"

"How well I know this is not New York," he said, glancing around at some of Main Street's more notorious businesses.

"Well, you're goin' back there soon," she retorted. "To your fancy New York. Here's the boardin'house. Get down."

He reined the wagon in front of Mrs. Johnson's Boardinghouse, and he and Caroline sat in silence for a moment, him staring at the horses, her clenching her jaw and looking off at the steady crowd in the street, then down at her lap.

"Go on. Get—"

"At first, Caroline, I *was* trying to charm you to get you to agree to sell me your family's land," Robert said. "I knew the way to your heart was through Clarence, so I was trying to charm him, too. But somewhere along the way I became snared in *your* charm—and in Clarence's and Rebecca's. I bought the house because I thought you would love it. There really is a stream some distance beyond that garden. I was trying to give your family a better life. For some reason, I thought you needed and wanted that. I'm sorry."

He watched her swallow. "That's sweet, Kingston, an' I reckon I know all that. I can't live there now anyway. I'd be thinkin' of all the time we spent upstairs an' I wouldn't like that."

"I love you, Caroline," he said softly.

She smiled weakly. "Yeah, well, you'd better scat. Fletcher an' Mrs. Johnson are probably wonderin' where you've been, too."

He reached for and squeezed her hand. She didn't respond other than to look down at her skirt again. He wanted to do more. He wanted to hold her, draw her close and press her head against his chest. He wanted to stroke her shoulders and back, soothe her, tell her everything would be all right.

But he couldn't. He wouldn't. He had come into her life, upset her entire world, turned it upside down in fact; he had tried to make the changes easier for her. But he couldn't promise her the one thing he knew would bring back her smiles and laughter. He just couldn't.

"Go on now," she murmured, squaring her shoulders, always brave Caroline. "Waitin' around ain't gonna make this easier."

She was right. He turned away and climbed down from the wagon scat.

She took the reins and started off almost immediately, unable to get away fast enough.

He watched her leave, watched her straight back and the way her hair curled so sweetly nearly to her waist, and he had the disturbing thought that he was letting the most remarkable woman he had ever met ride away. Simply ride away.

CHAPTER

TWENTY

"You're a damn fool, I don't mind telling you," Jacob scolded, kicking back in a chair positioned near the window in Robert's room. Robert sat at a nearby desk, looking over a sketch of the hotel and watching Jacob through the corner of his eye.

"I told you I didn't want to talk about it again," Robert fairly growled.

"For all her . . . eccentrities, she's an incredible woman. Devoted, thoughtful, kind—unless you cross her too many times. She's proud, almost noble." Jacob laughed low. "A knight in the disguise of an American farm girl."

Robert glanced at the window, where rain ran in rivulets down the panes. She *is* devoted, he thought. Fiercely protective of her family, committed to them. She'd never do something as disturbing as desert them.

She was thoughtful, too—bringing him cider for his hands that one afternoon, rescuing David from those ruffians, offering to have Clarence find the boy a place to live. Kindness, too, had been a factor in those actions.

And proud she was! Not so much that one was put off. Just enough to make a person gaze at her with admiration.

"She'd marry you," Jacob said. "I know she would—it shows in her eyes every time she looks at you. All you need do is ask."

"I can't ask," Robert said, and went back to studying the plans. Something was bothering him about them. Something.

"You love her, Robert."

"The third floor here . . . ," Robert said thoughtfully. "There's no bath."

"Would you . . . !" Jacob jumped up from his chair, hurried to where Robert sat, and snatched the plans from his friend's hands. "Would you stop thinking about these and looking at them for a few moments?" he demanded, peering down at Robert. "I haven't acted very nice, like my usual self, since coming to Dubuque. We found a different situation than what we usually find. My encounter with Caroline traumatized me, I don't mind telling you. I didn't like her much after she ran me off with her rifle. But I've known you nearly my entire life and I know there must be something special about her if you've fallen in love with her. She's not like Alexis, who blinded you with upper crust charm and beauty so much you couldn't see her faults. You know Caroline's faults—which also happen to be her strengths, in some cases. I didn't like Alexis, Robert. She was devious and full of herself. I tried to tell you that! But I'm glad you met her. Her leaving you alone at the altar was the best thing that's ever happened to you!"

"Have I asked"—his lips thin, Robert jerked the paper from Jacob's hands, tearing it in the process—"for your advice? Have I ever?" His hands were trembling, he hadn't eaten all day—the hour was now well past two o'clock in the afternoon—and he was disheveled, to sum up his appearance. He'd raked his hands through his hair countless times, his shirt was hanging open, and he was barefoot.

"You were drinking last night," Jacob observed, drawing back.

"So I was," Robert grumbled. But not enough. Not nearly enough. He wanted Jacob to get the hell out of the room.

Jacob gripped the edge of the desk and leaned forward, determined to make Robert see that his fear of getting married was keeping him from the most unusual woman he'd ever met, from a woman who loved him at least as much as he loved her. "There's nothing waiting for you back in New York. Only a life you've never truly enjoyed. I daresay you've enjoyed Caroline Watson. Immensely. If you're so frightened that she won't show up at the altar, don't get married in a church. Take the minister to her."

"I wouldn't do that!" Robert snapped.

"Why not?"

"Because that would be forcing her."

"Forcing her? How so?"

"By more or less demanding that she marry me right then and there."

Jacob pondered that and decided Robert was right. "Do you love her?"

Robert exhaled heavily, propped his peppered jaw in an open hand, his elbow on the secretary. "Yes."

"Do you think for a moment that she's anything like Alexis?"

"No!"

"Did you ever believe Alexis loved you?"

"Yes, but she never did anything as thoughtful as bring me cider for burned hands," Robert mumbled.

"What?"

"Cider for my burned hands. The lard made them sting worse. Caroline brought me cider."

Jacob chuckled. "I see. Cider . . ."

For a moment there was only the sound of rain pattering softly on the roof and window.

"Caroline hates people who are not what they seem," Jacob said. "She's direct, and she's fairly honest. Besides . . . I hate to point this out, but she's made a fool of you enough times already. Why would she make a fool of you by leaving you standing alone at the altar? She has nothing to gain, and she's not Alexis, so she wouldn't do it just to make you a laughingstock."

"I don't know," Robert murmured.

"She wouldn't, Robert. She wouldn't."

"Oh, Jacob, my friend, I just don't know."

Shouts drifted up from outside. Even with the window closed, the noise of the busy town still penetrated the room.

Jacob wandered back to the window, pushed his hands into his pockets, and stood there looking down. "There's something attractive about this awful place," he commented, and laughed in disbelief. "You were right—there's promise here. With all the businesses moving in, perhaps the gaming houses and saloons will stop dominating soon. I met a girl up from Davenport with her family, did I tell you?"

Robert lifted a brow. "No, you didn't."

"She's Swedish," Jacob said, tossing a grin over his shoulder. "Perhaps I'll be thinking of something permanent soon."

"You?"

"I said perhaps. I can't be a rogue forever."

Robert chuckled. "You *will* be a rogue forever."

Jacob turned around and leaned against the window frame. "I'm sorry I teased you so much about Caroline."

Robert shrugged. "I might have done the same if it had been you in the situation. I insulted you by insinuating that you hadn't tried hard enough to talk her and her family into selling their land."

Jacob pushed off from the window with the heel of his

boot. "I won't advise you anymore where she's concerned."

Robert fell silent again. He knew Jacob was right about Alexis being devious and full of herself, and certainly Jacob and Caroline were both right that Caroline was nothing like Alexis.

And he loved her. God how he'd come to love Caroline Watson. For her temperament, for her òddness, for her flashing eyes and unruly hair, for everything that she was—and wasn't. No parasol. No stiff manners. No phoniness. She was just Caroline—a special person.

"I'm going to brave the streets of mud to call on my new friend this afternoon," Jacob remarked, grinning.

Robert smiled. "What new friend is that?"

"My Swedish lady, of course."

"Of course. Just don't run away to Davenport before we finish the hotel."

"Promise." Jacob's grin widened. He started past Robert, pausing only to clap him on the shoulder. Seconds later, the door brushed open, then shut.

Robert had been looking over the hotel plans for the better part of an hour. He moved away from the secretary and toward the bed, wondering if he could sleep. Jacob had been right—he had been drinking last night.

Two days had passed since he and Caroline had parted outside the boardinghouse. He'd visited the site of the hotel, where the two saloons were now being torn down and the land cleared. He had visited it more to catch sight of Caroline, he suspected, than to see how things were progressing. But he'd seen only Henrietta, sitting back on her haunches near a corner of the cabin, watching him with slitted eyes. Ridiculous how that cat hated him!

He couldn't nap. He tossed and turned, seeing Caroline dancing, seeing her eyes cloud with passion, watching her assess the kitchen at the old Livingston home, smiling as she stared down at herself in the bedroom upstairs, discovering herself. He saw her lying in that bed of flowers, looking around in surprise like a nymph making a discovery. He watched sunlight reflect off her hair in the garden, heard her sweet voice tell him he would have to teach her about the flowers . . .

Caroline.

He thought about leaving here, leaving Iowa Territory, leaving her, and he felt such a hollow ache inside, he sat up on the side of the bed, leaned over, and put his head in his hands.

He wanted a warm home. He wanted her.

He *was* being a fool.

He stood, washed at the basin stand, shaved, and put on clean clothes.

He wondered if there was any place in Dubuque where he might find a rose. Or a rampion. Perhaps he might even find a dose of courage at the local apothecary . . .

Seated on a stool behind the cabin, Caroline moved the greens she'd harvested from the garden around in the tub of water before her, washing them thoroughly. She'd boil them soon and sell most of them to the miners.

Over near the barn, Grampa was tossing dried corn to the chickens, who clucked and ruffled about to get their share. Earlier, Clyde had come calling to apologize for more or less accusing Caroline the other day of having something to do with Hal Perkins's murder. He'd explained that a man in one of the saloons had had a little much to drink last night and bragged that he'd collected some money Hal had owed him for some time—he'd collected it the hard way, with a pistol. "A cowardly way," Caroline had muttered. She couldn't think of any worse crime than shooting someone in the back. Rain fell during Clyde's meek visit, as it had been falling off and on all day, and the sky was still just as gray as it could be.

So was Caroline's heart.

She wasn't going to cry and mope and feel sorry for herself. She just wasn't. She wasn't going to blame anyone but herself for Robert rejecting her, for the awful way she'd felt the last two days. She'd known why Robert Kingston was in town, and despite knowing why, she'd fallen into his arms; she'd fallen in love with him.

Henrietta had warned her away from the man. Hell, she'd warned herself away from him! But a magical afternoon, and an evening and night, hours filled with romance, had whittled at and finally crushed her determination not to get all emotional about him. She'd gone and fallen in love with him when she knew she shouldn't, when she knew they weren't right for each other. They were as different from each other as night and day, as sunshine and rain, and she shouldn't have let herself get caught up in believing that anything more than one night in a bedroom would come of their relationship.

She still felt so embarrassed and humiliated! She really had thought he'd bought the house for them to live in after they were married.

She gave a short laugh, one of disgust at herself.

Hearing a soft meow, Caroline pulled her hands from the water, dried them on her skirt, then reached to her left for Henrietta, pulling the cat onto her lap. She stroked Henrietta's belly, which swelled more each day.

"Right now I'm wishing I could be like you, Henrietta. You never seem to get your heart broken when a male comes, does his business, then leaves. If you do, you sure hide it good. I wasn't going to cry an' drag around, but honestly, Henrietta," Caroline said, nuzzling her friend's neck, "right now my heart is so swollen it's gonna bust if I don't let some tears out. I hate this feelin'. I never have cried too well. In fact, I hate to cry! You know that about me. You know these last two years I've had to be strong all the time. An' cryin' . . . well, Henrietta, that's a waste of time an' energy I've had to put into other things."

Her throat was feeling thick and her eyes were beginning to burn.

Oh stop it, she told herself. *Just stop it! You're not a baby who cries when she doesn't get something she wants!*

"At least you an' I, we have each other," Caroline whispered, her voice cracking. Her nose began to feel like it might start running.

Henrietta meowed again, low and sweet, and began licking Caroline's jaw and neck. Henrietta's love was unconditional and always there, and it was enough. It would always be enough.

The first tear fell slowly down Caroline's face, but the second, third, and fourth . . . If she hadn't known better, she might have thought someone was pouring a bucket of water over her head.

She didn't know how long she sat there and cried. Henrietta licked her face the entire time, trying to wash the tears away and make things better.

"He . . . he made me feel things I've never felt before, Henrietta. He made me feel like I was . . . like I was beautiful, like I was the only woman in the world. But you knew something wasn't right about it all an' you tried to tell me an' I should have listened to you better. I did at first, then my mind got all funny an'—"

"I'm glad you didn't listen to her better," a male voice said from nearby. "Will Henrietta forever dislike me, I wonder?"

Caroline's head popped up. Her eyes flew open and landed squarely on Robert, who wore a white shirt and dark trousers, and was clean shaven. He looked a lot like he had that first evening he'd come to supper. His eyes seemed deep today, full of thoughts and emotions. In Caroline's lap, Henrietta stiffened.

"Why do you care if Henrietta dislikes you?" was all Caroline could think to say. Her heart quickened—he held a basket filled with flowers. She spotted at least six red roses and several canterbury bells scattered among the numerous colorful blooms.

Caroline eyed the basket, feeling uneasy, feeling scared,

feeling a flicker of disturbing hope. She suddenly wished the clouds would open and rain would fall again and put the spark out. She'd cried enough for one day. Hellfire—she'd cried enough for the next five years! She didn't need to get her hopes up, then be left to cry again.

"Grampa's down in the chicken coop if you came to see him," she said, sniffing and shoving away what tears remained on her face.

"Caroline," Robert said so tenderly she wanted to jump up and throw herself at him. She felt more tears well behind her eyes.

She spoke roughly: "Talk to me without sayin' my name, Kingston. Think you could do that?"

"I love saying your name."

She jumped up, spilling Henrietta from her lap. The cat meowed, then rubbed against Caroline's leg. Caroline plopped her knuckles on her hips and glared at Robert. "What the hell are you doin' here, totin' flowers, lookin' all soft an' romantic again? I swear, I'm gonna march inside 'n' get the rifle! Scat, Kingston! Get out of here! Leastwise get away from me."

"I came to bring you these," he said, holding out the basket. He took a deep breath, then released it. "They're the courage I need, though if you keep being your usual belligerent self, that courage will sprout feet and run. This is difficult for me, Caroline, and the days ahead, the waiting, will be even more difficult."

"Courage?" she blurted. "Flowers give courage? Now, what's turnin' in that head of yours?"

He shrugged. "I grew up with them. I'm comfortable with them. Do you want them?"

She thought about saying no, she didn't want them, that taking them would only make her love him more because he was so sweet to bring them to her.

His sweetness made her weak, however, and she reached out and took the basket, trembling when their hands touched. Her gaze flew up and met his, and she had to blink back tears again.

"Robert Kingston, you're killin' me inside, do you know that?" she asked in a broken voice. "Why are you bringin' me flowers? Why the hell are you bringin' me flowers!"

"I need flowers close by when I ask you . . ." She watched him swallow, look off at the cabin, then back at her, then swallow again. Her throat suddenly felt parched, and she knew her eyes must resemble twin saucers. "When I ask you to marry me."

She sucked in a breath.

He glanced at the back of the cabin again, then at the stool where she'd been sitting, at the tub in which greens floated, at her feet, then at her face.

"Maybe, uh . . ." Now she swallowed. "Maybe you shouldn't give these to me just yet," she said, handing him the basket. "I love flowers an' those are real pretty. But maybe, just maybe, you should hold onto 'em a while longer."

He took the basket without objection and wrapped his arms around it, holding it close to his chest. "We could work through our differences, Caroline. I don't need china and gold-plated items around me. I simply grew up surrounded by them and having them around seems natural. But I don't need them."

"I reckon I know that. You've never once looked uncomfortable in our cabin, sittin' and smokin' with Grampa or seated at our table."

"I grew up learning that money solves problems. That thinking will be difficult to change, Caroline, but I will change it."

"It solves some—it durn sure pays fines—but I figure you know after your run-in with the Dubuque Watsons that it doesn't solve all problems, like whether or not you can get a piece of land you want. A lot of things matter more than money."

Nodding, he smiled a little at that. He shifted from one boot to the other, lowered the basket to one hand, then raised it again. He rubbed his thigh with an open palm. A second later, he rubbed his jaw.

"Maybe I'd better do the askin'," Caroline suggested. Seeing him look so uncomfortable was like having a hand squeeze her heart.

"That's not the usual way," he commented, giving a nervous smile.

"Reckon it's not. But then, I'm just full of surprises—or so I'm told. An' I ain't tryin' to wear the trousers here. I can see that this is real hard for you an' I want to make it easier. Besides . . ." She grinned. "Those greens are gonna get mighty soggy if I leave 'em in that water much longer. I plan on boilin' 'em, sure, but I hate handlin' soggy greens."

That pulled a laugh out of him. He shook his head. "I love you, Caroline. But if you ask me to marry you, I'm not facing my fear, am I?"

"I suppose not."

Meowing, Henrietta rubbed against Caroline's leg.

"Oh, I brought a little courage for Henrietta, too," Robert said, reaching into the basket. "A little gift to entice her into liking me, into rolling over and letting me pet her belly."

"You did?" Caroline asked in disbelief.

"Catnip, a mint, named so because cats love its aroma and flavor. I'm surprised she's not already at my heels."

"Well," Caroline said regretfully. "She really doesn't like you. You don't like her either so I can't figure why you brought her a gift."

"Call it a peace offering."

Caroline laughed. Seconds later, after he had lowered the basket to the ground, hunched beside it, and was reaching down beneath the flowers on top, she sobered. "This ain't like whiskey for cats, is it?"

"You mean will it make her drunk? No, no. She'll just enjoy it. It's a treat—like chocolate."

He pulled a plant from beneath the flowers, broke off a hairy, gray-green heart-shaped leaf, and rolled it between two fingers.

"Why are you doing that?" Caroline asked, watching him, still concerned.

"To bring out the aroma."

Henrietta stopped rubbing against Caroline's leg. She peered at Robert with her slitted eyes and flickered her tail.

"Well, hell, if you don't have her attention!" Caroline said in surprise. Henrietta took a step forward, dipping her head to smell the leaf, then stepped back and meowed again.

Caroline laughed. "She's nervous, too. Maybe you should put it down an' let her get it if she wants it."

"Then *she's* not facing her fear."

He was right, Caroline supposed.

Robert continued rubbing the leaf. Soon he put it in his palm and held his hand out toward Henrietta. "We could learn to like each other," he told her. "It wouldn't be so difficult as long as you don't invade the bedroom at the wrong time. If you do, well, it's outside with you. And no more tripping. That wasn't nice."

Caroline laughed. Her heart felt lighter now. She'd thought all was lost, but he'd come to ask her to marry him, and he was making a heroic effort to make peace with her best friend. But with a few conditions, of course.

Henrietta slowly but surely crept forward, sniffing, meowing, finally unable to resist the crumpled leaf in his hand. She tentatively licked his fingers, then snatched the leaf, stepped back, and chewed it eagerly.

"I can't believe my eyes," Caroline said in wonder. "You're sure it won't hurt her?"

"Now, hurting her is no way to win her mistress's hand, is it?" Robert queried, chuckling. "No, Caroline, it won't hurt her. Cats simply love catnip, that's all. Even the most stubborn of cats cannot resist it."

"Why didn't you bring her some before?"

"I didn't want to make friends with her before. I've decided that along with your unpredictable, sometimes irritating temperament, I must accept Henrietta."

"I ain't so bad!" Caroline propped her hands on her hips again. When Robert lifted his brows as if to say, "Now, think about what you just said and all the things that have happened these past weeks," she dipped her head sheepishly and dropped her hands. "Well, I reckon I can be mighty irritatin' sometimes."

He broke off another leaf and rolled it between his fingers. Henrietta didn't hesitate this time—when he placed it in his palm, she closed in before he had time to hold his hand out. Robert touched her head and stroked her back as she chewed the catnip. When she glanced up at him and meowed for more, he smiled at her. "So you like me now, hm? You've decided that having me underfoot might not be such a bad thing after all?"

"I think she's gonna enjoy havin' you underfoot!" Caroline observed. Hunching beside Robert, she, too, began stroking Henrietta's back.

Perhaps six inches separated her and Robert, and when she glanced up at him and smiled, he smiled back. She felt his warm breath as he eased a little closer. Her heart jumped.

"Caroline, would you marry me?" he asked, and he didn't even blink when he said the words.

She kissed him. She couldn't help herself. "I'll marry you today, right now, if that's what you want, if that would make you feel better."

"In your calico dress decorated with the red flowers?"

"Hell, I'd marry you in nothin' if you wanted me to!"

He pressed his lips to hers. "Now, that might be interesting."

She laughed. "It sure might be. Grampa wouldn't hide

behind his Iowa City paper to hoot—he'd just laugh out-right. You can follow me around all day if you want, to make sure I don't run off an' embarrass you."

"Caroline . . . ?"

"Yeah?"

"I trust you. I know you wouldn't run away. I know you wouldn't leave me standing alone. You pick the day for the ceremony—it doesn't have to happen today if you don't want it to."

"Oh, yep, it does!" she objected, kissing him back. "It does, 'cause I'm gonna drag you back to that house an' that bedroom tonight whether or not we're married. Ma was pretty shocked the other mornin' that I'd spent the night with you, so I reckon I'd better marry you first this time. I surely reckon I'd better otherwise I'll be havin' to redeem myself again—an' behavin' to cool Ma's temper is no fun."

Laughing, Robert sat back and drew her onto his lap. Henrietta rubbed against them both, purring contentedly. She flopped onto her back, then rolled around in the grass just as a ray of sunshine broke through a line of clouds to the west.

"I'll try my hand at managing the hotel, and I want to ask David if he'd like to come and live with us," Robert said, caressing Caroline's arm.

"Now, I was thinkin' the same thing myself."

His hand worked its way into her hair. He tipped her head back and spoke to her in the low, husky voice that had echoed in her head the last two very long and lonely nights: "I wish we were alone right now."

"Bless my eyes!" Clarence said from close by. "A person might think you two were gettin' friendly again!"

"Grampa . . . ?" Caroline said against Robert's lips.

"Yeah, honey?"

"You know that new Iowa City paper I brought you yesterday?"

"I sure do, honey. Done read it a time or two already."

"Go read it again, would you? An' in a little while, think about treatin' yourself to a shave at the barber. It's a special day, Grampa. Me 'n' Robert, we're getting hitched this evenin'. Tell Ma please, but tell her gently—I wouldn't want her to shatter the windows with her screamin'."

Robert chuckled, a deep rumble in his chest. Grampa gave a joyous yelp, and from the corner of her eye, Caroline watched him scamper away.

"Hitched . . . ," Robert mused. "Now, that is an interesting word . . ."

FREE
Romance
(a $4.50 value)

Send in the Coupon Below

To get your FREE historical romance and start saving, fill out the coupon below and mail it today. As soon as we receive it we'll send you your FREE Book along with your first month's selections.

---

*Come take a walk down Harmony's Main
Street in 1874, and meet a different resident of
this colorful Kansas town each month.*

A TOWN CALLED
Ꮿ HARMONY Ꮿ

__KEEPING FAITH by Kathleen Kane
0-7865-0016-6/$4.99

From the boardinghouse to the schoolhouse, love grows in the
heart of Harmony. And for pretty, young schoolteacher Faith
Lind, a lesson in love is about to begin.

__TAKING CHANCES by Rebecca Hagan Lee
0-7865-0022-2/$4.99

All of Harmony is buzzing when they hear the blacksmith,
Jake Sutherland, is smitten. And no one is more surprised
than Jake himself, who doesn't know the first thing about
courting a woman.

__CHASING RAINBOWS by Linda Shertzer
0-7865-0041-7/$4.99

Fashionable, Boston-educated Samantha Evans is the
outspoken columnist for her father's newspaper. But her
biggest story yet may be her own exclusive—with a most
unlikely man.